What People are Saying about the Left Behind Series

"This is the most successful Christian-fiction series ever."
   —Publishers Weekly

"Tim LaHaye and Jerry B. Jenkins . . . are doing for Christian fiction what John Grisham did for courtroom thrillers."
   —TIME

"The authors' style continues to be thoroughly captivating and keeps the reader glued to the book, wondering what will happen next. And it leaves the reader hungry for more."
   —Christian Retailing

"Combines Tom Clancy–like suspense with touches of romance, high-tech flash and Biblical references."
   —The New York Times

"It's not your mama's Christian fiction anymore."
   —The Dallas Morning News

"Wildly popular—and highly controversial."
   —USA Today

"Bible teacher LaHaye and master storyteller Jenkins have created a believable story of what could happen after the Rapture. They present the gospel clearly without being preachy, the characters have depth, and the plot keeps the reader turning pages."
   —Moody Magazine

"Christian thriller. Prophecy-based fiction. Juiced-up morality tale. Call it what you like, the Left Behind series . . . now has a label its creators could never have predicted: blockbuster success."
   —Entertainment Weekly

APOCALYPSE DAWN

BASED ON THE BEST-SELLING
LEFT BEHIND® SERIES

MEL ODOM

TYNDALE HOUSE PUBLISHERS, INC.   WHEATON, ILLINOIS

Visit Tyndale's exciting Web site at www.tyndale.com

Discover the latest about the Left Behind series at www.leftbehind.com

Cover photograph courtesy of U.S. Navy website: www.wasp.navy.mil

Author photo by Michael Patrick Brown

Written and developed in association with Tekno Books, Green Bay, Wisconsin.

Designed by Julie Chen

Edited by James Cain

Scripture taken from the New King James Version. Copyright © 1979, 1980, 1982, 1991 by Thomas Nelson, Inc. Used by permission. All rights reserved.

Published in association with the literary agency of Alive Communications, Inc. 7680 Goddard Street, Suite 200, Colorado Springs, CO 80920.

Published in association with the literary agency of Sterling Lord Literistic, New York, NY.

This novel is a work of fiction. Names, characters, places, and incidents are either the product of the author's imagination or are used fictitiously. Any resemblance to actual events, locales, organizations, or persons, living or dead, is entirely coincidental and beyond the intent of either the author or the publisher.

Left Behind is a registered trademark of Tyndale House Publishers, Inc.

Library of Congress Cataloging-in-Publication Data

Odom, Mel.
  Apocalypse dawn / Mel Odom.
    p. cm. (Apocalypse dawn #1)
  ISBN 0-8423-8418-9 (sc)
  1. Rapture (Christian eschatology)—Fiction. 2. End of the world—Fiction. I. Title.
  PS3565.D53A86 2003
  813'.54—dc21   2003007784

Printed in the United States of America

07 06 05 04 03
5   4   3   2   1

Covered in three days' worth of perspiration, filth, and fine yellow dust, First Sergeant Samuel Adams "Goose" Gander knelt beside the river that cut through the harsh land of southern Turkey. The stream was muddy brown, low for the season. Fish nearly as long as his arm swam slowly through the water.

Goose leaned forward and filled his canteen, wishing for cooler weather. He popped two water purification tabs into the canteen and shook it.

Then one of the fish he'd been watching jerked violently. Blood sprayed from a huge wound that ran through the creature's side. Water jumped from the river only a few inches from the dying fish, seeming to hang frozen in the air for a split second. A rainbow flashed through the spray and Goose knew a bullet had caused the splash.

"Sniper!" Goose yelled to his squad as he dove for cover. A second bullet slammed the metal canteen from his hand, leaving his fingers numb from the impact. Goose landed behind a shelf of broken rock.

The Rangers working the water supply detail flattened out against the harsh terrain immediately. Some of them ducked in behind the Hummers and cargo trucks and the big water-pumping unit.

Then the sound of three rifle reports rolled over their position.

"Anybody see anything?" Goose yelled.

"Nothing, Sarge."

"Thomas?" Goose asked over the headset. Cliff Thomas was the team scout.

"I don't see anything, Sarge."

"That's a heavy-caliber rifle," another Ranger said. "The sniper could be set up as much as a mile away."

Goose scanned the broken mountains in the distance to the south. "Anybody hit?"

A chorus of *no*s followed.

Goose breathed a sigh of relief. Syrian snipers had been something of a problem, but so far he hadn't lost any of his men. More shots ripped into the river. Two dead fish floated up in response.

Goose didn't think the shooter was actually aiming for the fish. The creatures were unexpected casualties. But the effect was a sobering one. It was a message of sorts, warning shots fired across the bow of the United States Rangers assigned to the area.

Switching frequencies on the headset, Goose said, "Base."

"Go, Phoenix Leader. You have Base."

"I've got a sniper hosing my water detail," Goose said. "I can't find him. Can you assist?"

"Affirmative, Leader. Base is looking." Base was the central Ranger command post. The intelligence teams there had access to spy satellites that could peer down into the country and read the time off a man's watch.

Goose remained pressed into the hard earth, feeling the heat soaking into his body. He listened as Base maneuvered their own sniper team into position.

"Got a line on your troublemakers out there, Leader."

"Affirmative, Base. Patch me through to the sniper team." Goose breathed out, blowing dust from the baked grit covering the bare areas where vegetation had given up the struggle to survive.

"Phoenix Leader, this is Sniper Team Romero."

"Good to have you there, Romero. Can you confirm Base's report of one hostile sniper team?"

"Not only confirm it, Leader, but we're in position to cancel their pass to the party."

"Negative on the cancellation, Romero," Goose replied. "The Syrians are baiting us. None of my team has been hit. But I wouldn't mind seeing them sit out the next few dances." Sliding his M-4A1 to the side, he took out his 10X50 binoculars and had the Ranger sniper team direct him to the hostile shooter's location.

After a brief search, Goose found the enemy team—a shooter and a spotter—stretched out on a rocky outcrop in the jagged mountains to the southeast. No one else was around. The digital readout on his binoculars estimated the distance at a little less than a mile.

"Romero," Goose said, "I have our sniper team in sight. Send them on their way."

"Affirmative, Leader. We'll send them packing."

An instant later, rock jumped from the outcropping around the two Syrian soldiers. They jumped for cover, obviously not expecting to be found so quickly.

The other Rangers cheered the sniper team on as they reported, "Leader, your water detail is clean and green."

"Understood, Romero. Thanks for the assist." Goose put his binoculars away and stood. He took up the assault rifle and felt fatigue eat into his bones.

Glancing at the dead fish floating on the river, he was reminded of an old army axiom, the military version of Murphy's Law: "It isn't the bullet with his name on it that a professional soldier has to fear; it's all those that are addressed 'To Whom It May Concern.'"

The 75th Ranger Regiment was stuck between a rock and a hard place. And it seemed more than their share of trouble was looking for them.

✷   ✷   ✷

Turkish-Syrian Border
40 Klicks South of Sanliurfa, Turkey
Local Time 0601 Hours

Death stalked the invisible line that separated Syria and Turkey.

Goose peered through his binoculars and adjusted the magnification as he scanned the border. He knew the balance that kept three armies from each other's throats was so tenuous that any change might tip it the wrong way. Even a shift in the slow, dry wind might trigger renewed hostilities. The hatred between the Turks and the Syrian-sponsored Kurdish terrorists had existed for too many generations to count. And Goose knew that the Turks' American allies would be in the thick of the fighting, no matter who started it.

The early morning light hurt Goose's eyes, and the rocks and sand around him absorbed the sun's rays and steadily rose to baking temperature. By midafternoon, he knew from hard experience, the arid land would be almost unbearable.

For the last seventy-two hours, he and C Company had been on constant alert in full battle dress, camped in the harsh, barren plateaus overlooking the border. He'd been awake for so long that sleep was a distant memory. The exhausted man inside him had no place here. The professional warrior had to stay sharp.

Despite the circumstances, he'd taken the time to stay clean-shaven, although he hadn't foisted the same expectation on his men. Leadership was often as much about image as about substance. A shade less than six feet tall, with wheat-colored blond hair that almost matched the desert around him and a body disciplined by nearly two decades of military training, Goose looked like a soldier. He kept his hair cropped high and tight, but sand still found a way to burrow into his scalp, where it itched furiously. Just one more irritant he had to ignore. The dry heat pulled at the half-moon shrapnel scar that ran from his right eyebrow to his cheekbone. The scar was less than six months old and still felt tight.

During the last few months, his border patrol assignment had turned nasty. The body count was getting serious for all sides. Of late, a few American casualties had been added into the mix, kicking up international scrutiny and drawing the attention of news media from all over the globe. There were other hot spots in the world, of course, and news service people were hunkered down like vultures around the various front lines, waiting to see where the bloodiest violence would erupt first.

Goose prayed some other place would win that lottery. He was sitting atop a powder keg that could leave dead soldiers piled high on both sides of the border—some of whom he might be responsible for.

Many months ago, the United Nations had sought the help of the United States to police a flare-up in terrorist activity along Turkey's borders. President Fitzhugh responded by sending in the troops. He explained to the American people that it was more than local terrorism that threatened the peace in that part of the world. Before long the Syrian army was facing off with the Turks at the border. Because of Turkey's role as a key Western ally in the turbulent Middle East, Fitzhugh had made sure help had been quick in coming. The 75th Army Ranger Regiment moved into the area on a peacekeeping mission. Rifle companies of the Third Battalion from Fort Benning, Georgia, an outfit with an illustrious combat history, had taken on their portion of the mission.

Goose hoped the American forces could keep the border nailed down until peace talks between Turkey and Syria and the Kurdistan

Workers Party could bear fruit. It was his job to see that the diplomats had the time they needed to keep people from dying.

But being so far from home for so long was hard. He missed his wife, Megan, and his boys, Joey and Chris. The last couple of years hadn't been kind to Goose—or to any American Special Forces troops. Terrorist activity around the globe had kept them in the field. Goose's five-year-old son, Chris, seemed to be growing up much too fast in the pictures Goose had received from home over the last few months. And his seventeen-year-old stepson, Joey, was on the brink of manhood. It nearly killed Goose not to be there for his boys and his wife.

According to the intel from HQ, the peace talks between Turkey and Syria were going to get serious any day. *Any day* had been more than a month in coming, and moving C Company from support capacity inside Turkey to the border wasn't a promising sign.

Dug in on the plateaus that made up the southeastern section of Turkey, Goose stared due south. The terrain wasn't as mountainous or craggy as in many places along the border. This had once been the gateway to Mesopotamia, home of some of the world's oldest civilizations—Babylon, Sumer, Persia, Assyria, Chaldea. The Tigris and Euphrates Rivers flowed from the mountains further north and spilled into the lowlands in the southeast, emptying into Iraq and Iran to form what had once been known as the Fertile Crescent.

Back when he was a young man, in a Bible class his daddy'd taught at church back home in Waycross, Georgia, Goose had studied this region. It was the place many Bible scholars believed had once housed the Garden of Eden. But now the green paradise was gone. Here the world seemed reduced to a sea of shifting yellow sand and gravel that sported islands of treacherous rocks and stubborn scrub bushes. And Goose, too, had changed. His easy acceptance of the church's teaching was long gone. He had seen too much violence to buy into the simple beliefs of his youth.

His faith, like the landscape around him, had been blasted.

"So, what do you think, Sergeant?" The voice of his commanding officer came via Goose's ear/throat headset. Satellite communications kept the teams in constant contact, and with HQ five klicks behind the front lines, that was good. As First Sergeant, Goose's headset was chipped for the main channel as well as four subset frequencies he could use for special team assignments. He was second-in-command and ranking NCO of a company consisting of for four rifle platoons ranged across the border, shoring up the exhausted Turkish soldiers on the front lines.

Despite the fact that the Syrian military hadn't shown signs of having audio-pickup equipment or signal-capturing communications antenna, Goose spoke quietly and evenly over the scrambled channel. "I think they're waiting on something, sir. Or someone."

"Nothing appears out of the ordinary," Captain Cal Remington replied.

"No, sir," Goose said, surveying the way the Syrian soldiers took refuge from the sun under vehicles and tarps. "The grunts are all business as usual. But I do see a little more spit and polish than normal today."

"'Spit and polish'?"

Goose grinned. "Yes, sir, Captain. An enlisted man, sir, he never forgets the dog and pony show he has to put on for an officer. Always cleaning. Always drilling. Always looking busy. The more important the officers, the more spit and polish."

"And you'd know that, would you, Sergeant?"

"Yes, sir. And if I recall, sir, there was a time before OCS when you knew that, too." Their friendship reached through nearly sixteen years of hardships and dangerous assignments, including Remington's choice to sign up for the army's Officer Candidate School. That long bridge of friendship more than spanned the gulf between officer and non-com.

Remington was silent.

Knowing the captain was back at headquarters, availing himself of the computer systems tied into the geosynchronous spy satellites twenty-three thousand miles into space, Goose waited. He shifted the binoculars slowly. Maybe Remington hadn't noticed the subtle change in the attitudes of the Syrian soldiers on the other side of the border.

The Syrian soldiers wore camouflage fatigues that looked a lot like the ones worn by the American and Turkish troops. The pattern was bigger, cleaner, and not as shaded. A civilian eye, Goose knew, probably wouldn't be able to differentiate between the three sets of battle dress uniforms in this part of the world, but Goose had no problem. His life—as well as the lives of his squadmates—could depend on that skill. It wasn't just a matter of finding and shooting the enemy. Like the old saying went, "Friendly fire isn't."

Syrian troop placement was heavy. Winning through intimidation, Remington called the effort, with his signature smirk of disapproval. Remington always said real warriors won wars by handing down a decisive victory that left no room for argument—not by saber rattling and trafficking in threats. Goose knew that for Remington, anything other than confrontation and aggressive action was NJ—no joy.

Goose didn't feel that way. If intimidation kept everybody from shooting, he was all for it. Putting on a good show could save lives. Remington may have had his reasons to prefer action. An officer's career advanced through victories, while an enlisted man simply wanted to do a good job and remain alive. Goose hoped the Syrians were willing to stick to intimidation for the foreseeable future.

The Syrian military boasted an assortment of Jeeps, Land Rovers, T-62 and T-72 main battle tanks, BMP-2 and BMP-3 armored infantry fighting vehicles, and BTR-60 armored personnel carriers. Farther back among the hills, Goose had seen self-propelled artillery and air defense units, as well as multiple rocket launchers. Satellite reconnaissance had confirmed all those weapons, as well as giving reliable estimates of troop numbers.

During the last week, the numbers had doubled. So the changes weren't all just spit and polish. Goose was getting a bad feeling about the future.

The Turks and the U.N. forces had their own array of weapons. The border area was crawling with Humvees, M-1 Abrams main battle tanks, and Bradley M-2 and M-3 APCs. Artillery and air defense units were bolstered by MLRs and Apache helicopter gunships. If that wasn't enough to handle the army arrayed against them, heavy-duty help was close by. The 26th Marine Expeditionary Unit—Special Operations Capable, or MEU(SOC), was on standby, poised for action on their three-ship amphibious ready group, anchored by the USS *Wasp*. The ARG sat on a 180-day float out in the Mediterranean Sea, ready to lend air and Marine support to the land-based forces at a moment's notice.

The Syrians knew that, and not just because of secret intelligence operations. The *Wasp*'s presence had been broadcast all over CNN and FOX News networks since the Rangers had moved in-country. The bad guys knew what they were up against—though not, Goose hoped, the specifics of all the goodies they had in their bag of tricks.

"Maybe they are waiting on something," Remington said.

Cal Remington wasn't one to drop hints and not pay off on them. "You got something, Cap?" Goose said.

"I don't know yet, Sergeant. But I may have a way to get something. I've got a maybe-mission for you, purely hide-and-seek with a chance at some action. If you'd rather bake in the sun and watch the

Syrian army corps sleep, I can use one of the staff sergeants for this little exercise."

Smiling despite the tension, Goose scanned the Syrian line again.
Lots of snoring soldiers. Even with the changes in the front line, many
Syrian troops were stretched out in the shadows under vehicles or
under small tents. In this climate, a nap in the shade made a whole lot
of sense. Goose felt it was a pity he and his men couldn't join them.

"I'm interested in a maybe-mission, Cap. Especially if it gets me
off this plateau and out of the sun. It'll give me a chance to stretch my
legs and clear my head."

"Not worried about leaving the troops there, Sergeant? As I recall,
you're usually the last one to leave the field when we're in a hot
zone."

"You've got sat-relays overlooking the play out here, sir," Goose
said. "You've got a clearer view of what's shaping up than I do. I figure
you must need me. I know you don't like me being away from the
front line any more than I do."

"That I don't, Sergeant." Remington's banter was light. "I may
have eyes and ears in space, but I'll take your gut over technology any
day. Anyway, you'll be back in place soon enough. I'm looking at a
short hop that will give you the chance to show your stuff. Maybe if
you get away from that standoff for a little while you'll get a different
read on it when you get back."

"Yes, sir. " Goose peered along the mountainous area and at the
tarmac road that crossed the border. The Syrians and the Turks had
checkpoints for vehicles as well as pedestrians. So far there had been
nothing to see today. "Who do I need, and when do I go?"

"Take a squad. Yourself and ten. Two vehicles. And you're leaving
now."

❋   ❋   ❋

Captain Cal Remington stood behind the four-man unit that handled
the communications relays for his present operation. Nervous energy
filled him, pushing him to act. Instead, he waited and watched the
eight computer screens spread in front of his team. Waiting was not
his forte and never had been.

The computers in the cinder-block building that had been re-
vamped into a command HQ five klicks behind the border made the
chill air-conditioning necessary. Gasoline-powered generators sup-
plied the juice to run both the computers and the air-conditioning.

Thick bundles of cables snaked across the chipped stone floor. An assortment of bullet holes scarred the walls, offering mute testimony to how many times firefights had taken place in this building. The building had once been part of a small village, a place where farmers and artisans had met to swap goods and talk, but it was mostly rubble now. Only three of the small cinder-block buildings remained intact.

The satellite feeds came in beautifully, panning down over the Turkish-Syrian border. The signals actually came from two different satellites, but Cray computers relayed those signals into the systems so they could be handled independently at each of the four workstations manned by Remington's tech support unit.

OCS hadn't revealed all the secret machinations of its cybernetic systems, and Remington was amazed at the computer surveillance program's abilities. Still, he knew how to use the intel the programs provided. Even though the information they gave him would have been a commander's dream just a few years ago, he needed more. Three shifts of four operators kept twenty-four-hour surveillance on the border over different overlapping fields.

After three days of close scrutiny, Remington was of the opinion that there wasn't much they hadn't seen, photographed, cataloged, and archived along C Company's section of border country. The tech teams had accumulated gigabytes of information and pumped it out to army databases in Diyarbakir, where the general command in-country was situated, to the ARG headed by the USS *Wasp* out in the Med, and to the Pentagon. None of the information gathered so far offered any indication of what was behind the increased terrorist attacks within Turkey. Something was up. Watching just wasn't enough; Remington wanted—needed—to know what the enemy was thinking.

"Captain Remington, sir."

Turning, Remington studied the man in civilian clothes who stood between two Ranger escorts. The man was tall, over six feet, but Remington stood two inches taller. The Ranger captain was also broader through the shoulders than the new guy, and at thirty-eight, probably a handful of years younger.

"Sir," the corporal said, throwing a sharp salute while standing at attention, "this is Central Intelligence Agency Section Chief Alexander Cody."

The CIA agent didn't look happy about the announcement. He seemed to be fit, and his mouth looked habitually stern. He had short-cropped dark hair going gray at the temples. His light-colored slacks, white dress shirt, and tie showed a layer of dust, as did the tan jacket slung over one arm. Beneath a painful looking wind- and sunburn, his skin was pale. Dark sunglasses hid his eyes.

"Come in, Agent Cody," Remington said. "Corporal, Private, you're dismissed."

The corporal saluted again, spun smartly, and departed with the private in tow.

"Not exactly the kind of introduction I usually get in my line of work." Cody crossed the room and held out his hand. "Or one that I would want."

Remington shook the offered hand. Cody had a firm grip and a callused palm. "In the regular army, we stand on formality, Agent Cody. Except for sometimes on the front lines, where a salute is considered to be a sniper magnet by our more experienced troops."

"I can understand their caution. I start to feel exposed when I get the full treatment. You can call me Alex," Cody offered.

"Fine. You can address me as Captain, or Captain Remington."

If Cody took any insult, he didn't show it. "Very well, Captain. You've been briefed on our situation?"

"Only that you've had an agent go missing, and that we're supposed to help you get him back. If possible."

Cody reached into his shirt pocket and produced a miniature CD in a plastic case. "I've got an image of the agent here."

Remington took the disc and handed it to Lewis, one of the young techs. "Get this up for me."

"Yes, sir." Lewis took the disc, pushed it home into a CD-ROM reader, and tapped the keyboard.

Instantly, the monitor on the left scrolled. Thumbnails of images spread out in a simple information tree. All of the images were of a young, dark-complexioned man who looked Middle Eastern. He might have been Turkish, Kurdish, or Syrian; in fact, he could have been from any of a dozen countries in the area. He looked all of twenty years old.

"He's one of ours?" Remington asked.

"Yeah." Cody gazed at the young man's photo. "An American, Captain. Not a recruit or paid informer."

"What kind of assignment has he been on?"

Cody hesitated. "You don't have clearance."

Remington mastered the wave of anger that flooded through him. "I just detailed a squad of men to handle the intercept your agency asked for, Cody. If my men are going to be in danger, then you'd better clear me."

Cody pursed his lips and removed his sunglasses. "Icarus is a covert operative we've managed to get into one of the PKK cell groups."

The PKK, Remington knew from his own briefings regarding the border patrol assignment, was the Kurdistan Worker's Party. Organized in 1974 by Abdullah Ocalan, the PKK planned to establish an independent Kurdish state from land within Turkey, Iraq, or Iran. Over the years, the organization had turned to terrorism aimed at destabilizing the Turkish government. Often the PKK terrorists killed as many Kurds as they did Turks.

"Infiltrating a single terrorist cell doesn't seem like a good investment of manpower," Remington stated. "The cells are kept small and independent, with relatively no interaction among other cells or the parent organization. The intelligence you'd get would be infinitesimal at best."

"Icarus penetrated the cell assigned to assassinate Chaim Rosenzweig," Cody said. "Thanks to Icarus, the members of that team were . . . *dissuaded* from that action."

"How dissuaded?"

"Five of the eight men assigned to the assassination are dead," Cody said. "The other three escaped our sweeps. They have apparently taken Icarus with them."

Remington nodded. He hadn't heard about an assassination team being intercepted, but he wasn't surprised that Rosenzweig was a target. The Israeli botanist whose synthetic fertilizer had turned his country into a veritable Eden almost overnight was reviled by most of the Arab nations, although Israel's neighbors had made their peace with Israel. In the end they'd had no choice, but peace at the end of a gun barrel was still peace.

Rosenzweig had been given the Nobel prize in chemistry for his efforts, and he'd been handed a death sentence by terrorist organizations scattered around the Middle East, who now faced a concerted Israeli effort to put them out of business.

That shift in prosperity in the Middle East, especially since it also affected the global balance of trade and power, had triggered a Russian surprise attack that had caught Israel and the world off guard fourteen months ago. When he'd heard of the attack, Remington had figured Israel's existence would be measured in minutes.

Instead, the Russian air force had suffered a massive systems failure. Their attacking force had self-destructed, its crumpled remains raining down from the sky in flaming chunks. Military experts and analysts agreed that the Russian air force had grown lax and that the fleetwide systems failures were caused by poorly maintained, obsolete equipment. Remington wanted to be sure that such a disaster never occurred to his forces on his watch.

"If this assassination attempt is off the books," Remington asked, "why is your covert agent still with the PKK cell?"

Cody stared at the young man's face on the computer screen. "We haven't been successful in exfiltrating Icarus."

"Maybe he didn't want to be exfiltrated."

"We don't feel that's the case."

Don't feel, Remington knew, wasn't a definite answer. "How long has Icarus been under?"

"A year and a half. He penetrated the PKK almost seven months ago. We were about to pull the plug on the op at that point but he managed to get inside the cell." Cody paused. "Captain, there is no question about this man's loyalty. That's why I'm here talking to you today. He's a good man in a bad situation. He gave us the assassination team when they were ready to strike, and he endangered himself by doing so."

"He could be dead already."

Concern creased Cody's face for just a moment then flickered out of existence. "I refuse to believe that."

"You've asked for help," Remington pointed out. "I'm risking the lives of my men. Sell me on what you believe."

The CIA agent nodded at the computer terminals. "I can log your computers in to the link we've set up for your team."

Remington excused Lewis from the chair and Cody sat. The CIA chief's fingers clacked against the keyboard in rapid syncopation. The monitor screen scrolled and scrolled again.

"What am I looking at?" Remington asked.

"I'm downloading a satellite feed. We have a lock on the vehicle Icarus is being transported in."

The screen image changed, revealing a ten-year-old Subaru Legacy. Battered and pale blue, the vehicle stood out in sharp relief against the yellow sand. A billowing amber dust cloud trailed behind the Subaru.

Remington watched the station wagon jerk and bounce across the rough terrain. The road was ancient, a whisper-thin memory that probably was constructed for carts and foot traffic, or military Jeeps.

"You're sure he's in there?" the Ranger captain asked.

Cody tapped more keys. The feed changed to a thermal image view. The station wagon registered as purple, and the road and the desert became a sheet of pale yellow. The human body temperature of 98.6 degrees was lower than the ground temperature, making the four figures actually register cooler than the land around them. The four people inside the car became outlined in dark yellow and orange.

"We've had a lock on this car since it left Ankara this morning," Cody said. Ankara was Turkey's capital city. "We've tracked Icarus since the group left Jerusalem."

"The assassins got close," Remington observed.

"Yes. Icarus has been closely watched."

"They suspected him?"

"The group watched each other. Since we decided to take them down in Jerusalem, we created an opening for Icarus to feed us information. However, we couldn't get a message back to him."

"What message?"

"We wanted him out," Cody said. "Icarus has reached an untenable position. If those other men don't suspect him now, they will soon. Or whoever they're going to meet in Syria will."

"When your teams swept the other members of the cell, seems Icarus should have jumped ship."

"Unless he thought he was about to get more information we needed. We would have gone after Icarus ourselves, Captain Remington, but given the state of alert in Turkey and Syria, the decision was made that it would be more feasible and prudent to have your men handle the exfiltration."

Remington silently agreed. While the United States Army's peacekeeping effort was welcomed in-country, CIA agents weren't. Especially since they didn't operate with Turkey's permission in many cases.

Cody tapped the keys, changing the view back to normal.

The perspective also pulled back, revealing movement high in the hills overlooking the road. Cody tapped the keys again, narrowing the focus to the eleven Rangers huddled in two groups on either side of the narrow road. Another keystroke put the group's geographic location in longitude and latitude under them.

"These are your men?" the CIA section chief asked.

Though he recognized the Ranger camo fatigues, Remington checked the location of Goose's group. The figures matched. Goose had brought his unit into position after a fifteen-minute hop from the front lines. They now sat seven klicks north-northeast of the border face-off.

"Yes," he replied, moving back to Cody's screen.

"They're good?"

"They're Rangers," Remington answered. "They're *my* Rangers. They're the best."

"Well," Cody replied noncommittally, "in three or four minutes, we're going to find out."

The pale blue station wagon continued bouncing across the broken terrain, closing on the Rangers' positions.

Turkey
37 Klicks Southeast of Sanliurfa
Local Time 0621 Hours

Goose hunkered down behind the rocks on the west side of the road he'd decided had probably served as a pass through the mountains back in the days of the Silk Road. These days it was so little used Goose figured the only reason it wasn't grown over was that nothing would grow in the sand and bleak rock.

A half mile away, a dust cloud closed on their position.

Moving slowly, letting his dust-covered camo do the job it was designed to do, Goose lifted his M-4A1 and peered through the scope. He checked to make sure the digital camera mounted underneath the assault rifle had a clear field of view.

The digital cam hooked into the modular computer/sat-com feed on his load-bearing frame, spreading the extra weight across his shoulders. After two years of training with the rig for special urban warfare operations, Goose didn't even notice the extra weight on the rifle.

In most instances, the M-4A1 carbine was a better weapon than the M-16A2 Goose had been given when he entered the Army sixteen years ago. He'd been a rawboned twenty-one-year-old fresh from the backwoods country of Waycross, Georgia. Both assault rifles fired the 5.56mm round, but the M-4A1's barrel was fourteen and a half inches long, nearly six inches shorter than the M-16A2. Along with the collapsible butt stock, the M-4A1 offered quicker reaction speed as well as the ability to use the weapon in more compact places.

Goose lay prone on the hot ground. Before taking up his position, he'd scraped away the top layer of sand and rocks, exposing the cooler earth below. It made lying down on the scorching desert surface more bearable. Only a minute or two of being exposed to the dry heat had turned the layer he'd exposed the same color as the land around him.

He adjusted the telescopic sights, bringing the image of the pale blue Subaru station wagon into proper magnification. The image sharpened. He kept both eyes open, the way he had been trained to do, mentally switching between both fields of vision. His father, a woodsman who had hunted all over the Okefenokee Swamp and had pulled a tour of duty as a Marine in Korea, had first taught him the technique. Drill sergeants and sniper specialists had refined the skill during training.

Dried mud covered the station wagon's windshield except for the arches carved out by the wipers. Streaks of dried mud stained the car's body. Tie-downs held two spare tires and two five-gallon jerry cans on the roof.

Goose played the scope over the vehicle's windshield. The driver and the man sitting in the shotgun seat looked Middle Eastern. Evidently the vehicle's air-conditioning wasn't working because they were both drenched with perspiration that left damp stains in the armpits of their shirts.

"Base," Goose said, speaking into the pencil mike at the left corner of his mouth.

"Go, Phoenix Leader," Remington called back. "Base reads you five by five."

"You got vid?"

"We see what you see, Leader."

"Can you confirm your package?" Goose asked, sweeping the M-4A1's sights from the driver to the passenger.

Remington hesitated an instant. "Neither of those men. They are confirmed hostiles. Repeat, we have positive ID of hostile nature. Don't take any chances with these people."

Shifting the rifle slightly and refocusing the scope, Goose ran the sights over the two men in the backseat. He knew the agent immediately because the man's face was battered and bloody. Gray duct tape covered his eyes, wrapping around his head. From the uncomfortable way the man was sitting, Goose guessed that his hands were tied or cuffed behind him.

"Is this the package, Base?" Goose asked.

"Affirmative, Leader," Remington said. "You have visual confirmation."

The station wagon had come within a quarter mile of the Rangers' position. The rough terrain kept the vehicle's speed down to about thirty miles an hour.

Goose switched over to the team frequency. Remington and HQ remained part of the loop. "We've got ID. Our save is located in the rear seat. Passenger side, not the driver's side. Copy?"

The ten men in the unit responded quickly.

Glancing over his shoulder, Goose looked at Corporal Bill Townsend. The corporal had been the first man Goose selected for the ten-man unit.

Bill had just turned twenty-eight. He was young, easygoing by nature but quick on the fly on an op. Like Goose, he wore load-carrying equipment, an LCE, that supported his gear. Combat webbing held extra magazines and rounds for the M-4A1/M-203 combo he carried. The M-203 grenade launcher fired 40mm grenades and added a wallop to a squad's force.

During the eight years he'd known Bill, Goose had never seen him perturbed. Things didn't always go the way Bill thought they should, but he worked through any situation, be it smooth sailing or total chaos, with better grace than any man Goose had ever known. Bill was totally relaxed and at peace with himself. Goose figured it had something to do with the corporal's faith. Bill was a devout Christian who spent time with squadmates who were having personal troubles. He was good at easing the burdens down to some manageable load. If Bill hadn't been such a good soldier and adamant about making a difference in the world in that fashion, Goose would have recommended the corporal for a counseling position on base.

Seven years ago, when Goose had met Megan Holder at Fort Benning and fallen in love with her in spite of his best efforts not to, Bill had counseled him. Goose had always promised himself that he'd remain single till he finished his twenty years and retired, reminding himself that a dedicated career soldier's family often got short shrift by the very nature of the job. He hadn't wanted to put anyone through that. But Goose had been torn in his resolution when he saw Megan trying bravely to raise her son—*our son*, he corrected himself—Joey, all by herself.

Bill had known Goose was troubled and had talked to him without really talking to him for a while. At least, that was the way it seemed. Looking back on things now, Goose had the distinct impression that the young man knew exactly what he was doing.

In the end, Bill helped Goose get over his cold feet and follow his heart. Bill had been best man at their wedding, a position Goose always thought would belong to his old friend Cal Remington. After all, Goose had been best man at two of Remington's weddings. But for some reason Remington hadn't been able to participate on the date Goose and Megan had chosen. In the end, Bill had been the perfect best man, and he had stayed close to Goose's whole family. These days, Remington seldom visited the Gander household, while Bill was often around. He frequently baby-sat Chris.

"I'm here," Bill told Goose quietly. "When you move, I've got your six."

"You get your prayers said?" Goose tossed off the question in a lighthearted way, but he'd been around Bill when the man had prayed over injured soldiers and during disastrous situations. It seemed to Goose that God paid special attention to Bill's words. Although he'd never talked about his feelings with anyone else, Goose had always felt the strength and conviction in Bill's prayers. While he had a few doubts of his own about God, Goose leaned on Bill to put in a good word for him with the Big Guy.

Bill nodded. "Prayers said. Mine. Yours. The squad's. We'll make it home okay, Sarge."

"I hope you're right."

An easy grin touched Bill's lips. "You can't just hope. You gotta have faith."

"I do have faith."

"Nah." Bill shook his head. "If you had faith, you wouldn't have to reach for hope."

"Then I'm working on it. Best I can do. Thanks, man." Goose turned from Bill.

It wasn't often Goose felt the difference between the younger man and himself, but today he did. They often attended the same prayer groups while they were in the field. Or, more accurately, Goose joined the ones that Bill headed. And even back on base, Bill had found the church that Goose's family attended. Bill spent some of his free time working as a youth minister for athletic events there.

"Phoenix Three," Goose called out.

"Three," Bobby Tanaka responded. He was the unit sniper, young and cool under pressure. "Go, Leader."

"I want the package protected, Three. Your primary target is the hostile in the backseat with him."

"Affirmative, Leader." Tanaka lay in a prone sniping position behind an M-24 bolt-action sniper rifle.

The station wagon closed on the gap.

"On me," Goose ordered. He tracked the vehicle with the M-4A1.

Twenty yards in front of the Rangers' position, the Subaru's front wheels hit the portable spike barrier concealed under the sand. The tires blew as the spikes shredded the rubber. Before the driver could hope to regain control over his vehicle, the rear tires hit the spikes and went to pieces as well.

"Go!" Goose commanded, pushing himself up and racing down the hill. Sand, gravel, and rock tore loose under his combat boots, throwing up dust. He skidded twice, dragging a knee both times to stay upright while he cradled the M-4A1 in his arms. Bill pounded along behind him.

The station wagon driver tried to keep going, but the tire rims sank into the soft sand and chewed through the hard-packed earth. In less than five feet, the station wagon had mired up to its chassis. The engine roared as the driver tried to use the four-wheel drive to fight free of the earth. The churning rims threw rooster tails of sand and rock behind the vehicle, then reversed and threw them forward.

Skidding down the hill, Goose closed on the vehicle. He watched the movement in the station wagon, tracking his unit as well as the targets. Years of combat training, discipline, and action in several deployments stood him in good stead. He kept his finger on the trigger guard. Until he knew he was going to have to shoot and he had a confirmed target, he never touched the trigger.

Dust filled the air around the station wagon, obscuring his vision. The man getting out of the passenger side looked blurred, but there was no mistaking the Uzi submachine gun clenched in his fists.

"Weapon!" Goose yelled, throwing himself forward and down. He brought the M-4A1 up and slid his finger into the trigger guard, squeezing the trigger three times. The butt stock shoved against his shoulder with each shot.

Hit by the rounds, the terrorist fell backward. The passenger window erupted in a spray of glittering shards.

Even as the terrorist fell to the ground, Goose spotted the station wagon's driver lifting a semi-automatic pistol in his fist and pointing the weapon at the CIA spy. Goose tracked the man but couldn't fire because one of the Rangers was in his field of fire.

Then the driver's head snapped back.

For Goose, time seemed to slow down. His senses whirling, his mind driven to adrenaline-charged razor awareness, Goose noted the starred hole that had formed on the windshield, then heard the heavier 7.62mm report of Tanaka's M-24 sniper rifle roll into the gap around the road.

As he died, the driver fired a pistol round that punctured the station wagon's roof and the jerry can on top. The jerry can exploded in a seething mass of hungry orange and yellow flames that spread across the top of the vehicle. The second can, already propelled by the first can's explosion, detonated in midair. A sheet of flames arced over two of the Rangers standing ahead of the vehicle to the left. Both soldiers hit the ground and rolled to extinguish the flames that clung to their fatigues and helmets.

The heat wave generated by the blast hammered Goose. Through tearing eyes, he stared through the pool of flames that clung to the station wagon. Flames poured down over the vehicle's side and formed fiery puddles on the ground.

The third terrorist was fumbling for the door.

The battered CIA agent screamed, "Kill him! Kill him!"

Managing to hit the door release, the terrorist vaulted from the Subaru and ran. He pulled a sat-phone from his pocket even as he brandished a 9mm pistol in his other hand. The man hit the dirt and crawled for cover.

"Kill him!" the CIA agent yelled from inside the burning car.

Goose transferred his M-4A1 to his right arm and pushed himself up. The car blocked his line of fire. He ran toward the station wagon. The windshield, covered in flames, imploded and blew back over the body of the dead driver. Fire rushed into the vehicle's interior.

Ducking to avoid the tongue of flame that spat from the open passenger door, Goose reached into the burning car and hooked a hand inside the agent's elbow. He yanked the man from the vehicle, nearly sending both of them sprawling before getting his feet under him.

Bill rushed in and grabbed the agent's other arm. They had to drag him back from the burning Subaru because his feet were taped together.

"You've got to get that guy!" the agent yelled hoarsely. Fresh blood trickled from his split lips and broken nose. Bruises showed all across his face.

"Our mission is to get you out of here alive. That's our first priority." Something else in the car blew, sending waves of blistering heat over them. Goose quit talking and helped Bill drag the guy farther from the flames.

"Take it easy," Goose said. He stood, cradling the M-4A1 and looking for the terrorist.

Bill flipped a combat knife from his LCE and slid the sharp blade through the duct tape securing the man's ankles and wrists.

The agent reached for the tape covering his eyes but couldn't manage to pull the strips from his face. The binding at his wrists had been tight enough to cut off his circulation, and his hands probably remained numb. Goose knew that when the man started to get the feeling back he was going to be in a world of hurt.

The terrorist was out of sight, invisible in the cloud of black smoke spewing from the burning station wagon.

"Don't you understand me?" the agent bellowed. He tried a couple different languages while Bill pulled at the duct tape over his eyes.

"We understand you," Goose replied. "We're U.S. Army Rangers. With the 75th out of Fort Benning. Our mission is to get you out safe. Why do we have to kill him? Give me a good reason to risk my men to do it, now that we've done what we came here to do." As a soldier, Goose had killed, but always to protect himself or others. He had never killed indiscriminately or allowed any man under his command to do so.

The agent blinked his eyes against the harsh sunlight. Tears rolled down his dusty cheeks. "That man will transmit to the Syrian forces. They'll know you've saved me. They know that I know they're planning to launch a major offensive against the Turkish and U.N. forces, especially the American military. If he gets his message through, they'll launch that strike immediately. Your refusal to kill him will take away days and hours we might have had to prepare."

Fear raced through Goose. He'd known something was up on the border. He'd felt it in his bones.

"Three," Goose said as he threw himself in pursuit.

"I've got him," Tanaka replied.

The wind changed. The terrorist materialized out of the concealing smoke with the sat-phone clasped tightly against his head. Then he spun, his legs flaring out wildly as he fought to keep his balance. The phone against his head went to pieces. Blood showed on his hand. He turned just as the sound of Tanaka's sniper rifle slammed across the sound of the burning car.

The wind carried the twisting black smoke across Goose's vision, smudging the sight of the terrorist as he raised his pistol. The station wagon exploded, bits of it launching into the air, its body buckling into a wrenched mass of flaming metal.

Goose twisted into a profile stance, offering the smallest target possible to the terrorist. He flicked the M-4A1's fire selector over to a three-round burst. "Put the weapon down!" he ordered. "We're the United States Army! Throw down your weapon and step away!"

Instead, the terrorist screamed in rage and opened fire.

One round slapped against Goose's Kevlar-lined helmet. It hit hard enough to knock his head to one side like he'd caught a punch from a professional boxer. The bullet ricocheted from the helmet, though. Goose took a half step to the right to recover. His sights on the terrorist never wavered. He squeezed the trigger, aiming for the kill zone.

The terrorist staggered backward just as the report from Tanaka's sniper weapon echoed around Goose. It was over.

Goose assigned Williams and Clark to secure the third terrorist's body and confirm the kill, then turned back to the CIA agent.

The agent stood with difficulty, leaning heavily on Bill. Holding his assault rifle in one hand, Bill put his other arm around the man's waist to support him.

Flipping over to the secure command frequency, Goose said, "Phoenix Base, this is Phoenix Leader."

"Go, Leader. Base reads you."

"Can you confirm the story we're getting here?"

"Affirmative, Leader," Remington said in a cool voice. "My translator at this end tells me the man was telling someone that the group had been attacked by American Rangers."

"Was he alerting Syrian forces or the PKK?" Goose asked. He thought of his team. The front line was only seven klicks away, but suddenly it felt like a million miles.

"He was transmitting a warning, Leader," Remington said. "We haven't been able to confirm the destination of the signal. There wasn't time to get a lock on it."

"Did he get through?"

"We don't know."

❈ ❈ ❈

United States of America
Fort Benning, Georgia
Local Time 11:21 P.M.

Megan Gander stabbed a hand out, palmed the handset, and had the cordless phone to her ear between the first and second ring. The real trick was being awake and semicoherent by the time the chill plastic touched her ear and cheek.

Her thoughts flew immediately to Joey. She'd fallen asleep on the couch waiting for him to get home. She looked at her watch. Joey had a 9 P.M. curfew on school nights, and he knew it. It was way too late for her boy to be out. Her anger came awake with her, and she was ready to unload on her seventeen-year-old son if he was calling with *any* excuse as to why he hadn't been home at curfew.

If Goose were home, Joey wouldn't push his luck so hard, she thought, and at the same moment she prayed the call wasn't from the police to tell her something had happened to Joey. Or from the army, telling her something had happened to Goose.

That was her second thought as she awoke. Maybe the call was about Goose. Her husband had sounded calm and casual during their phone conversation the previous day, and she knew he wouldn't call her late at night or during her scheduled shift at the base's counseling center. Goose was just that way. No matter what time zone he was in, Goose always knew what time it was in her world and what she had going on.

Just as she thought the call might be about Goose, she dismissed the possibility. While Goose thought things might heat up along the Turkish-Syrian border, he'd assured her that nothing had happened yet. And if something had happened to Goose, there would have been a uniformed officer at her door to inform her, not some impersonal phone call.

"Megan Gander," she said, then covered the mouthpiece while she cleared the sleep from her voice.

"Megan, this is Helen Cordell."

"Yes, Helen. What can I do for you?" Helen Cordell was the current night shift supervisor at the counseling center where Megan worked. Megan sat up on the living-room couch. She wore pink sweats that were a favorite of hers from her high school days eighteen years earlier. Other than during her two pregnancies, her size had never changed. She'd been gifted with a fast metabolism and worked hard to stay in shape. She and Goose shared mutual interests in tennis and hiking, as well as other team sports supported on base, and that helped make scheduling activities easy.

"I know it's not your scheduled shift," Helen said, "but we have a situation."

"It's no problem. I was just grabbing a nap." Megan got up and moved through the small three-bedroom base house she and Goose had filled with comfortable furniture and personal items. She walked past the master bedroom and down the hall to Joey's room. "I'd have been up anyway in a few minutes."

"Is something wrong?"

"It's my son, Joey." Megan opened the door and peeked into the room. The room was a mess—the walls covered with posters of extreme sports icons in midstunt, CDs scattered everywhere, and schoolbooks gathering dust on the small rolltop desk Goose had given the boy as a birthday present a few years ago. The bed was empty. "It's past curfew and my teenager still hasn't made it home." Megan walked to the other bedroom. "He was supposed to be home by nine. If he's not home by midnight, I get to go out and look for him."

"Now I really hate having to call you," Helen said. "I know how nerve-wracking it is waiting up on a teenager. I've done that myself."

"I know. Joey wouldn't pull something like this if Goose was at home." Megan eased her other son's door open.

Chris lay swaddled in blankets featuring his favorite cartoon heroes. He slept on the top bunk of the bunk bed, which he'd had to have because "sometimes me and Daddy like to have guy time to play video games and watch videos and stuff-like-that-PLEASE-Mom."

The night-light on the dresser bathed him in soft golden illumination that highlighted the wheat-colored hair he'd gotten from his father. The night-light was a scene that showed Jesus with a shepherd's crook telling stories to a group of children gathered at his feet. It had been a gift from Bill Townsend, who sometimes spent the night with them at the base when the weather turned bad or when he and Goose had to make an early morning jump. On those nights, Bill read to Chris from the big book of children's Bible stories he had bought for the boy, giving the characters unique voices that delighted Chris and left him imitating Bill for days.

It helped knowing that Bill and Goose had each other over in Turkey. *But who do you have, Joey?* Megan couldn't help but wonder.

"Maybe this can wait," Helen suggested.

Megan sighed. She knew she wasn't going to be able to get back to sleep. Worrying about Goose and Joey was getting to be too much, and that wasn't even taking into consideration the caseload she was currently working at the counseling center.

"If you called this late," Megan said, "I know you thought it was important. Now spill."

"Gerry Fletcher is in the infirmary," Helen said.

Megan's stomach lurched. Gerry Fletcher was one of the special projects Megan had taken into her heart. Helen was well aware of that. *Everyone* connected to the counseling center—half the base—was aware of that.

For the last fourteen months, since Private Boyd Fletcher had moved to Fort Benning with his wife and son to become a Ranger, Megan had been aware of the abuse Gerry underwent. Most of it, she'd gathered, had been psychological in nature: unkind words, sarcastic comments, anything to wreck the eleven-year-old boy's self-esteem.

But occasionally there had been bruises on Gerry's arms and legs and shoulders. None had ever shown up on the boy's face, though. Boyd Fletcher had evidently declared Gerry's face off-limits.

Megan had tried several times to get Gerry out of the home. She'd failed. No one had ever seen Boyd Fletcher punish Gerry in any way. Gerry was, according to staff at the base schools, one of the best students a teacher could hope for.

Megan had urged Gerry to come forward with what happened. No dice. He always smiled at her and tell her that he was just "accident-prone." Boyd Fletcher had refused steadfastly to talk to her, other than the one time he had been ordered to by the base commander.

Gerry had gone more than a month without a bruise after that; then he'd suffered a devastating bicycle wreck that had broken his left arm. Or so Gerry and Boyd had claimed. Somehow, though, the wreck hadn't taken any skin off the boy's knees or elbows the way such an accident normally would have. When Megan had asked for another interview with Boyd Fletcher, the base commander had denied it, telling Megan he would only enforce such a visit if she could offer proof of physical abuse.

It had gotten so hard going through channels that Megan had gone to Goose with the situation months ago. That was something she almost never did. He had listened and soothed her because he was Goose and that was what he did. However, during the past months, until Goose's unit had been pulled out to reinforce the Turkish troops, Gerry had seemed to relax and even be happy most days. Megan couldn't prove it, and she wouldn't ask, but she felt certain Goose had done something to affect the situation in the Fletcher household.

"How is he?" Megan asked.

"Bruised. Shaken up. He says he was outside on the roof with his telescope. He says he slipped and fell."

"How bad is it?"

"The doctor says he's dislocated his shoulder, but the physical pain is only part of it. That's one scared little guy, Megan," Helen said. "Gerry doesn't want his dad to know."

"Where's his father?" Megan always thought of Boyd Fletcher as Gerry's *father*. A *dad* was someone like Goose, someone who cared.

"At home."

"Does he know Gerry's in the hospital?"

"No. Gerry's with Dr. Carson."

Megan relaxed a little. *Thank You, God, for that.* Craig Carson was a friend and one of the best pediatricians on the base.

"Dr. Carson and I are *electing* to have a busy night and phone trouble until you get a chance to see Gerry," Helen said. "If you want to come in to see him, that is."

"Of course I want to see him," Megan said. "I'll be right there."

Turkey
39 Klicks Southeast of Sanliurfa
Local Time 0643 Hours

Belted in tight, Goose sat in the shotgun seat of the Ranger Special
Operations Vehicle. The vehicle's powerful diesel engine growled as
the all-terrain tires dug into the sand and propelled the team across
the desert back toward the Turkish-Syrian border.

Based on the Land Rover Defender Model 110, the RSOV offered
seats all the way around that faced outward rather than forward, giving passengers 360-degree visibility. The Rangers had adopted the vehicles after the Gulf War. With ten inches of clearance, heavy-duty
suspension, and four-wheel drive, the RSOV was a mover and shaker
on a cross-country run.

Tanaka drove while Clark handled the top gunner position where
the M-249 SAW was mounted. Bill sat with the CIA agent on the rear
deck, which was the most protected point on the RSOV. Williams and
Cusack occupied side seats. The rest of the Ranger unit rode in a second RSOV. Both vehicles charged and leaped across the broken terrain.

Goose scanned the countryside continuously. Nothing else appeared to be moving on the desert. He glanced over his shoulder and
saw the CIA agent staring apprehensively south to the border.

"Phoenix Leader," Remington said.

"Go, Base," Goose responded. "Leader reads you."

"Do you have a headset on Special Project?"

"Affirmative, Base. Special Project, do you copy?"

"I copy," the agent replied.

"I'm Captain Cal Remington, son. I'm glad we were able to get you out of there in one piece."

"So am I. Until your guys showed up, I thought I was dead."

"You probably would have been. They tell me you're the main reason Chaim Rosenzweig isn't lying in a box right now."

"I suppose so, sir."

Goose listened to Remington work. In a few short sentences, Remington had managed to remind the agent what he owed the Rangers, and Remington in particular, while at the same time acknowledging the agent's potential worth. Goose didn't always agree with the captain's methods, but they were effective.

"I need to know about the offensive the Syrians have planned, Son," Remington said.

The agent hesitated. "Is Section Chief Cody there, Captain?"

"Yes."

"Could I speak to him?"

"This is a military operation," Remington said. "Mr. Cody has been sidelined for the moment."

Sidelined? Goose thought. *More likely Cody had been thrown out by his boot heels.* If the Rangers had known there was a chance that a transmission might result in a Syrian attack, they would have handled the rescue mission differently. The CIA section chief hadn't been up front with them, and Goose knew Remington wouldn't have stood for that. Cody had probably been cleared from HQ in that moment.

"The information I have is sensitive," the agent said.

"If the Syrians are planning to attack the Turks and the company I've got stationed there, I can guarantee you, no one is going to be more sensitive than me."

"With all due respect, sir, the information is highly classified."

"Let me ask you a question, Son. If the bullets start flying across that border in the next few minutes, are we going to be seeing dead CIA agents hitting the sand? Or dead Rangers? *My* dead Rangers."

The agent still hesitated.

Looking back at the man, Goose noticed how young he was. Surely no more than a handful of years older than Joey, probably less than that. It was strange to realize. Joey still fought and complained about taking out the trash, and this agent had been responsible for penetrating a terrorist cell and preventing the assassination of an international figure.

"Rangers, sir," the agent replied. His voice broke and Goose felt a little sorry for him. When he glanced back over his shoulder, he saw that Bill had a hand on the young man's shoulder.

"If you can," Remington said, "I'd appreciate it if you'd help me save some of those Rangers, Son. The same way we saved you."

For a moment, the RSOV's engine droned into the silence that followed Remington's plea.

"I guess Section Chief Cody told you it took a long time to gain the PKK's trust," the agent stated.

"Almost a year," Remington agreed.

"The reason they let me in was because I crack software. I don't know if you realize this, Captain, but hackers aren't the real deal when it comes to penetrating firewalls and security countermeasures surrounding computer systems."

"I work with intelligence," Remington replied. "I know the difference between crackers and hackers."

Goose checked his watch. The Chase-Durer Combat Command Automatic Chronograph had been a gift from Megan and the kids. The watch was solid and heavy, and its cost had been excessive when matched against the family budget. But Megan had insisted on giving it to him, especially since he was gone from home so much these days. As first sergeant, time was always a consideration, so he was always looking at the watch, always thinking of the family he left at home.

Now, though, Goose felt time working against him. He figured they could be no more than five minutes out from the front line.

"I impressed the men I was with," the CIA agent went on. "I managed to crack into several security areas that held Chaim Rosenzweig's movements and finally located the target in Jerusalem. Thankfully, I was also able to alert the agency team there to set up the intercept. I don't think Rosenzweig or his people even knew he was in danger."

"Why didn't you shake loose then?" Remington said.

"Because while I was inside the hotel system, using the computer the PKK cell had given me to use, I found out they had another man on me, piggybacking every move I made."

"They made you?"

"Yes, sir. I think so. I don't know how far back they made me. Maybe the day I stepped into the cell. In order to crack Rosenzweig's security, I had to use agency resources. Every time I was inside the system using the tools I keep stashed there, the PKK cracker was shadowing me. I discovered him two weeks before the assassination attempt was scheduled."

"He found out information about the agency?" Remington asked.

"Yes. In the beginning."

Goose waited for the other shoe to drop.

"That wasn't the guy's major interest, though," the agent said.

"What was?"

"The United States Army buildup along the Turkish-Syrian border."

Cold dread spread across Goose's back, neck, and shoulders. He remained calm and quiet, letting Remington handle the questions because he knew the captain would be asking the same things he would.

"What did they get?" Remington asked.

"Everything," the agent answered. "They know where the U.S. military forces are, and they know where the Turkish forces are. Exact locations."

Goose glanced at Bill, knowing the man could overhear the conversation even though he wasn't linked to the frequency through the headset. Bill looked grim but he didn't say anything.

"I tried backtracking the guy," the agent said. "I put a trace on him through the sat-com relays I was using, a relatively simple snooper program that masks itself as a digital enhancement viewer. Using the information I received through a dozen traces, I triangulated the guy's location through ground-based satellite relays."

"Where was it?"

"In Aleppo, Syria. Do you know where that is?"

"I know where Aleppo is," Remington said.

Goose digested that. Aleppo housed the Syrian Missile Command. They had three mobile surface-to-surface missile brigades there that included one battalion of FROG-7 surface-to-surface missiles and one battalion of SS-1 SCUD-B missiles.

The FROG-7s were unguided rockets but capable of carrying nuclear, chemical, or biological payloads seventy kilometers in from their point of launch. The SCUDs had limited guidance systems that made them somewhat reliable but certainly more dangerous than the FROG-7s.

"When did you know for sure the cell had made you?" Remington asked.

The agent took a deep, shuddering breath, then knuckled fresh blood from the corner of his mouth. Goose believed the young man might have a cracked rib. If it had punctured a lung, thankfully the arterial flow seemed minimal, only coloring his breath now and again.

"The minute the assassination started to go badly," the agent said, "I was locked down by the three men your team rescued me from. After the sweep, they were the only ones left standing. They took a ship around Syria, sailing from Israel to Turkey so they wouldn't draw attention to themselves. They knew the U.S. military was observing the coastal cities and didn't want to take a chance on someone identifying me."

"Why didn't they kill you?"

"Killing me would have been simpler. But they wanted to use me to continue digging into military placements around the Turkish border. We sailed to Izmir, then took a car to Ankara to one of the safe houses they had set up. I suppose the agency picked me up there and told you."

Goose watched the southern horizon. Tension knotted his stomach. If the Syrians had the information they needed to attack the border armies, and they knew the CIA agent they'd been waiting for was now in American hands, there was nothing holding them—

"Phoenix Leader," Remington said.

"Go, Base," Goose responded.

"I need you to delay your return to the front lines."

Goose bridled at that. The last place he needed to be during the coming engagement—an engagement he had unknowingly triggered by rescuing this CIA agent—was away from the front line.

"But, sir—"

"That's an order, Sergeant," Remington barked. "I want you and your team to head to Glitter City. You'll need to take control of the evacuation there."

Goose glanced at his watch, thought of Megan, Joey, and Chris, and did the necessary math. He was three minutes from Glitter City and ten minutes from the front line.

Glitter City was basically a tent city built of Quonset huts and leftover buildings from small towns that had been bombed and shelled out of existence years ago during border hostilities. It was located halfway between the border and Sanliurfa. During the past few weeks, as armament on both the Turkish and Syrian sides had built up, reporters from FOX News and CNN had taken up transitory residence in the tent city, becoming media nomads reporting on soldiers in the field, weaponry, political and sociological issues, and the possibility of war or peace.

During the previous weeks, at Remington's insistence, Goose had done two interviews. He hadn't enjoyed doing them. So far, as near as he could tell, neither of the pieces had aired. Which was fine with him, though he considered the possibility that he wasn't very interesting or very photogenic. Maybe he was just too boring for TV. Still, he and Megan had enjoyed a laugh about them. She had threatened to tape them and play them at family gatherings.

"Sir," Goose said, curbing his impatience and his anger because he knew Remington maintained a no-fly zone for those emotions, "Sergeant Michaels can take care of the evacuation. His qualifications—"

"Make the adjustment now, Sergeant," Remington said. "That's an order."

"Yes, sir." Stung, Goose gave Tanaka the order, then reset the GPS heading himself while Tanaka made the course correction. "New course has been laid in, Captain."

"Goose," Remington said in a quieter voice, "I need you there. The Syrians launched a wave of short-range missiles eighteen seconds ago. Glitter City is one of their targets." He paused. "Do what you can to save whatever's left of them, Goose."

❖ ❖ ❖

United States of America
Fort Benning, Georgia
Local Time 11:57 P.M.

"Mommy, I don't want you to go! I don't want you to go!"

Megan's heart shattered at the unhappiness in her five-year-old son's plaintive cries. She wiped tears from Chris's cheeks and looked into his china blue eyes that were so much like his father's.

"It's going to be all right, little guy," Megan said as she carried Chris in through the double doors of the staff support building. She'd called ahead to arrange emergency baby-sitting. She'd also left messages on Joey's pager and forwarded all incoming calls to her cell phone.

"Daddy calls me little guy," Chris said petulantly. "Not you, Mommy."

"I know. I just felt like calling you little guy. So you can be my little guy the way you are for Daddy. You're just going to be here a little while. Then we'll go home."

Megan carried Chris on her hip, surprised at how big he'd gotten since the summer. The thought that Goose wouldn't even recognize his son when he returned from his current tour swept into her mind and brought new pain.

Extended absences during active tours were a hazard of the kind of soldiering Goose did. He and Megan had talked long and hard about those absences, about how much they affected a marriage as well as any children of that marriage. That was the biggest fear Goose had had about getting married. He'd seen military careers destroy families, and he believed too much in what he was doing to back away until he had finished the career he'd promised himself to deliver.

And compromise was a hard thing for Goose. He loved his family as fiercely as he loved his country. Having to choose between them would have destroyed him, and Megan knew that. So she chose to be strong for him, to be the woman she had trained herself to be after her first husband had abandoned Joey and her, and to wait for the time that Goose would be home again.

God willing, she prayed softly. *Please, God, be willing.* She always kept Goose close in her prayers.

"No, Mommy! No!" Chris wailed. He butted his head against her shoulder in frustration.

"It's going to be all right, Chris," Megan said. "It'll only be for a little while. Then I'll take you home and we can cuddle in my bed. I don't work in the morning, so we can watch your favorite videos together. I'll make pancakes. I promise."

Right after I get through grounding your brother for the rest of his natural life, Megan thought. Leaving Chris asleep in his own bed would have been so much easier than getting him up, getting him dressed, and getting him upset. If Joey had been home when he was supposed to be, she could have done just that. Her frustration and anger at her older son grew.

"Okay," Chris said sleepily. He lay against her more contentedly, and his breath whispered soft and warm against the hollow of her throat. "I love you, Mommy."

"I love you, too, baby," she told him.

One of the three women on duty in the emergency baby-sitting facilities met her at the door. Since Megan had used the services before and was on file, all she had to do was show her military ID to check Chris in. Megan politely refused the young woman's offer to take her son and carried him inside the room herself.

The room was filled with cradles and small beds. The constant state of readiness around the world was taking a terrible toll on military families. Emergency baby-sitting had become a necessary thing in these troubled times.

As Megan looked around, she was surprised to see that most of the beds were filled. She glanced at the woman who had checked her in. "Busy night, huh?"

"Yeah. Military support personnel got called in a few minutes ago," the young woman said. "There's been some kind of attack."

A cold rush in Megan's chest took her breath for a moment. "Where?"

"Turkey," the woman said.

"What happened?"

She shook her head. "I don't know. I heard the news from one of the men who dropped off his daughter a few minutes ago." She looked at Megan. "Do you have someone over there?"

"My husband." Megan held Chris tightly. It hurt to think about putting him down and walking away from him. With Goose in danger, and Joey gone, she couldn't think of being absent from her younger son.

But Gerry's in danger, too, she told herself. Reluctantly, she placed Chris in one of the empty beds and pulled the sheet over him.

He looked up at her with those wide, blue eyes. "Night, Mommy."

"Good night, baby." Megan was surprised at the lump in her throat. "I love you. Say your prayers, honey."

"Now I lay me down to sleep," Chris said. "I pray the Lord my soul to keep."

"He will, darling. He will." Megan ruffled her son's hair and kissed him.

"I'm just going to sleep for a little while, Mommy, so you can come and get me soon."

"I will, Chris. I'll be right there for you. Promise."

Yawning, his little nose wrinkling, Chris rolled over on his side and closed his eyes. He was asleep in the space of a drawn breath.

Megan kissed her son once more, thankful for such a precious gift, and left the nursery. Her thoughts spun, filled with Gerry and Boyd Fletcher, wondering where Joey might be, and hoping that Goose was all right, because if she knew her husband, he would be in the middle of things.

The Mediterranean Sea
USS *Wasp*
Local Time 0657 Hours

Alone with the dead man in the small, refrigerated room next to the medical department that was sometimes used as a morgue, U.S. Navy Chaplain Delroy Harte gazed at the stationery before him and prayed that the proper words would come to him. *God, help me. How do you write to a woman and tell her that her husband is dead? How do you write to his children and tell them that their father no longer lives?*

Those were things agencies within the Department of Defense had been set up to handle. Even knowing that those agencies had already contacted the dead man's family didn't help him. Dwight's family would expect a letter from his chaplain and good friend; a sad announcement would carry a more personal touch than the standard military communications. But the emotional cost of writing that letter was higher than Delroy had believed possible. He'd never, in his years in the military, been put in the position of writing one like it before. Letters for the dead, yes; he'd written those. But never a letter for someone who'd been his best friend.

The chaplain closed his eyes, aware of the familiar noises of *Wasp* coursing all around him, and tried to remember how his father had handled deaths within his small Baptist congregation in Marbury, Alabama. But Delroy Harte found no solace there. Josiah Harte had known every member of his congregation, all those souls who sat in the pews every Sunday to hear the hard-fisted, hellfire-and-brimstone sermons his father had delivered. His father had also known all of the townspeople who never darkened the door of the church till they were carried inside in a box.

Delroy had known the man who now lay in the black body bag on the stainless steel table a few feet away. Known him well and admired him greatly. He shifted and gazed at the body bag, hoping that an answer would somehow appear there. But it didn't.

His father had been ten times the pastor Delroy had turned out to be. Josiah Harte had watched over his congregation and his family with love and wisdom, leading them with a stern hand and a gentle touch, guiding so many of them to fulfilling lives enriched with a sense of purpose.

Tense and fatigued, a condition that was hard to get into and almost impossible to escape, Delroy stood and stretched his legs. He stood six feet six inches tall. In high school, he'd been a power forward, one of the greatest basketball players the school had ever seen. People had believed he'd never make it through college without being drafted by the NBA. But that had been before he lost his father. Somehow in the deep and terrible confusion of that loss, Delroy had found the Lord in ways he had never imagined.

But you didn't stay walking close to the Lord, did you, Delroy? No, you turned away from Him. And you are too afraid to tell anyone because you don't know what would become of you without this mission in your life.

He rubbed his chin. The stubble that had grown there let him know he'd been at his task much longer than he would have guessed.

His eyes burning with exhaustion, he gazed at his blurred reflection in the stainless steel table where he'd been working. His skin was dark, nearly blue-black, and his image flowed like a dark pool across the metal surface. His hair was cut military style, high and tight, as it had been for thirty years, since the day he'd entered the navy. He wore his chaplain's service dress blue uniform, but he'd left his white gloves and his tie in his pocket. The tie would go back on before he left this room.

Officially, he was off duty right now. Writing the letter to the dead man's family was something he was doing at the request of the dead man himself. Back in sick bay, before the emergency surgery that had been ordered after Dwight had complained about severe chest pains and shortness of breath late last night, Dwight had asked him to take on this task—just in case . . .

Waiting in the medical department while the medical personnel worked on his friend, Delroy had expected to sit for hours till the doctors and nurses performed the surgery and got Dwight stabilized. The medical staff told Delroy there was nothing to worry about outside of the normal risks of bypass surgery—and given Dwight's comparative youth and overall fitness, those were pretty small. At least, that was what they told him before they started cutting.

Delroy had believed them. Dwight had been in great shape, he was only fifty-two years old—only three years Delroy's junior—and the doctors were top-flight military surgeons tempered by previous service in combat conditions. When she was in home port in Norfolk, Virginia, *Wasp* was counted as the fourth largest hospital in the state. She was part of the state's disaster relief plan. Military medical aid didn't come much better than the facilities on USS *Wasp*.

But the doctors were wrong this time. Fifteen minutes into the surgery, Chief Petty Officer Dwight Mellencamp had died on the table. Thirty minutes after the surgery had begun, the surgeon had been out in the waiting room, explaining everything to Delroy, and despite his personal grief, the chaplain had followed most of the medical jargon. The docs had done their best.

But it was still nearly impossible to understand that Dwight was gone. No longer would he play chess or share historical mystery novels or argue religion with the chaplain. Dwight had been a Christian of the old school—believing every word of the Bible as the literal truth. The book of Revelation had been a hot topic between them as they tried to imagine what the world would be like after the Rapture. Dwight was convinced that they were living in the end times, that the world had reached the point of no return when believers and nonbelievers would be separated by God's own hand.

Delroy didn't believe that, and their arguments had sometimes grown heated because Dwight believed so fiercely. Dwight had accused Delroy of hiding his head in the sand, of denying a truth so obvious that any child should be able to see it. Dwight had been growing in his faith, seeing things and making connections that Delroy was just unable to accept. Delroy thought that by debating the future with Dwight, he was defending the faith. Sometimes, though, after one of their discussions, he wondered in the dark of the night if Dwight was right. Perhaps he was the one hiding the lack of strength of his faith. Maybe he was only giving lip service to the beliefs his father had taught him so long ago.

"God help me, Dwight," Delroy said in a choked voice. "I am going to miss you so much." He placed a hand on the body bag, knowing that a few of the young Marine corpsmen and navy sailors on board *Wasp* would never have thought of willingly touching a corpse, even through the body bag.

Being with the dead man didn't bother Delroy the way he knew it had bothered some of the other men who helped carry the corpse into the room. Back home in Marbury, the farming community he had grown up in, sitting up with the dead before the burial was a long-established practice. Delroy had sat up many nights, with his grandparents and his father and the people of his father's parish.

But you didn't get the chance to sit up with Terrence, did you? Despite the long years that had passed, tears stung Delroy's eyes. Remembering was so confusing. Images of Terrence as a baby, as a gap-toothed four-year-old holding a chamois and helping Daddy wash the family station wagon, as a young man playing high school basketball, and finally as a Marine corporal in a dress uniform festooned with ribbons and medals. *No chance at all.*

Five years ago, his son, Lance Corporal Terrence David Harte, had come home from the Middle East sealed in a box that had never been opened. The military had handled the burial with pomp and splendor and brevity. Delroy, stationed elsewhere, had been flown home in time for the funeral.

After the funeral and most of the requisite bereavement leave, Delroy had opted to return to his post sooner than required. His wife had never understood that he couldn't stay there in the home that he and Terrence had remodeled. Terrence had been everywhere in that house—in the pictures hanging on the wall, in the sink stand that was a half-inch longer on the right than it was supposed to be because Terrence hadn't cut the exact center from the countertop. The mistake had been his and Terrence's, and they'd waited years for someone to notice. Delroy's wife never had.

Tenderly, Delroy folded the old memories and put them away. He enjoyed them because they were all he had left of the son he'd loved so much, but he resented that they could intrude into his thoughts, into his life, without warning and sometimes without provocation.

Today, though, there had been plenty of provocation. He returned to the tall stool next to the stainless steel table where he had been composing the letter Dwight had charged him to write. It had almost been a joke between them last night as Dwight was prepped for surgery.

"Write to her, Chaplain Harte," Dwight had said. "Write to my wife and my kids. Tell them how much I love them. If this thing goes sour, I want them to know that I was thinking of them. And that I'm sorry I couldn't be there more."

Delroy had tried to allay his friend's fears. Serious military man that Dwight was, he had been torn between family and duty all his

life. He had always said God would let him know when he'd had
enough of the navy—or when the navy had had enough of him.

Someone rapped on the door to the small room.

"Come," Delroy said. He set his face, automatically reaching for
the tie in his pocket in case the length of time he'd spent with the
dead man had attracted the captain's attention. Captain Mark Falkirk
was a by-the-book navy officer, but he was also a man who realized
his crew and staff were human.

The door opened and a hesitant young man stuck in his head.
"Chaplain Harte."

"You know I don't stand on formality when I'm not at post, Tom."
Delroy's military rank was commander, but the proper verbal address
for all military chaplains remained *Chaplain*.

"Yes, sir." The young midshipman stepped into the room. Tom
Mason was one of the aides Falkirk had assigned to coordinate between the chaplain and the staff. "It's just that . . ." He looked at the
sheet-covered corpse, then back at Delroy. "You're working."

Delroy shook his head. "I'm just doing a favor for an old friend.
Come on in."

The midshipman held up a cup. "I brought you coffee. Cream,
two sugars. Shaken, not stirred." It was an old joke, but he meant
well.

"Bless you." A real grin twisted Delroy's face. He accepted the cup
Tom handed him.

Tom stood between Delroy and the door, coming no closer to the
corpse than he had to.

Delroy sipped his coffee, finding it sweet and hot. "You don't have
to be nervous, Tom. He's dead. He can't hurt you."

Tom scratched at his shirt collar with more than a little nervousness. "I know that, Chaplain Harte."

"You watch too many horror movies." Delroy knew that several of
the crew passed DVDs around the ship, sharing and trading with each
other as they did with books and video games. Tom was a horror
movie aficionado.

"Yes, sir," Tom agreed. "I do."

The men aboard *Wasp* had seen a lot of action in recent years, even
if most of it had only been lying in wait off the coast. They were familiar with death, but most of them weren't comfortable with it.

The matter wasn't helped by the fact that Chief Petty Officer
Dwight Mellencamp had been aboard ship for years and was a per-
sonable man. Over twenty-six hundred men and women crewed

aboard *Wasp* since the ship had been retrofitted with fem mods, up-grades that allowed the quartering of the female Marines and sailors that amounted to 10 to 25 percent of the crew. But most of that crew had known Dwight, or known of him.

Delroy put the coffee cup down. "What brings you here?"

"Captain Falkirk."

Delroy examined the paper in front of him. He'd chosen not to use the notebook computer he had back in his quarters. A message like this needed the personal touch. Dwight would have wanted a letter, not a fax or an e-mail, sent to his family.

"And what did the captain want?" Delroy asked. He thought Falkirk was going to suggest strongly that he stand down for a time.

"A eulogy," Tom answered.

Delroy frowned, feeling overwhelmed.

"A lot of people knew Chief Mellencamp," Tom explained. "Captain Falkirk feels that addressing the situation, what happened to the chief, with a small service would be better than letting the crew deal with it alone. As big as *Wasp* is, we're like a community. The captain believes everybody aboard ship would feel better if we said a proper good-bye to the chief."

Despite the additional pressure the situation put on him, Delroy had to agree with the captain's assessment. The situation along the border between Turkey and Syria was gut-churning for Marine troops and navy crew, who lived with the fact that they might be called into immediate service at any time. *Wasp*, with nearly twenty-seven hundred souls aboard her, not counting the crews of the other six support ships in the ready group, held almost the same population as Marbury, Alabama. But the crew aboard *Wasp* lived on a world that measured 820 feet long and 106 feet wide, a very small island. Marbury was spread out considerably more, and folks still managed to keep up with each other's business. When Delroy had been a boy there, all the funerals were standing room only, the pews packed with family and friends.

"All right," Delroy said. "Does the captain have a time frame in mind?"

"Captain Falkirk said to leave it up to you. But he also said that something like this, it's better to deal with it sooner than later."

Delroy nodded.

"The captain said to take your time," Tom went on. "He knows you and the chief were close." The midshipman hesitated. "I suggested that the captain get someone else."

"No." The reply was out of Delroy's mouth before he knew it, and the answer was also sharper than he'd intended. *There's no one else I would assign this to.*

Tom took a step back.

"Easy," Delroy said. He rubbed the back of his neck with a big hand, hoping in vain to ease some of the tension there. "Nobody's going to do that eulogy but me. Tell the captain to give me a call at his convenience later. We'll iron out the details then."

Before Tom could reply, a warning Klaxon screamed. The banshee wail filled the room, echoing in the larger medical department on the other side of the open door.

It was, Delroy thought, loud enough to wake the dead. But it didn't this time. The flesh that had once been Dwight Mellencamp lay unmoving in the body bag.

Tom turned and charged out the door.

Delroy followed at the younger man's heels as they pounded through the medical department and ran out into the hall. A stream of men and women hurried through the halls and climbed the stairs leading up to the flight deck. They strapped on protective gear—vests and helmets—as they quickly filed upward.

"What's going on?" a sailor asked a Marine.

"Dunno," the Marine corpsman said. "Our general orders are to assemble on the flight deck and stand ready to deploy."

"Deploy?" The sailor caught the stair railing and yanked himself around. "Deploy where?"

"The border," the Marine replied. "That's where the heat is. Don't you keep up with current events?" The Marine shook his head.

"Man, that's crazy."

Pausing, Delroy let the last of the crewmen and Marines climb the stairs. He fell in behind them, sprinting up through the 02 level. In seconds, he was on the flight deck, coming up inside the island that housed the bridge.

Delroy surveyed the activity that swept the landing helicopter dockship. Movement filled the LHD as deck crews dressed in color-coded jerseys—primarily red for fuel and ordnance and yellow for spotters—ran to their assigned posts. Marines erupted from flight deck ramp tunnel, moving at a dead run with their gear tied securely around them and their assault rifles held at port arms before them. In the old days, military Jeeps had been able to drive up those ramps, but the Humvees they used now were too wide. The next generation of landing helicopter dockships had already worked appropriate changes into the redesigns.

Fighter jets, AV-8B Harriers, rolled off the flight deck, dropping out over the dark sea then rising like kites caught by the wind. *Wasp* had nine takeoff and landing positions on the deck for helicopters, six to port and three to starboard. The port and stern elevators brought up CH-46E and CH-53E helicopters and the Harriers two at a time.

The CH-46Es, designated Sea Knights, had the distinctive twin prop design. The CH-53E Sea Stallions had the more traditional appearance of a main rotor backed by a tail rotor and were currently ranked as the fastest helos the Marines handled. As soon as the helos were in place and had been boarded by Marine troops, they leapt into the sky.

No voices could be heard over the din that filled *Wasp*'s flight deck. Jet turbines on the Harriers screamed, competing with the whirling rotors on the cargo helicopters used as troop transports. Navy crew outfitted the aircraft as they rolled on deck from the elevators.

Delroy kept moving toward the island, which was what most of the crew called the bridge structure on the ship's starboard side. As chaplain for the ship, Delroy had to remain available to help out where he could. He raced up the stairs and through the coded doors leading to Primary Flight. Pri-Fly was *Wasp*'s nerve center for air operations.

Commander Kelly Tomlinson stood watch this morning. Designated the air boss, he'd served in the same capacity for a handful of years. He was tall and muscular with a shock of blond hair and a surfer's tan. He also held the current record for bench presses down in the ship's fitness center and had been a fierce surfing competitor in Hawaii before giving up that dream and stepping into the military life.

The commander glanced at Delroy then resumed watching the deck activity through the heavy-duty glass. "Good to have you, Chaplain."

"Thank you, sir." Delroy moved to his usual place back of the shipboard computers. He stood with Lieutenant Gabriel Morales, who was in charge of the Landing Signals Officers. They'd shared stories in the galley about small towns and family.

Morales's LSOs remained grouped and ready to assist with aircraft landing. Each man and woman was clothed in deck gear, including helmets and goggles. The lieutenant was lanky but muscular. He had grown up on a working cattle ranch in west Texas and sported a mustache that pushed the envelope on navy regs.

"What's up, Gabe?" Delroy asked.

"The Syrians just launched a full-blown attack across the border," Gabe said in a low voice. "They took out the communications towers with SCUDs and FROG-7s. From what I understand, the U.N. peace-keeping forces and the 75th Rangers are taking a beating."

Delroy glanced at the state-of-the-art weather forecasting equipment that was the heart of the Pri-Fly area. Weather affected every operation. A small television monitor mounted next to the computer screens showed a battle in progress. The tagline read TURKISH-SYRIAN BORDER.

"What triggered the attack?" Delroy asked.

Gabe shrugged. His dark brown eyes flashed as he watched the aircraft lifting off Wasp's flight deck. "Who knows? It was waiting to happen, Del. Only a matter of time. The intel I was looking at, man, you just knew the Syrians were gonna jump some time."

"What are we doing?"

"Air and troop support. Those gunships are herding jump troops. We're also providing medical corpsmen to handle on-site wounded. Once a triage is established, the wounded that can travel will be sent back here. From what we've heard so far, there are a lot of casualties. Gonna be a lot more."

Glancing at his watch, Delroy did the math. With the border two hundred miles away, give or take a handful, the trip in-country would take time. "The border is an hour and a half away."

"An hour and twenty minutes," Gabe corrected.

As Delroy watched the television screen, coverage shifted to Glitter City. Several of the specials about the ongoing conflict had been shot there and in the field featuring military men involved in the border patrol, and almost everybody in the ship had watched them when they aired. Over the last few tense months, Delroy—as well as the rest of the world addicted to news services—had watched the dead city rise from the dust and become a thriving if threadbare metropolis of journalists and local residents trying to make a living from the meager opportunity the media invasion had brought them. One of the news-magazines was planning to do a special on the impact the journalists' presence had on the area.

The camera panned down the single road that cut through Glitter City. People were panicked, some of them abandoning vehicles while others loaded gear and passengers aboard, evidently thinking they were going to flee before the missiles reached them.

In the next instant, absolute carnage tore through Glitter City.

SCUDs landed in the small town, and the resulting explosions collapsed a building.

Dwight's voice came to Delroy in that moment. *"We're living in the end times now, Del. God is going to deliver his people from the war and strife that's going to consume this world. We're going to live to see the Rapture."*

Dwight had been wrong, of course. He hadn't lived to see it. But as Delroy Harte watched the stark images relayed on the television monitor, the chaplain found the idea of the Rapture being close at hand much easier to believe.

But then, Delroy denied that, refused to believe it. This was just a military engagement, not the end times. Perhaps a war would even come of it. Men would die and he would pray for them because that was what he had signed on to do.

Turkey
30 Klicks South of Sanliurfa
Local Time 0657 Hours

A SCUD-B surface-to-surface missile's rockets burned for eighty seconds, more or less. While in the air that eighty seconds, the SCUD-B traveled one hundred and seventy-five miles.

The distance to Glitter City from Aleppo, Syria, was less than eighty miles, less than half the distance the SCUD-Bs were capable of. When he'd gotten the call from Captain Remington, Goose had been three minutes away from the tent city that housed support personnel as well as media. Even picking up the pace in the RSOVs to the point of risking life and limb, the Rangers arrived two minutes and forty-eight seconds after the first wave of SCUDs blasted into the landscape.

Goose sat buckled into the passenger seat and peered at the huge dust cloud that had been raised around the area from the impact and detonation of the SCUDs. Bobby Tanaka whipped the vehicle hard to the left just as Goose yelled, "Something's in the road!"

The yellow dust cloud had concealed the long steel body of an unexploded SCUD missile. Goose knew from hard experience that SCUDs didn't always detonate. The failure rate for the Russian-designed weapons was something U.S. military forces would never have allowed. But the thirty-foot-plus missiles remained in the Syrian army's arsenal. And they had done their share of damage today.

The RSOV skidded wildly in the loose sand. The rear quarter panel came around and smacked the SCUD. When he heard an ear-splitting blast at almost the same time, Goose figured that he and his unit had just been blown to smithereens.

Instead, the RSOV skidded in the opposite direction from the impact as Tanaka overcorrected. The SCUD in the roadway remained a dud. It would have to be removed by bomb disposal teams later.

Glancing over his shoulder, Goose watched the second Ranger vehicle avoid the SCUD by several feet. Then realization kicked in that if the detonation he'd heard hadn't occurred at their twenty it had to have happened elsewhere. He glanced forward again and saw a new cloud of dust curling up a hundred feet and more from the desert.

Clods of hard earth and debris tumbled back down from the sky. They drummed against the RSOV with the force of sledgehammers. The cacophony rolled over Goose, deafening him.

Holding his left forearm over his face, Goose took as much cover as he could from his helmet and Kevlar vest. Rocks and clods pinged off armor as well as flesh, leaving welts, scrapes, and bruises. Goggles protected his eyes from the grit that swirled in the air, but the yellow dust matted and stuck to the kerchief he'd pulled up over his nose and mouth. Perspiration and saliva had made the kerchief wet enough to turn the dust to mud.

The fallout from the SCUD detonation continued for a few seconds, then immediately started again as at least two more missiles struck the high ridges of broken earth that surrounded Glitter City. Ages ago, when the town had been little more than a trading post for travelers, small stone buildings had been constructed against the sides of the bowl that contained the meeting place. The surrounding hills forming the natural bowl had always protected the village and the traders from the wind and the sandstorms that sometimes rose up. The town had provided a place of relative peace, a little shade, and a natural spring that was work to get to but had provided the townsfolk with their share of cool water.

Since the arrival of the American troops and the international media, Turkish traders had opened up a market again. They offered local cuisine and trinkets for souvenirs, bartering those things for American and European products such as cigarettes, Coke and Pepsi, and even military MREs. Most American fighting men only accepted the meals-ready-to-eat when nothing else was available, but Turkish traders found a ready market waiting to sample the meals.

Several buildings had existed on those hillsides, some of them decades old. Most of them were in some state of disrepair. After the media had encamped there, local construction teams had been hired to provide more adequate shelter. With things heating up on the border, most of the reporters wanted to stay on-site rather than make the trip between Diyarbakir and Sanliurfa, the closest metropolitan cities.

The repaired buildings had filled with the international reporters, enterprising Turkish merchants, and support personnel subsidized by the spending habits of the Turkish and American troops. When members of the U.N. relief crews and peacekeeping efforts had arrived, the overflow had been set up in tents. The tents ranged from cutting-edge technology to sheets of canvas put up with sticks. All of them offered shade from the unforgiving sun.

No one knew who had hung the sobriquet *Glitter City* on the place. But everyone knew the reference was to the Hollywood-style atmosphere of the place. Some news agencies had rolled out what were, in effect, microproduction companies that shot day-by-day footage of the military buildup on both sides of the border, managed day trips to local religious sites such as the Ulu Cami—the Grand Mosque of the Suljuk Turks—the brick beehive cities of Harran, and the Pool of Abraham, and interviewed anyone and everyone willing to talk to them.

During conversations with other Rangers who had visited Glitter City, Goose had learned that several newscasts now featured segments spotlighting the potential for disaster between Turkey and Syria. Several investigations had been made into the roots of the PKK and their effect on Turkey's relations with its neighbors.

Other writers prepared books and took photographs, laying out chapters that were edited and readied for printing as soon as they were e-mailed to New York publishing houses. There were even a few releases being done about Turkey, the Turkish-Syrian conflict, terrorists, and historical events and places, pieces that would be aired on the Travel Channel, The History Channel, and on the Discovery Channel, then released straight to video.

War—or at least the threat of impending war—had become big business in media, politics, and economics. Politicians used those threats to shepherd legislation through Congress and to fund budget increases for military spending. The military needed the money— U.S. troops were deployed at every hot spot imaginable, going after everything from terrorists to the bankers who financed them to drug dealers to the country's traditional enemies.

Not every politician was pushing for more and bigger weapons and more and bigger armies. Goose had heard of a United Nations representative from Romania named Nicolae Carpathia. Surprisingly,

Carpathia was pushing for disarmament in his own country. At the time he'd heard that, Goose had never thought it would happen. Romania was part of Eastern Europe, left orphaned by the failed Soviet Communist government, and host to a series of bloodthirsty dictators who had only been driven from office by equally bloodthirsty military uprisings. Most military analysts had figured that the country would be awash in political unrest and military action for decades to come. Instead, Carpathia had begun to quiet Romania down, almost as if by magic.

"Incoming!" Bill yelled from the back of the RSOV.

Instinctively, Goose looked up and saw another SCUD plunge from the air like a blunt spear. Although the missiles lacked a lot in targeting systems, this one streaked almost into the smoke- and dust-covered heart of Glitter City.

The preexisting clouds of smoke and dust prevented Goose from seeing the actual impact. But a heartbeat later, a fairly new blue van erupted into the air, turning and whirling like a child's toy. Flames wreathed the vehicle and then the gas tank blew, ripping open the vehicle's side.

The van reached the apex of its arc and had started earthward again, disappearing into the smoke and dust before the sonic boom of the explosion reached Goose's ears. A moment later, a wave of concussion rattled the RSOV's windshield.

Merciful God, Goose prayed. *Spare the innocent. Because if You don't, they're all going to die here today.*

Bobby Tanaka glanced at Goose. Fear lit the young man's eyes. He put his foot over the brake and slowed.

"Get in there, soldier," Goose said.

"Gonna be suicide to go in there," Tanaka said. But he grinned a little as he pressed his foot harder on the accelerator and drove the vehicle over the edge of the bowl. "Ah, well, I always did like a wild ride." The RSOV juked and shuddered as the tires fought for traction on the hillside. They'd run out of road, roaring out over loose layers of sand and rock.

Goose sat in the shotgun seat with his left foot braced against the dash. He cradled the M-4A1 with both hands and kept the assault rifle canted up at the ready. Closer to ground zero now, he raked his gaze across the field of destruction the SCUDs had left in their wake.

Huge craters had opened up from the bomb blasts, turning the desert floor under the shifting sands into a lunar landscape. Stone buildings lay in tumbled wrecks or nearly covered by a deluge of de-

bris that had slid free of hillsides. Flattened tents and flaming tents littered the area, and none had been spared. The concussions from the
SCUDs had ripped the tent pegs from the ground and flung the tents
around like used tissues. Cars and trucks and vans sat abandoned,
blown over or apart, or wrapped in flames that sent spikes of twisting
black smoke up through the dust cover.

People, dead and dying and badly broken, covered the ground.
Other people hunkered in the false safety of the few remaining buildings or behind boulders on the ground and the hillsides. Several people shouted and cursed and cried out for help. Incredibly, some of the
reporters were still working, standing in front of cameramen who had
managed to hang on to functioning equipment.

A familiar sickness twisted greasily through Goose's stomach.
He'd been on battlefields, had scenes etched inside his skull that he
knew would never leave him. Today was going to add to that library
of carnage.

"Base," Goose called over the headset.

Only white noise answered. Remington and his support staff were
off-line.

Goose wasn't surprised. Any staged attack against the American
site would include strikes designed to take out the communications
relays. It wouldn't last, though. Cal Remington was nothing if not a
man who planned for every eventuality. Backup systems were in
place; they would be on soon. Goose believed that. Until then,
though, they had their orders.

"Stop here," Goose ordered.

Tanaka ground the big vehicle to a halt.

A single road running north and south bisected Glitter City. Everyone who arrived there was on their way somewhere else.

"Off," Goose yelled. Raising his voice was almost unfamiliar after
being accustomed to the headsets. He unbuckled and jumped to the
road.

Flames crackled around the broken and battered husk of a van
that had been gutted and made over into a small restaurant on
wheels. A Turkish man had operated the van, parking somewhere
within the vicinity of Glitter City every morning and selling the *borek*
and *doner kebab* lamb rolls his wife made every night. The *borek*—thin
rolls of pastry filled with cheese, minced meat, or spinach and potatoes—was one of Goose's favorites and he'd always stopped by the
man's van when he was in town. The menu had also included pilaf,
baklava and *kadayif* pastries, and thick, dark Turkish coffee.

Although the man spoke only rudimentary English and Goose spoke no Turkish at all, they'd communicated well enough to conduct business. During those times, Goose had also seen the man's two sons, looking perhaps eight and ten, who worked inside the van with him. Both boys had been bright and energetic, their eyes shining and quick, picking up English words and phrases like sponges. Every time they had seen Goose and other Rangers in uniform, the boys had yelled, "Hoo-ahh," just like a Ranger, letting Goose know that the van had evidently become a favorite feeding place for the 75th.

The man lay on his back, half covered with sand and rock from a nearby explosion that had left a ten-foot-wide, three-foot-deep crater in the ground. Blood covered the man. One arm was missing and one leg half gone. He stared sightlessly at a sky that couldn't be seen through the dust and smoke hanging in the air.

Goose walled himself away from the panic and fear that vibrated within him. Soldiers knew fear, but they also knew control.

A few feet away, the oldest of the two boys lay in a crumpled heap.

Heart thumping in his chest, Goose crossed to the boy. He knelt, eyes scanning the surrounding area as his personal combat radar, developed through training and on battlefields in the Middle East and Africa, kicked into life. Cupping his left hand around the boy's small shoulder, Goose pulled him over gently.

From the slack way the boy moved, Goose knew immediately he was dead. As the body came over, the metal shard that had pierced his chest showed, standing out from his flesh nearly a foot.

Goose's mind screamed. Images flickered behind his eyes, scanning visual data into his brain, contrasting the boy's slack, dead face with the grinning kid he had seen only a couple days ago. The boy couldn't be dead; he had been too *alive* to be dead like this.

It isn't fair, Goose couldn't help thinking. *God, there's no way You can make this right. Children are not supposed to die like this.*

But children did die. Goose had seen it in countless other operations. Children were always some of the first to die when war touched civilized areas. They were too weak and vulnerable to protect themselves, and they were so unskilled in taking care of themselves. Professional soldiers died in those circumstances. Goose had seen them. What chance did a child have?

"Sarge." Bill Townsend's calm voice came from behind.

Goose didn't answer, drawn into the dead boy's dark brown eyes that were cold and distant and lifeless now. The Syrians had known there were children in Glitter City, and women, too. And they had brought their war to those innocents just the same.

"Sarge," Bill said again.

Trapped by the violence before him, feeling guilty because he hadn't managed to stop the PKK terrorist from placing the sat-phone call, Goose had to struggle to tear his attention from the dead boy. He couldn't help thinking about his son, Chris. How would it feel, he wondered, knowing that Chris would never again offer a hug or a smile or a turn at one of his favorite video games? Goose banished the thought. It was unthinkable.

Goose glanced at Bill. "He's dead."

Bill nodded. "I know. A lot of people are."

For the moment, the SCUD shelling seemed to be on hold. Goose knew that starting up the second wave would take almost an hour and a half. In addition to being terribly inefficient as WMDs, weapons of mass destruction, SCUDs took a lot of reload time.

"Then let's save the ones that are left," Goose said, more for his own focus than his team's. "This boy had a brother. If we can, I want him found."

Bill nodded.

Goose glanced back at the dead boy. "This isn't right, Bill." His voice caught at his throat.

"He's in a better place, Sarge," Bill stated quietly and politely. "That's what you have to focus on."

"It's hard."

Bill was quiet for just a moment; then he said, "Not if you believe, Sarge. It only gets hard when you have doubts."

A kernel of anger exploded inside Goose. His voice came out sharper than he intended. "Then I'm a doubter."

"I know, amigo. I'll pray for you. Acknowledge that and work on it, but never accept it."

For a second, Goose thought his anger was going to spill over onto Bill. He barely restrained it. He knew Bill was right, but believing he was right was another thing entirely. Acceptance was a small thing to talk about, Goose knew, but it was a chasm in spirituality.

"Hey!" someone called. "Marines!"

"We're Rangers," Dewey Cusack called back automatically. "We're the 75th." The Ranger hailed from Kansas, a corn-fed country boy with an easygoing manner and a fierce pride in his unit.

Goose stepped forward, the M-4A1 still clenched tight in his fist.

He peered through the haze of dust and smoke, brushing at the mask of wet sand that impeded drawing his breath through the kerchief.

"I need help," the speaker went on. "My friend has been shot." He was young and compact, carrying sunburn from recent exposure to the harsh desert climate that stood out starkly against his white-blond hair. His accent was Australian.

"Break out the medkits, Bill," Goose said.

"You got it, Sarge."

Using every iota of command that he had learned in his career, forcing a calm he definitely didn't feel, Goose stepped into the center of the wreckage of what had been Glitter City.

"I'm First Sergeant Samuel Gander of the United States Army Rangers," he declared in a loud and proud voice. "We're going to get you out of here."

United States of America
Fort Benning, Georgia
Local Time 12:13 A.M.

Megan held up her ID as she stopped at the military checkpoint in the
base hospital. Since the recent terrorist attacks around the globe, security on base had become a big issue. She carried Gerry Fletcher's file
in her hand. After dropping Chris off, she'd stopped by her office to
pick up the file. If she was going to have to argue with Boyd Fletcher,
she wanted to have every weapon in her arsenal to do battle with.
Nothing she had weighed as heavily as the man's history.

The uniformed Rangers working the security desk checked for her
name in the computer while she waited.

"Cross-check with the ER list," Megan suggested when they didn't
find her name immediately. "Helen Cordell called me in for an emergency. This wasn't a planned visit."

"Yes, ma'am," the young corporal replied. His name badge identified him as Grady.

The soldier was, Megan knew, only a few years older than Joey,
and yet the young corporal already carried an air of responsibility
about him that her eldest son rarely showed. *That's not fair*, she
chided herself almost as soon as she had the thought. *The military
trains that air of responsibility into the soldiers it turns out.*

Many of the younger Rangers were still kids in some respects. In her
counseling capacity, Megan had talked with some of them, helping
them get over failed relationships and relaying news about deaths in
the family and other tragedies. Those same young men looked rigorous
and potentially lethal in the BDUs, helmets, and Kevlar vests while

carrying assault rifles. But she'd also seen them crowd the base basketball and volleyball courts in their downtime discuss video games and
PC games over lunches in the cafeteria. She had counseled them as
they dealt with life's setbacks and pain during the lonely hours.

Megan used her cell phone again, dialing Joey's number and again
getting the mailbox. She didn't bother to leave a message. She glanced
back out the door she'd entered, spotting her reflection and staring
through it. She couldn't help wondering where Joey was, if Goose was
all right, and if Chris was still asleep.

She also wondered what Boyd Fletcher was going to do when he
found out they had his son in the ER. As a matter of fact, she wondered what she—

"Ma'am."

Startled, Megan turned to the young corporal. "Yes."

"Your ID checks out, ma'am. You're on the list for Ms. Cordell.
You can proceed."

"Thank you," Megan said. The television behind the desk caught
her eye. A FOX News anchor was talking, the flags of Turkey and Syria
on the wall behind him. SPECIAL BULLETIN hung ominously on the
screen. The audio was too low to hear. "Are you watching what's happening in Turkey?"

The corporal grimaced. "We're trying to, ma'am. We're not getting
much from over there right now."

"What's the problem?"

An uncomfortable look covered the young soldier's face.

"My husband is over there," Megan said. "I'm concerned about
him. He hasn't told me much about his circumstances, but I know my
husband, and I know when he isn't telling me something he thinks
will worry me."

The other soldier glanced at her, then at the roster the corporal
held. He looked back up. "Mrs. Gander?"

"Yes."

"Private Malone." The young soldier rose to his feet and took off
his black beret. "I know Goose, ma'am. He's a good man."

"Yes, he is."

Malone hesitated for just a moment. "We received a phone call at
oh-four-hundred advising us not to talk about the trouble over there.
In case the media showed up. I doubt we'll see anybody here, but general orders are passed around to everyone. Scuttlebutt moves through
the ranks pretty quickly, as you probably know."

"I do," Megan said. That was why she had asked.

"Right now, ma'am, we don't know much more than the media does. There was an attack along the border. There are casualties. We don't know anything more than that. The Syrians evidently took out the communications systems, including Glitter City."

Megan remembered Glitter City from her conversations with Goose. "That's where the reporters and media people are gathered."

"Yes, ma'am. There have been casualties there, too, but we haven't got much information. The Department of Defense has satellites keeping an eye on things there, but they're only giving out information on a need-to-know basis. I wish I could tell you more."

"So do I, Private."

"Are you going to be on the premises for a while, Mrs. Gander?"

Megan thought about Gerry Fletcher and the coming confrontation with his father. "Yes." *Unfortunately.*

"Right now," the private said, "all the media seems to be off-line, too. Maybe it's just the confusion."

And maybe it's something more. Megan was certain they both thought that, but neither of them wanted to say it.

"I was thinking that if I heard something," the private said, "I could let you know."

"I'd appreciate that," Megan said.

"Yes, ma'am."

Walking away from the young private, Megan began to focus her thoughts on the task at hand. She couldn't do anything about Goose's situation except pray for him. She was helpless to do anything more right now about Joey's actions except pray for him—and ground him for life the next time she saw him. And she had done her best by Chris. Her baby was sleeping in a warm bed, well cared for. She'd done all she could for her family. Now it was time to do what she could to save the kid she'd been called in to help. Megan strode down the hallway toward the ER.

Gerry Fletcher, she reminded herself. *I can help Gerry Fletcher.* It was important to focus on the attainable things in the face of chaos. That was, she remembered, one of the things she'd learned from Goose— and one of the things she liked best about her husband, and most respected. Goose was bedrock, and he'd had to be patient to teach her to trust again after everything she had gone through with Tony, her first husband.

The waiting room outside the ER held a handful of people. Two soldiers sat in army sweats and looked worried. Another soldier, who looked about thirty, sat with three small children in chairs on either side of him and a little blonde-haired girl asleep in his lap. Another young soldier paced the floor.

Megan said a quick prayer for all of them. Whomever they were waiting on and worrying over, those people were in good hands. The doctors and nurses at the base hospital were well trained and they were committed to their jobs.

"Hey, Mrs. Gander," the young, redheaded receptionist behind the desk said cheerily.

"Hi, Tammy," Megan replied. "Still got you on nights?"

Tammy frowned and rolled her eyes but couldn't sustain the effort and grinned. "Yeah, but I'm getting used to the hours, and I've learned how to program the VCR. I've worked a few of the day shifts, subbing for other people. You know, the nights are a lot quieter."

Most of them, Megan agreed. But tonight, she felt certain, was going to be different. "Do you know where I can find Helen?"

"Here." Helen Cordell stepped out from behind the wall at the back of the receptionist's office. She was trim and neat. Of African-American descent, her skin was so dark it appeared blue-black under the fluorescent lights. She kept her hair cut short and straightened. Her patterned dress, in deep greens, blues, and occasional purple, fit her perfectly.

Besides being a fantastic hospital shift supervisor, Helen was also a seamstress. She claimed to have learned the knack purely through self-preservation. Her husband was a drill instructor on base nearing the end of a thirty-year hitch. Together, Helen and Marvin Cordell had raised five sons and two daughters, and Helen had sewn all their clothes, making up with her skill the budget deficiencies of an enlisted man's pay. She also tailored her husband's uniforms and sent him out every morning bristling with fresh-starched crispness.

"Coffee?" Helen raised the cup she held.

"Please," Megan said.

Helen disappeared around the corner. "Cream. One sugar."

"You've got a good memory."

"Nope. I've just learned that good people like to be appreciated in little ways. Remembering how a person takes his or her coffee is a small courtesy." Helen reappeared with two full cups. "The good male doctors that I work with? They never have to remember their anniversaries or their wives' or girlfriends' birthdays. I do that for them. I hate pulling a shift with a good doctor dealing with heavy guilt or last-minute-gift panic. Of course, the bad ones can just live with their problems. I figure it's a learning experience for them."

"Where's Gerry?"

"In the back. Out of the way so you can be more or less alone for a while."

"His parents haven't noticed he's missing?" Megan followed Helen through the twists and turns of the hospital corridors.

"Please," Helen said with a sarcastic tone that Megan had heard from her only a handful of times over the years they had known each other. "They're not going to know Gerry is gone until somebody tells them."

"Gerry's still sticking with the story that he fell off the roof?"

"Tighter than a tick on a hound's ear," Helen replied.

"But you don't believe him?"

"I raised seven children with a husband who was in the military and gone from home a lot," Helen said. "I know every way there is to fib. When something got broken in the house, it didn't take me long to find out who did it. And once my Amazing Mom powers—more powerful than Superman's X-ray vision or Spider-Man's spider sense—were a proven thing to my kids, they gave up trying."

Megan believed that, too. Helen had a reputation as a straight shooter around the base hospital. Sometimes, though, she was painfully so.

"Even my husband, whom I love with all my heart and who never did anything to hurt me, was sometimes known to stay out with his buddies a little longer than we agreed on. I knew when something had really come up and when he'd just gotten pressured into staying longer by being afraid of losing guy-points." Helen glanced at Megan conspiratorially. "Sometimes I let Marvin get away with it. Just to throw him off, you know. It's okay for a child to know how Mom's going to react every time, but a woman has to retain part of her mystery for her man."

In spite of the tense situation ahead of them, Megan couldn't help grinning. She and Helen saw each other professionally, and those times usually were seldom and short. Still, the rapport that existed between them was real.

Helen turned a final corner and stopped. She pointed at a room at the end and on the right. "He's down there. I've already delivered a snack to him. Chocolate milk and Oreos. Decidedly and deliberately unhealthy. That kid can use the extra calories. He's skinny as a rake handle."

"I know," Megan said. She took a deep breath. "Thanks, Helen."

A troubled look twisted Helen's features. "Something you should know."

Megan waited, guessing that she knew what the woman was going to tell her.

"I asked Dr. Carson to wait out of respect for you because I like you and I like how you do your job," Helen said in a quietly serious voice. "And because I think it will help if you talk to Gerry about it before it happens." He let out a breath. "The doctor and I are reporting his father this time, Megan."

"For what?"

"For beating that child," Helen said. She crossed her arms and lifted her chin. "I couldn't do anything about the bicycle wreck Gerry claimed to have had. But this." She shook her head. "I know he's not telling the truth tonight."

"How?"

"Those bruises and that dislocated shoulder are hours old. Even the blood on the scratches was so dry it was flaking. Gerry waited a long time before he came here."

Megan digested that. The thought of the small boy lying in his bed, hurting and scared, waiting for his father to go to sleep to steal off quietly to the hospital hurt her. One of Boyd's pet peeves, brought out in conversations with Gerry, was that his son wasn't tough enough and got mollycoddled by his mother. It was things like this that Megan had seen in her practice that sometimes caused her to question her faith in God. Children were so innocent, and yet they were victimized in so many ways.

"I think his father beat him earlier," Helen said quietly, "and I think Gerry knew his arm was hurt badly enough that he had to do something about it. He was in a lot of pain when he got here."

"Is he afraid to go home?"

"No. As a matter of fact, he was ready to leave as soon as Dr. Carson finished putting his arm in a sling. I told him we were waiting on X rays."

"He doesn't know I'm coming?"

Helen shook her head. "I was afraid if we told him that he might panic."

"He's going to panic when he sees me."

"Yeah. Probably." Helen put her hands on Megan's shoulders. "You're a good counselor, Megan. I know you can handle Gerry and his fears just fine. The trick is to get him to tell the truth about his father."

"That's going to be hard," Megan said. "As much as Gerry is afraid of his father, he loves him just as fiercely."

"I know. But if you can get him to talk, do it. To save this kid, we're going to need his testimony."

"His dad is going to go ballistic when he finds out that Gerry came to the hospital."

"I'm going to make sure we have MPs here when we have to deal with him," Helen promised. The military police took care of all criminal matters that occurred on the base.

"How is Gerry now?" *That's the main thing,* Megan told herself. *Start there. Don't think about Boyd Fletcher and how bad things are going to get when he shows up.*

"The doctor has him stabilized and relatively pain-free. He's even got him amused. ESPN runs twenty-four hours a day. There's a big basketball game from out on the West Coast." Helen smiled sadly. "Kids are incredible, you know? They go through so much, and they love so completely in spite of whatever bad things they endure." She sighed. "I just can't imagine what this world would be like without children."

Megan thought of Chris, picturing her son sleeping in the borrowed bed as she'd last seen him. Before Goose, she'd never imagined having another child. In fact, she'd never imagined being happy again. Yet, here she was.

The fact that Gerry Fletcher was waiting for her darkened her thoughts. She looked at the other woman. "How long do I have before you and Dr. Carson file a report with the MPs?"

"I'll give you thirty minutes."

Megan winced at the deadline. "Thirty minutes isn't enough time to prepare Gerry for the things he's going to have to go through in addition to what he's already been through."

"Megan," Helen said, "I'm sorry, but it's what we've got. I don't want to deal with this any more than you do, but I will. I don't want to see Gerry taken away from his parents even for a few days, but Boyd Fletcher has to get some counseling."

"I know."

Helen pushed her breath out. "Hey, I'm not mad at you."

"I know that, too. This is just a bad situation all the way around." Megan glanced at her watch. "Thirty minutes. Starting now?"

Helen nodded. "If you need anything, there's an intercom in the room. Let me know."

"I will." Megan turned and walked toward the room. She focused her thoughts, drawing in a deep breath then emptying her lungs. She wished she were less tired, more awake. She wished Joey and

Chris were both home. She wished Goose was safe. Then she prayed that what she could do tonight would be good enough to change Gerry's life for the better.

Working with the quick efficiency that military life had trained him for, Goose divided his team into two five-man units that began organizing the rescue and evacuation. Each team was equipped with a complete medkit from the RSOVs. He placed Dean Hardin, a no-nonsense Texan with more than a decade of service—including combat experience—in charge of the second unit. But Goose kept Bill with him.

Hardin's group took the east side of Glitter City while Goose's took the west. "Keep your weps up at all times," the sergeant told his men. "Until we're told otherwise, we're going to believe we're in a hostile zone and the Syrians are just about to top the ridge."

Despite the cries of the wounded, the sounds from burning vehicles and structures, the exploding thunder of artillery in the distance that spoke of continued conflict along the border, Goose heard silence. He missed the constant flow of information that streamed down through military channels over the headset. That noise had been with him for years, at once aggravating and reassuring. Although his father didn't often talk about his own tours as a special forces Green Beret, Goose had always been aware that he fought a different battle than his father had. The modern fighting warrior lived and died by the flow of information.

From what Goose could tell on his preliminary survey, nearly 80 percent of the people who had been in Glitter City at the time of the attack had been wiped out. Goose guessed from the craters in the hillsides as well as the SCUDs lying around that hadn't detonated that less than half the missiles had struck the town. But the ones that had made it had almost been enough to do the job.

Nearly half of those who had survived the attack were wounded. Most of the injuries were serious and would require hospitalization. Sanliurfa, the closest city with medical care, lay thirty klicks to the north and east. If a medical convoy took care, they could make the trip in twenty to forty minutes, but they were already twenty-four minutes into the ninety-minute window of opportunity they had to escape the next wave of SCUDs.

And that was only assuming the Syrians had fired everything they had loaded in the first attack. Goose wished again that the communications were back on line. They hadn't received any reinforcements to help handle casualties, and that—along with the constant rolling barrage of artillery—led him to believe that fighting along the border was hot and heavy. The need inside him to be back out there on the front lines with his men was almost overwhelming.

"Over here," someone yelled. "I'm trapped."

Goose swiveled, tracking the voice. A coughing fit followed, breaking up the repeated cry. The haze of dust continued to eddy around the area. Goose was beginning to doubt that the dust would ever settle entirely.

Eight people had joined Goose's five-man team. Thirteen was an inauspicious number, and he couldn't help thinking that most people thought the number had become unlucky as a result of Jesus' last supper with the apostles. Judas Iscariot had been the thirteenth man at the table, and Judas had betrayed Jesus for thirty pieces of silver. The number bothered Goose a little. He didn't consider himself overly superstitious, but that number of able-bodied men seemed to stay the same and never grow.

Further irritation came when some of the cameramen and reporters refused to help aid the wounded and search through the dead, choosing instead to shoot footage of the bombed town. Some of them claimed to be concerned about the possibility of AIDS, while others simply couldn't deal with the reality of sorting through corpses for survivors. Goose wanted to order the men to work, but he knew his likelihood of success in getting them to help was remote.

By now, Goose carried a crowbar in addition to the M-4A1 slung over his shoulder. His knuckles and palms were torn and bleeding, barked raw from handling broken rock, jagged metal, and shattered glass.

"Here," Bill called, crouching beside a tumble of rock that had once been a building.

Goose joined his friend, listening to a reporter's voice breaking in the background as the man tried to relate what had just happened to a cameraman. Shifting his LCE, Goose slid his M-4A1 from his shoulder and handed the weapon to Steve Dockery, a battle-seasoned corporal. Taking a moment to survey the pile of debris, Goose hefted his crowbar.

"Gonna have to be careful," Bill advised. He hooked a finger into his kerchief, brought it down past his chin, and shook off the mud that clung to the material. His face, protected by the kerchief, looked clean and white against the dirt that covered his goggles and the rest of his face. "We move this wrong, the whole thing's gonna come down."

Goose nodded in agreement. He turned to his group. "Dockery, Cusack, stand guard. Evaristo, you're with Bill and me. The rest of you people form a line. We're going to shift the small stuff, then try to pull this wall section back without toppling it."

The eight civilian volunteers, two of them women, formed a line. During the last few frantic minutes of rescue operations, they had learned the drill.

Bill took point on the salvage, having the steadiest and surest hands, the quickest eye, and an unshakable faith that they were going to be able to rescue the people who were left. He selected rocks from the jumbled stone and started passing them back, uncovering the wall section that had fallen precariously into the V-shaped corner of the building that remained.

Sand had rushed down the hillside in a wave, running over the back of the building and flooding the interior through the windows. The sand had become a threat to the person inside, but it was probably the only thing that allowed the man to survive.

Bill handed rocks back like a machine, able to make his selection from the myriad of stones before him, seize it, heft it, and pass it to Goose.

Standing almost knee-deep in the loose sand, Goose grabbed the chunk of rock. His hands burned and ached with the effort. Muscles cramped in his back. Sand and small debris had managed to get inside his BDU and under the Kevlar vest. Anchored by the constant stream of perspiration that covered him, the sand and grit chafed at him. He pushed himself past the discomfort, thinking of the people they had yet to save and the ones who would be lost if they didn't hurry.

The next person in the rock removal line was a woman in her late twenties. She was a brunette with dark eyes, dressed in torn khakis and a light purple blouse. Her hair was cropped short, ending at about the nape of her neck. She was slender, and the way she handled herself told Goose that she kept in shape.

She took the chunk of rock from Goose's hands. Pain and fear registered in her eyes as she looked at his face. The rough use had torn skin from her hands and forearms. Bloody patches held clots of sand that Goose knew had to be uncomfortable. But she kept at the work, swinging around and passing the rock to the next person in line.

Goose took the next rock Bill handed him. He handed it to the woman.

"Danielle," she said as she took the rock. She turned to pass the stone on, then turned back to Goose. "My name."

"Oh." Goose handed her the current rock, swiveled, and reached for the next.

"Danielle Vinchenzo. I'm a reporter with FOX News." Danielle coughed, choking on dust.

"Sergeant Samuel Gander, ma'am," Goose responded.

"I work this hard for you, Sergeant," Danielle said, "I'm going to want an interview." She coughed again but kept shifting rock.

"If we get out of here alive," a heavyset man with a florid face said.

"We'll get out alive," Goose said with conviction.

The man made a show of looking around at the carnage that had been left of Glitter City. "A lot of people haven't."

Goose didn't have anything to say to that.

A few minutes later, Bill had finished clearing the leaning wall section. He surveyed what was left, then looked at Goose. "We could try to dig him out, Sarge. Sand's loose enough, and it would make quick work."

"But the sand's helping hold the wall back," Goose said, realizing the difficulty they faced.

"Yep." Bill took his helmet off, wiped his forehead with a grimy arm, and clapped it back in place. "We're gonna have to get it off."

"We'll bring the section up with the crowbars," Goose instructed, his mind quickly providing a possible solution to the problem. "Brace the section with rocks, then keep raising till we get the clearance we need." He chose a relatively flat rock, hollowed out a place under the fallen wall, and set the rock into place.

Bill did the same.

"Hurry," the man cried out from under the rock. "It's getting . . .

hard . . . to . . . breathe . . . in here." The voice sounded weaker, and constant fits of coughing and retching echoed within.

When both crowbars were in place, Goose swapped looks with Bill. "On three," Goose said. He counted. On three, he pulled up on the crowbar, straining everything he had. Black spots swam in his vision and he felt dizzy.

Slowly, inexorably, the wall section shifted, coming up a few inches. Sand flooded in from the sides, filling the cavity that had been left by the partial collapse.

The man inside screamed in terror. "It's falling! It's falling!"

❀   ❀   ❀

United States of America
Fort Benning, Georgia
Local Time 12:18 A.M.

"Gerry," Megan said softly.

The boy sat up in the middle of the hospital bed. His unruly auburn hair stuck out in places from uncontrollable cowlicks. Freckles spattered the bridge of his nose. His hazel eyes remained fixed in awe on the television suspended from the ceiling in the corner of the room. His right arm hung in a clean white sling. Gauze pads covered scrapes on his arms and legs. He wore sweat pants with the knee out and a long-sleeved sweatshirt.

Megan knew Gerry had worn the sweats to try to hide the bruises on his arms, legs, and back. She sat quietly beside the bed, trying to keep herself relaxed in spite of everything rocketing through her mind. Watching the basketball game on television was grueling when she knew Goose was in action—in danger, she amended. She wanted to switch over to one of the news channels, but she tried to convince herself that if ESPN wasn't interrupting the live game broadcast with news of the military engagement in Turkey, things couldn't be too bad.

"Gerry," Megan tried again.

The boy pointed at the television screen. "Did you see that?" he asked excitedly. "Did you see that?"

During the past twelve minutes of the precious thirty Helen Cordell had graciously allotted, Megan had talked basketball with the boy, mostly listening. She had picked up some of the players' names. Only a minute or two ago, Gerry had bemoaned the fact that the

Knicks guard was scoring on the Lakers player. Gerry was a *major* Lakers fan.

"Gerry," Megan said in a slightly sterner voice. "We're going to have to talk about what happened tonight."

Without looking at her, Gerry drew away, curling himself into a ball. He drew his legs up, wrapped his uninjured arm around his knees, and protectively cradled his injured arm between his stomach and his thighs. His attention never wavered from the screen.

Thankfully, the Lakers called for a time-out and the station shifted to a commercial.

"Gerry, are you listening to me?"

"Yes, Mrs. Gander." The boy reached for the half-empty bottle of chocolate milk on the tray beside the bed. He made certain the cap was on tightly, then shook the bottle vigorously.

The action reminded Megan of Joey at that age, and sometimes even now. When she saw him. Between school, his friends, and the part-time job at the small café in Columbus, whole days passed lately that she and her eldest son spent only minutes together. But where Joey took chocolate milk as a given, Gerry seemed to treasure the bottle he had, doling it out to himself in small sips.

"We need to talk," Megan said.

"About what?" Gerry kept checking the television screen, but he was studiously ignoring her. He took an Oreo from the small pile of cookies on the paper plate and unscrewed the treat. He licked at the white filling.

"Your fall."

Gerry shrugged. A twinge of pain flashed across his face, blanching his cheeks white under his freckles. "I just fell."

"From the roof of your house?"

"Yeah." He licked at the cookie again tentatively.

"What were you doing on top of the house?"

"Looking at the stars."

"Why?"

"I don't know. I guess because I like stars."

Megan went with that patiently, knowing the clock was working against her and that the commercial on television couldn't last forever. "What do you like about stars?"

"I don't know."

"Have you looked at them before?"

"Yeah. All the time."

"You've never mentioned that in one of our sessions."

"So?"

"We've talked about other things you like. Basketball. Biking. It just seems kind of strange that you've never mentioned an interest in astronomy before." Gerry preferred to talk about *anything* other than his father and his relationship with the man. During some sessions, Gerry had even stooped to talking about homework problems and assignments.

"Maybe," Gerry said, "it's 'cause you didn't ask."

Megan let that statement sit between them for a moment. By assigning the blame to her, Gerry was trying to distance himself from the conversation. She remained silent, knowing from experience that arguing the point was the wrong thing to do. Gerry was a good kid. Not all of the ones she worked with were, but Gerry Fletcher was one of the good ones in a bad spot.

Looking at her, guilt flashing in his eyes, Gerry said, "Sorry. You ask lots of questions. It's not your fault you didn't know. You just didn't ever ask that question."

That was a start. "Tell me about your telescope."

A trapped look creased Gerry's thin face. For the first time, Megan saw the deep purple bruise that marred his left jawline. *The back of a hand?* she wondered. *Or a collision with something else?*

Her stomach turned and she had to push back from the line of thinking and the images that came to mind. Boyd Fletcher was a big man physically, and he lived on adrenaline. A definite type A personality filled with anxiety, tension, and aggression.

"What about it?" Gerry asked defensively.

"What kind is it?" Megan started slow, working with small details that would gradually tear away the fabrication Gerry was presenting. If she did it, here and now, with him knowing she was on his side, maybe it would go easier when the MPs presented their questions and Helen and Dr. Carson accused Boyd Fletcher of abusing his son.

Gerry carefully raised and lowered his thin shoulders. "I don't know. It's just a telescope."

"How long have you had it?"

"A while."

"Did you get it for a birthday or Christmas?"

The presentation of the choice brought home to Gerry that he was going to have to be careful and more attentive to his answers. "Does it matter?"

"I don't know. Is the telescope broken?"

"Probably," Gerry replied. "It was a long fall from the top of the house. I mean, the fall banged me and my arm up pretty bad." He nodded, more to himself than to her. "Probably the telescope got broke."

The television had returned to the basketball game, but Gerry's attention was riveted on his cookies and milk and the questions Megan had for him. He nibbled at one of the cookie pieces.

"Did you check on the telescope?" Megan asked.

"No."

"I was just wondering. You know how your dad is about your things." Boyd Fletcher had a history regarding his son's property. If Gerry broke or damaged something, the boy was made to pay a price. But if Boyd were mad at his son, he broke or disposed of Gerry's toys.

When Gerry had claimed he'd had a bike wreck, Boyd Fletcher had gotten rid of the bike, which had upset Gerry terribly. The brief—very brief—conversation Megan had shared with Boyd Fletcher had been harsh and to the point: Maybe Megan could require the sessions, but she couldn't require him to provide a bike for his son.

"He won't care about the telescope," Gerry said.

Megan nodded. "That's good. Who got the telescope for you?"

Hesitating, Gerry said, "My dad." During the sessions, he always tried to build his dad up in her eyes. He was eleven years old and he knew that she didn't feel good about his father even though she had tried to hide that fact.

"Is your dad interested in astronomy?" Megan asked.

"I guess so."

"How is he going to feel about the telescope getting broken?"

"He's probably not going to like it."

There's an understatement. Megan sometimes got the feeling that Boyd Fletcher deliberately gave his son breakable things or items that were hard to manage just so he could find fault with him.

"Probably not," Megan said. "So what are we going to do about it?"

Panicked, Gerry looked at her. "What do you mean? It's broken. There's nothing we can do about it."

"Don't you think we're going to have to tell your dad?"

Gerry was quiet.

"You know your dad doesn't like it when you do something wrong and then hide it from him," Megan said. Several of Gerry's more severe punishments, including physical as well as mental ones, resulted from the boy's attempts to conceal things from his father.

"I'll tell him," Gerry said. "Promise."

"I appreciate you being willing to. But I think this might be some-thing we'd do better together." Megan slipped a glance at her watch. Only eleven minutes remained of her allotted time. It was time to turn up the pressure. *Help me here, God. I'm getting in over my head, and there's not going to be any turning back.* She kept her voice casual. "We can tell him about the telescope at the same time we tell him about your visit here tonight."

"I can tell him in the morning."

Megan shook her head. "Sorry, guy. No can do. A visit to the hos-pital in the middle of the night requires Dr. Carson to report this."

"To my dad?"

"And possibly to other people."

Gerry gnawed his lip. "The doc called you, didn't he?"

Megan thought about Dr. Carson. The man was young and bright and caring, and she thought Boyd Fletcher would probably rip through him like a buzz saw. No, Boyd Fletcher needed a more sub-stantial target, someone who could stand up to every withering sec-ond of the argument that was surely forthcoming. Someone who could dish it back.

"Actually," Megan said, "Mrs. Cordell called me."

Gerry seemed to relax a little. "Mrs. Cordell is a tough lady."

"Yes," Megan said. "One of the toughest I know."

"She doesn't believe I fell off the roof, does she?"

Megan didn't hesitate. One of the bonds she had with anyone who saw her was unflinching honesty. "No, she doesn't."

"Do you?"

"No."

Gerry glanced at the thick file on the Fletcher family that Megan had brought in with her. The boy deflated with a long sigh, finally giv-ing in to the realization that events had progressed past the point of his ability to control them. "How much trouble is my dad in?"

"I don't know, Gerry," Megan said. *A lot, for starters.* But she hon-estly didn't know how much more. She glanced at her watch. *Six min-utes. Help me, God, because that's not nearly enough time.* She looked at the intercom on the wall, torn between begging more time from Helen and Dr. Carson now and panicking Gerry.

The boy sat on the hospital bed and looked apprehensive.

Keep it nice and easy, Megan decided. *Give it a couple minutes. See how things go. There'll be time to call Helen.* She smiled a little to ease Gerry's mind. "Why don't you tell me what really happened, and we'll take it from there?"

Turkey
30 Klicks South of Sanliurfa
Local Time 0718 Hours

On the other side of the collapsed wall in Glitter City, the trapped man's horrified screams continued to assault Goose's ears, spurring in him an instinctive need to react—now. Only his training as a professional soldier—think first, have a plan, and stick with it—kept that impulse in check as the wall section collapsed further.

"It's okay, buddy," Bill said calmly to the man as he maintained his hold on the crowbar shoring up his end of the heavy wall section. "Just the sand shifting. We've got the wall. We're not going to let it fall on you."

Goose didn't know where Bill found the strength or the wind to speak. He felt all but done in from his exertions to uncover the trapped man. The crowbar felt as though it were about to pull his arms from their sockets. He wasn't the only one feeling the strain. The heavyset man and one of the other volunteers had bailed on the line, dropping out of the rescue effort, collapsing, exhausted and wheezing, to the sand.

Danielle and one of the other men rushed forward with rocks to put under the edge of the wall to brace it up. Then Goose and Bill added a second flat rock to the first and fought for another fistful of inches.

The wall section shifted more, letting sand cascade in again. Under the ton of dead weight, the man screamed, then his cries were cut off abruptly. Several cubic yards of sand and rock around the V-shaped section of the building's corner left standing broke free and sped under the elevated wall section like mercury rolling across a flat surface at room temperature.

Anxiety flooded Goose as he realized the man they had been trying to rescue had probably been buried in that avalanche. He squatted and drew his Mini Maglite from his LCE. Clicking the flashlight on, he dropped prone to the ground and peered under the monstrous slab, praying to God that their efforts had not inadvertently crushed the life from the man they were trying to save.

The high-intensity yellow beam barely cut through the haze of dust that squirted out from under the slab in a boiling rush. The hollow under the wall section left an area almost seven feet long and four feet wide. Just about the dimensions of a grave, Goose couldn't help thinking. Hackles stood up on the back of his neck. The man they'd been working to rescue was nowhere in sight.

In the center of that space, something writhed under the sand that had rushed in. For a moment, Goose was reminded of a cow he'd seen sink in a pit of quicksand in the Okefenokee Swamp while on a hunting trip. He'd been sixteen at the time and out hunting with his buddies. They'd tried to save the cow, but in the end they'd had to watch the terrified creature sink into the bog until it disappeared.

Bill threw himself forward but was too broad to get through the gap. On his knees, he began scooping at the loose sand with both hands.

The wall shuddered and sank an inch, and the sand continued to flow.

Watching the struggling figure in the middle of the space, Goose stripped off his helmet and his LCE. "Let me."

Bill kept digging. "You're the last man that should go under there, Sarge. That wall could come down any second. We redistributed the weight, but we can't get it shored up on the hillside."

"I'm the only man that will fit. Now move, Corporal." Goose pulled his kerchief down and shoved the Mini Maglite between his teeth.

Reluctantly, Bill gave ground.

Goose slid by his friend. The flashlight beam jostled and jarred across the sea of sand that filled the hollow space. Dust flooded Goose's lungs at once, choking him down so that he couldn't draw a breath. He scooted forward on hands and knees, clawing through the sand. Something more solid than the sand and considerably less dense than one of the stones he'd been handling took shape under his right hand. Turning, he found he'd uncovered the face of a dead man.

Sand had filled the man's eyes, nose, and mouth. He lay partially on his side, his hair black and stringy against the fine yellow sand.

God help me, Goose prayed as he forced himself to push the corpse from his mind and concentrate on the struggle ahead of him. There was no way of knowing—yet—how many people had been in the structure when it had come down. Later, if there was a chance to excavate the bodies, authorities would learn the number of casualties—and who they were.

Later, he'd have the luxury to wonder how many families were going to be devastated by the news today.

Reaching the writhing pile of sand, Goose tried to push to a kneeling position but couldn't. The wall was less than two feet above him. He worked from his stomach, arching his back and using both arms like a swimmer, shoving sand from the person who had been buried.

Even as he pushed the sand away, he became aware that still more sand was sliding in from the wall's edge where it butted into the V-shape of the building's corner. Their efforts had lifted that portion of the wall enough to allow the sea of sand to slither in. A moment later, the wall itself shifted, grinding across the rocks they'd placed to create the gap Goose had crawled in through. Even as he watched, the wall dropped at least two inches.

"Sarge," Bill called.

Goose didn't answer, concentrating on his efforts to save the man. Sand flew into his mouth around the Mini Maglite he held between his teeth. He resisted the urge to spit it out because he would lose the flashlight, and the ambient light from outside the wall wouldn't be enough to work by. But the dust felt thick in his throat, gathering weight and threatening to trigger a purge reflex.

The wall section shifted again and dropped enough to slam into the back of Goose's head.

"Sarge!" Bill sounded a little more panicked now.

A hand grabbed Goose's ankle and yanked. He slid backward a short distance. "No!" he said around the flashlight as best he could. He prayed fervently, wishing he believed with the same intensity that Bill did, but the face of the dead boy he'd seen only moments ago kept haunting him. How strong did faith have to be? Beneath the goggles, perspiration trickled across his face, washing small bits of grit into his eyes, making them stream and burn.

Then a hand reached up from the sandy grave and wrapped around the back of Goose's neck like something out of a horror movie he'd seen as a kid. Fingernails tore into his flesh. Concentrating, thinking quickly, Goose followed the path of the arm that held him in a death grip. Ramming his hand through the shifting sand wasn't easy, but it was doable.

Reaching down the length of the arm, Goose hooked his hand under the armpit and managed to secure a strong grip on the man's shirt. For the first time, Goose realized that the man had been standing up in the building. The sand had come in so swiftly that the deluge had filled the structure with him standing.

Goose tried desperately not to think about the number of people that had been caught in the building. Overhead, the wall fell again, sinking into the deep sand, coming far enough down now that it pressed against his back. He spat out the flashlight, caught it in his free hand, and yelled, "I've got him! Pull!"

"Get him out of there!" Bill yelled. "C'mon! Pull! Put your backs into it!"

Even as Bill shouted, the massive stone slab over Goose's head dropped another few inches, pinning him against the sand.

❈   ❈   ❈

United States of America
Columbus, Georgia
Local Time 12:28 A.M.

Basso booms of speed metal music, delivered with hammering intensity, rocked the interior of the nightclub. Out on the large dance floor, young men and women writhed and practically fought one another. To someone not familiar with the club scene, it probably looked like they were vying to claim more territory.

Most of the club's dancers favored leather and lace, barely-there shorts, crop tops, slinky dresses that were painted on, and leather pants so tight—on both sexes—they just had to cut down blood circulation. The laser light show burned red, blue, green, and livid purple beams through the air and swirled multicolored patterns over the dance floor. The dancers' dangling earrings and ornamented piercings in their eyebrows, lips, and noses glinted in the garish colors of the laser lights.

Many of the dancers sported intricate tattoos. Some of them were temporary, courtesy of a street artist working with fluorescent paint who'd set up shop in his van outside the club. Others wore glowing necklaces and armbands that the band had thrown out a few songs back.

"Are you having a good time?"

Mesmerized by all the action in front of him, Joey Holder looked down at the young woman at his side. "Yeah," he said.

She gave him a puzzled look and leaned closer.

Realizing that he hadn't spoken loudly enough to be heard over the music, Joey raised his voice. "Yes. Great time."

Jenny McGrath smiled up at him. She rocked to the beat, popping her shoulders and clenched fists to the rhythm. "Cool. I thought you would."

"Yeah. Me, too." As soon as the words left his mouth, Joey realized how dumb they sounded.

"You're a funny guy, Joey."

"It's not all natural talent," Joey replied loudly. "Sometimes I have to work at it."

She grinned at him, and in that flash of white teeth, Joey fell in love with her all over again. At an inch or two over five feet, carrying a woman's full body with slender lines, her short-cropped spiky hair dyed purple, Jenny McGrath was beautiful.

Stonewashed low-riding jeans sheathed her hips, and her midnight blue camisole top revealed enough milk white skin that it threatened to fry his brain cells. Her nose ring and eyebrow ring glinted in the laser lights.

She so totally fit into the club, reminding Joey again that he didn't. His nervousness over the fake ID in his pocket increased. Someone was going to find him out, then there'd be all kinds of trouble. Jenny didn't know how old he really was, and she was twenty-three. His mother, if she had known where he was, would have gone crazy.

"Want to dance some more?" she yelled.

"Sure," Joey shouted back.

She took his hand and charged out onto the dance floor. At the outer fringes, she stopped, cupped her hands around her mouth, and shouted, "Leonard!"

A shaggy-haired behemoth turned to face her. He was dressed in jeans and a loose plaid shirt over a concert T-shirt. He looked like he was in his thirties. Tattoos featuring flaming skulls marked his bared arms.

"I want to surf," Jenny shouted.

Leonard grinned, revealing that he was missing his two front teeth, then bent over slightly and folded his hands together to make a stirrup. "Come ahead, darlin'." He raised his voice in a thundering shout. "Surf's up!"

Immediately the nearby dancers turned and raised their hands.

Without hesitation, Jenny threw herself forward. She stepped into Leonard's clasped hands, then let him hurl her into the audience. Waiting hands caught her above the heads of the crowd, balanced her, then propelled her toward the stage.

Jenny surfed on her back, flailing wildly to make sure the other dancers knew she was coming. "Joey! C'mon! See if you can make your way to the stage!"

Still grinning, Leonard held out his clasped hands. "You up for it, little man?"

The challenge in the words was evident, and Joey felt himself bristling in response. Steeling himself, he nodded and ran at Leonard. He put a foot into Leonard's hands and leaped. In the next instant he was airborne, shooting up onto the crowd of moshers.

Dancers below Joey shouted at him as he passed. Some of them congratulated him while others cursed at him. Both responses, and even mostly neutral expressions, usually came couched in acidic obscenities that Joey had seldom encountered. He felt thrilled and embarrassed at the same time.

Vacation Bible school had never been like this. As soon as that thought raced through his mind, Joey felt an immediate surge of guilt and was reminded how the youth minister had always told him the best way to know what God wanted in a person's life was by paying attention to the small niggling doubts that often turned into guilt if left unchecked. His preacher said that a sense of right and wrong was placed within every person, but it was up to that person to fine-tune that sense and keep his or her covenant with God.

An old anger surfaced in Joey again, triggering the rebellion that had claimed him. No one knew what was right for him. He didn't even know, but he sure wasn't going to let someone else tell him. He'd loved his dad, but Tony Holder had left and seldom showed up these days. Joey had liked the youth minister, Mr. Lewis, but Mr. Lewis had moved away.

Joey had deeply liked, admired, and respected Goose, especially in the early days of Goose's marriage to his mom. Those times had been great. Then, in no time at all it seemed, The Squirt had been born. Chris's arrival into the family had changed everything for Joey. Goose's attention had been divided between the boys, and he wasn't able to do as many guy things with Joey as he had before Chris had been born. The pickup basketball games and racquetball games Joey had loved stopped as Goose stayed home more to take care of Chris.

Part of that time spent together before Chris arrived, Joey knew, was because his mom worked long hours in the counseling center helping other people's kids. That hadn't been a problem before Chris had been born. Then, Goose had told them they were going to "bach" it, and they'd go take in a movie and grab dinner at a café off base. If they didn't do a movie, they'd go to the rec center, shoot some hoops, or play racquetball till they were both too tired to stand.

Chris had spoiled all of that. Goose hadn't been able to go as much when Joey's mom wasn't home to take care of the baby. And it was like Goose never even noticed how much things had changed. It was then that Joey realized that he was, and always would be, Goose's stepson, not his real son. When he was feeling generous, which wasn't often these days, Joey supposed that it wasn't Goose's fault. After all, Goose couldn't have known how he would feel about having a real son until he had one.

But Joey felt lied to and taken advantage of. Like he'd been replaced. He pushed away those thoughts and concentrated on the moment. The music was loud, the lights were dizzying, and the crowd was *wild*. And he was in the middle of it.

The crowd shoved him toward the stage. Tossed and hurled across the surface of the crowd, Joey craned his neck around and spotted Jenny ten feet ahead of him and quickly approaching the stage. Most of the hands shoved him forward, but he caught more than a few punches to his back, ribs, and thighs. Anger ran rampant through much of the crowd. The hard music gave their rage a voice, and the various chemical stimulants they were imbibing gave people free reign to act on the primeval violence that moved within them. After this night, Joey was certain he'd be carrying bruises for a week.

Jenny reached the stage easily. She was a girl. Girls always reached the stage. But she was met by two burly security guards wearing band T-shirts with SECURITY stamped across the chest and back of the shirts. They wore black paratrooper pants, but none of the guys looked like the military government-issue guys that Joey had been around.

As Joey closed on the stage, the two security guards confronted Jenny. Usually, the security people pushed the crowd surfers back from the stage, and the dancers swept them back to the other end of the dance floor. But this time the lead guitarist—a guy with a tattooed face, skinny arms, and obscene T-shirt—stepped forward and spoke to the security people.

The guitarist started on a throbbing, ear-splitting solo and spoke to Jenny. Unbelievably, Jenny started dancing onstage, gyrating her body in a manner that filled Joey with lust and jealousy all at the same time. If she had danced for him like that—alone—he would have been thrilled. But dancing in front of guys who hooted and yelled and screamed encouragement was horrible. He also felt it was incredibly stupid.

Joey reached the stage. Anger burst loose inside of him. He tried to run across the stage and get to Jenny. He didn't know what he was going to do when he reached her, but he was determined to reach her.

Two security guards caught him before he took his third step. With embarrassing ease, the security guys flung Joey back into the crowd. Once he landed atop the crowd, the dancers shouted in eager derision at his failed attempt and started shoving him to the back of the dance floor.

"No!" Joey yelled, wanting to get to Jenny and get her off the stage or at least let everyone know she was with him. But the crowd wasn't listening or couldn't hear him. He fought and twisted and grabbed on to people. In the end, his efforts didn't matter. He was swept along the top of the crowd like a piece of flotsam driven before an aggressive tide.

Turkey
30 Klicks South of Sanliurfa
Local Time 0725 Hours

As the tide of sand shifted around him, hands—Goose didn't know how many—pulled at his feet and worked up his legs. He slid out from under the collapsed wall section as the sand rushed in to fill the empty space. But he kept his grip on the trapped man. Rough stone rasped and cut into Goose's shoulders and the back of his head. His arm felt wrenched from its socket as he drew the trapped man from the sand, but he hung on.

As soon as the man came free of the sand, Goose shot out from under the wall. He managed to wrap his free arm behind the man's head in an embrace to strengthen his hold. Someone grabbed his belt and the speed of the rescue attempt increased again.

Bright sunlight ripped into Goose's eyes as he emerged. Bill reached for the rescued man. In the same instant, the wall section collapsed with a *whumf* that spat out a roiling mass of dust. The group of rescuers turned away from it.

"It's okay, Sarge," Bill said, dropping to the ground beside Goose. "I've got him. I've got him. He's gonna be okay. You're gonna be okay."

Goose released his grip on the man and rolled over. The coughing fit he'd been holding back erupted, and for a moment he thought he was going to cough up a lung. His head felt near to bursting. Then, just as he thought he'd never draw another breath, enough of the dust cleared from his lungs that he could suck in a gasp of relatively fresh air.

Weak and shaking but recovering quickly, Goose forced himself to his feet.

"Are you all right, Sergeant Gander?" Danielle Vinchenzo stood at his side. Blood streaked one side of her face, leaking from her temple to her chin.

"Yes, ma'am," Goose answered, then went through another coughing fit.

She offered him a canteen of water.

"Thank you, ma'am."

"Are you always this polite?" she asked. "You nearly got crushed under that slab."

Goose felt a little flustered. The question had come from left field and wasn't connected to anything that had been going on. He uncapped the canteen and filled his mouth. Rinsing the dust from his mouth, he spat the water out. Then he took a drink. He glanced around at the bombed-out city.

"Sorry, Sergeant," Danielle said with a wry grin that looked totally out of place on her bloody face. "A reporter's professional curiosity, I'm afraid. I always try to understand the people and the stories I cover. And maybe I'm a little irritated that anyone can be that cool under pressure."

"I'm from Waycross, Georgia, ma'am," Goose said. "My daddy raised me to be respectful, and the military has kept it that way. As far as being cool under pressure, it's just an act." He smiled back at her.

"Golden Globe all the way, Sergeant."

"If you'll excuse me, ma'am, I've still got to see to getting these people—and you—out of here." Goose turned from the reporter with a polite nod, then joined Bill at the side of the man they'd rescued.

The man looked to be in his late forties. The yellow dust clung to him, as thick as the confectioners' sugar on a powdered donut, graying out his pinched features. He was bald and had firm features, the face of a man that an audience would trust as he delivered the nightly news. His lightweight gray suit was ripped and torn. His eyes rolled wildly in their sockets. From the crooked angle of his left foot, Goose knew the man's leg or hip had been broken. Maybe both.

Goose thought he recognized the man from one of the television networks, either American or European, but he couldn't be sure.

Bill tilted the man's head back and poured water into his mouth from a canteen. "Easy there, mister. You'll want to spit that out. If you swallow that mouthful without getting clear of all that sand, you'll just be sick."

The man rinsed his mouth and spat, getting most of the water on himself because he lacked the strength to spit far enough to clear his body. He pushed away Bill's offer of the canteen again and croaked, "Teresa's still down there."

"Teresa?" Bill asked.

The man nodded. "She's my producer. We took shelter when the missiles struck. She was standing right beside me when the building collapsed and started to fill with sand."

Sorrowfully, Bill shook his head. "We didn't find her."

The man clutched at Bill's uniform. "You've got to go back. You've got to find her. She was there. The sand pulled her away from me."

"Sir," Goose said, "we can't."

The man looked at Goose. Fire danced in his eyes. "Sergeant, that woman may be down there dying."

Goose spoke patiently. "If she was down there, sir, then there's nothing we can do for her. She's in God's hands." He said the words, but he didn't really believe them. And he hated the fact that the woman's survival had been taken out of his hands before he had even known she had been at risk. It wasn't fair.

Exhaustion and shock overcame the man. He fell back and sobbed helplessly, putting a hand over his face.

"Sarge." Cusack trotted over with a section of canvas tent he'd cut.

The Rangers had salvaged pieces from the tents and used them to drag wounded over to the decades-old deuce-and-a-half that had escaped the wholesale destruction that had swept through the rest of the town. Flames had blistered the vehicle's camo paint and left a layer of black soot over it, but it was still serviceable. An enterprising Turkish man had ended up with the ex-military vehicle and had hired it out to the media to transport equipment back and forth from the airport. The roads to Glitter City were few, and only called *roads* in polite company.

Dockery gave Goose his assault rifle back, then helped Dewey organize the litter bearers to carry the man they'd rescued to the big truck. Together, the two Rangers hauled the injured man away, leaving a smooth concave trail in the sand behind them.

Goose pulled himself back into his gear, gazing across the single road that divided Glitter City and seeing that Hardin's team had found another survivor. There were getting to be fewer and fewer of those, and most were too injured to help out with the rescue operation.

Hardin, Goose noticed, had also started a scavenger pile, throwing items he considered salvageable and marketable into a pile near the edge of the hard-packed earthen road. The man had a knack for finding things. Hardin was a good soldier but not a career-minded one. He remained military because he knew how to play the options that came to him and because he could follow orders. But Hardin also had a tendency to involve himself in barter and trade that bordered on black market. Still, his skill could be priceless in places like this.

During their last deployment, a peacekeeping mission in East Africa, Hardin had become the go-to guy to locate hard-to-find materials. That was the up-side. The down-side was that Hardin had also muscled his way into being something of a black market kingpin while the 75th was stationed there.

Goose had wanted to bust the man down in rank from corporal to private when he'd discovered the illicit trade he'd gotten involved in. But Remington, a company sergeant then, had smoothed the waters and kept Hardin at rank. When Remington had made officer, he'd brought Goose along with him, but he'd also brought Hardin along. There were times when Goose didn't agree with Remington's line of thinking.

But there was no mistaking Hardin's value in a firefight or any op that needed a man who was cool, was quick under pressure, and never hesitated to make a life-or-death decision.

Sudden static in Goose's left ear shot a bolt of white-hot pain screaming through his brain. His radio hissed, popped, and crackled, then cleared.

"Phoenix Leader," a man's voice said. "Phoenix Leader, this is Base. Do you read? Over."

Goose put a hand to the headset and adjusted the volume. Static continued to ripple through the connection, but the communication remained steady. "Phoenix Leader reads you, Base."

"Stand by, Leader. I'm connecting you to Base Commander."

Knowing that the com officer was alerting Remington to the fact that he had Goose, the sergeant glanced toward the south. The booms of the heavy artillery continued. *C'mon, Cal,* Goose urged. *Get with me. Let me know how bad this is and what we have to do to fix it.*

❊   ❊   ❊

United States of America
Columbus, Georgia
Local Time 12:35 A.M.

Leonard met Joey at the other end of the journey back across the dance crowd as the dancers surfed him away from Jenny and the stage. At the end of the ride, the final dancers unceremoniously dumped Joey onto the floor. Caught unprepared, still distracted by the stage show Jenny was putting on, Joey hit the floor hard.

"Hey," Leonard said, grinning broadly and pointing. "Looks like you lost your girl." He pointed toward the stage. "Guess she's throwing the small fish back tonight, minnow."

Joey was so mad and hurt he couldn't speak. Slowly, and with some effort because he was sore from being beaten during the surfing, he forced himself to his feet, rubbing the elbow he'd smacked on the floor. But he couldn't help staring back up at the stage where Jenny was still dancing.

A baby spotlight picked her out. She had become the center of the show while the lead guitarist continued his solo. She was beautiful, and Joey was sure every guy in the club knew it.

"She's flauntin' it, man," Leonard crowed. "That's harsh to watch, dude. I mean, if you're all caught up in her like you seem to be."

"She's just dancing," Joey said defensively. "She likes to dance. She dances all the time." The excuse sounded lame and he regretted it instantly.

"Yeah," Leonard agreed. "Jenny's always been that way."

Remembering the way she had called on Leonard to help her start her surf run, Joey asked, "You know Jenny?"

Leonard nodded. "A couple years now. Maybe." He scratched his big, shaggy head. "Kinda hard to remember. Hey, I'm gonna grab a beer."

Joey glanced back at the stage where Jenny was still breaking the frenetic beat down into popping dance moves that brought cheers from the crowd. She wasn't like any of the girls he'd known back at the base. Clouded with angry disgust and confusion, especially since part of him enjoyed that Jenny was such a hit because he had brought her, he followed Leonard to the bar.

"Man," Leonard said, looking back at the stage, "Jenny's stealin' the show." He grinned and shook his head. Then he looked at Joey. "I always feel sorry for the guys she dates."

"Why?" Joey asked. A few weeks ago when he had met Jenny, he'd thought she was the sexiest girl he'd ever met.

"She's fickle, man. Don't stay with nothin' or nobody for long." Leonard ordered a beer from the tattooed bartender dressed in holey jeans and a sweatshirt with the sleeves ripped off. Laser lights gleamed against his shaved head and glinted from his piercings.

The bartender looked at Joey.

"Beer," Joey said, digging money out of his pants pocket.

The bartender tossed his bar towel over his shoulder and leaned on the bar. "You don't look old enough, kid."

"I got ID," Joey argued. He was seventeen. The club, Ragged Metal, had a mandatory minimum age of twenty-one.

"You're twenty-one?" The bartender grinned in disbelief.

"Yeah." Joey fought to keep his eyes locked on the bartender. That was one of the things that Goose had taught him: always look another man in the eye. Tony, Joey's real dad, had never stuck around long enough to teach him anything about being a man. Maintaining eye contact was still hard for him, and for a moment Joey had the sick feeling that he was going to cry or look away.

"C'mon, Ace," Leonard said. "Get off him. He's got ID or he woulda never got past Turco at the front door."

"Looks young to me," Ace argued.

Joey knew he looked young. He couldn't help that. He got his slim, dark looks from his dad, who'd looked like a kid well into his twenties. Dressed in torn stonewashed jeans that his mom would have so totally freaked over and a red muscle tank top under an unbuttoned chambray shirt, he figured he looked a lot older. If his mustache or beard would ever come in heavier, that would help.

Until then, he had the fake ID that David Wilson, one of the other base teens, had made for him. Living on base wasn't all bad, David would say, because some of the best computer equipment going was there and easy to access. Fake IDs were only part of the services the clever fourteen-year-old provided—for a fee. Joey's ID had cost some cash and some baseball cards that he had collected with Goose. That had been back before Chris was born, back when Goose still had time for him.

"He comes from over at the base," Leonard said. "You know how the Army guys make their kids dress."

"Not all of them go for the conservative look," Ace argued.

Leonard gestured with his beer. "Your dad a career guy?"

"Yeah." Joey didn't bother to mention that Goose was his stepdad. And he was surprised that Leonard had pegged him as a military brat so quickly. Joey had thought he was disguised. "Almost twenty years." Or more. Joey couldn't quite remember. He just knew that with Goose the time seemed like forever. He couldn't imagine Goose being anything but a soldier, although Grandpa Gander told stories from time to time about Goose as a kid.

According to those stories, Goose had always been a Goody Two-shoes, which gave Joey and him less to talk about now that Joey was deep into his teen years and wanted more out of life than Goose evidently had. Goose had worked with his father as a carpenter in Waycross, hunted and fished the swamp, and signed with the army almost right out of high school.

"Officer?" Leonard asked.

"Non-com," Joey answered. "First Sergeant." He was surprised at how he said it and at the pride he felt. He hoped Leonard didn't notice because that was pure geek.

The bartender pulled a beer up, opened the bottle, and slid it across the bar while taking the folded money Joey had placed on the counter.

"Tough guy?" Leonard turned and placed his back to the bar, hooking his elbows over the edge.

"Goose? He's one of the toughest." Joey sipped his beer. The taste was awful and he worked hard not to grimace because Ace was still watching him suspiciously. He'd only tasted beer a handful of times. None of those times had been pleasant and he really didn't see why people bothered to acquire the taste. But they did, and if he wanted to be cool and fit in with the crowd Jenny hung with, he knew he'd have to acquire that taste, too.

"So where did you meet Jenny?" Leonard took out a pack of cigarettes and lit up. He blew blue smoke into the air and a purple laser light shot through the cloud for just a moment.

Joey glanced over his shoulder and felt another wave of anger. There was so much of it in him that it worried him sometimes. It worried his family, too. That was one of the reasons his mom had first started making him go to church. She was a counselor, and yet she was too close to this problem to completely solve it. So she'd dumped the problem into God's lap. Terrific solution. Maybe church had helped her as a kid, but it wasn't working for him. He felt picked on by life, by his real dad, by the fact that he and his mom had to survive on so little, not get to do so many things, and by Goose going away so much. He just felt abandoned.

His mom had hoped that church would help him get over those feelings. She talked to him about faith, but so much of what she said had come across like counseling stuff. He didn't have faith, and he knew it. Everyone had abandoned him, and God had never showed up in his life.

When things had finally started to get better, after Goose married his mom, Chris—"one of God's most precious gifts"—showed up and took everything away from him again. Even Bill's kind words and well-meaning approach to the situation didn't put a different spin on things. And Bill was one of the most insightful adults Joey had ever met.

The harsh thing about having a little brother dropped into his life was that Joey couldn't hate Chris. He'd wanted to, but his little brother was so cool and loving and looked up to him so much while Goose wasn't around that Joey knew he could never really hate his little brother. Still, there were moments that resentment crept in between them. But the love was real, maybe the realest thing Joey had ever felt, because Chris didn't seem to expect anything back.

In fact, thinking about Chris now, Joey felt guilty that he wasn't home to make sure his little brother was tucked in. That was one of the things that Goose had asked him to do.

But there'd been this date tonight with Jenny.

He watched her up on the stage. Some date. He didn't know how he was going to handle the present situation.

"I met Jenny at work," Joey replied, answering Leonard's question.

"Wick Dreams?"

Joey shook his head. "Kettle O' Fish. It's a restaurant. We're both servers."

Leonard drained a third of his beer. "Last I heard, Jenny was working at the candle place in the mall."

Joey shrugged. He didn't know about that. In fact, it seemed like there were a lot of things he didn't know about Jenny. "I met her at Kettle O' Fish. We worked a few shifts together, then she told me about this place and asked me out." He felt pretty good about that. He'd never had a girl ask him out before. The girls he knew on base usually found a way to let him know they were interested in him and wouldn't mind being asked out. He'd dated a lot, but he'd never met a girl like Jenny McGrath.

"Yep, that's Jenny." Leonard finished his beer, set the empty on the bar, and asked for another. "She always goes for guys that are younger than her. And definitely more innocent."

Joey almost argued the point on that one, but he didn't. Leonard was a big guy. Besides that, he had information about Jenny that Joey wanted.

"Want a word of advice, kid?" Leonard asked.

The black anger Joey felt got the upper hand for a moment, making his voice sharp and quick. "Do I look like I need advice?"

Leonard glanced at him in surprise. For a minute, Joey got the impression the guy was going to jump him. Then Leonard grinned, and there was a trace of evil in the expression. "Yeah, you do."

Joey swallowed and kept back the immediate response that formed in his mind.

"My advice to you," Leonard said, "is to enjoy tonight. Maybe a couple other nights, and some real nice times. But don't get hung up on Jenny. She ain't forever, man. She's just out to amuse herself, and you're just the flavor of the week."

Leonard's words slammed into Joey. He bridled against the prediction. The guy didn't know that. Jenny had come on really strong, talking to him, making time to be with him. The attraction wasn't one-sided. Joey was certain he wasn't the only one to feel it.

But Jenny was still dancing with the band, still in the spotlight and apparently loving it.

Feeling kind of sick, no longer able to tolerate the beer taste in his mouth, Joey turned back to the bar, intending to ask for an order of cheese nachos. Ace stood at the television mounted on the wall behind the bar. Channels cycled as the bartender used the remote control. The news broadcast caught Joey's attention.

On the screen, video footage of troops rushing across windswept desert sands bore the tagline SYRIAN-TURKISH BORDER. Explosions ripped across the stark landscape in the next instant.

Ace cycled past the news channel.

"Hey," Joey shouted.

The bartender turned around. "You want something, kid?"

"That news channel," Joey said. Goose! Goose was over there! "Let me see that again."

"You got somebody over there?" Ace asked.

"My dad," Joey answered without hesitation. "My dad is over there."

"That's harsh, man," the bartender said sympathetically as he switched the television channel back. "Looks like those guys on the front line are taking a beating."

"My mom and dad got into an argument this evening."

"Before you came to the base hospital?"

"Yeah. A long time before."

As Megan watched Gerry Fletcher, her heart went out to the boy. Remaining professional in light of everything that had gone on so far tonight, especially after having to drop Chris off and not knowing where Joey was or if Goose was all right, tested her emotional control to the max. At the moment, with the clock ticking here and who-knew-what going on with her menfolk, she felt in over her head dealing with both Gerry and her own family crises. As she always had in other times of overwhelming stress and uncertainty about what course she should pursue, she quietly prayed to God.

She felt a little guilty just now because it seemed like she was praying to Him lately only to intercede on her behalf or her family's, not just to accept and talk and give thanks. But that was when she most needed Him: when things—like Gerry's situation—got the better of her. And when those things—like Gerry's situation—continued, sometimes she couldn't help feeling that God didn't care.

Upon occasion, Megan had unburdened herself to Bill Townsend when he had been visiting. Bill had always seemed so understanding, so seemingly in tune with God's ways, that he had been easy to talk to about her work and about her faith. She'd told Bill about the bad things she had dealt with while counseling the base kids, and Bill had told her that God's plan took everything into account, that no sparrow fell without notice. He couldn't explain why those terrible things happened, but he did believe they served a purpose that wasn't always within human understanding. From the way he had talked, Megan knew that Bill believed that. But she had her doubts, and times like tonight brought those doubts to the forefront.

Gerry sat in the bed with his back to the headboard. He held his good arm wrapped around his injured arm, his knees doubled up. Although he stared at the television set where the Lakers had just returned to the court after the half, Megan knew the boy no longer saw the game. He was reliving the night, reviewing another section of the never-ending nightmare his life had turned into these past few years.

"Your parents got into an argument," Megan prompted after a short while.

"Yeah," Gerry said.

"I'm sorry."

Gerry shrugged a little, taking care with his injured shoulder. "It's not your fault, Mrs. Gander. It's my fault." Tears ran down his scratched cheeks. "It's always my fault. That's what you don't understand. That's what I've been trying to tell you all this time, and you just don't listen. If you just listened and believed me, maybe we could fix me. Make me better."

"I know you, Gerry," Megan said softly. "You're a good person."

Stubbornly, sniffling and wiping at his tears, Gerry shook his head. His voice came out as a hoarse whisper. "I'm not. I can't be. If I was good, my mom and dad wouldn't fight so much over me."

"Your mom and dad haven't just fought over you," Megan said. "During our sessions, you said they've fought in the past over money and over jobs your mom has taken."

"Yeah, but they'd have more money if they didn't have me," Gerry said. "I've heard Dad say that. And if they didn't need more money because of me, Mom could be at home more."

"We've talked about this before. I thought we both agreed that your mom works because she likes work. She makes friends there." And, Megan suspected, Tonya Fletcher worked outside the home to get away from her controlling husband. Megan believed the abuse issue ran deeper than just Gerry. During her conversations with the woman, though, Megan had never gotten Tonya to open up.

"Maybe she wouldn't need friends if things were better at home." Gerry rested his chin on his knees. Tears continued to cascade down his cheeks. "Maybe she'd be happy with my dad."

"You don't think she's happy with him?" Megan pried at the situation as delicately as she could. Normally, she would have been tempted to wait until Gerry was better able to deal with the situation, but with the MPs about to be notified, she couldn't afford to do that. Boyd Fletcher was going to go through the roof when he found out what was going on.

"I don't know," Gerry answered. "I think they'd be fine. If it wasn't for me." He choked back a sob, faking a cough. "I've heard my dad say that. I told you he's said that."

Megan knew. When Gerry had told her he'd heard his dad say that, she'd felt sympathetic and angry all at once. No child should have to hear or endure the things Gerry had. But there were others out there that had things as bad and worse.

"Did you do something to cause the fight tonight?" Megan asked. The MPs would want to know, and it was better to know the answers to the questions those men would be asking so she didn't get blindsided.

"No." Shivers coursed through Gerry. "It just started over dinner."

"How did it start?"

"They were talking. About going out. Mom was tired. You could see that she was tired. Dad said he wished they could go to a movie, the way they used to before they had me. But they didn't have anyone to watch me and he didn't want to take me."

Megan forced herself to remain silent.

"Mom told Dad to go ahead and go, that she would stay with me while he got out of the house and relaxed for a little while. He said that going out wasn't the point, that he wanted to go out with her, that they never got to do anything together anymore."

The Fletchers rarely went out as a couple, Megan knew. But some of the gossip around the base was that Boyd liked to hit the bars, and having a fight with his wife gave him a good excuse to go.

"Dad got mad then," Gerry went on. "He started cussing and throwing things. He broke one of the vases Mom had made in her art class."

Evidence for the MPs, if it hasn't been cleaned up, Megan thought and felt immediately guilty that she had to think like that. Tonya Fletcher hadn't gotten to finish her art class due to her husband's reluctance to watch Gerry by himself. When Gerry had suffered his "bike wreck" during one of the art classes, Tonya had stopped going.

"After the vase got broke," Gerry said, "Mom got mad. She started yelling back at Dad. She hardly ever dares to do that. She said if anybody deserved to get out of the house, it was her because she was stuck there all day just waiting for him to come home and find something wrong with everything she did." The boy's voice lowered. "Then Dad said the way he heard it she wasn't there by herself all the time."

Megan measured the question carefully, then asked, "Your dad suspects your mom sometimes has company at home when your father is gone?" That was a new wrinkle in an already volatile situation.

Gerry wiped at his reddened eyes. "Dad says she does. But, Mrs. Gander, I've never seen anyone else there. I come home every day right when I'm supposed to, and I've never seen anyone. Mom just sits there alone." He sniffled, a little more under control now because he was so physically exhausted. "Sometimes, Dad asks me if I've seen anyone around the house when he's gone. He gets me by myself and asks me. But there's never been anyone there. I don't think he believes me, though. Most of the time he just tells me I'd lie for her because she's got me trained to do that." He wiped at his eyes and looked at Megan. "Tonight, Dad said he thought Mom was up to something. Then he started talking about how I don't look anything like him. Or her, even."

That, Megan knew, was true. Gerry was much smaller than his father, but that could have been just genetics, a throwback to another part of the Fletcher family, or to Tonya's family.

"Dad said I looked like someone else," Gerry said, "and that someone else was probably really my dad. Mom yelled at him, telling him he should never say something like that in front of me." He gnawed his lip. "I think Mom was really embarrassed and that's why she did it."

"Did what?"

"She threw a pot at him. Just picked it up from the stove and heaved it at him. He was so surprised that it hit him in the head. I couldn't believe it. Then he crossed the room and slapped her."

Megan forced herself to remain under control. From the sound of things, the Fletcher situation had dropped into complete chaos.

"Mom fell," Gerry said. "Dad drew back like he was going to hit her again. Before I knew it, I ran at him." He started crying again, covering his face with his hands and shaking his head in denial. "I hit my own dad, Mrs. Gander. I never thought I would do something like that." He sobbed brokenly. "What kind of son would do that?"

Megan swallowed the lump in her throat. "A son who cares about his mother and wanted to protect her."

Still shaking his head, Gerry buried his face against his knees. His shoulders shook with silent grief.

"Is that when your father hit you?" Megan asked. She hated having to push the boy, but she needed as many details as she could get.

Gerry hesitated for a moment, then nodded.

"How many times?"

"I don't know."

"Was it once?" Megan asked. "Twice? More than that?"

He looked up at her, his eyes still pooling with tears of helplessness, hurt, and shame. "I don't know, Mrs. Gander. He hit me and hit me. Mom had to get him to stop. She threatened to call the MPs. She told him she would tell the base commander."

Horrible images of the violence that had taken place in the home filled Megan's mind till she felt she wasn't going to be able to handle them. *Why, God? Why put a child through this?* And at the same time she wondered why she had to be the one to deal with the child. Guilt ripped through her an instant after that thought.

"Did your dad stop then?" Megan asked.

"Yeah. But the house was wrecked. There were broken dishes everywhere. That's how come my arms and legs are scratched up."

"What happened to your shoulder?"

Gerry shook his head. "I don't know. He grabbed me or something. I know he didn't mean to hurt me. He said he was sorry."

Megan felt like screaming. After beating up his family, Boyd Fletcher simply handed out an apology.

"He doesn't mean to be that way, Mrs. Gander," Gerry said. "He really doesn't. But if my mom did something wrong—" his voice broke and he sucked air noisily for a moment—"if I'm really not his kid, then he shouldn't have to pay for me or take care of me. Should he?"

No answer came to Megan. In all her years of counseling, no child had ever asked her a question like that.

"You see," Gerry said desperately. "This might not be his fault at all."

"Listen to me, Gerry," Megan said as calmly as she could. "After tonight, some things are going to have to change."

The boy shook his head. "I don't want them to change. I just want them to go back to the way they were. I never should have come here."

"Yes, you should have." Megan paused, gathering her thoughts, hoping she was making herself convincing. "Gerry, this thing that happened with you and your mother tonight might have gotten worse if you hadn't said anything. You and your mom might have gotten hurt. You still might get hurt—the next time it happens.

Staying quiet when things are this.wrong.in the household isn't good. People who can help you have to know what's going on."

"No one can help me. No one cares."

Megan took a breath, listening to the commentary of the basketball game coming from the television, not believing how ordinary the sound was when there was so much pain in the room. It seemed like a reminder that no matter how bad Gerry Fletcher's life got, the world didn't care.

No one cares, Megan thought. *Or I could have stopped this long ago.* Tears leaked down her cheeks, triggered by sadness and anger and confusion. *Do You care, God? Do You see what You've let happen in this poor child's life?* She felt bitter and angry then, and she knew her tone toward God was accusing. Guilt stung her, but in a way she forgave herself. She felt that tone was deserved even if God wasn't ultimately to blame.

"I can help you," Megan said in a husky voice. "I'm going to help you. First, though, we're going to have to get you and your mom someplace safe."

Panic filled Gerry's face. "I don't want to leave my dad."

"Just for tonight." *For starters,* Megan thought. She was certain she could get the base commander's office to push Boyd Fletcher into getting more and deeper counseling after this episode.

"How much trouble is my dad in?"

"Some."

"It's all my fault, isn't it?"

"No," Megan said. "It's not your fault, Gerry. Please believe that."

Gerry shook his head. "I shouldn't have told." He rocked back and forth against the bed's headboard, unable to stay still. "I knew I shouldn't have told."

"You needed medical care."

"My arm isn't broke. I thought it was broke. I got scared. I should have just stayed in bed instead of sneaking out. I should have known my dad would never break my arm. This is all my fault."

Before Megan could say anything, a familiar bass voice reverberated in the hallway outside the door.

"Where's my son?" Gerry knew that voice and trembled. Megan knew it, too, and braced herself. A string of curses exploded after the nurse answered the question. Loud footsteps, the result of heavy combat boots worn by someone big enough to make them really crash into the government-issue linoleum floor, rang out in the hallway, coming closer with every footfall.

Turkey
30 Klicks South of Sanliurfa
Local Time 0743 Hours

Goose jogged as he talked over the headset, running tandem to Bill on the other side of the road. They secured the perimeter the unit had established around what was left of Glitter City during the evac op, taking their turn as the others had in two-man groups. The other eight men kept working with the wounded when they weren't walking patrol. Goose was also certain Hardin was busy squirreling away salvaged goods every chance he got.

Thick yellow dust still hung in the air. Sunlight slashed through the haze. Perspiration caked dust, smoke, and debris to Goose's exposed skin. His lungs ached for clean air and labored hard to suck what he got through the wet dust filming the kerchief he had wrapped around his face. They avoided craters left by the SCUD explosions and the clouds of thick smoke streaming from buildings that continued to burn.

"How bad is it?" Goose asked Cal Remington. After their initial radio contact, the captain had stated that he would have to get back to him. Cal had only—at first—wanted to ascertain that Goose was still alive and that the unit was relatively intact. Goose had had his hands so full with the rescue/evac operation that Remington's curtness had been fine with him. But now that they'd done what they could, Goose checked in with HQ. He wanted to know more about the big picture. A lot more.

Remington sounded tense. "The Syrians are not holding anything back, Sergeant. This is shaping up to be a major land grab, and the

Syrians obviously want to nail down as much territory as they can as soon as possible before the Turks, and we, get a chance to recover and pin down their advance."

The grim news that the border units were still under attack pounded at Goose's conscience. The crash and thunder of the artillery strikes south of his current position continued mercilessly. The need to be on the move thrummed inside him.

"Diyarbakir is the nerve center for Turkey's military base against the PKK," Remington continued, "but they're geared for counter-terrorist operations and action against riots. Not to take on the whole Syrian army."

"That's correct, sir," Goose agreed. The great walled city had been built back in the twelfth century and was known for the beautiful mosques within the huge black basalt walls that surrounded the metropolitan area. In addition to its key military role, Diyarbakir was one of Turkey's prized cultural possessions, filled with history.

"I think the Syrians are going to try to reach Diyarbakir and sack the city to make a statement. And to gain an important piece of real estate. The only thing standing between them and that city is us." Remington breathed out angrily. "This isn't simply an escalation of border warfare, Goose. This is a commitment to work some changes in the status quo between these two countries." Frustration echoed in his voice. "The Turkish military intelligence guys should have seen this coming."

Although he hadn't seen any stats on Syrian troop movements, Goose figured Remington was right in his assessment of the situation. There was no other reason for Syria to so suddenly and so solidly go on the offensive. Chaim Rosenzweig's economic miracle had calmed down some of the tensions in the Middle East, but Israel's new and greater prosperity had also triggered jealousy in Syria and some of its neighbors.

It wasn't just jealousy that was the problem. All that money pouring into Israel had also given rise to feelings of renewed threat in the country's neighbors, as if the past tensions in the region hadn't been bad enough. Many of the Middle East nations hadn't believed Israel would be generous with her newfound wealth.except when it came to buying arms and armor. And where could the Israelis aim all of that newfound weaponry? The Arab nations had all envisioned themselves with a target circle right in the center of their borders. Even though Israel had been keeping a low profile lately, the shift in the balance of power had destabilized the region. And with that much tension in the air, something had to snap.

The Syrians had to have a goal for their aggression, and the city of Diyarbakir was the most logical goal. If the Syrians proved successful in taking Diyarbakir, they would gain a lot of raw materials and a nice piece of strategic territory—including control of the Tigris River, known as the Dicle River locally—as well as a good staging position for further military ops and missions against Turkey and the U.N. peacekeeping efforts. It would be an excellent base for an attack on Ankara, the capital city of Turkey and a center for the country's international business. Also, the Turks would be more careful about destroying the walled city of Diyarbakir than the Syrians would. All that history made a great protective barrier, if the Syrians could take it.

"The Turkish command doesn't believe that the Syrians will reach Diyarbakir." Remington's tone—at least to Goose, who had known him for years—held a note of doubt and sarcasm. "They believe we can hold the line at the border."

"What do you think, sir?" Goose went to the deuce-and-a-half and helped load an unconscious woman who had suffered an abdominal wound. They had gotten the bleeding stopped and enough plasma into her to maintain blood pressure, and she was still breathing. But she'd lapsed into unconsciousness, and Goose didn't like the look of her. He was afraid that the woman had slipped into a coma.

Bill sent the next two men out on patrol.

On the other side of the makeshift gurney made from slashed tent canvas, Danielle Vinchenzo talked on a cell phone, evidently turning in a story. Like Goose and his men, she wore a piece of cloth tied over her lower face to keep out the worst of the sand. Because of that, her voice was muffled as she talked to her network. The phone lines had come back up with the mil-sat network. When she saw Goose and Bill, she nodded a quick thank-you at them. Goose's men aboard the deuce-and-a-half helped to pull the wounded woman aboard.

"I believe we can hold them," Remington answered. "But the cost is going to be high. We're losing men out there by the minute, Goose. My men."

"Yes, sir." A bleak coldness touched an unreachable spot between Goose's shoulder blades at the thought of all those men falling beneath enemy weapons. So many of them were young, hardly more than boys. Not much older than Joey.

Even as he thought that, Goose realized he, too, might not make it back home, might not see his wife and sons again. Then he steeled himself, knowing he couldn't afford to think like that. As a soldier, he faced that risk every day of his career. He always kept the possibility in perspective. But today, that possibility was up close and personal once more, and he was reminded that there were no guarantees. The image of the dead boy passed through his mind. Why did things like this happen? Goose couldn't believe that it was part of God's plan. Faith in God could never explain the carnage he'd been witness to, today and through his long military career.

"Have you got any good news for me?" Goose asked his captain.

"We've got additional backup that the Syrians might not have been counting on," Remington said "Five minutes after the first SCUDs were launched, USS Wasp was cleared for action. President Fitzhugh didn't hesitate about making the call. Wasp lost communication with us shortly after that, when the SCUDs took out our primary communications stations, but not with the Pentagon. Air support lifted from the Wasp's flight deck and is on the way in right now."

Goose checked his watch. He'd automatically logged the time of the attack as 0706 hours local time. The Wasp was nearly two hundred miles away. The CH-46E chopper was the slowest of the aircraft that would be in the reinforcement group. The Sea Knight helo class moved at something less than 170 mph. He did the math quickly.

"The ETA of those ships is roughly twenty-two minutes," Remington said, showing that he still knew how Goose thought and when he thought it. "I confirmed that before I got back to you. Might go ten minutes earlier or later, depending on whether they run into any trouble with the locals."

That news heartened Goose somewhat. USS Wasp was the lead ship in the seven vessel Amphibious Readiness Group (ARG). That team was designated as the 26th Marine Expeditionary Unit/Special Operations Capable (MEU/SOC). Wasp was currently stationed on a 180-day float in the eastern Mediterranean not far from Cyprus, Greece.

The six other ships that supported Wasp carried more men, weapons, and materials, including Cobra helicopter gunships in addition to cargo helos that mainly transported Marine troops. Goose knew about the sea-based unit because he always made it his business to know as much as he could about anything that helped or hindered whatever mission he was currently assigned to.

In addition to nearly two thousand Marines and over a thousand sailors, Wasp also transported forty-two CH-46E Sea Knight helicopters and five AV-8B Marine Harrier aircraft. All of them were capable of making the jump to the Turkish-Syrian border. The aircraft could also be refueled in midair by KC-135 Hercules Stratotankers, so they could remain on constant patrol and provide support.

"How bad is our line, sir?" Goose asked.

"We've taken some big hits along the border. The casualty lists are going to be high." The captain's tone was somber but confident.

During his career, Cal Remington had seen down-and-dirty action around the globe, and he'd never been a man to knuckle down before a challenge. More than anything else at the moment, he would be planning on delivering a counteroffensive that would hurt the Syrians as badly as the Turks, Americans, and the rest of the U.N. peacekeeping effort had been hurt.

Goose heard the captain talking in a low voice to someone else, then Remington switched his attention back to Goose. "How much longer is your team going to be needed at that twenty?"

Goose swept the rescue effort with his gaze. All the wounded had been loaded onto the deuce-and-a-half. There were fewer than he had hoped and more than he had expected. News stations around the world were going to be in mourning, and international attention would be on the events shaping up between Turkey and Syria.

Smooth snake tracks that crisscrossed marked the paths the rescuers had made through the sand while using canvas sleds to pull people too heavily injured to move on their own. Smoke eddied and spun through the dust haze like pulled taffy, black against the deadly floating gold.

"Not long," Goose answered. "We're loading the survivors now. And the dead that we can manage."

"Leave the dead," Remington said. "They're wasted time, effort, and space. Your wounded are going to have a hard enough time getting out of that area before the next attack launches."

Goose bristled at the command. Remington's order came across as callous, but Goose's inherent rejection of the plan of action ran deeper than that. As Special Forces, as a Ranger, he was trained and committed to leaving no one behind—dead or alive.

"You don't have time for anything more, Goose," Remington said in a softer voice. He obviously knew the reservations Goose had about the order. "Sending you there was a mistake. At least, sending you there was a mistake in retrospect. Who would have guessed the Syrians would have attacked the border so quickly or without restraint?"

Goose silently agreed. He stared at the corpses littering both sides of the road that cut through the small heart of Glitter City. One of those bodies, he knew, belonged to the boy who had helped his father serve meals. They had never found the other boy.

Distancing himself from that image, Goose tried not to look too closely at the bodies that had been too disfigured to immediately identify. He didn't want to carry those memories with him from the battlefield. He already knew that the nightmares from today would always be with him. That was one of the prices he paid for being a warrior in the service of his country.

Several of the reporters and cameramen walked along the lines of the dead, filming the bodies and commenting on the attack. Their stories went out live. When the military radio communications had come back on line, so had several channels for the media. Some of the satellite-equipped vans were still in one piece and a few of the media people had gotten them operational. The vehicles now pulled double duty as media relays and ambulances as more wounded and survivors were loaded onto them.

"I need you at the front line, Goose," Remington went on. "Every minute you spend at that rescue op is a minute that I don't have you where I need you most."

Goose sighed and rubbed his jaw. His body ached from the physical demands. "I know, sir." Despite the conversational tone Remington had adopted, Goose felt more at home keeping the line between officer and non-com clear and defined. "As soon as we can clear this twenty, we'll be on our way."

"We're holding our own along the border for the moment," Remington went on. "We're rerouting the com frequencies and sat-relays to bring all the teams up to speed again. Communications between here and the Pentagon continue to be hit-and-miss. But those troops hunkered down there know we've got help on the way from *Wasp*. I've made sure they know it."

"The air support and the extra troops are going to be a welcome addition, sir," Goose said. He was interrupted by an explosion at the far end of Glitter City where an overturned sedan burst into flames. "But those pilots are going to be taking their lives in their hands if they attempt landings near the border. The Syrians have got plenty of ack-ack guns to knock them down."

The number of anti-aircraft guns brought into the area over the last few weeks was impressive. Part of every Ranger's job was reconnaissance, and Goose and his teams had sent plenty of numbers and stats back for the officers and computers to crunch. Military thinking at the time had been that the AA guns had been brought in due to

Wasp's arrival in the Mediterranean Sea. No one had seen the additional guns as an arms buildup before a sudden strike.

"I'm aware of those gun emplacements, Sergeant," Remington said. "Those are going to be some of our first targets as we organize our retaliation. Captain Falkirk, *Wasp*'s commander, has informed me that the Marines plan on putting in just behind our forward line. They will be relatively secure there, then they'll hump up to join the Rangers along the front line. The Harriers and the Cobras will try to punch holes along the Syrians' front perimeter and take out enemy ships invading our airspace. The Syrians have air force units on the way as well. They've been holding them back."

The thought of the men he helped command getting pounded by an aerial-based assault falling on the heels of the SCUD launch filled Goose with dread. The enemy air teams were new. The Syrians had held the planes and helos in the rear to keep from tipping their hands. And maybe to keep from losing them to friendly fire. The known unreliability of the SCUDs always made them a question mark in a battle.

"They're also moving armored cav into the area, Goose," Remington said. "Tanks and APCs as well as field artillery. We've got units in place ourselves, so they're going to wait to see how their air strikes and the SCUDs do before making that commitment. If our center holds strong along the roads crossing the border, we'll be able to keep them back."

"Understood, sir," Goose said.

"In the meantime, I've got a helo en route to pick up you and your team."

"Sir," Goose said, looking at the two RSOVs parked near the tallest building left standing in Glitter City, "I've got two vehicles here. Leaving them behind—"

"—isn't going to happen," Remington interrupted. "That helo is carrying drivers that will get those vehicles back where we can use them most. In the meantime, I want you and your team back to the front line as soon as I can get you there."

"Yes, sir."

"The helo pilot is on your team's frequency," the captain said. "He's code-named Leapfrog. He's maintaining radio silence till you're ready for him."

Goose peered through the shifting layers of dust and smoke but couldn't see anything.

"Is there anything else, Sergeant?" Remington asked.

"What about an escort for these people?" Goose asked.

"They'll be on their own. They can get to Sanliurfa."

The idea of the few surviving civilians and media people pushing forward on their own didn't appeal to Goose. The military situation could change in an eye blink. And those vehicles, especially the deuce-and-a-half, weren't going to be able to outrun another phalanx of SCUDs.

"You got them out of there, Goose," Remington said. "That's more than a lot of them could have accomplished on their own."

"Yes, sir." Goose couldn't argue with that. If the survivors hadn't been given concrete instruction and direction, far fewer of them would have survived.

"I'll be in touch, Goose. Just get yourself and those men where I need you as soon as you can."

"Yes, sir." Goose clicked the headset back over to the team frequency. "Two."

"Two," Bill answered. He stood near the deuce-and-a-half's cab, turning to face Goose. They could have shouted across the distance, but the headset communications made conversation easier.

"What's the sit-rep?"

"Convoy's locked and loaded, Sarge. Ready to roll."

"Then get them sent out."

"Who do you want with the deuce-and-a-half?" Bill asked.

"No one," Goose replied. "We've been given orders to await air transport to the front. Courtesy of the captain."

"Can't get along without us, huh?" Bill's tone was light, but Goose knew that the day's events had worn on him despite his show of calm. But the calm was an essential part of Bill, the result of Bill's beliefs. No matter how bad things got, Bill always believed that God had a hand in things.

But how could he say that this is part of God's plan? Goose scanned the war zone that lay in shambles around him. "Can't get along without us? Evidently not," he replied in answer to Bill's jibe. "Who do you have heading up the civilian effort?"

"A guy named Murdock. He and his crew have been working construction in the area."

Goose vaguely remembered meeting the man. "I'll talk to him and let him know where he stands."

"He's a good guy," Bill said. "For an ex-jarhead."

An ex-Marine? Goose took that as a sign that things were going to be better. He jogged toward the deuce-and-a-half. "Phoenix Team, this is Phoenix Leader. Hold perimeter positions until the air unit arrives. And the first person to see it, let me know."

A chorus of responses echoed over the channel.

"Leapfrog," Goose called. "Are you there?"

"Affirmative, Phoenix Leader," a young male voice answered. His confidence seemed unshaken. "Looking for the LZ, Sarge."

"Put the bird down inside town," Goose advised. "We'll come to you, and the drivers can pick up the ground units here."

"Affirmative, Leader."

Goose paused at the deuce-and-a-half's side. He peered up at the driver. "Mr. Murdock?"

Murdock was grizzled and gray haired, the lines in his face ironed in by time and strength of character. He was stoutly built and looked to be in his fifties. Blood spotted his torn khaki shirt.

"I'm Murdock." The man extended a hand down.

Goose took the man's hand, and even though he had been prepared, he was surprised by the strength of the construction man's grip. "Good to meet you, sir."

Murdock shook his head. "Don't 'sir' me. I mustered out with sergeant's chevrons that weren't much different than yours."

Nodding, Goose took his hand back and looked at the deuce-and-a-half. "You can handle this rig?"

"Like I was born to it," Murdock said. "You got no worries there."

"We've got a dust-off coming up," Goose said. "We're not going to be escorting you."

Automatically, Murdock glanced at the sky. "Going back to the front line?"

"Yes."

"From what I've seen, and from what I've heard from the reporters," Murdock said, "it's a nasty place down there. You keep your head low."

"I will."

Murdock looked at Goose. "You and your men did a good thing here today, Sergeant. A lot of people wouldn't have gotten out of here without you." A smile twinkled in his blue eyes. "The only thing I can see wrong with the lot of you is that you ain't Marines. Things get back to normal soon, come look me up. I'm good for a dinner and a good word with the Marine Corps."

Goose agreed.

"Until then," Murdock said, "I'll drive this rig on into Sanliurfa and get these people squared away. I'll be saying prayers for you every mile."

"Thanks," Goose said. "I'd appreciate that. So would the rest of the unit." He stepped back and waved Murdock into motion, yelling at the passengers in the back to settle in.

Despite the huge size and the power of the vehicle, the deuce-and-a-half glided into motion. The large tires crunched across the rocks, broken mortar, glass, and other debris littering the road.

Movement on Goose's right drew his attention to the reporter and cameraman approaching him. He had noted the two men earlier as they'd talked to Bill only a short distance away.

"Get that man's picture," the reporter said, waving to a camera-man bleeding from one ear and a scalp wound. The reporter was bloodied but appeared sharp and driven. "He's the commanding offi-cer."

Camcorder resting on his shoulder, the cameraman approached Goose. The reporter trotted after him with a wireless mike in his hand. The reporter was young and wild-eyed, obviously not nearly as focused as his older partner.

"Sergeant," the reporter said as he jogged to keep up with Goose. "I'm George Hardesty, with Viewpoint Action News."

Goose didn't recognize the affiliation, but he wasn't surprised. His news watching was limited primarily to FOX and CNN, and lately when he'd been at home, his viewing channel of choice had been cartoons with Chris. With the memory of those cartoons, Goose missed his youngest son. Of course, he missed his wife and oldest son as well. But there was nothing like a hug from Chris, so innocent and so freely given, that seemed to make sense of the world and set everything straight in about three seconds flat.

"Mr. Hardesty," Goose stated calmly, "the convoy is leaving. I suggest you and your cameraman load up and get moving before you're left behind."

Hardesty shook his head. "I won't be left behind. I've been around this business for a long time. Besides, I can always go with you and your men. That's where the story will be."

Goose faced the man. "We're not retreating, sir. We're returning to the front line."

"I can go with you."

Before Goose could politely respond, Hardin's voice came over the headset, calling for his attention. "You've got Leader," Goose said, turning away from the reporter.

"I've got our bird," Hardin said. "South-southwest."

Glancing up into the hazy sky, Goose made out the familiar wasp shape of the UH-60 Black Hawk troop transport helicopter. The helo was marked in desert camo tans and browns.

"Acknowledged," Goose said. "Leapfrog, we have a visual on you."

"Good to hear, Phoenix Leader. I can't see anything down there in that soup." The UH-60 settled in, dropping quickly earthward.

"Captain," Hardesty tried again, extending the wireless microphone. "Anything you'd care to say about today's attack? Anybody you'd like to speak to back home?"

Goose knew the reporter didn't know his rank. In the field, the Rangers kept rankings hidden so the officers and non-coms couldn't be picked off by enemy sniper fire.

Turning to the reporter, Goose put an edge on his voice. "Mr. Hardesty, either you get in one of the vehicles that are transporting these people back to Sanliurfa or I'm going to put you on one."

"I only need a minute of your time," Hardesty complained.

"Leader, this is Leapfrog," the helo pilot broke in. "I've got three bogeys coming in from the west. Repeat, three bogeys coming in from the west."

"Affirmative, Leapfrog. What do you see?"

"Three vehicles, Leader. Jeeps. Small trucks. Can't quite make them out with the dust flying around. Want us to take a look-see before we settle in?"

"Have we got a sat-relay that can look for you?" Goose asked.

"Negative, Leader. We're still in a dark zone out there till all the sat-repeaters are put back in place."

"Eyeball the bogeys," Goose said. "But stay clear. If they're coming to help, use the PA to let them know the evacuation is taking place now."

"Will do, Leader. Could be scavengers, too. I heard there's bandits in the area."

Goose watched as the helicopter rose into the sky once more, then soared across Glitter City. A wake of thunder from the big rotors followed. He radioed the rest of the team and got them moving toward a common meeting point along the ridgeline. He glanced at his watch and saw that it was 0750 hours. The air support from *Wasp* was still ten or twelve minutes out.

"Captain."

Irritated by the reporter's continued insistence on not following orders, Goose turned to face the man. He took a deep breath to calm himself because the cameraman was fully focused on him.

"Not captain," Goose stated as patiently as he could. "Sergeant."

The reporter opened his mouth to speak again.

"Phoenix Leader," the helo pilot called out. A note of concern was in the young man's voice.

"Go, Leapfrog." Goose turned in the helo's direction. The Black Hawk shot through the air then heeled up like a falcon turning into a stiff breeze.

"Leader, we have problems. These bogeys look a whole lot like Syrian troops. I see—"

"Rocket!" another man at the helo end of the communication yelled. "Get us out of—"

In the distance, the Black Hawk exploded into an orange and black fireball that stood out against the smudged blue sky. The aircraft lost altitude at once, dropping like a wounded duck. Before the UH-60 disappeared from sight over the ridgeline, another explosion detonated aboard the aircraft, blowing the helo into flaming pieces.

Holding his M-4A1 in both hands, Goose ran for the ridgeline, the sound of the explosions reaching him only heartbeats later. In the next instant, the first Jeep that the helo pilot must have seen shot over the ridgeline, airborne for several feet before plunging back down. Two others followed the first, with scarcely a heartbeat of time between them.

Nearly to the remains of the building at the outermost west end of Glitter City, Goose recognized the camo pattern of the Syrian troops that manned the three Jeeps. "Phoenix Team, fall back!" he yelled.

The gunner on the rear deck of the lead Jeep saw Goose and opened fire with the 7.62mm machine gun mounted on the vehicle's roll bar. Steel-jacketed rounds slapped the sand at Goose's feet, chased him as he changed directions, then cracked rock from the leaning wall that had survived the fire and the bomb that had destroyed the building.

Goose leaped forward, threw his right hand out, and came up in a forward roll. Taking cover behind the leaning wall, he hefted the M-4A1 in both hands and stepped around the corner, snugging the assault rifle into his shoulder.

"Private Fletcher!" Helen Cordell called down the length of the hospital corridor. "You will come back here now!"

"Not without my son! You can't keep him from me! You people shouldn't have had him here without my permission anyway!"

Megan heard the vehemence and anger in the man's words. Unconsciously, she started to draw up, preparing to defend herself.

"The MPs are on their way," Helen warned.

"Fine," Boyd Fletcher roared. "They'll be here when I bring charges against you and the doctor for treating my son without my consent."

Gerry got out of the bed before Megan could stop him. She was a step behind the boy as he ran out into the hallway. He froze, like a deer in headlights, and stared down the corridor.

Megan put her hands on the eleven-year-old boy's shoulders, feeling the tremors of fear shiver through him.

Boyd Fletcher saw his son immediately. He was a big man, blocky and solid, a handful of inches over six feet. Short black hair with a pronounced widow's peak formed a skullcap over his broad head. Hazel eyes as flat and cold as a pit viper's sat on either side of a nose that had had been broken repeatedly in the past. He wore fatigues. Light glinted against his dog tags.

"Private Fletcher, I am ordering you to stand down this instant!" Helen stood at the other end of the corridor. Two nurses and a doctor stood with her. None of them made an effort to stop Fletcher.

From the slightly unsteady way Fletcher was walking, Megan felt certain the man had been drinking. Whatever limited control the man had on his emotions when he was sober would have been partially lifted by the alcohol. Keeping her hands on Gerry's shoulders to hold him in place, she stepped in front of the boy and pushed him behind her.

"Private Fletcher," Megan said sternly.

Obscenities littered the hallway as Fletcher kept coming.

The language didn't bother Megan. She didn't approve of it, but on an army base she'd developed a certain familiarity with it. And her work with teens had been occasionally rife with it. Of course, it wasn't a universal problem. Many soldiers, including Goose, never cursed. Or at least never cursed around her.

"Private Fletcher," Megan tried again. She kept Gerry behind her, making it apparent that he would have to go through her to get to her son.

"Get out of my way," Fletcher ordered as he closed on them. "What has he been telling you?"

Megan knew the man wasn't going to stop.

"Whatever it was," Fletcher declared, "it doesn't matter. He's a little liar anyway. You can't believe a word he says. I told you that when you first started seeing him."

Gerry tore free of Megan's restraining hand and darted forward. "Dad! Stop! Please, stop!"

Stepping forward again, Megan once more placed herself in front of the boy.

"Mrs. Gander, don't!" Gerry pleaded. "He doesn't know what he's doing when he gets like this! Please!"

Before Megan could think of anything to say, the two uniformed Rangers from the security desk arrived at a full run. Helen yelled to them and pointed at Boyd Fletcher, loosing them like hounds on a fox. Their footsteps, closing at a drumming double beat, alerted Fletcher that he wasn't the only big guy in the hallway.

The bleary-eyed private turned around, snarling curses.

"Soldier," Corporal Grady barked in a loud voice, "stand down now or we'll stand you down."

Fletcher grinned drunkenly. "My lucky day, boys. Unless I'm seeing double, I'm getting a two-for-one tonight if you decide to open the ball on this one. You pups had better back off if you know what's good for you."

Grady and Malone hesitated.

"I came here to get my son," Fletcher said. "He's mine. Nobody can keep him from me. He's not supposed to be here. He's not supposed to be talking. I'm taking him home."

"No," Grady said. His voice cracked slightly, and there was a tense edge in it. "You're going to leave the boy here, and you're going to come with us."

Fletcher cursed again, then turned and advanced toward Megan and Gerry. Grady and Malone launched themselves at the drunken private. They tried to restrain him, but Fletcher closed his hands into fists and viciously hammered both of the younger men, driving them down to the ground in seconds. The meaty smacks of flesh against flesh rocketed through the hallway.

When he'd shaken free of his would-be captors, Fletcher aimed himself at Megan again. He cursed Gerry and in his diatribe blamed everything wrong in his life on the boy.

Megan stood her ground, fear rattling inside her like an insane beast. She felt Gerry cowering behind her and heard his whimpering sobs. *I will not falter,* she told herself. *I will not step away from him.* She thought of Goose somewhere out there on the Turkish border, dealing with God only knew what. Surely she, too, could hold her ground in a hostile situation.

Before Fletcher could reach Megan, though, Malone and Grady—bleeding and bruised—rose from the floor and threw themselves at him. Malone went low, wrapping his arms around Fletcher's ankles while Grady hit the man waist-high.

Driven off-balance, Fletcher fell forward, slamming into the floor at Megan's feet. He screamed and raged, shouted curses, and struggled to get to his feet. His face, when he looked up, was covered in blood.

Megan stepped back and turned around. Gerry was no longer standing behind her. She watched helplessly as the boy ran to the other end of the hallway and crashed through the emergency exit. A warning Klaxon shrilled in his wake, but he was gone out into the night before the door closed.

❋   ❋   ❋

United States of America
Columbus, Georgia
Local Time 12:55 A.M.

"Hey, Joey, what are you doing? I thought you came here to dance."

Mesmerized by the action on the television screen behind the bar at the heavy metal club, Joey didn't recognize Jenny McGrath's voice at first. The news anchor was saying that the current footage had been taped, that the live transmissions had been lost, and that the station hoped to re-establish a live transmission within the next few minutes.

Goose is over there in that! The thought screamed through Joey's mind like a banshee wail.

"Joey?" Jenny's voice took on a plaintive note. "I didn't come here with you to be ignored."

A television anchor hunkered down behind a wall of sandbags. He held a microphone in one hand and squinted against the dust and smoke that eddied across the screen. "—what we understand is that there's been a full-scale assault upon the Turkish army and U.N. peacekeeping forces."

"Do you know what precipitated the attack?" an offscreen anchor-woman asked.

A tremendous explosion sounded nearby before the reporter could reply. The man in the field dropped prone and covered his head with both arms. Sand and earthen chunks rained down, pelting the newsman mercilessly. The cameraman took cover a moment later, dragging the camera behind him. The view from the field tumbled along the desert floor. The scene shifted immediately, showing footage of SCUDs streaking through the sky, then a line of explosions leaping up from the distant horizon.

"Joey," Jenny called again.

Aggravated with the girl for interrupting him, still smarting over the way she had deserted him to dance with the band, Joey said, "I'm trying to listen to the television."

Jenny's voice turned cold. "Catching up on the Lakers game?"

Aware that Jenny wasn't at all happy with him, Joey said, "No. It's a special bulletin. The Syrians just attacked Turkey."

Crossing her arms, Jenny didn't appear mollified by that explanation in the least. "So instead of a guy who's a sports fan, I'm trading up to one who's totally a political science nerd? And what, exactly, is so fascinating about that?"

Memory of the way Jenny had danced on stage only moments ago rattled around inside Joey's skull. Looking at her, he realized that he wasn't as happy to be out with her as he'd thought he would be when she first asked him.

"I told you my dad was a soldier," Joey said, biting back his retort. "He's stationed over in Turkey." He pointed at the television. "He's one of the guys over there in the middle of that right now. His unit, the 75th Rangers, was assigned there. He could be hurt right now, or maybe worse." He couldn't bring himself to say that Goose might have died in the initial assault.

"Oh." Her features softening somewhat, Jenny glanced at the television. "There's nothing you can do about what's going on over there. I mean, whatever's going to happen is going to happen."

Joey looked at her in disbelief.

A frown creased Jenny's forehead and lips. "Don't give me that look. I work five nights a week at Kettle O' Fish, which is a dead-end job no matter how much you seem to like it. Do the math. I work five nights. That leaves two nights off. On those nights, I like to dance." She paused. "This is one of those nights, Joey, and we're not exactly dancing here."

Overwhelmed in the face of such an uncaring attitude, Joey didn't know what to say.

"Besides," Jenny said, "I thought you said your dad was in California."

Tony Holder had lived in California for the last half dozen years. He had been a small-time filmmaker in L.A. since divorcing Joey's Mom and leaving Columbus.

"It's Goose," Joey said. "My stepdad."

Jenny frowned again and shrugged. "So what? You said yourself that the guy hardly has any time for you these days. Why should you worry about him?"

Because I care about what happens to him, Joey thought immediately, but he didn't say it. *Maybe he's forgotten about me, but I still don't want anything to happen to him. Mom would go crazy. And Chris would lose his father.* Joey knew all about that and didn't want his little brother to experience something as bad as that. He glanced back at the television screen and took his cell phone from his pocket.

When he'd left the family house that evening, he'd turned the device off, knowing his mom would call to check on him after he stayed out past his curfew. He intended to tell his mom that he had forgotten to charge the phone and had left the power cord adapter for his car's cigarette lighter on his desk. The car was his mom's, so his stuff wasn't always in the vehicle. It was a fib he'd used in the past, and taking the battery out and discharging the power before he arrived home was no problem.

"Joey," Jenny said.

Ignoring her, Joey watched the television, noticing that Leonard and Ace were both keeping track of the conversation between him and Jenny. Punching in his number, Joey quickly cycled through the menu options and opened his mailbox.

There were two messages, both of them from his mom. The caller ID indicated that five other messages had been missed between the first and last message. The first three had been from the Gander home phone number. The last four had been from his mom's cell phone.

"Joey," his mom said calmly, "you're out past your curfew. You are going to be so grounded when you get back home."

In a way, his mom's promise of punishment was reassuring. If she was only thinking of grounding him, then things couldn't be that bad. But the call had been logged in before the time when the news channel said the hostilities had started.

"Are you listening to me?" Jenny demanded.

"Give me a minute," Joey said, looking at the television. The news footage cycled through again. Evidently the reporters had been caught pretty much flat-footed and hadn't been able to send much in the way of footage before the communications lines had been cut. He punched up the second message.

"Joey," his mom said. Her voice sounded tight and controlled, the way it did some days when things got really hectic at the counseling center. "I don't know where you are, and I don't know what you might have seen on the television. All I can tell you is that I haven't received any information about Goose."

Some of the tightness inside Joey's chest relaxed. *Thank You, God.* The sentiment flooded through him, but at the same time he felt like a hypocrite, one of those people who reached for God in times of need but never simply gave thanks to Him all along the way. But there hadn't been a lot to be thankful for lately, had there?

"I know Goose's unit was involved in the action along the border," his mom went on. "I've been called in to the base hospital. An emergency has come up regarding one of my patients."

That, Joey knew, wasn't a good thing. The last time his mom had gotten called in to the base hospital had been when one of the teens she was counseling had tried to commit suicide. Even as he thought that, he remembered Chris.

"I had to drop Chris off at the emergency child-care center," his mom said. "I don't know how long I'll be at the hospital. If you get this message, please go by and pick Chris up. He wasn't happy about being left there." There was a pause. "I'm really ticked at you for not being here and for causing me extra worry, Joey, but I want you to know I love you. Get home and we'll get this sorted out."

The message clicked off. Before the automated message could prompt him to replay, delete, or save the message, Joey punched the asterisk to end the session. He dialed his mom's cell phone number but got only her message box. Fear crept through him, swamping him with thoughts of what might have happened to his mom or Goose or Chris. He was worried to the point that getting yelled at for blowing off his curfew actually sounded good to him.

"Joey." Jenny sounded totally miffed.

Looking at her, Joey said, "I gotta go."

"What?" she asked sarcastically. "Did you hear your mom calling?"

"As a matter of fact," Joey said, "I did. There's been an emergency. I brought you here. I can drop you back by your house. Or do you think you can find a way home from here? I'll pay for a cab."

"You're leaving me here?" A look of disbelief covered her beautiful face.

"I'm trying not to."

"Do you care?"

"Actually," Joey said, "I do. Goose—my step-dad—taught me that you don't just ditch someone you brought with you. And I don't want to just leave things like this between us. I want to see you again. If that's okay." *And, boy, doesn't that sound lame.* But the thought didn't linger in his mind. He was thinking totally of his family.

Jenny stayed silent for a moment. "I can find a way home."

Her answer slashed through Joey's knotted guts. His anger coiled inside him, and he wanted to stand there and argue with her, to tell her how much her actions had hurt him. But he thought of Chris in the child-care center with some stranger, and he knew how wigged out his mom would be with Goose in the thick of things over in Turkey.

"Fine." Joey shelved his anger and hurt for the moment. Sorting them out with all the confusion spinning through his head at the same time was almost impossible. That was another thing Goose had helped him work on when he was just a kid. He'd been confused over his dad's abandonment and his mother's remarriage. As a result, some of his anger had been targeted at Goose, who had taken everything in stride. They had worked through most of that one step at a time—until Chris had been born.

Chris.

Joey turned and walked away.

"Hey, man," Leonard said solemnly, dropping a hand on Joey's shoulder for a moment. "Hope everything turns out okay with your dad."

"Me, too," Joey said. "Thanks." He kept moving.

"Hey, Joey," Jenny called from behind him.

He stopped and watched as she ran to join him. "What?" he asked.

"Want company?"

"You?" Joey couldn't figure her out. She had been so hard on him, then this. Her behavior didn't make sense.

"Yeah."

"Why?"

She shrugged. "Because you're a friend. And I think maybe you could use a friend for a little while."

A *friend*. That was one of the last things Joey wanted to be with Jenny McGrath. He almost groaned in frustration.

"Look," Jenny said. "For what it's worth, I'm sorry for the things that I said. I'm not always a nice person."

"No," he agreed, and part of him wanted to be a little mean about accepting her offer. However, he regretted his response immediately.

She sighed. "It's a twenty-minute drive back to the base. Your dad is obviously involved in something really bad, wherever he is."

"Turkey."

"Whatever. And I don't know what your mom had to say—"

"There's been an emergency. My little brother got dumped in the child-care center on base because I wasn't home." *Like I should have been.* "Chris likes to be in his own bed at night. Mom said he wasn't happy about being left there, and if he wakes up there, he's going to freak."

"Then let's go get him," Jenny said, taking Joey by the arm.

Joey didn't move.

She looked at him, locking eyes. "It's a twenty-minute drive, Joey. You're upset. At least, I'd be upset in your shoes. You don't need to be alone. And the fact that you wanted to make sure I was going to be okay if you left me here was kind of cool." She shrugged. "Let me return the favor by riding along with you. I take care of my friends, too. When I get over being temporarily self-involved."

Joey melted at her hesitant smile, and he got a peek behind the usual confident and distant air Jenny McGrath broadcast to everyone. He got the feeling she was actually afraid he was going to turn her down. But thinking about that twenty-minute drive back to Fort Benning, he knew he'd be a basket case by the time he arrived if he was alone.

"All right," he said.

Over her left shoulder, the television at the bar changed its programming with no warning. The words LIVE BROADCAST—GLITTER CITY, TURKEY started streaming across the bottom of the screen.

Even across the distance, Joey recognized Goose's haggard features. Goose wore a kerchief over his lower face, but the scar by his right eyebrow that curved down toward his hidden cheekbone marked him immediately. Sand coated his face and gear. A helicopter flew through the air in the distance behind him.

Goose was obviously short of patience with the reporter talking to him. The camera shot only showed his head and shoulders, but Joey could identify the emotion by his stepdad's stance. Then Goose turned away from the camera, one hand going to the headset. The helicopter exploded.

Stunned, not believing what he was seeing, Joey's breath stopped dead and tight in his lungs and his mouth turned dry as chalk. On the screen, Goose advanced toward the ridge where the flaming fragments of the helicopter had fallen. In the next instant, a Jeep sailed over the ridge and landed on the desert floor. The vehicle swung dangerously close to the burned-out husk of a building as the driver overcorrected. The gunner on the rear deck swung his weapon in Goose's direction and started firing.

Joey watched as Goose reversed directions and took cover behind the broken, smoke-wreathed fragment of a wall. Bullets threw up sprays of sand and chewed pockmarks in the stone. Then the camera view changed as the Jeep gunner's next sweep of deadly fire caught the cameraman and punched him backward.

A sheen of bright crimson blood covered the camera lens before everything went black.

Turkey
30 Klicks South of Sanliurfa
Local Time 0755 Hours

As Goose centered the M-4A1's sights over the Syrian gunner on the Jeep's rear deck and squeezed the trigger, he watched in helpless frustration as the machine gun swiveled in the reporter and cameraman's direction. Hardesty threw himself flat, but the cameraman never had a chance.

A fusillade of bullets slapped into the cameraman, shredded the camera, and dropped a bloody corpse to the hot, smoke-stained ground already strewn with debris.

Taking aim, Goose slipped his finger over the M-4A1's trigger, took up slack, and pulled through. The assault rifle bucked against his shoulder. He fired two more three-round bursts, unsure of which one raked the machine gunner from the rear deck. A body tumbled from the vehicle and fell in a limp-limbed sprawl to the ground.

Noticing that there had been a casualty, the Syrian soldier driving the Jeep took immediate evasive action.

No mercy existed in Goose's heart. He thought of all the unsuspecting people who had been killed in the brutal attack only moments ago. When he had to take the lives of people killing innocents, he figured he was on the side of the angels. He fired again, putting his next rounds into the driver, watching as the man slumped over the steering wheel.

Out of control, the Jeep weaved and drove into the flaming hulk of a building. As high as the flames were, Goose knew the third man in the Jeep wasn't going to make an escape from the building.

Hardesty, the news reporter, lay on the ground and raised his head only briefly to look at the dead cameraman. Then he began shouting for help.

"Three," Goose shouted hoarsely, not knowing if the headset connection was still intact. "This is Leader."

"Three reads you, Leader," Bobby Tanaka radioed back.

"Take the high ground, Three. You're our cover."

"Affirmative, Leader. Three has the high ground." As the squad sniper, Tanaka could provide covering fire.

Goose watched as the other two Jeeps roared into Glitter City. "Four," he said.

"Four reads you, Leader," Dean Hardin replied.

"Get one of the RSOVs up and running, Four," Goose ordered. "If any crew from that 60 survived, I want to know. Eight and Ten, you're with Four."

"Acknowledged, Leader," Hardin said. "Gonna be tough getting through to them."

"We'll give them something else to worry about." Goose's mind raced. From years of training and self-discipline, he knew where every man in his unit was. A shaky plan came together between heartbeats.

The two Jeeps reached the other end of the town and came back around. The machine gunners raked the hillside where Phoenix Team was hunkered down, letting the Rangers know they had the range and the firepower to get the job done.

"Two." Goose rose, sucking his breath in to charge his lungs with oxygen. Adrenaline fired through him, temporarily erasing all fatigue and fear.

"Two copies," Bill said.

"You've got the 203," Goose said. The M-203 fired fin-stabilized 40mm grenades with a variety of purposes.

"Affirmative."

"If I give you a target, can you hit it?"

"Leader, don't—"

Taking his M-4A1 firmly in both hands after swapping out magazines, Goose sucked in another breath, then pushed it all out. "Load up with an HE round. No fragmentation. Let's cut the risk of friendly fire."

"Goose," Bill protested. "This isn't—"

The two Jeeps rumbled closer. The lead Jeep headed for Goose's position, obviously confident of engaging him.

"I've got no choice, Two," Goose said. "They're on top of me. You're in an exposed position. One of us has to be at risk, and if you're taken down, we lose the 203's punch."

"All right, Goose." Bill didn't sound relaxed.

"Now." Goose broke cover in a rush, running toward the opposite side of the street. He drummed his combat boots hard against the sand, knowing that if he were back on base, in sneakers or in baseball cleats, he could make better time. Combat boots were prized by soldiers for endurance and protection, not for being fleet.

The machine gunner of the lead vehicle opened fire at once. A brutal line of 7.62mm bullets cracked the wall where Goose had been hiding, then chopped through the sand after him as the Syrian soldier compensated for his motion.

The rattle of machine gun fire filled Goose's head. He knew the Syrian soldier almost had him in his sights, felt certain he heard the harsh whisper of the steel-jacketed rounds cutting the air just behind him. His heart slammed against his rib cage like an enraged beast seeking escape. He thought of Megan and Joey and Chris, and he thought about God and Jesus, the way his father had talked of them in the Sunday school classes he'd taught back in Waycross when Goose was growing up.

The Lord is my shepherd, Goose thought. *I shall not—*

In the next instant, Bill's aim with his M-203 proved dead on target. The 40mm HE grenade slammed into the front of the Syrian Jeep. Hammered by the high-explosive grenade, the Jeep's hood buckled and the three Syrian soldiers seated in the vehicle blew out into the road. One of the Jeep's tires exploded, turning into a whirlwind of shredded rubber. Continuing to roll, the vehicle turned hard to the right and crashed into a pile of debris.

"Two is down!" Tanaka yelled. "Repeat, Two is hit!"

Only then realizing that the remaining Jeep's machine gunner had been firing at the Rangers staggered along the hillside and that Bill must have taken a round while he'd exposed himself to fire the grenade launcher, Goose saw that he'd exhausted his own options.

A line of 7.62mm rounds chopped into the sand before him, cutting off further escape.

Goose spun, digging his boots in, turning sideways to present his left profile and—God willing—a smaller target. He brought the M-4A1 up, aiming by instinct and years of training rather than seeking the sights. The instant he stroked the trigger, he knew he'd missed. He didn't get another chance.

A pair of 7.62mm rounds thudded into his chest and stomach, driving him down and backward.

"Leader is down!" Tanaka yelled. His voice came loud and rushed over the headset.

At the same time, the sniper's voice sounded like it was coming from a million miles away to Goose. He was dimly aware of crashing into the sand, but he hung on to his assault rifle. He'd been shot before. He'd been knifed and blown up. He knew he had no time for panic. Even temporary panic killed good Rangers dead.

Less than forty feet away now, the remaining Syrian Jeep drove straight for Goose. The driver obviously intended to run him over, finishing what the machine gunner's rounds might have only started. Thankfully, but only just, the driver's impulsive action also kept the rear deck machine gunner from firing another burst into Goose.

Unable to breathe, not certain if the bullets had penetrated flesh or had been stopped by his body armor, Goose pushed past the pain and forced himself to move. His whole chest felt numb. He threw his right leg left and rolled a full 360 degrees.

"Goose!" Tanaka called. "Goose!"

Do your job, Ranger, Goose thought.

Sand covered his face as he came over on his back with the Jeep over him, its undercarriage only inches above his face. The clearance was about the same as the Ranger four-wheel-drive vehicles had. He felt the heat of the Jeep's exhaust against his left cheek for a second, then bright sunlight stabbed into his eyes as it passed him by.

Knowing the machine gunner would probably turn to pick him off, that he would never get to his feet before the man could kill him, Goose threw his left hand up and caught the Jeep's rear bumper. He curled his fingers around the bumper's edge, hoped the edge wouldn't cut into his flesh too badly, and grunted in pain as his arm nearly jumped from his shoulder socket.

He trailed behind the Jeep, too close for the machine gunner on the rear deck to tilt his weapon down. Dragged by the Jeep across the rough landscape at thirty miles an hour or more, Goose skidded and went airborne like a sled hitting fresh powder, skipping the uneven terrain.

The Syrian soldier manning the machine gun peered over the back. A surprised look creased his features.

Holding on to the M-4A1, Goose lifted the assault rifle and squeezed the trigger at pointblank range. The 5.56mm round punched into the soldier's face and tore him from the rear deck.

The corpse thudded into the sand and didn't move.

Battered and bruised by the rough ride across the sand, his lungs still feeling like they were bound by constricting iron bands, Goose released his hold on the Jeep. He slid to a stop in the sand. *Bill was hit.* The memory whipped through his mind even as his strained shoulder screamed at him. He put his left hand out and rolled to his feet. His shoulder felt weak, like it was made of broken glass.

"Leader's up!" Cusack yelped excitedly. "Tanaka!"

"I've got him," Tanaka replied in a quiet, controlled voice.

Pushing himself, focusing on the battle at hand with the professionalism he'd developed after seventeen years in the military, Goose brought the assault rifle to his shoulder. He dropped the sights over the driver's chest. From his peripheral vision, he saw the Syrian soldier in the passenger seat point his AK-47 at Goose. Before he had a chance to fire, the Syrian soldier pitched forward and Goose knew that Tanaka had found his target.

Goose fired a series of three-round bursts. Bullets chopped into the Jeep's grill, then across the hood, and smashed into the driver just above the steering wheel. The dead man's foot slipped from the accelerator and clutch. A moment later, the Jeep stuttered to a halt.

Head spinning, lungs aching, Goose swayed. For a moment, he thought he was going to fall. Abruptly, the iron bars constricting his lungs dropped away. He took a deep, shuddering breath, then coughed and almost threw up. Flames coursed across his chest. No blood showed on his chest. Intact. He'd been pounded, but the bullets hadn't penetrated. He said a silent prayer of thanks.

Keeping his assault rifle up at the ready, slightly canted down so he could sweep the weapon up, Goose advanced. He sucked in another breath, feeling as though his chest were busted up inside but not feeling any grating of bone that would have indicated shattered or splintered ribs that could pierce his internal organs and compromise his breathing. His lungs appeared to be intact.

"Two," Goose called as he closed on the stalled Jeep. Neither of the Syrian soldiers moved. "Two, do you copy?"

One of the RSOVs raced up the hillside. Evidently Hardin and the two men with him had managed to get the combat vehicle and were rolling to check on the downed helicopter.

"Two copies, Leader," Bill replied. The weakness in his voice offered proof that not all was well with him.

"What's your status, Two?" Goose grabbed the driver by the shirtfront and dragged the man from the Jeep's seat. The corpse dropped to the sand. "Confirmed kill."

"I'm hurt," Bill replied. "But I'm still standing."

Goose pulled the man from the passenger seat and dumped his body to the ground. "Confirmed kill. How bad is it, Two?"

"Patchwork, Leader. Leg shot. Bullet went through and through."

"Do you need assistance?" As Goose walked back toward the hillside, he checked on the three-man crew from the second Jeep. The HE round had blown them in a semicircle from the point of impact.

"I need a medkit," Bill replied. "Having a tough time getting the bleeding stopped."

"I'm on it, Leader," Cusack offered. "I've got a medkit."

"Take care of it, Six," Goose acknowledged.

"Leader, this is Base." Captain Remington's voice.

"Clear my channel, Base," Goose ordered. "I'm in the middle of a busted op and you can't help me."

Remington took no offense. "Affirmative, Leader. I'll be standing by."

"Understood, sir." Goose approached Hardesty, who still lay on the ground. "Get up."

Hardesty got up uncertainly. He stared at the dead cameraman. The man was so young to be so dead that the fact was offensive to Goose.

"Four," Goose said, reminding himself that other young men were selflessly giving their lives along the border even then. The artillery fire continued without cease. "What's the sit-rep at your twenty?"

"Leapfrog is officially scratched, Leader," Hardin replied. "I've got five survivors from a sixteen-man crew aboard the 60."

"*Four* survivors," Evaristo said in open disgust.

"One of the survivors is a chaplain," Hardin said. "All of these guys are banged up, Leader. Gonna be more of a detriment to the cause than any kind of help."

Artillery fire rolled to the south, crossing over Goose in a wave of echoes.

"Get them squared away," Goose ordered. "We're leaving in two minutes."

❖ ❖ ❖

United States of America
Fort Benning, Georgia
Local Time 1:10 A.M.

Heart thudding, Megan ran out into the base hospital parking lot. Only a dozen or so cars occupied the striped slots. She stopped in the center of the lot and spun around, looking for Gerry Fletcher.

Fort Benning kept security lights on all through the night where they were needed, so the area around the hospital was relatively lighted. Lamps illuminated high-traffic areas, but the residential areas remained dark except for lights along footpaths between the buildings. The military base was a safe area, a place where married couples and families with children could live in peace.

But tonight those safe places harbored shadows where a scared eleven-year-old boy could easily hide.

"Megan."

Turning, Megan spotted Helen Cordell standing in the open emergency door. The bleats of the alarm blasted out into the parking lot.

"Have you found Gerry?" Helen asked.

"No." Megan tried to push away the frustration she felt. "I didn't know he was running till he was already gone."

"Neither did I." Helen gazed around the parking lot. "He can't have gone far."

"I know. I just don't know where he could have gone."

"Do you know his mother's number?"

"Yes." In that moment, Megan felt foolish. It was her job to keep it together, to know and to be ready to act one step ahead of anything the kids in her care could come up with. Gerry had been terrified of his dad. That much was evident. But she was good at her job. Maybe she wasn't thinking at her best tonight, but she was prepared. "I've got Tonya's phone number in my cell phone memory."

"Check there," Helen suggested. "As scared as that kid is, the first place he'd probably go is home."

Especially if he knows his father isn't there, Megan silently added. "What about Boyd Fletcher?" It was important when she talked to Gerry that she be able to honestly tell him what had become of his father. Telling Gerry what was going to happen to him next, that he would probably be removed from his home and placed in foster care, was going to be hard. Megan had been forced to do that before, and those situations had never gone well.

"He's going to the hoosegow for the night," Helen said. "Resisting arrest is going to guarantee that. Then I'll be adding new charges in the morning."

Megan took her cell phone from her pocket. "I'm going to keep looking out here. And I'll call Tonya."

Helen nodded. "I've got to shut this alarm off and call it in to base security as a false alarm before I have a platoon of young men waiting to be the next Bruce Willis arrive here. I'll pass the word along to the MPs. They can help look for Gerry."

"Thanks, Helen." Megan was grateful for the assistance and the positive attitude that the other woman brought to the situation. With Helen around, nothing seemed impossible.

Helen closed the door and took away the yellow rectangle of light that spilled out onto the parking lot from the hospital's emergency exit. Under the mercury vapor lights that illuminated the parking lot, the landscape and the cars appeared in grays and blacks, as lifeless and alien as the moon.

Megan pressed the cell phone's keypad. The screen flashed on, ghastly green-gray. She'd missed three calls. While she'd been talking to Gerry, she'd muted the ringer out of habit. She mentally harangued herself. She was out of the house, Goose was in danger, Joey was God-only-knew-where, and Chris was in child care. What had she been thinking?

But she knew what she'd been thinking about: Gerry Fletcher sitting in the hospital emergency room. That was one of the aspects about her life that got really confusing: how could she be a mom and a wife and a counselor and expect to do a good job at any of those?

During one of the infrequent sessions with Bill when he'd been visiting, she'd talked about trying to balance her life. Bill, relying on his faith, of course, had said that all works God intended for a person to perform would be given balance. The key was to trust in His guidance in all things at all times. That was hard to do because she cared so much about her man, her sons, and the kids entrusted to her care.

With a little guilt, she realized that she hadn't even considered the time needed to be spent being a good Christian.

She stared at the cell phone screen where Joey's number stood out in sharp relief. So what was it to be: mother or counselor?

Joey, she decided, and felt a twinge of guilt. With so many things out of her control, she needed to know that her son was all right. She would be able to focus more on Gerry when she found him.

The phone rang once before Joey answered. "Mom?"

"Joey, are you all right?" Megan walked toward the far end of the parking lot. Three young men sat in a dark blue muscle car she felt certain Goose would have identified in an instant.

"I'm fine, Mom."

Thank You, God.

"Mom," Joey said, "I'm sorry I missed curfew."

Remembering how Gerry was afraid of his father, knowing that she had never had—*would never have*—a relationship like that with either of her sons, Megan kept calm, reminding herself how thankful she was that Joey was okay.

"We'll talk about that later," Megan said. "I'm just glad you're all right."

"I know."

Megan heard traffic over the phone connection. "Where are you?"

"Just a few minutes from the base," Joey said. "I'm on my way to pick up Chris."

"Thank you, Joey. I appreciate that a lot."

He was silent for a moment. "I'm sorry that I wasn't there for him."

"You can be there for him now," she said. "That's the important thing. I don't know when I'm going to be home, and I really didn't want him waking up in a child-care facility."

"I got it covered, Mom." Some of the hesitation and guilt faded from Joey's voice.

Megan knew that was because he was in his element as oldest child. He had a task and a responsibility. "Thank you, Joey." She stared at the muscle car where the three young men talked. From their haircuts, she deduced that they were soldiers.

"Have you heard anything about Goose?" Joey asked.

Megan had to halt herself from automatically correcting her son and telling him to refer to Goose as his dad. For a while, before Chris had been born, Joey had started calling Goose "Dad," but that had gone away within weeks after Chris's birth.

"I haven't heard anything," Megan replied.

Joey was silent for a moment.

"Honey," Megan said, "I've really got to go. This is an emergency situation. I'll tell you about it in the morning. After tonight is over, I think I'd like to talk to someone about this."

"All right, Mom," Joey said. "You know I'm there for you."

Both of them, Megan was certain, felt uncomfortable with that customary response after the missed curfew tonight. "I love you, Joey."

"I know, Mom." He hesitated just long enough for her to know that he wasn't alone. "I love you, too. I'll see you whenever you get home. If I'm not there by the time you need to get to school—"

"I'll get The Squirt off and get myself to school," Joey said. "Promise."

"You still have lunch money?"

"Yes, Mom." The exasperated tone in his voice told her that she'd just stepped into one of those child/adult potholes that made the journey through the teen years so rocky for the parents and children.

Megan curbed her own response. Pointing out that Joey hadn't been adult enough to hit his curfew would have done no good and only destroyed the good rapport they'd had up till that moment. Until they could both be adults in the relationship, she had to be the one.

"I'll try to be home as soon as I can," she said. "I'll call in the morning if I can't be there. So Chris can talk to me."

"Okay, Mom."

Megan said good-bye and broke the connection. She halted in the parking lot and flipped through her phone book index, stopping on Boyd and Tonya Fletcher's phone number. She punched the *Talk* button.

Six rings later, the phone was answered. The clanks and clunks that carried over the connection told Megan that the person who answered the phone was having a hard time.

"Hello," Tonya croaked in a sleep-filled voice.

"Tonya," Megan said, "this is Megan Gander." She paused to let the young woman take the information in. Even at her best, Tonya seemed a step behind the rest of the world. She had her hopes and dreams, but she didn't quite seem in touch with all the realities of her life.

"Come on, Mrs. Gander," Tonya protested. "Do you know what time it is?"

"Yes," Megan assured her. "There's been a problem, Tonya."

"What kind of problem?" Worry and anxiety filled Tonya's voice.

Megan heard the creak of the bed. She knew the younger woman was probably sitting up and only then learning that her husband wasn't there. The time was early for some of the bars and the after-hours clubs that remained open illegally.

"Can you tell me if Gerry is there?" Megan asked.

"He's in his bedroom," Tonya said.

"Are you sure?"

"I put him to bed, Mrs. Gander. I should know where my own kid is."

Yes, Megan silently agreed, *you should.* Instead, she said, "Gerry was at the base hospital just a short time ago, Tonya."

"No way." Tonya sounded angry and confused at the same time. "He's in his bed."

Megan listened to the change in the phone's pitch, knowing that

Tonya Fletcher was walking through the house. She waited patiently, hoping that the woman was going to tell her that Gerry had returned home. If he had, Megan was content to let things at the Fletcher home gel for the moment and concentrate on getting Boyd Fletcher blocked from being around his son without proper supervision.

A moment later, Tonya's voice took on a note of hysteria. "He's not here, Mrs. Gander. He's *not* here. His bed is empty. Where did you say he was?"

"He was here at the base hospital," Megan replied as calmly as she could. If Gerry hadn't run home, where had he gone? He didn't have good friends at school, there were no other families or kids that Gerry talked about. Boyd Fletcher hadn't let his son get close to anyone else. Except for the base-assigned youth counselor who wasn't quite able to do her job well enough to save him.

"Where is Gerry now?" Tonya demanded.

"I don't know, Tonya," Megan admitted. "But we're going to find him."

"How could you lose my baby?" Tonya was sobbing now, the draining noise broken intermittently by hiccups.

"We didn't lose him," Megan said patiently. "He checked himself in for emergency care. He was treated, and he's fine. A couple bumps and bruises."

"He fell," Tonya said quickly. "He fell again. You know how clumsy he is, Mrs. Gander. He's always falling."

"We'll talk about that later."

"I've got to get off the phone," Tonya said. "I've got to call Boyd."

"Boyd's here," Megan said. She was conscious of the attention she was getting from the three young men in the muscle car.

One of them got out of the vehicle. The slim young black man wore gray sweat pants and a red muscle shirt that showed off tattoos on his deltoids. Megan couldn't be sure because of the uncertain light, but the tattoos looked like West Coast gang symbols, dark blue ink barely standing out against the ebony.

"Boyd's there?" Tonya's tone indicated that made no sense to her. "What is he doing there?"

"He came looking for Gerry."

"He knew Gerry was in the hospital?"

"I don't know how he knew Gerry was here," Megan replied. She filed the question away because it was a good one, and one that she wanted the answer to herself. "Boyd assaulted two of the security men at the hospital. He's been arrested."

"That . . . that's *crazy!*"

"Tonya," Megan said. "I need you to listen to me." She spoke like she was talking to a child, like she was explaining to Chris why he couldn't watch some of the violent cartoons on the networks. "Can you listen to me, Tonya?"

"Sure. Sure, I guess. Did you have Boyd arrested?"

"No," Megan answered.

"Because you don't know what he can be like when he gets upset."

Megan thought about the damage she'd seen done to Gerry, how Boyd Fletcher had fought the two young Rangers. She figured she could guess how Boyd Fletcher was. "You don't have to worry about your husband for a while, Tonya. He's been taken to lockup. I'm going to need to talk to you."

"About what?"

"About what happened to Gerry tonight."

"Nothing happened to Gerry. He fell. I told you he fell."

"Then why didn't you bring him to the hospital?"

"He wasn't hurt bad."

"He came to the hospital," Megan pointed out. *God, please help me here. Thank You for letting me know Joey is okay, but there's still Goose out there, and Gerry is lost. Please help me deal with this the right way.*

"He was just overreacting," Tonya said defensively. "He knows how you like to baby him. He's probably just acting out to get your attention."

"Then he beat himself up severely to get my attention." Megan didn't mean to drop that on the woman, but she was beyond self-restraint and control. Where would an eleven-year-old boy run after seeing his father, the man—no, the *thing*—he most feared in the world, get hauled down by two Rangers? Gerry was still at a young age. He wouldn't believe that the two Rangers would be able to stop his father. He'd believe that Boyd Fletcher was like one of the monsters in the teen movies, the ones that just will not stop, cannot be killed. That was the kind of thing Gerry believed he was dealing with.

"No," Tonya said in a choked voice. "That's not true."

Megan took a deep breath. "I know it's not true, Tonya. I know what happened to Gerry. Now I need to know where he is."

"I don't know, Mrs. Gander. I really don't know." Tonya started sobbing again. "Help me. I don't know what to do."

"It's okay." Megan hated the guilt that she felt. While dealing with Gerry and his problems, it was easy to lose sight of the fact that there were two victims in the Fletcher household. "I'll tell you what you can do, Tonya."

"What?"

"Check the house," Megan instructed. "Maybe Gerry came back but he's not in his room. Maybe he's hiding there somewhere. Some secret place he has. Check outside the house. With everything that happened here tonight, he might be too scared to come in."

"He wouldn't be afraid of coming into his own house."

"He was pretty scared tonight, Tonya. I don't know for sure, but I think Boyd had been drinking."

"Maybe I should come down there and try to bail Boyd out."

"After what he did tonight," Megan said, "they're not going to let him out for a while. Trust me. You'll do more good there."

"Okay." Tonya sounded completely defeated.

"If you find Gerry," Megan told her, "call me immediately." She waited till Tonya found a pen and paper, then gave her the cell phone number. "If I find Gerry first, I'll call you." She punched the cell phone's End button.

The young black man stood nearby, giving the easy appearance of waiting patiently.

Megan looked at him, then turned and started to walk back to the hospital building.

"Ma'am," the young man called.

Calmly, Megan turned, punching 911 into the phone and slipping her thumb over the Talk button. If things went badly, she was a thumb twitch away from immediate help—theoretically. "Yes."

The young man crossed his arms over his chest and made no attempt to come closer. "I don't mean to alarm you, ma'am. Got a good friend inside about to have his first baby. I'm Private Trevor Newman. I'm with the 75th."

"Private," Megan said, "my husband is Sergeant Gander."

"Yes, ma'am. That's what I thought. I know Goose. I shoot hoops with him and Joey now and again at the gym. I've seen you there a couple times. You and your baby."

Those times hadn't been very often of late. "How can I help you, Private?"

"Actually, I thought it might be me was able to help you, ma'am. Didn't mean to eavesdrop, but I couldn't help hearing you talk about a little boy you're looking for."

"Do you know where he went?"

"Yes, ma'am. I believe so." Newman nodded toward the nearest on-base apartment complex. "He went up there."

Megan looked at the squat, four-story building. Several of the lights were still on in the apartments. She guessed that several of the military guys still on base were watching the Lakers game as Gerry had been trying to do or were screening movies.

"He went to one of those apartments?" Megan asked. She sorted through the names of the people Gerry had mentioned but knew of none of them that were in the immediate area.

"No, ma'am," Newman said. "I mean, he went *up* there. There's fire escapes on that building, ma'am. That boy hauled himself up one of them to the rooftop."

Megan stared at the building. For the life of her, she couldn't imagine why Gerry would do such a thing. "Are you certain?" she asked the young private.

"Yes, ma'am. I do a lot of recon work for my unit. I see what I see, and I'm telling you what I saw." Newman turned. "Hey, Pete."

"Yeah." A slim Hispanic man stepped away from the muscle car.

"Use that spotlight on your Jeep, bro. Light up the roof of the res building over there." Newman pointed.

"You're going to make a lot of people very unhappy," Pete warned, but he crossed to the Jeep Wrangler decked out for off-road driving that occupied the slot next to the muscle car.

"Gotta check something out," Newman said. "Mrs. Gander here is looking for a kid. I saw him go up on that building."

"I didn't see anything, man."

"That's why they got you lugging that M-60, grunt," Newman replied with a grin, "and why I run point or wing."

"Anybody comes to me with a beef over the light," Pete promised, "I'm sending them to you." He flipped on the spotlight.

Megan shielded her eyes, blinking against the sudden pain, then followed the white tunnel the beam cut through the night. At first, she believed the young soldiers were only earning themselves a world of trouble that would lead to a severe dressing-down by the base commander, maybe a few visits from other Rangers, and possibly even demerits entered in their files.

Then her doubts disappeared, becoming an arctic cold spear that pierced her heart when she saw Gerry Fletcher standing at the edge of the building's roof four stories above the ground.

Turkey
30 Klicks South of Sanliurfa
Local Time 0759 Hours

The explosions that had ripped the UH-60 Black Hawk helicopter from the sky had scattered the machine over two hundred yards of desert sand. Flames still clung to some of the bigger pieces, and turgid black smoke curled up from them.

Goose was amazed that anyone had survived the destruction and the tumble from the sky, let alone four of the crew. He stood in the passenger seat of the other RSOV as Tanaka parked the vehicle fifty feet away from the one Hardin and the two Rangers with him had used to get to the site. Tanaka pointed their RSOV in the other direction, giving the Ranger teams overlapping fields of fire as well as a perimeter.

"Phoenix Leader," Remington called over the headset.

Goose assigned men to perimeter watch. Cusack stayed in the RSOV to finish tending Bill Townsend, who had taken a round through his upper thigh. Luckily, the 7.62mm bullet had cored through the outside of the leg. The wound was debilitating, but the steel-jacketed round had missed both the thighbone and the femoral artery. Contact with the bone would have broken the leg, and slicing through the femoral artery might have caused Bill to bleed out and die before they could get the flow stopped. Either way, he had been lucky.

Or had God watching over him, Goose amended, feeling certain that was more reason than the other.

"Go, Base," Goose said as he stepped out of the RSOV and dropped to the sand. "Leader reads you five by five."

"How bad is it?" Remington asked.

"The helo is gone, sir." Goose surveyed the bulk of the wreck. Fire wreathed the Black Hawk, burning off the excess fuel. Whatever equipment remained aboard that might be salvageable wasn't going to be approachable for some time. "We've got four survivors. All of them are wounded."

"What about your squad?"

"Mostly intact, Base. One walking wounded."

"Your vehicles?"

"We're in motion, sir." Goose surveyed the wounded men.

The chaplain wore an identifying armband that guaranteed recognition but not safety from enemy fire. He was in his late forties, his dark hair peppered with gray. Hard lines made his face look haggard. Quietly, he held one wounded man's hand and spoke in a low, confident voice.

Hardin stood beside the chaplain, out of the line of sight of the wounded man. With an impassive expression, Hardin locked eyes with Goose and slowly shook his head.

"There's something you should know, Sergeant," Remington said.

"What, sir?"

"The reporter that was talking to you, Hardesty, was sending out a live transmission at the time the helo went down and your squad was attacked. The television stations carried that transmission in real time. No delay."

Goose took in the statement, automatically logging the ramifications. If Megan or Joey was awake, and if they knew that war along the Turkish border had broken out, they might have seen the footage on television. He felt guilty that his wife and son might be sitting home worrying about him.

"I'm sending a message through channels," Remington said. "Fort Benning will send a dispatch to Megan to let her know you're all right."

For the moment, Goose thought. He was enough of a realist to know that Remington might be sending a message that might not be true twenty minutes from now. "Thank you for that, sir."

"We're fighting wars in unusual times," Remington said. "Battle has never been a televised event before. Yet that's where we're finding ourselves. I didn't want you distracted from your mission."

Goose checked his watch. "I've still got a window on the arriving aircraft, sir."

"Yes, you do. Can you get there?"

"Yes, sir. We'll be carrying wounded. I'd like a medical team to meet me if possible. I've got one man here who's touch and go."

"Affirmative, Leader. I'll pass the request along, but I can make no promises. Those people are busy. We've got wounded and casualties scattered all along the border."

"But we're holding."

"Yes, Sergeant. Those men at the front are Rangers. *Our* Rangers. They'll stand. And once those Marines arrive and we get the air support we're expecting, Syria is going to be sorry she opened the ball on this one."

Goose cleared the channel and switched back to the squad frequency. The sat-relay vids weren't up yet, but he thanked God the com channels held up through the emergency rerouting.

"Hardin," Goose called.

"Yeah, Sarge."

"Let's get loaded up. Take the two wounded. We'll handle the chaplain and his charge."

"We're on it." Hardin trotted back to the RSOV he commanded and got his four-man team to transfer two of the wounded helo crewmen to the vehicle.

Goose surveyed the burning remains of the helicopter. Occasionally the flames shifted and he could see the bodies of the two pilots still strapped into their seats. Both dead men were burned beyond recognition.

"Sergeant."

Turning at the sound of the soft voice behind him, Goose faced the chaplain. "Chaplain," Goose said.

"O'Dell," the chaplain said. "Timothy O'Dell." He spoke with a New York accent and offered his hand.

"First Sergeant Samuel Gander." Goose took the man's hand, finding the grip solid and reassuring.

O'Dell nodded. "I know who you are, Sergeant. We were briefed before we jumped from the border."

"We're pressed for time here, Chaplain."

"I know, but I wanted to talk to you about Private Digby over there." O'Dell paused, looking back at the young man lying unconscious on the OD field blanket that was pockmarked with ember charring. "If we try to transport him across the desert, I'm afraid he's not going to make it. Shrapnel from one of the shattered helicopter rotors pierced his right lung. It's pretty much filled with blood. There are other injuries, but that one is the most serious."

"The only other option is to leave him here," Goose said. He kept emotion from the decision, though he knew if anything happened to the young soldier he would feel guilty later. Command came equipped with harsh decisions.

"I could stay with him," O'Dell offered.

Goose looked into the man's eyes. "I can't guarantee a medevac, Chaplain. I can't even guarantee there will be one when we get to the other end of this jump."

"God will provide, Sergeant. He always does."

For a moment, Goose was almost swayed by the chaplain's quiet words. They carried the same certain conviction that Bill's counsel often had. But the stark desert surrounding them weighed heavily on him.

"I can't let you do that," Goose said. "If I leave you out here, we could lose you both."

"Sergeant, I'm willing—"

Goose cut the man off firmly but politely, having to talk a little louder because the fresh assault of artillery fire thundering to the south. "Chaplain, I appreciate that, but it's not going to happen. I don't want to lose anyone, but I'm not going to risk two."

The chaplain looked like he wanted to argue, then he stood respectfully. "All right, Sergeant. We'll do it your way. I'll pray for success for us all."

Goose nodded a thank-you and turned from the man, focusing on the mission, concentrating on the need to get to the front where he could perhaps start saving lives instead of losing them. He walked to the wounded man's side, listening uncomfortably to the wheeze and rasp of the young soldier's breathing as his chest labored. Blood streaked the wounded man's face and his left eye was swollen shut.

Calling Cusack, Evaristo, and the chaplain over while Tanaka manned the RSOV, Goose gripped the edge of the bloodstained field blanket under the wounded man. On the count of three, they lifted the young soldier from the ground. He groaned in pain but didn't wake.

Goose felt like yelling with the wounded man. The exertion pulled at his strained shoulder and brought back the sensation of the iron band around his chest, cutting his breath short. Together, they carried the injured man to the back of the RSOV.

Bill reached out and helped guide the soldier onto the rear deck area. Cusack had cut away Bill's left pant leg to get to the wound. Heavy gauze bandaged the leg.

"Don't bust that dressing loose," Cusack warned. "We had a hard time pulling everything together."

Bill's face blanched white and a sick sweat poured from his skin. Gingerly, he returned to a sitting position. "I like being a soldier," he said with a grin that was only a shadow of the usual effort. "I don't even mind getting shot *at*. It's part of the service. But this getting shot, you know, I have a real problem with that."

The moment of levity, even as out of place as it was, lightened the mood. The young soldier lying on the RSOV's rear deck even woke long enough to gasp, "Tell me about it."

As the other Rangers belted in around the RSOV, Goose took his position in the passenger seat. "Let's roll," he told Tanaka.

Tanaka let out the clutch and the four-wheel drive kicked small rooster tails in the sand for a moment before catching better traction.

Glancing over his shoulder, Goose saw the second RSOV flank them, staying behind and to the right. He checked the western skies, knowing the aircraft from USS *Wasp* was inbound from that direction.

Except for the smoke and dust haze rising from Glitter City, the blue sky remained empty.

C'mon, Goose thought, *be there. We've got a lot to do.*

❀ ❀ ❀

United States of America
Fort Benning, Georgia
Local Time 1:12 A.M.

"Gerry." Megan grew short of breath as she sprinted up the steel fire escape that zigzagged back and forth across the outside of the resident building. She was in shape from the sports she and Goose played, but that didn't prepare her to be at peak condition during one of the most intensely stressful situations of her life. "Gerry."

The boy didn't answer.

Below, out in the parking lot, Private Newman and his friends kept the spotlight on the boy. They also stayed back at Megan's request. At this point, with everything that had happened to him tonight, she wasn't sure what Gerry Fletcher was capable of doing.

"Gerry." Megan's feet drummed against the metal fire escape steps. The clanging noises rang and echoed against the apartment building.

One of the windows above on the third floor opened and a young, bare-chested man leaned out. His dog tags glinted in the spotlight. Rap music with unintelligible lyrics blared out into the night. "Hey! What's going on out here?" he demanded.

Without pausing to answer, Megan ran past him. The vibration of her passing tipped over a wrought-iron stand containing three potted plants. Potting soil and vegetation scattered across the landing and leaked through the holes in the grilled landing.

"Hey," the guy in the window called again. He started climbing out.

"Back off, soldier," Megan ordered, putting all the steel she could muster into her voice. During her observations of Goose in his element, she'd seen him bark commands in the same kind of tone. He'd told her that the voice of authority was something a soldier often responded to without identifying the source, if the speaker could carry off the role. The ability to produce that voice was one of the first deciding factors in choosing non-coms and officers.

The soldier froze halfway out of the window.

Megan grabbed the next rail headed up and took the steps two at a time. She looked up at Gerry Fletcher. The boy still stood transfixed in the bright spotlight. His face was wracked with anguish and fear. Tears glistened like silver as they ran down his cheeks to his quivering chin.

Heartbroken, Megan thought as she hurled herself up the flight of steps. *And terrified.* She couldn't help wondering how much of Gerry's life had been spent feeling that way. *Later. Think about that later. Get him down from the building now. Why did he come up here? Why is he standing near the edge? God, that boy shouldn't be up here.*

But she was afraid she knew.

God, I need Your help here. I hope that You're listening. Please be listening.

In the parking lot below, a military Jeep with flashing security lights pulled to a stop beside Newman and his friends. Two uniformed MPs got out with flashlights and shined the beams over the Jeep, highlighting Newman and his friends.

Megan ran. Her breath burned the back of her throat and her lungs seemed too small to drag in the air that she needed. *Calm,* she instructed herself. *Gerry needs you calm. You need to be calm for yourself.*

She pulled up the final few steps. Her body felt like lead. Everything seemed to be going too fast and too slow at the same time. She stepped out onto the rooftop. Gravel cracked and crunched under her feet. She had to be trapped in a nightmare. This had to be a night-mare. God help her if it wasn't.

Gerry Fletcher stood farther down the same wall she'd come up on. The spotlight on his body turned him almost ghostly white in the front and made his back half as black as night.

"Stay away, Mrs. Gander," Gerry said in a voice that broke. "Please stay away."

Megan stopped immediately. In a situation like this, the potential victim needed to feel in charge. Many suicides took their own lives in an attempt to prove they had some control left to them. She held her hands out to her sides.

"All right, Gerry," she said in a calm voice. "I've stopped."

Gerry looked back out at the parking lot.

The MPs shined their lights up at the roof, adding to the intensity of the spotlight. Then they started for the building.

"Gerry." Megan forced herself to sound calm. She didn't feel that way, but she could sound that way—with effort. Years spent counsel-ing troubled youths had honed that skill within her. "You've got to come away from the edge of the building, Gerry. If you don't, the MPs are going to come up."

Gerry shook his head, peered over the edge, and looked like he was going to throw up. But when he faced her, he still looked reso-lute. "If they do, I'll jump."

The calm way he stated his planned action scared Megan. Gerry sounded broken in spirit, filled with a quiet desperation that ran bone deep. "You're breaking the law, Gerry. They can't just walk away."

"I'm planning on jumping anyway." Gerry's voice remained calm and matter-of-fact. "When they get too close, then I'll jump."

"Let me try to stop them," Megan offered. She lifted her cell phone and punched in the number to the security office.

The dispatch officer came on in a crisp, efficient tone.

"This is Megan Gander," Megan said, watching the MPs jog across the parking lot. "You've got men monitoring a situation near the base hospital. A boy on an apartment building roof."

"Who are you, Mrs. Gander?" the dispatcher asked. Other voices sounded in the background, other dispatchers working other calls.

"I'm the boy's counselor," Megan said. "You can verify that through Helen Cordell at the base hospital. She called me in. Dr. Car-son is the attending physician in the ER tonight. He's aware of the sit-uation as well."

The MPs had jogged to the base of the building.

"I'll do that now, Mrs. Gander," the dispatcher replied. "Until then, the MPs—"

"Back them off," Megan said, watching as one of the MPs started up the fire escape. "If they try to come up after him, he's threatened to jump."

"Ma'am, I haven't confirmed who you are or what the situation—"

"Do you want to confirm all that after he's jumped?" Megan interrupted with desperate anger.

The brief pause that came after her challenge seemed elastic, like it would stretch on forever. Then he said, "All right, Mrs. Gander. You've got a point."

Listening closely, her eyes on Gerry, Megan heard the dispatcher order the MPs stand down. The transmission through the MPs radios came from below, lagging a half second behind the cell phone connection.

"Gerry," she said, turning back to the boy. "They've stopped. See? You're in control here. We're going to do what you want to do." *God, please give me the time and the skill to convince him that he wants to live. I've asked You for a lot in the past, but I really need Your help here.* She stepped toward the edge where the MPs could see her.

Their flashlights played over her. Light seared into her eyes and she turned away. The MPs pointed their lights to the side. Looking down again, she experienced immediate vertigo. How far up was four stories? She didn't know. But she was certain that the height was more than enough to kill an eleven-year-old boy.

"Step back away from the building," Megan called down to the MPs.

The young soldier leaning out the window of his apartment remained in that position below. The rap music continued to blare. Unbelievably, the soldier held a small camcorder in his hands. The intense light sprayed through the dark night, mixing with the blinding glare of the spotlight.

"Mrs. Gander," one of the young MPs said. The tone indicated that he wanted verbal confirmation.

"Yes," she answered in a firm voice. "I need you to step back. Please."

"Yes, ma'am. If you need any help, just let us know." The MP stepped back from the building. He cupped the walkie-talkie microphone clipped to his right shoulder and spoke briefly.

"I will. But I think Gerry and I are quite capable of getting ourselves out of this situation." Megan looked at the boy. Tears still cascaded down his face. "We can handle this, can't we, Gerry?"

Gerry didn't answer.

Megan waited, then talked more softly, as if she didn't want the MPs to hear. Actually, she intended the effort to bring Gerry and her together, to let the boy know he was helping someone else. Sometimes by helping someone else, a person better learned to help himself.

"They need to hear you, Gerry," Megan said. "They need to know that you're in control of the situation. They have to tell the dispatch officer that they're confident that you know what you're doing."

Gerry didn't move, didn't speak.

"Gerry, I need your help. They need your help. I've got to try to do my job, and they've got to try to do theirs."

The boy swallowed hard. "It's okay. Me and Mrs. Gander are gonna talk."

Thank You, God, Megan thought. But she knew the quick response on her part was just lip service. She didn't believe God had anything to do with the present situation. She didn't see how. If God were paying attention, He would never have allowed Gerry Fletcher up on the roof.

"That's fine," one of the MPs called up. "You guys talk all you want to. But if you could move away from the roof's edge, it would help."

Megan looked at Gerry, putting the response back onto the boy.

"No," Gerry said. "I'm not leaving, Mrs. Gander." He wiped his face with a shaking hand. "I'm going to jump. I really am."

"So, you and your mom."

Joey braked to a halt at a stoplight that had turned red right before he reached it. He turned to look at Jenny McGrath in the passenger seat. Since they'd left the club, they hadn't talked much. During his cell phone conversation with his mother, he had noticed Jenny was being really attentive while trying not to get caught eavesdropping.

"Yeah?" Joey prompted.

Jenny looked at him. The stoplight threw red light over her face, revealing her right profile in red highlights and leaving the left side of her face buried in shadow. It was like she was trapped between two worlds.

Joey didn't know where the impression had come from, but once the thought had come to his mind he couldn't get rid of it.

"You and your mom are close," Jenny said.

"Yeah. Mostly."

"Mostly?"

Joey looked away, aware that the young woman's eyes were boring into his, seeming to see past so much of the image that he had built up to impress her. "I kind of blew curfew tonight. Not exactly a step designed to build closeness."

Surprisingly, Jenny laughed. "No," she agreed. "Definitely not."

"What about you?" Joey said, thinking that if an opportunity presented itself he should capitalize on it.

"What about me?"

"Are you close to your mom?"

Jenny looked away. "She's dead."

Joey felt horrible. The night just wasn't going well at all. He felt like he couldn't do anything wrong without making a mess of things. "I'm sorry. I didn't know."

"No," Jenny agreed. "You didn't." Her face turned green. She waited a beat, then pointed at the traffic light. "Green. We can go."

Feeling even more inadequate, Joey took his foot from the brake and placed it on the accelerator. He sped up, following the familiar streets back to Fort Benning.

"You didn't do anything wrong by asking, Joey," Jenny said. "You couldn't know. It's just me and my father."

"No brothers or sisters?"

She shook her head, then a smile twisted her lips. "But you have a little brother."

"Chris." Joey nodded. "Yeah."

"So how old is he?"

"Five," Joey said. "And don't try to tell him any different because he can count."

"Five's a cute age."

And seventeen's not? Joey wanted to ask. But he didn't. He was afraid of the answer. Especially since he'd told Jenny he was twenty-one. "How do you know about cute ages for kids?" he countered. "If you don't have a younger brother or sister?"

"Before I became a server, I worked in a child-care center. I liked working with the creepers."

"Creepers?"

"Kids ten to fourteen months old. The daycare center staff called them creepers because they just started to pull themselves up on things and walk."

"Oh."

Jenny looked at Joey and smiled again. "And you were thinking?"

"Horror movie stuff. Aliens. Predators. Creepers." Joey shrugged. "Just seemed to fit."

"So what's your little brother like?"

Joey slowed and took a left through the intersection, making certain he had plenty of room before the oncoming traffic reached them. A pang of jealousy ripped through him. Jenny didn't even know Chris and already her attention was zeroing in on him, leaving Joey way behind.

Struggling to mask his hurt and disappointment, Joey said, "Chris is great. Everybody likes him." *Can't you tell?*

"Must be nice."

"What?"

Jenny looked away from him, turning to play with her hair in her reflection on the side window. "Having a little brother."

"Some days," Joey admitted. "Other days, I wish I was an only child."

"Why?"

Joey shrugged. "Kinda miss all the attention." *Miss it a lot, actually.*

"You do, huh?" Jenny turned her attention to him.

Really regretting all the scrutiny he was getting, and feeling more than a little defensive, Joey said, "Yeah. I mean, you have to work your tail off at home to get your parents to notice you because all your cuteness points faded back in a past you can barely remember, and your little brother just has to step into the room and—*pow!* He's the center of attention."

"That happens a lot?"

"Yeah," Joey said. "All the time." A kaleidoscope of images swirled through his mind, stinging with each memory of how Chris had so nonchalantly taken the full attention of both parents and any other adult who happened to be around. "I mean, it's like Chris is a magnet for attention."

A brief, tense silence stretched between them. Joey had the feeling he had done something incredibly stupid, but he couldn't for the life of him figure out what it was.

"I thought you lived in an apartment with a roommate," Jenny said. Her voice turned cold and hard. She slid away from him, pressing herself up against the door. "That's what you told me at Kettle O' Fish."

Too late, Joey realized that one of his lies had been found out. And they were all tied together. Sick apprehension filled him.

"What else have you lied about?" Jenny demanded.

❉   ❉   ❉

Turkey
37 Klicks South of Sanliurfa
Local Time 0810 Hours

Artillery fire peppered the ridge of desert rock Captain Remington had chosen as Goose's observation point. Goose braced himself as Tanaka hit the brakes. The RSOV skidded through the loose sand and broken rock that covered the area from the explosions that had turned the border region into a moonlike landscape.

Keeping his head low and his helmet cinched up tight enough to keep it on, Goose stepped from the RSOV and sprinted over to the com team Remington had waiting for him. The two men pressed themselves into the lee side of a rocky outcrop that thrust up to a broken point twenty feet overhead.

Despite the preparation he'd had for the scene and the occasional glances of the border he'd gotten while racing for the observation point, the carnage strung along the border nearly froze Goose's heart. In all his years as a soldier, Goose had never seen anything that could have left him ready for the horrible consequences of the clash that lay before him.

The Syrian infantry remained too far away to see with the naked eye. According to Remington's reports while Goose had been en route, after the initial flurry of SCUDs and FROGs had landed within Syrian occupied territory, the enemy army—at this point that was the only way Goose could think of them—the Syrians had abandoned their posts and pulled back.

If the Turkish government and the United Nations could have agreed with President Fitzhugh's desire to send the troops into Syria, a beachhead could have been established. Recon posts and maybe even search-and-destroy missions against specific targets identified from earlier intel could have been organized. But that hadn't happened. Now, if those same operations had to be done, the cost in lives was going to escalate.

Goose raked his gaze over the death and destruction that filled the border area. Artillery shelled the area, harrying the men dug in along the invisible front line. Smoke and dust swept across the land, carried in clouds that swirled slowly in the dry breeze. Exploding mortars and rocket fire hammered those clouds, blowing them to smithereens or causing them to twist in new and violent gyrations.

The dust and smoke looked like wraiths, Goose realized, and his neck prickled at the thought, though he wasn't usually prone to an overactive imagination.

Men and pieces of men were scattered in all directions. As bad as Glitter City had been, the border units had been hit worse. Soldiers hustled through the burning APCs, Hummers, tanks, and cargo trucks, all overturned and strewn about like an angry child's toys. The uninjured men were working to separate the quick from the dead. A few of the men had medical bands on their arms to identify them for and protect them from enemy snipers. However, the Syrian artillery fire recognized no Geneva Convention edicts and had no conscience. From Goose's vantage point, it looked as though the corpsmen were being targeted *because* of those armbands.

Three men carried a fourth to a waiting truck marked with a Red Cross insignia. Just as they reached the truck, a group of four MiGs, the Russian-made aircraft the Syrians used, appeared in the south. The jets streaked out of the blue sky, looking like camo-colored darts.

Goose switched over to the frequency used by the troops in the field. Before he could say anything, cries of, "Incoming! Incoming!" filled the headset. Knowing he couldn't offer anything more, he clicked back to the command frequency Remington had designated to him.

Below, men scattered all along the border.

The MiGs peeled out of the tight diamond formation they had been in. Looking like high-tech vultures, the jets fired a salvo of air-to-surface missiles that rocketed toward the entrenched positions of the Turkish, U.S., and U.N. forces.

The missiles struck the ground and unleashed thunderclaps of noise, as well as unbelievable destructive fury. One of the missiles struck the medical transport truck. Goose wasn't certain they'd intended to hit that target or not; with the clouds of smoke and dust and the speed at which the MiGs were flying, it was possible that the pilot never saw the truck's Red Cross markings.

The missile struck the truck broadside, piercing the ribbed canvas and not exploding till it struck the ground. Later, Goose never knew if he actually saw the missile pass through the truck in one of those moments of crystal clarity that sometimes happened on the battlefield, or if the analytical processes in his mind that he tapped into while making decisions told him that was what had happened.

In the end, it didn't matter.

The resulting explosion lifted the truck from the ground, whirling it end over end thirty feet into the air. The gas tanks ruptured and caught on fire. In the next instant, the truck was a flaming comet that descended on an M-1A1 Abrams tank. As the twisted hulk of the truck rolled from the tank, bodies of soldiers spilled out in its wake. Some of the corpses wreathed the Abrams.

The three men who had been carrying the fourth had been blown several yards away. None of them got up.

One of the few surviving anti-aircraft emplacements opened fire. A collection of American Rangers and Turkish soldiers operated the double-barreled weapon, tracking black clouds of flak across the blue sky. In the space of three or four seconds, the AA gun crew had the MiG's range. The AA cannonfire struck the MiG like a giant's fists, crumpling the warbird. Trailing oily black smoke, the MiG turned and tried to limp back south of the border. Another salvo of AA cannonfire caught up with the jet, and the resulting explosions broke it into fiery pieces.

"Boo-yah!" Tanaka yelled a short distance from Goose. The young man stood and shook his fist at the falling debris that had been the enemy aircraft.

In the next instant, one of the three surviving MiGs wheeled in the sky, flipping over in an inversion that took it away from the AA gunners' sights. Still inverted, the Syrian pilot triggered his 20mm guns. The cannon rounds pounded the desert ground, opening harsh tears in the earth and throwing up spiraling double plumes of dirt, sand, and smoke. The pilot flipped over 180 degrees, never pausing on the 20mm cannon.

Even as they realized the danger they were in, the AA crew was struck by the hammering bursts of 20mm cannonfire. Dead soldiers dropped, torn and bloody, like rag dolls. None of the brave crew that had brought the enemy jet down remained alive.

Continuing to rain destruction down on the border, the MiGs slammed air-to-surface missiles into vehicles and groups of men. A direct hit by a missile blasted past the reactive armor covering an Abrams and tore the turret loose.

A moment later, a surviving member of the tank crew tried to scramble from the rolling stock only to get caught by the next missile that flipped the Abrams over. The small American flag attached to the radio aerial burst into flames and incinerated.

Goose watched the destruction helplessly. Hitting the MiG with a round from the M-4A1 would have been an amazing feat. *And a waste of ammo,* he thought bitterly. With supply lines cut up and in danger, there was no telling how much time would pass before the survivors could resupply.

"Look out!" Tanaka yelled. "Incoming! Nine o'clock!"

Goose swiveled his head to the left and spotted the MiG sweeping in from the east, running a nap-of-the-earth course. "Down!" he yelled. "Take cover!" He turned and ran, spotting the chaplain with the grievously wounded young soldier. "O'Dell!"

The chaplain glanced up just as the first cannon shot tore up the desert terrain, heading for their position. "Help me! Please help me!" He gripped one side of the dust- and blood-covered blanket and started dragging the unconscious man toward the nearest RSOV.

Shifting his assault rifle to his shoulder, Goose ran and caught the other side of the blanket. Adding his strength and speed to the chaplain's efforts, together they humped the blanket toward the RSOV. Then the cannon fire echoed all around them, and Goose knew that if he could hear the destruction at nearly the same time as the rounds hit the ground that the enemy fire was almost on top of them.

Five feet out from the RSOV, Goose yelled, "Under! Now!" and threw himself forward in a skidding dive. His strained shoulder screamed in renewed fury as he desperately clung to the blanket. O'Dell had gone to the ground at the same time, maintaining his hold on the blanket and the soldier as well.

Gravel tore at Goose's lower face. He arched his back, riding his Kevlar chest armor hard. Pain lanced his left knee, biting into his flesh. His mouth opened to yell, sucking in the dust-covered kerchief, and then a whirling maelstrom of sound drowned out any sound he might have made.

❋ ❋ ❋

United States of America
Fort Benning, Georgia
Local Time 1:16 A.M.

Helplessly, Megan watched as Gerry Fletcher remained standing on the roof's edge. *God, where are You when I need You? We can't let this happen! God, please don't let this happen!*

The wind picked up, pulling at Gerry's clothing with invisible fingers. He threw his arms out, and for a moment Megan thought he was going to throw himself over; then she saw that the movement was instinctive, made to keep himself from tumbling over the edge.

The boy remained standing on the roof's edge. The spotlight turned his auburn hair the copper color of a new penny. For a moment, in the harsh light, his hair looked like a red-gold halo.

"Gerry," Megan said. "I've got a phone here. Why don't we call your mom?"

Gerry hesitated, then shook his head. "I don't want to talk to her."

"I think it could help." Megan thought about taking a step forward, slowly cutting down the distance separating her from the boy. But she knew if she encroached on him there was every chance she could scare him over the edge.

New tears coursed down Gerry's face. He trembled. "You don't understand, Mrs. Gander. You never understand. I try and I try to tell you, but you just don't get it. I'm a jinx to my mom and dad."

Megan knew that the words the boy used were his father's.

"I was born," Gerry said, "and I screwed up their lives."

"That's not true."

He turned to face her, his face angry. "It *is* true! All you gotta do is ask them!"

"If your father feels that way—"

"He does. And you know it."

"Your father is wrong," Megan said.

Gerry stared wild-eyed at her, as if he couldn't believe she had said what she had.

Never in one of her counseling sessions had Megan dared interfere so directly with the relationship between parent and child. She had always tried to mediate, to help one or both parties come to an understanding that worked for all of them. That was her job; the performance that she had agreed to undertake. Relationships healed best that healed together, when both or all parties took on some of the guilt and undertook a portion of the effort required to put things back together.

But there is no guilt on Gerry's side, God. Surely You see that. Of us all, You have to be able to see that. Don't be blind to that now. Deep inside herself, though, Megan was afraid that God wasn't listening, that He had turned a blind eye to the sparrow perched on this roof's edge.

"You can't say that about my dad, Mrs. Gander," Gerry said. "He's a good soldier. He's my dad." He wiped tiredly at his eyes.

"I didn't say your father wasn't a good man," Megan replied. "I said he was wrong. Everybody can be wrong. We're supposed to be wrong sometimes. That's the best way we learn. From our mistakes."

"I'm the mistake," Gerry sobbed. "There's something wrong with me, Mrs. Gander. Something bad wrong. Before I was born, my mom and dad were happy. Now they're not. It's all my fault."

"Gerry, please. Let's call your mom. I talked to her earlier—"

"You did? Why did you do that?"

"Because you ran from the hospital. Because I was worried about you."

"You shouldn't have done that, Mrs. Gander." Unable to remain calm, Gerry started pacing along the building's edge. His arms shot out from time to time, and he nearly fell twice.

"Gerry." Unable to stop herself, Megan stepped forward.

"*Don't!*" Gerry screamed. "*Stay back!*" He turned and faced her so abruptly that he almost fell.

Megan froze. Her heart beat so frantically it nearly burst. "Gerry, I'm stopping."

"Stay right there!" he commanded in a shrill voice.

He's afraid. Megan clung to that realization. As long as he's afraid of falling, he won't jump.

"Gerry," she said calmly, "I talked to your mother just a few minutes ago. She's worried about you. She knows you've been to the hospital."

"Where is she?"

"At home," Megan said. "I told her to wait there in case you came home. She doesn't know you're up here. But I think she'd like to. I think she'd like the chance to talk to you." She paused and took a deep breath, knowing she was about to push another of Gerry's hot buttons. "I think you'd like to talk to her, too."

Stubbornly, Gerry shook his head. "When she finds out my dad got arrested because of me, she's going to be mad."

"Your dad didn't get arrested because of you. He got arrested because he attacked those other two men."

"I shouldn't have gone to the hospital."

"You had to go to the hospital." Megan slowly lifted her cell phone. "I'm going to call your mom." *And you're going to push him to the point of no return.* She hated that. But she felt certain there was no other way she was going to get Gerry from the rooftop. She pressed the Redial button, ringing the Fletcher home number.

"Don't!"

Megan held the phone out, turning the volume up. "It's ringing, Gerry. Do you hear it?"

"No!"

"Hello?" Tonya Fletcher's voice sounded frantic. "Megan! One of my neighbors came over. Her husband is one of the MPs. What is Gerry doing up there?"

Calmly, her breath feeling tight inside her lungs, Megan pulled the phone back to her ear. "Tonya, it's Megan. I need you to be calm."

"*Calm!* My son is up on a rooftop! Where, I've been told, you chased him! How can you expect me to be calm! My husband is in jail, my son is in danger, and this is all because of you!"

"Tonya." Megan made her voice forceful. "We can sort out whose fault this is later. Right now Gerry needs to know that you want him safely down from here. Do you hear me?"

"I hear you! But this isn't my fault! This isn't Boyd's fault! We can't help how Gerry is! Don't you understand that? You've seen how he is! You've seen how he always wants attention!"

Too late, Megan realized that Gerry heard every word his mother said. The rooftop was silent and still, and the tinny voice from the cell phone traveled easily to Gerry's ears.

"Gerry," Megan said, covering the phone's mouthpiece. Before she could say another word, a belligerent voice bellowed up from below.

"Gerald Fletcher, you had better move your sorry self off that rooftop right this minute, mister! Don't make me come up there and get you!"

Megan recognized Boyd Fletcher's voice. She was still a half step behind Gerry. The boy wheeled around at the roof's edge, and fear filled his features. He seemed to regain his balance for a moment. Then his left foot shot out from under him.

Megan was already in motion, watching as Gerry flailed his arms in a doomed effort to regain his balance. He toppled over the edge without a word.

"Do you even have a little brother?"

Joey felt angry and scared all at the same time. Jenny was acting totally weird. *She's not just mad. She's scared. Real scared,* he amended. But he had no idea what she was scared of.

"What's wrong with you?" he demanded. Then he wondered if someone who evidently had that much wrong with them could even have a clue that something was wrong.

A car horn blared.

Yanking his attention back to the street, Joey discovered that he had wandered across the center line and was now traveling halfway in the oncoming lane. He pulled the wheel hard, overcompensating as he steered back onto the proper side of the road.

His tires squealed. Another car horn bleated behind him. Bright harsh light flooded his back window, splashing against the rearview mirror and stabbing into his eyes to blind him.

"Let me out!" Jenny demanded.

Eyes tearing, mind scattered, Joey frantically tried to figure out where the street was. He couldn't even remember where he was, but he knew he was close to the military base. The bright yellow car parked along the street appeared in his view like a ship pushing through a dense fog.

"Stop!" he yelped.

"You stop!" Jenny countered. She slapped him, hitting his arm and the top of his head.

Joey raised the arm blocking the laser beams from the car on his rear bumper to protect himself. The bright lights zapped his eyes again. The car horn behind him blared once more, longer and louder this time.

"Jenny!"

She hit him again.

"Jenny! C'mon! I can't see! I'm gonna wreck!" And if his mom wasn't already going to go through the roof, wrecking her car would definitely do it.

Desperately, Joey reached up and twisted the rearview mirror out of his eyes. Almost too late, he spotted the red SUV at the side of the street. He pulled away from the collision course he was on, narrowly avoiding locking bumpers with the SUV. He didn't even know if his mom's insurance would go high enough to cover an expensive vehicle like that. And he was certain there wouldn't have been much of his mom's car left.

Shifting in the seat, somehow snaking loose from the seat belt, Jenny got a leg up and kicked Joey in the side. "Let me out of this car! Let me out now!"

"Ow!" Joey tried to cover his side. "Jenny, stop!"

"You shouldn't have lied to me! I get tired of being lied to! Everybody lies to me!"

Man, she's totally losing it! Tears leaked down Joey's face. He was hurt and scared and probably madder than he had ever been. From the corner of his eye, he spotted a side street. He swerved the car, somehow escaping the merciless onslaught of the lights from the vehicle and the idiot driver behind him.

Jenny slapped Joey in the head again.

"Stop!" Certain he was out of the flow of traffic now, Joey stomped the brakes. The car came to a rocking halt. He raised both hands and caught Jenny's wrists.

She kicked him in the face hard enough to split his lips.

"Let me go!" she demanded. "Let me go *now!*"

"All right, you psycho!" Joey shouted back. "I'm letting you go!" He tasted blood as he released her wrists.

Jenny popped the door release and got out of the car.

In dazed disbelief, still trying to figure out what had just happened and what had set Jenny off, Joey watched her walk down the darkened street away from the car. For a moment, he just wanted to drop the car back into drive and leave her there. But the street looked like part of a residential area. There were no public pay phones around. And it wasn't the kind of neighborhood where a stranger could bang on a door at this time of night and expect to borrow the phone.

Frustrated, feeling so totally trapped, Joey popped his door open and stepped out into the night. "Jenny. Wait! Where are you going?"

"Away from you." She wrapped her arms around herself and kept walking.

"Why?"

"Because you lied to me, Joey. If that's even your real name."

"C'mon. I didn't start to work at Kettle O' Fish under an alias."

"It wouldn't be the first time."

"My name really is Joey." Unable to just leave her, feeling pressured because he'd promised his mom he was going to pick up his little brother, Joey sprinted after her. "I really do have a little brother named Chris. I've got pictures." At his age, he'd thought carrying pictures of his little brother—especially one that got all of the attention—was kind of a dumb thing to do, but Chris was the only little brother he had. Besides, not everybody got to open his wallet so his secret was usually safe.

Jenny kept walking.

In a half-dozen long strides, Joey caught up with Jenny. She swiped at him with a fist. He ducked back, only inches out of her reach. For a girl, she could really throw a punch.

"Would you please look at my wallet?" Joey held it out, open to his driver's license and base ID. "Look. I've got military ID, too."

"Go away, Joey. Or whatever your name is."

"This is stupid." Joey stopped. *Let her go*, he told himself. *You can't stop stupid people from being stupid.* People his age always said that. His anger stirred in him again. "You know, if anybody should be upset about tonight, it should be me. I took you to the club and watched you dance with every guy in the place but me."

Jenny whirled, then marched back to him, staying carefully back out of his reach. "What?"

"You heard me. You." Joey pointed at her. "Me." He pointed at himself. "Not exactly a fun date."

"Oh, man," she said. "You are so full of it. What? You think because you ask somebody out you get to own them?"

"No." Joey sighed. "No, I don't. But I think it should give those two people a chance to get to know each other."

"Really?" Jenny arched a brow. "And just exactly who was I supposed to be getting to know? Joey who lives on his own? Or Joey who lives with his mom?"

Joey took a deep, shuddering breath. Man, tonight had been so totally messed up. He sucked on his split lip and offered his wallet. "I'm Joey Holder. My mom is Megan Gander. My stepdad's name is Sam. Samuel Gander. His friends call him Goose. I call him Goose. He's the one over in Turkey right now that we saw on the television. My dad, Tony, he lives in L.A. I haven't seen him in ten years. I haven't even got a phone call in five years." He took in a breath and let it out. *About the time Chris was born*, he realized, and he couldn't help wondering if his little brother's birth had something to do with that. He shoved the question out of his mind, knowing it would haunt him later. "I'm seventeen. Not twenty-one."

She stared at him for a minute. "So you lied about your age?"

"Yes."

"Why?"

"To meet you." Joey shrugged. "Things didn't work out exactly the way I wanted them to."

Quiet and intense, her arms wrapped around herself, Jenny stared at him.

Joey felt incredibly uncomfortable. He was also suddenly aware of the chill that was in the air. It was March. Even in the South, spring was chilly without a jacket.

"For the record," Jenny said, "you asked me to go to the club with you."

"Okay."

"That's not asking me for a date. If you want a date from someone, you ask them for a date. I thought maybe you hadn't been to the club before and wanted someone to go with."

"I hadn't," Joey said.

Jenny sighed and shook her head. "You're seventeen. Of course you hadn't." She held her hand out. "Let's see your fake ID."

Reaching into his pocket, Joey produced the fake ID he had been so proud of only a few days ago when his great plan had begun. He put the ID in Jenny's hand.

She looked at it and smiled a little. "Good picture."

"Thanks." Unable to help himself, Joey grinned a little. Suddenly, all the trouble that had been gathering all night didn't seem so heavy.

"Dumb idea." Jenny ripped the fake ID into quarters and let the pieces blow away.

"Oh." Joey's smile melted.

"Do you really have a little brother?"

Joey opened his wallet and flashed Chris's picture again.

"Cute kid," Jenny said.

"Everybody says that," Joey replied glumly.

"How do I know the picture didn't come with the wallet?"

Reaching behind the top picture, Joey showed her an older one of him and Chris together.

Peering more closely, Jenny said, "He looks a lot like you."

Joey almost asked her if that meant he was cute, too. But he didn't. Tonight, thankfully, he was not going to be that dumb.

"So your little brother," Jenny said, "he's still at the child-care place on the base?"

Joey nodded.

"And your stepdad really is over there in all that mess in Turkey?"

Joey nodded again.

Jenny sighed. "Okay. Let's go get the little brother. I bet your mom is going nuts."

"Yeah."

"The curfew thing isn't helping."

"No," Joey agreed.

"You picked a really bad night for all of this, Joey."

"You're telling me."

Jenny started back toward the car. Caught by surprise, Joey had to step quickly to catch up. He reached past her to open the passenger-side door. It was something he'd seen Goose do for his mom for years and couldn't remember his dad ever doing. Few guys did something like that anymore, and Joey had liked the idea of showing that kind of respect. Thinking of that reminded him of Goose, and uncertainty filled him again. He slipped behind the steering wheel and got the car moving again.

He paused at the corner, waiting on the light as traffic passed. "About the seventeen-years-old thing," he said.

She looked at him. "What?"

"If I'd told you I was seventeen years old and wanted to go out on a date with you, would you have gone?" After all, once he was un-grounded—if ever—maybe there was the possibility of getting a real date with Jenny.

"No."

Joey tried to accept that. "Because I'm seventeen?"

"Because I don't date," she stated in a flat voice. "I haven't dated in a long time. I don't let anyone that close."

Just shut up, Joey advised himself. *You're ahead of the game. Just shut up and be glad you're not alone right now when it seems like the world is falling apart.*

But, of course, he couldn't. Smart and lucky just weren't in the cards for him tonight. "Why don't you date?" he asked.

"Look," Jenny said, "that's something I don't want to talk about. I—"

When she screamed and leaped at him, Joey figured he had set her off again and he was about to have his head beaten in. Then lights of an approaching vehicle flashed against the window to his left. Turning from Jenny, wanting to protect his face, he caught sight of the huge camo-colored Suburban coming straight at him.

His scream got lost in the screech of tearing metal, his head slammed into the window, and his vision blacked out.

❋   ❋   ❋

Turkey
37 Klicks South of Sanliurfa
Local Time 0819 Hours

The earth moved.

Lying under the RSOV, Goose felt the ground quiver and roll from the massive explosions of the 20mm cannon rounds blasting craters into the ridgeline. For a moment, all sound went away as he temporarily turned deaf. Then he heard the drumming rain of rocks and dirt clods against the RSOV.

"You okay, Sarge?"

Glancing up, Goose saw Bill Townsend crowded in under the fighting vehicle beside him. "Yeah. Anybody hit?"

"Not yet." Bill grimaced as he shifted his wounded leg. "But they've got us in a tight spot."

Goose checked the wounded man and saw Chaplain O'Dell pressing his fingers against Digby's throat.

O'Dell looked up. Blood seeped from scratches on his face. "Thank You, God—this boy's still with us."

And if we could get a medical team in to him, Goose thought, *he might actually have a chance.* He crawled under the RSOV, turning around so he could survey the battlefield again. Switching to the main tactical channel, he heard the lieutenants and sergeants ordering their men to hold their positions, to wait out the attack as much as they could.

Clicking back to the command frequency attributed to him, Goose said, "Base, this is Phoenix Leader. Do you copy?"

"Base copies, Leader," Remington answered.

"We're taking a beating up here," Goose said. "I'm looking for good news."

"Good news is on its way, Leader," Remington replied. "Let me introduce you to Blue Falcon Leader. He's heading up a contingent of Marine Harriers that have been running nap-of-the-earth. The Syrians don't know these guys are even close."

Goose grinned grimly and took out his binoculars. "Glad to have you, Blue Leader."

"Pleasure is ours, Phoenix. Gonna be serving up a little dish I like to call extreme prejudice on those three Syrian flyboys that have dared invade your company's airspace."

The Marine pilot's casual confidence was infectious. Goose felt a little better about the situation the Rangers were in. He scanned the border with the binoculars. The three Syrian jets strafed the area again. In his mind, he was already working on plans to shore up the defense and hold the line once the Syrian air strikes were removed and the wing support provided by USS *Wasp* and the rest of the 26th MEU(SOC) arrived.

"Phoenix, this is Blue Falcon Leader."

"Go, Falcon," Goose replied.

"We have those rascally rodents in view and have carefully identified them as definite hostiles. We are preparing to engage."

"Good luck, Falcon, and Godspeed." Goose put his binoculars away and glanced up into the sky. He figured he must have seen the Harriers at about the same time the MiG pilots did.

Pound for pound, minute for minute in the air, the Harriers were some of the deadliest military birds of prey in close air support maneuvers. Navy fighter pilots didn't care for the smaller and slower warbirds, but Marine pilots knew how to eke every plus out of their chosen craft.

Powered by Pegasus-vectored thrust engines manufactured by Rolls Royce, the jets measured forty-six feet, four inches long. Their swoop-winged design made them immediately recognizable to anyone who knew aircraft. The vectored thrust could be turned to ninety degrees, giving the Harrier the startling ability to lift off straight up, then launch forward. The VTOL, or vertical take off and landing, craft handled much better in short takeoff and vertical landing (STOVL) mode. The rolling takeoff made possible by short jump ramps aboard short aircraft carriers enabled the jets to take to the air like their name-sake, a deadly British Isles marsh hawk.

The MiG pilots tried to turn tail and beat a hasty retreat back across the border. Mercilessly, the Harriers swooped up, rising above the hard deck with thunderous roars. AIM-9 Sidewinders , air-to-air missiles designed for taking out other aircraft, launched from the Harriers.

With unerring accuracy, the Sidewinders locked on to the super-heated jet engines of the Syrian aircraft. Two exploded only a heart-beat apart, turning into a roiling mass of orange and black flames that elongated into ovals of destruction .

The third Syrian pilot heeled over hard to starboard, trying desper-ately to evade the Sidewinder rapidly closing the distance. A second later, the air-to-air missile slammed into the MiG and ripped the fighter aircraft to shreds. Flaming debris pinwheeled from the sky, plummeting to the ground on the Syrian side of the border and disap-pearing into the smoky haze that drifted across the battlefield.

"Phoenix Leader, this is Blue Falcon."

"Go, Falcon, you have Phoenix," Goose responded. "That was quite a morale booster you delivered there, Falcon."

"Our pleasure, Phoenix. We've heard you men have been hard up against it. We're spearheading a bunch of leathernecks that are ready to get their land legs back if you want to invite them to the ball."

"Affirmative, Falcon. I'm looking forward to meeting those men."

"Set up for the meet and greet, Phoenix. You should have them in your view to the west-southwest. Blue Falcon has your point."

"Thank you, Falcon." Goose crawled out from under the RSOV. A gaping hole in his left pants leg showed deep, bloody scratches in the bruised flesh beneath. When he moved the knee, he felt twinges of pain, but they weren't as bad or as deep as the aches in his strained shoulder. He didn't believe either injury would require any kind of hospital treatment. If he had a couple hours of rest, he was certain he would be fine.

But he was also certain that a couple hours of rest wasn't going to be possible for a long time. Thankfully, the artillery barrage launched by the Syrians slowed. Maybe those crews were preparing for an as-sault by the Harriers.

"Phoenix Leader," Remington called over the headset, "can you confirm visual on the arriving relief teams? *Wasp* reads them five by five on the sat-scan."

Goose scanned the sky, pulling his M-4A1 back into his arms, where the assault rifle felt most natural. "I'm looking, Base."

Behind him, the Harriers opened fire across the border. "Phoenix, this is Blue Falcon Leader."

"Go, Falcon," Goose said.

"You've got a hostile unit moving on your twenty, Phoenix. We haven't confirmed the numbers yet, but you've got rolling stock and cav as well as groundpounders coming under cover of all the haze. We're going to discourage them as much as possible, but we're not going to be able to stop them all."

"Affirmative," Goose replied. He clicked back into the general communications channel. "Bravo Platoon. Echo Platoon."

"Go, Phoenix Leader. You've got Bravo Leader." Bravo Leader was Lieutenant Matthew York, a not-quite-thirty graduate of OCS after a hitch in college and ROTC. He was still a little green to command after only brief combat exposure, but he was a good soldier.

"Phoenix, this is Echo Platoon Two." Riley Bernhardt's voice was grim and steady. Like Goose, he'd been in since high school and worked his way up to three stripes, second-in-command of Echo.

"Echo Two," Goose said, "where is One?"

"One went down with the AA gun, Phoenix," Bernhardt said. "I couldn't stop him."

Lieutenant Hector Dawson had been commander of Echo. Like York, Dawson had come up through OCS. But Dawson had turned out ambitious like a lot of young officers, certain his commanding skills and station in life had blessed him with luck and a certain amount of John Wayne movie hero invulnerability. A sergeant working with a new lieutenant, as Bernhardt had been, had his work cut out for him. Goose had been in that position, too, and had lost a young lieutenant in East Africa.

"All right, Two," Goose said, knowing Remington was listening in and would hear everything he was saying, "you're taking a field promotion and moving to command of Echo. Understood?"

"Affirmative, Phoenix."

Goose knew the promotion would have a positive effect on Echo rifle company. Professional soldiers, even raw recruits, often valued a sergeant's guidance more than an officer's. A sergeant lived in the same air they did, wore the same dirt, and shared the same blood. Officers had to go a long way to prove that to the men they led, and most didn't bother because they were busy trying to earn their next posting and battle their way up the military ladder of success.

"Bravo, Echo," Goose said, "coordinate your efforts with the

Turkish military. I want a pincer set up to close off the access route the Syrians are using for their advance."

"Affirmative, Phoenix," Bernhardt agreed.

"Understood, Phoenix," York answered.

According to the information Goose had gotten from the lieutenants and sergeants in the field, those two rifle companies were more intact than Alpha or Charlie companies. He turned and found Bill at his side, stubbornly limping along to keep up.

"You should stay put before you tear that wound loose," Goose said.

"I lay up, a lot of good Rangers are going to get killed. As long as I can stand, I can help."

Goose looked at his friend, unable to stop thinking that none of them were going to be able to stand much longer if the reinforcements didn't arrive soon.

"It's gonna be all right, Sarge," Bill said. "We're on the side of the angels."

"I wish I had your confidence, Bill."

Bill shook his head. "It's not confidence, Sarge." He had to speak in a loud voice to carry over the sudden onslaught of 25mm cannonfire from the Harriers' GAU-12 fuselage guns. The General Electric–made weapon sported a five-barrel rotary design that was nothing but lethal on the battlefield. Carrying three hundred rounds in the magazine pod slung under the fighter jet's fuselage, a trained pilot could blast a swath of destruction in seconds. The advancing Syrian troops were in the process of seeing that firsthand. "I keep telling you, it's belief."

But it was hard to believe God cared about Rangers today. As soon as he had the thought, though, a wave of guilt rocketed through Goose. He shoved the feeling from his mind, clearing his focus as he scanned the skies.

"Phoenix Leader," Remington called.

Bill threw out an arm. "There! There they are!"

Shading his eyes, still nearly choking on dust that somehow made it through the drying kerchief across his lower face, Goose spotted the specks in the sky. Six wasp-shaped AH-1W Whiskey Cobra helicopter gunships led the arriving aircraft.

"Base," Goose called over the headset, "Phoenix has confirmation of *Wasp*'s wing. Pass on our appreciation to *Wasp*'s captain."

"Affirmative, Phoenix," Remington responded. Despite his attempt to have no change of tone in his voice, Goose still heard the relief in his friend's words. "Get those Marines down in a safe place and let's sort this out. Not one inch of that border is going to be given up on my watch."

"Understood, sir. We're going to take care of it for you." Goose stood under the advancing line of Cobra attack helicopters. The Marine aircraft were similar to the AH-64A Apache gunships Goose was more familiar with. Their shadows hugged the ground and flashed over him. The sound of their passing hit him a short time later.

Once the Whiskey Cobras whipped over the ridgeline Goose had used as his observation post, the Harriers pulled away. Evidently, the two teams communicated on their own wavelength.

Besides the 20mm autocannon mounted under the nose, the Whiskey Cobras were also decked out with two LAU-68 rocket pods on the inside pylons that were flanked by two Hellfire antitank missiles and four antipersonnel bombs. The Whiskey Cobras, guided by instrumentation, sped into the cloud of smoke and dust that nearly obscured the battlefield.

A moment later, the rocket pods spat flames and carnage, ripping into the landscape and the Syrian army troops. The Hellfire missiles struck a staggered line of tanks, fast-attack vehicles, and armored personnel carriers. Goose's hopes lifted more as he saw the mass of destruction the Marine pilots left in their wake. Despite the differences in the branches of service, Goose respected the other soldiers and their equipment. After today, he felt certain the Syrians would as well.

Bravo and Echo rifle companies kept moving to secure the border along the craters and wrecked vehicles.

Turning, Goose sprinted back toward the LZ he had marked off for the team. The landing zone was on the flattest terrain available, but the smoke and dust hanging in the air lowered ground zero visibility drastically.

"Phoenix Leader," an unfamiliar voice called over the headset. "This is Excaliber Leader. We are at your twenty but can't find the LZ. Repeat, we do not see the LZ."

"Affirmative, Excaliber. Phoenix has you in sight. We're rolling out the red carpet." Goose switched over to the frequency his team was using. "All right, mark it off. Pop smoke."

In response, preset smoke grenades detonated electronically, marking off a trapezoid-shaped LZ that Phoenix team had verified as being clear of large boulders, broken ridges, or other landing hazards.

"Excaliber," Goose called, "do you have the target LZ in sight now?"

A heartbeat passed.

"Affirmative, Phoenix. Excaliber has your LZ in sight. We'll rendezvous at your twenty."

"Understood, Excaliber. I'll be the Ranger with the big grin on his face." Goose ran, heading for the LZ.

"Incoming!" Hardin yelled.

Instinctively, Goose went to ground. He held on to the M-4A1 with one hand and grabbed his helmet's chin strap with the other. His face skidded across the hard-packed ground, losing hide as well as the kerchief masking his lower face. He breathed in and choked on the dust an instant before the artillery rounds collided with the terrain.

The radio communications crackled and spat through Goose's headset. Making sense of the garbled lines was difficult.

"Where is that artillery crew?"

"Don't know, Blue Falcon Leader. We're searching."

"Find them." The Marine pilot cursed. "Those men and those transport helos are going to get blown to bits."

"I'm hit! I'm hit!"

More artillery shells continued to land, chewing into the turf. Craters opened up in the LZ. One of the CH-46E helicopters took a direct hit while the group held back rather than charging into the LZ the Syrians had targeted.

Peering up with his arm shielding his face, feeling the sting of the skinned cheek, Goose saw the helo sag drunkenly. Orange and black flames whooshed from the cargo door, blowing the group of Marines from the cargo space like flaming puppets. Their arms and legs pinwheeled as they fell at least seventy feet. There would be few—if any—survivors.

The CH-46E was distinctive because of the twin rotors, one at either end of the fat-bodied aircraft. The model was primarily a cargo helicopter, giving it the CH designation, but could be used as a troop carrier. Originally, the CH-46 had been built to carry twenty soldiers, but increased armor and structural upgrades had cut that number to between eight and twelve men.

"Phoenix Leader," Bernhardt called.

Goose barely heard the man over the garbled dialogue coming through the headset. "Go, Echo. You have Phoenix."

"We've got the artillery company in sight, Goose."

"Understood. Can you shut them down?"

Battling the indefatigable pull of gravity, the damaged CH-46 slid toward the merciless ground. An instant later, the rotors chopped into the hard earth and shattered on contact. Shards of composite metal sliced through the air.

"It's no-man's-land out there, Phoenix," Bernhardt replied. "Our air support has us cut off."

"Blue Falcon Leader," Goose called. "Can you see those Rangers?"

"Negative, Phoenix," the Marine pilot replied. "It's duck soup down there. We've stayed true to our line of demarcation."

Goose thought furiously as the fierce shelling continued virtually unabated. If the Harrier pilots had been able to see through the smoke and dust to see Echo Company, they could have targeted the enemy artillery. "Echo, can you put a smoke round near the artillery?"

"That's pushing two hundred meters, Phoenix."

"Understood," Goose replied. The M-203 grenade launcher's accuracy was only good out to a hundred and fifty yards. "Put a round out there."

"Will do, Phoenix."

"Blue Falcon Leader, did you copy?" Goose asked.

"Affirmative, Phoenix. Blue Falcon will be watching for smoke."

"Your target will be fifty yards south of the smoke," Bernhardt said. "Mark—*now!*"

Turning, Goose peered back across the border. A second later, a plume of violet smoke shot up from the ground, coloring the dust and smoke like ink from a startled squid.

"Echo, Blue Falcon Leader marks your target designation and I have a verified lock," the Marine pilot said. Target lock required laser spotting from another source. Goose guessed that one of the other Harriers or the Whiskey Cobras had pinpointed the target. "Pull your team back and take cover. Gonna be a big blast over in that twenty."

The Harrier heeled over in the air above Goose's head, splintering sunlight for a moment, then diving back toward the battlefield. The pilot kept his deadly craft low, charging into the teeth of the artillery fire. Then a pillar of fire launched up from the ground whirling orange flames and black smoke from the Hellfire missile's double detonation.

The artillery fire stopped immediately.

"Way to fire, Blue Falcon Leader!" Bernhardt called.

"Phoenix, Excaliber is coming in."

"Come ahead, Excaliber. We're clean and green as it's going to get." Goose pushed himself to his feet, feeling the weakness in his knee and shoulder.

"Affirmative. We've got troops here that are ready to rock and roll."

"Goose! Goose!"

Bill Townsend's voice rolled out of the smoke and dust to Goose's right.

"It's Dockery, Goose," Bill said. Under the dust and blood, his face was ashen. "He's hit."

Goose followed Bill as the thunder of the arriving CH-46Es filled the air overhead again. The pilots juked their helos around, bringing them down in a compact spread. Then the dust and smoke cleared in front of Goose. Seeing Dockery nearly took Goose's breath away.

Corporal Steve Dockery had eight years in as a Ranger and had seen some of the worst that the terrorist campaigns had to offer. He was a good man, a good soldier.

Now Dockery sat on his knees in a mockery of obeisance. A two-inch-wide, six-foot-long shard of the downed helicopter's shattered rotors impaled him, sticking through his back and nailing him to the ground in a crouching position. His assault rifle lay beside him. Blood colored the kerchief over his lower face. His hands gripped the piece of steel that jutted from his chest and into the earth between his knees. Crimson ran down his arms, darkening the sleeves of his BDUs.

The man tried to speak. His mouth came open, but only blood poured out.

Goose didn't know why the soldier wasn't already dead, but over the years he had seen men cling tenaciously to life because they were afraid there wasn't anything afterward. His eyes made contact with Dockery's.

Dockery's mouth moved again, pleading.

Bill knelt beside the wounded man and took one of Dockery's hands in his. "We're gonna be okay, buddy," Bill said, his voice unnaturally calm. "We're gonna be okay. Just look up in the sky. Look at those helos coming in to us. We got help now. We'll get you out of here."

Goose shouldered his rifle and dropped to one knee. He opened his medkit and took out an ampoule. Ripping the plastic away with his teeth, he stabbed the needle into a vein in Dockery's arm and hit the plunger. He hoped the anesthetic was enough to knock the man out, but at the same time he felt bad that Dockery might not even be conscious the last few minutes of his life.

Bill took out gauze and tried to stem the flow of blood around the wounds in the Ranger's back and chest. "Sarge. Goose. I need help. Please."

"Excaliber, this is Phoenix," Goose called, holding a bloody and shaking hand to his mouthpiece. "Are you prepared to take on wounded?"

"Affirmative, Phoenix. Excaliber is ready, willing, and able to transport wounded back to *Wasp*. The cap'n has the ship's hospital standing by if we can't make use of local resources in Sanliurfa."

Not feeling in the least relieved, knowing that a great number of good men were going to be dead very soon and some were already dead, Goose looked back at Dockery. The Ranger's eyes had glazed, but his breath still pulled at the kerchief covering his mouth. He was conscious, but barely so.

Goose took some of the gauze Bill handed him. He took a deep breath and tried to steady his hands as he worked to staunch the bleeding. The shadows of the descending helicopters filtered through the swirling smoke and dust haze to cover them.

"The shrapnel missed his heart and both lungs," Bill said. "At least, I think it missed both—"

When his friend's words cut off abruptly, Goose looked up from Dockery's back. Bill wasn't on the other side of the wounded man. All that remained was a set of crumpled of BDUs, the LCE, the assault rifle, and gear.

Alarm jarred through Goose. He'd only taken his eyes off Bill for an instant. There was no way Bill had time to get out of his clothes and then—then—then *what?* Take off across Turkey?

The superstitious paranoia that Goose had grown up with as a child, part of that feeling stemming from stories of the Old Testament and part of it from all the tall tales of ghosts and monsters that lived in the Okefenokee Swamp around Waycross, Georgia, raised goose bumps across the back of his neck. He fisted the pistol grip of the M-4A1 and glanced around.

"Bill?"

"He . . . vanished," Dockery croaked.

Goose glanced at the wounded man, noting the pinprick-sized pupils, symptoms of the drugs in his system.

"'S'truth, Sargh. Saw 'im . . . disappear."

A dozen questions filled Goose's mind. Before he had a chance to ask any of them, metal screamed overhead. He glanced up, spotting the black silhouettes of the helicopters through the dusk and smoke haze framed against the sun and the blue sky. Tears ran down his cheeks, brought on by the stabbing brightness of the sun.

But then he saw at least half of the CH-46Es slide out of control across the sky. They collided with other helicopters, shredding rotors and sending deadly shrapnel through each other and the vulnerable troops inside.

Then the troop transport ships rained from the sky like dying flies, breaking open and scattering troops and gear across the hardpan. In a handful of seconds, the relief effort sent by USS *Wasp* had become a broken necklace of casualties spread across the battlefield.

※   ※   ※

United States of America
Fort Benning, Georgia
Local Time 1:20 A.M.

Megan threw her upper body out across the roof's edge. She'd moved before she'd thought about the action, and she knew that was the only thing that had saved Gerry Fletcher. She had never moved so quickly in her life. By some miracle, she managed to grab the boy's left wrist and stop his plummet down the side of the building to the hard ground four stories below.

Men cursed in the parking lot below, in stunned amazement as well as fear. Megan recognized those emotions because she felt them within herself as well. She couldn't believe she'd caught the falling boy.

At the same time, she knew she wasn't going to be able to keep Gerry from falling. She didn't have the mass or the strength. Her arm felt torn from the socket.

The spotlights from the vehicles trained on her and Gerry, pinning her shadow and the boy's against the side of the building in hard-edged relief. The MPs broke loose first, sprinting for the fire escape.

"Somebody get up there!" Boyd Fletcher squalled. "She's going to get that boy killed!"

Megan tried to pull Gerry up but couldn't. She lacked the upper-body muscle it would take to pull the boy up. At the same time she wondered who had brought Boyd Fletcher out into the parking lot. If the man hadn't startled Gerry—

But he did, she told herself. *You're dealing with that now. No! God, we're dealing with this! You and me! You helped put Gerry out here on this roof tonight, and You're going to help me get him back down!*

Metal rang as the MPs pounded up the stairs. "Hold on, ma'am!" one of them called. "Just hold on!"

I am! Megan thought. *God help me, I am! God, please help me!*

Megan could see an explosion of fear go off inside Gerry as he dangled above the waiting ground. Whatever he'd thought when he stepped off the roof, he'd clearly changed his mind now. He kicked and whipped his other arm up to grab hold of her forearm.

"Pull me up, Mrs. Gander!" the boy pleaded. "Pull me up! I don't want to fall! Please don't let me fall!"

At least we're on the same page now, Megan thought. She pulled at her arm. Abruptly, she slid across the roof's edge. Her shirt buttons rasped against the rough surface. *No! God, no!*

She kicked her legs back and barely managed to stop herself from continuing to skid over the edge. From the sound of their steps on the metal treads, the MPs had reached the second landing now. She breathed as deeply as she could, forcing herself to be calm.

"Somebody stop her!" Boyd Fletcher yelled. "She's going to get my son killed!"

My son. Megan heard the words, but she didn't believe it. Boyd Fletcher hadn't ever called Gerry by his name in her hearing before. He'd referred to the boy as a possession; the same as saying "my car."

Pain burned through her arm. She focused on Gerry. His eyes were wide with panic. His fingernails clawed into her arm, leaving bloody furrows. Her own fear allowed her to ignore the burning pain of the deep scratches, as if it were someone else's flesh that was getting torn.

"Mrs. Gander! Mrs. Gander! Please help me!"

"I am, Gerry. I am." Megan tried to keep the tears from her eyes but she couldn't. She was going to drop him. She'd never be able to hold him till help arrived. He seemed to get heavier with each passing second, a weight like a blacksmith's anvil kicking and yelling at the end of her arm.

"Stop her!" Boyd Fletcher yelled. "She's going to kill him! She's crazy!" He struggled, trying to break away from the two MPs who had stayed with him, even though his hands were cuffed behind his back. One of the MPs slapped his stick at the backs of Fletcher's legs, knocking the man into a crumpled kneeling position. He leaned down, pinning Fletcher with one hand against the small of his back.

Fletcher screamed curses.

"Calm down, Private," one of the MPs ordered.

To Megan the voices, even Fletcher's yells, seemed like they came from a million miles away.

"Mrs. Gander!" Gerry hung on to her desperately.

Megan slid another couple inches, getting dangerously close to losing her scant purchase at the roof's edge. "God," she shouted, "please help me! Please help me with this!"

But there was no answer.

There had never been an answer when she had asked for help. Sometimes, most of the time, she had to admit, the situations she prayed over had gotten better. Bill told her that God acted in the world, gave signs that built faith if people trusted enough to look for them. Even in the Old Testament, when God had spoken to His prophets on a regular basis, those ancient men had struggled more to disbelieve and discount than to accept. Bill had suggested that was why idolatry had sprung up, that man had a self-defeating need to reach out to things that didn't exist rather than admit God's love was there for them.

Idols couldn't hold a person accountable for his or her actions. A person couldn't break faith with an idol. An idol was a fabrication, a thing a person chose to believe in because she could exercise some control over the idol by choosing to worship it or not worship it. Blame could be placed on an idol, payoffs withheld from that idol, a new idol found.

But what about God's love? Megan asked herself frantically as she slid another inch. *Where is His hand in this? I'm going to lose this boy, God! I'm not strong enough to hold him! Please! You can see this! You have to be able to see this! Help me!*

"Mrs. Gander!" Gerry slipped another inch.

Megan's grip on the boy's hand loosened. Her hand grew numb and ached miserably from her sustained effort. Goose could have pulled the boy back up. She felt certain of that. Goose was strong, stable. He could handle anything the world threw at him and keep going. She had seen that.

Gerry slipped again, and Megan slid forward across the roof's edge. She knew that if she didn't release him his weight was going to drag her into a free fall with him. Part of her—the animal part that lived in the lowest recesses of her brain, still afraid of fire and storms and any kind of change—screamed at her to let go. No one could blame her for saving herself. She had already risked her life. Saving Gerry Fletcher was impossible—*Nothing is impossible with God's help*—it would have been better if she had missed him—*Why didn't I miss him?*

Gerry's hand slipped from her forearm, no longer able to hang on, his clasp sliding from her arm to her hand.

"Mrs. Gander!"

"I've got you, Gerry. I've got you. Just hang on. Just hang on a moment longer."

The MPs were on the final landing, headed for the rooftop. They were big and strong. They could hold Gerry and make him safe. All they had to do was—

"We just have to hang on a few more seconds." Megan's arm felt like fire had invaded the joint. "Just a little longer." Tears blurred her vision and she knew she was crying. *God! Why? Why have You abandoned us?*

The blood from the scratches along her forearm threaded down her hand and onto Gerry's. The grip they shared became slick and uncertain.

"I'm falling!" Gerry screamed. "I'm falling!"

"No," Megan said, stifling the urge she had to scream as well. "I've got you, Gerry. I've got you." She felt the rooftop shake under her as the MPs raced toward them. "Just don't let go. Don't let go, Gerry."

Thin as a whisper, silent as snow, gone in the blink of an eye, Gerry's hand slipped through hers.

"No!" Megan screamed as she felt his fingers glide through the blood that coated her hand.

Gerry wailed in terror. And he fell, plummeting toward the unyielding concrete in front of the apartment building.

17

United States of America
Fort Benning, Georgia
Local Time 1:21 A.M.

Time slowed as Megan watched Gerry Fletcher fall. Time slowed but never stopped, moving inexorably on in horrifying tiny ticks rather than in a brain-numbing rush.

Gerry dropped like a rock, tumbling over backward, his arms stretched out and reaching helplessly for a handhold, his legs bicycling. A scream stretched the boy's mouth wide, but Megan couldn't hear it over her own yell of anguish. She'd had him . . . and she'd lost him.

Why, God? Why did You let both of us come up on this roof tonight? If everything happens for a reason, if I'm supposed to believe that, what good was it for Gerry to be up here? Why did I have to be up here? The last bit was selfish. She knew that and regretted the thought in the same moment she had it.

Gerry tumbled, turning to face away from her.

Tears blurred Megan's vision. She blinked them away unconsciously, and when she opened her eyes again, she saw Gerry hit the ground. At least, she thought the boy had hit the ground. But looking down now, she knew that something was wrong.

The pile of clothes at the bottom of the building didn't look big enough to be a boy. They only looked big enough to be—to be a pile of clothes.

That's denial, Megan told herself, knowing that had to be true because nothing else made sense. *My mind is shutting out the real sight of Gerry down there, shutting out the true image of blood and broken pavement. He fell. He hit. O God, what have I done? Why did You forsake us? He was just a baby.*

The two MPs on the rooftop grabbed Megan's legs. She hadn't even noticed she'd still been falling, skidding slowly but surely over the side of the roof. Gerry's certain death had paralyzed even the lizard's instinct for survival in the back of her brain.

"Mrs. Gander," one of the MPs said. "Mrs. Gander, relax. We've got you. It's over."

Stubbornly, Megan clung to the roof's edge. One of the MPs guarding Boyd Fletcher ran toward the impact area. *Impact area? Is that what you call it?* She didn't know how she could be so callous. The MP reached the pile of clothes and stared down. His head swiveled around, looking for something.

"Where is he?" Boyd Fletcher yelled. "Where is Gerry? I saw him up there. She hid him. Check the rooftop. He can't have gone far." He struggled to get to his feet, but the MP holding him down never moved, grinding him down on his face.

In the end, Megan couldn't hold on to the roof's edge. The MPs proved too strong. They talked softly to her, like she was a child or a trauma victim. Shaking and shivering, not certain that she was strong enough to walk on her own two feet, Megan allowed the men to hold her from either side.

"Mrs. Gander."

Megan tracked the voice, turning to the man on the right when she wanted to go look over the roof's edge again. *It's only clothes. Only clothes.* And that made no sense at all.

"Yes?" Her voice came out as a croak.

"Are you all right, ma'am?"

She tried to speak, found she couldn't, then tried again. "I think so."

"Do you feel strong enough to take the stairs, ma'am? If not, we can probably get a rescue unit to come take you off the roof. It would be a lot easier if you could make it under your own steam." The MP was in his fifties, a black man gone gray at the temples, with a seamed face that offered strength and support.

Megan nodded.

"I'm sorry, ma'am, but I need you to audibly answer me. I need to know that you understand what I'm asking." The MP's grip on her arm was gentle but firm.

"Yes," Megan said. "I can walk."

"Then—when you're ready, ma'am."

Megan started forward, aiming for the fire escape.

"Have you got her, Dave?" the other, younger MP asked. "I gotta look for that kid."

"Yeah," the big MP answered. "I can make it. If not, we'll stop partway down and you can catch up, or one of the others can come up here."

Megan stopped and turned to the younger MP. "What did you say you were going to do?" She couldn't believe she stopped, but what the man had said had jarred her.

The man stared at her. "I'm gonna look for that kid, Mrs. Gander. Do you know where he got off to?"

Megan made herself breathe out. "His name is Gerry." That was important. He wasn't just some chattel of Boyd's, a possession; he wasn't just his abusive father's property.

"Yes, ma'am," the MP answered politely. "I've gotta look for Gerry."

"He fell," Megan said. *God, he slipped right through my fingers. How could You allow something like that to happen?* "He's down there on the pavement."

"No, ma'am," the young MP insisted. "All that's down there are his clothes."

Megan stared at the man. "His clothes?"

"Yes, ma'am." The MP nodded and shined his flashlight around the rooftop. Nothing came into view. "Can you tell me where the kid—where Gerry is, Mrs. Gander? Things will probably go easier if we can bring him in."

"We won't let his father at him," Dave, the older MP, promised. He obviously mistook Megan's shocked silence as trepidation. "Private Fletcher is going to be in lockdown tonight. He won't touch that boy."

The young MP grimaced and glanced at his partner. "Is there another way down off of this roof?"

Dave shook his head. "This is it."

"The kid couldn't have flown down from the roof, Dave. He's either up here or he's down there."

"Pete." The older MP licked his lips. "Maybe the boy was never up here."

"I saw him," Pete said. "I *saw* him." He glanced at the roof's edge, trailing the flashlight beam along it. "And I swear, Dave, I swear I saw that kid fall from the building."

"If you did, he'd be down there," Dave said. "All that hit the ground was clothes. You heard Mitchell and Rick the same as I did. You only saw clothes hit the ground. Nothing else."

"Then we're looking for a naked kid?"

"Maybe he was never up here. Maybe Mrs. Gander only had his clothes."

Megan couldn't believe what she was hearing. Why would anyone think she'd only been up on the building with clothing? Why did they think only clothing had hit the ground?

"That sounds kind of weird, don't you think?" Pete asked.

Dave shrugged. "You look. I'll get Mrs. Gander to the ground, then I'll come back up and help you look some more."

"You saw the kid, didn't you, Dave?" Pete looked desperate. "You saw him up on this rooftop, didn't you?"

Dave let out a long breath and Megan saw the fear in the man's eyes. "It was dark," the older MP said. "I don't know what I saw."

Dazed, not comprehending what was going on, Megan allowed herself to be led away. She descended the metal stairs mechanically, barely noticing the bright light of the camcorder trained on her from one of the building's windows.

"Get that camera out of here," Dave growled.

Reluctantly, the young soldier filling the third-floor window did as he was ordered. He was shirtless, and his dog tags gleamed in the reflected illumination. The camcorder light died. "Did you see that boy disappear, Sarge?" the young soldier asked.

"Be quiet, soldier," the MP snapped. "You look like you've been drinking tonight. You sure don't want someone prowling around inside your apartment if you've got a shift in the morning. You'd get a referral in no time flat."

The guy stood his ground but didn't say anything.

As she descended the stairs, Megan kept staring at the pile of clothing that Gerry Fletcher had been wearing only moments ago. She tried to comprehend what she was seeing, trying to make some sense of it. How could there only be a few clothes left from a young boy that had fallen from a four-story rooftop?

But when she reached the ground level, those clothes were all that was left of Gerry Fletcher. The memory of the boy's screams as he fell haunted Megan.

"What did you do with my son?" Boyd Fletcher yelled. He arched his back and turned to look at the man holding him down. "Make her tell you. Make her tell you what she's done with my son. That's your job."

"I didn't do anything with him," Megan said, staring at the clothing. She remembered the garments from when she'd first seen them in the hospital, then again when Gerry had slipped from her grip and twisted through the intervening distance. God help her, she thought that was one memory she'd never forget.

"She's lying!" Boyd Fletcher screamed. "You all know my son was up there. He's still up there. Find him!"

In a daze, Megan approached the clothing. She knelt and touched the sweatpants with the tattered knee, the sweatshirt, the smudged socks and sneakers. Silver gleamed in the combined lights of the MPs and the curious onlookers that had gathered from the nearby apartments. She moved the socks and shoes, revealing the silver necklace Gerry's mother had gotten him last year. Almost hypnotized, she lifted the necklace in her fingers. The small sterling silver cross hanging from the necklace spun and caught the light.

"Get her away from those clothes!" Boyd Fletcher bellowed. "Get her away from them now! They aren't hers! She has no business with them!"

On her knees, Megan stared at the cross. She remembered how proud Gerry had been of his necklace. He wouldn't have left it behind. She wrapped her hand around the cross, thinking that she could still feel the warmth of the boy's body in it even at the same time knowing that had to be impossible.

Gerry wouldn't have left the necklace. He wouldn't have left his clothes. *He didn't leave. He fell.* The words thundered through Megan's mind, overriding even Boyd Fletcher's loud curses and demands that someone find his son.

"Mrs. Gander."

Megan was suddenly aware of the big MP at her side. His hand was once more on her arm. This time his grip wasn't just supportive; it constrained her as well, letting her know she wasn't leaving unless he agreed to it.

"Mrs. Gander," the MP said, "I'm afraid you're going to have to come with me."

"I can't." Megan rose, feeling the MP's hand tighten around her arm. *He's afraid I'm going to try to run.* The realization flooded through her like cold water, triggering an instinctive impulse to do precisely that.

"Ma'am," the MP said with polite determination. "There are going to be a lot of questions."

"I can't," Megan said. "I promised my son I'd come for him."

"Where's your son?"

"At the child-care facility."

"Then he'll be fine," the MP said.

"I told him I'd be there. I told him I'd be there when he woke up." Unexpectedly, new tears and a fresh wave of panic ripped through Megan. She felt sick and her knees buckled. If the MP hadn't been holding on to her arm, she would have fallen.

"Come with me, Mrs. Gander," the MP suggested. "I'm sure we can sort this out in a little while."

"Cuff her," Boyd Fletcher snarled. He called Megan several unkind words, struggling against the man who held him and against the handcuffs that held him. "Cuff her. She did something with my son. Find out what she did with him."

Megan opened her palm and gazed at the tiny silver cross. She prayed. She prayed harder than she had prayed in years. Without another word, the big MP guided her toward the security Jeep. The flashing lights whirled through Megan's vision. She felt like she was in a terrible nightmare and she couldn't get free.

❁ ❁ ❁

The Mediterranean Sea
USS *Wasp*
Local Time 0821 Hours

Only minutes after the last of the aircraft had lifted from *Wasp*'s deck, Delroy Harte had returned to his private quarters to watch the unfolding development of the engagement along the Turkish-Syrian border. The combat information center had been reduced to using long-range satellite images because the carefully orchestrated Syrian attacks had taken out the primary communications lines with the first wave of SCUDs. Glitter City, with all its media personalities and support crews, had become a casualty less than three minutes after that.

Captain Falkirk and his intelligence teams had been reduced to tapping into the video feeds being pumped out of Glitter City. Those hadn't lasted long either. With the second wave of SCUDs, the feeds from Glitter City had been lost as well.

Delroy had barely switched on the television in his private quarters and started flipping through the news channels before those services were lost, too. He had sat quietly for several minutes, trying to take solace in the growl and thunder that was *Wasp* twenty-four hours a day, seven days a week. The ship had been the major portion of his world for years.

Sailors green to *Wasp* hated the constant barrage of noise. Old hands took comfort in the sounds, knowing them all individually.

Within minutes, though, Delroy had known he couldn't stay in his quarters. He had taken his portable television set and returned to the medical department to try and attack the letter once more. His prayers to God weren't going very well either. Thinking about the young warriors in the field dying so far from home reminded the chaplain too much of Terrence.

The loss of his son was never far from Delroy's mind, nor was the fact that the loss and his own inability to deal with it had shattered his marriage after twenty-seven years. Actually, he was still married. He had never filed for divorce, and Glenda had never pressed him for one. He had simply stopped going home. He'd effectively cut off his ties to his family, though they still sent cards and letters.

But it was Glenda's ability to believe that their son was taken from them for a reason approved of by God's will that mocked his own belief. And yet, tattered and broken as that belief was, it was all Delroy had to cling to. He had put on a good face and made the best he could of his career and his life, but Glenda knew him as no one else ever had.

Except for my father, Delroy thought. *Josiah Harte would have known what I'm thinking at a glance.*

Glenda's own belief had shamed Delroy. And her ability to deal with his own decision to effectively end the marriage three years ago, two years after Terrence's death, had shamed him further. He still sent money home to help with the bills, but less than a year after he had stopped going home, Glenda had opened an account at the bank and put the money there. She rented the house out to make the mortgage payment and moved into a small apartment. She continued teaching and worked at Carl Bynum's produce market during the summers.

Seated again at the stainless steel table with the blank paper that was supposed to be the letter he was going to write to Dwight Mellencamp's family, Delroy stared at the television. *Wasp* had satellite hookups for television throughout the ship. The crew traveled in relative comfort.

Only moments ago, some of the news feeds in Turkey had come back on line. There had been a bit about a U.S. Army Ranger outfit that had helped evacuate Glitter City, then that feed had gone off-line when Syrian troops had arrived and started shooting. The cameraman had evidently been one of the first fatalities.

Now the television channels were full of late-breaking stories. Some of those stories centered on first-person accounts by reporters concerning the evacuation of Glitter City, the horrifying convoy back to Sanliurfa, and the attacks that had gone on within Sanliurfa. Some came directly from the border where reporters were pinned down by enemy fire just as the domestic troops, the U.N. peacekeepers, and the U.S. Army Rangers were.

Delroy glanced at the body bag that contained his dead friend. The chaplain couldn't help feeling that in a way Dwight Mellencamp was lucky he hadn't lived to see this day. It was certain that several of the Marines the chief had known and loved like sons wouldn't be coming back. By the time what was left of their people got back, *Wasp* would feel like a ghost town.

The body bag suddenly sagged, collapsing in on itself.

Goose bumps prickled across the back of Delroy's neck. His breath caught at the back of his throat. At first he thought he'd imagined the sagging, but as he looked at the body bag, he knew that he hadn't. Dwight had been a big man. There was no way he could fit in the body bag in the shape it was in now.

For a moment, Delroy was back in his grandfather's house, listening to the old man tell stories to his grandchildren that triggered fussy arguments from his wife. Grandpa Smith, on Delroy's mother's side, had been a constant joker. One night when the grandkids had been visiting, he'd explained about sitting up with the dead, and how sometimes in the old days before mortuaries embalmed the bodies and prepared them for burial, that sometimes the dead would sit up as well.

The first time Delroy had sat up with the dead with his father a few years later, he'd been frightened out of his mind, thinking the corpse of his great-uncle Darmon would sit up at any moment, maybe even come crawling out of the casket like a mummy in one of those old monster movies. His father had noticed Delroy's discomfort at once.

Reluctantly, Delroy had explained his fears. Quietly and patiently, as was his way except when frightening nonbelievers with visions of hell and eternal damnation in that roaring lion's voice of his, Josiah Harte had explained how in the old days the unprepared body would sit up. He had described in detail how the reaction was caused by rigor mortis setting in and tightening muscles due to the dead body's inability to process sugar. Sometimes, his father had said, trapped air was even expelled from the corpse's lungs, but the person was not actually alive, as uneducated and superstitious people thought.

Even though his father had been kind and understanding and informative, and even though Delroy was nearly fifty years older, he suddenly felt like that small eight-year-old boy sitting in near dark with only candles for light. He forced himself to breathe again.

Using his remote control, he muted the television and pushed up from the chair. His heart beat frantically as he made himself approach the much flatter body bag. Hand shaking, he pressed his palm against the body bag.

The bag sank beneath Delroy's hand, giving way immediately and not stopping till his palm reached the table.

"No." He didn't even recognize his own voice at first.

Quickly, struggling with all the emotions that were suddenly cascading within him, Delroy slid his hand down the length of the body bag. It was empty. At least, it was empty of a corpse. However, there *was* something inside the bag.

Before he could stop himself, Delroy reached for the zipper and tugged it down, freeing the zipper's teeth so the bag could fall open.

Empty. The realization filled the chaplain with a mind-numbing cold that the refrigerated room couldn't even begin to compete with.

With the bag open, Delroy saw the clothing lying inside. The lump he'd felt had been Dwight's favorite shoes, a pair of Birkenstocks that his wife had given him a few Christmases ago.

Stunned, his mind reeling and snatching at possible reasons for this unbelievable turn of events, Delroy left the empty body bag and crossed the room. He pulled the door open and stepped into the main hallway of the medical department.

Cary Boone, in his mid-thirties and one of the ship's best surgeons, stood in the hallway with a puzzled look on his face and a PDA in his hand. Tall and powerful with short dark hair, and right now a heavy five o'clock shadow, Boone was one of the regulars in Delroy's pickup basketball group when *Wasp* was in her homeport.

"Chaplain Harte," Boone greeted him distractedly.

"Dr. Boone," Delroy replied. Navy doctors were called "doctor" until they reached the rank of commander. "Do you know if anyone moved Chief Mellencamp's body?"

Boone looked irritated. "Why would anyone do that?"

"I don't know. But Dwight—" Delroy halted himself. "The chief's body is missing."

"I thought you were in there with him." Boone covered ground rapidly, opening hatches along the hallway and peering inside.

"I thought I was, too, but just now, when I checked the bag, the chief's body was missing."

"I'll ask around." Boone tried another door. "Have you seen Nurse Taylor?"

Jenna Taylor was a favorite among the crew and the doctors. She was a vivacious young redhead from Ohio and one of the most level-headed, kind, and considerate people that Delroy knew.

"No," Delroy answered.

"I swear that she was right here," Boone said distractedly. "I was going over these files with her, in preparation for the wounded we expect to take on from the border skirmish, and Jenna was talking to me from one of these rooms. She stepped in here to get something."

"She's been working this morning?" Delroy asked.

"Yes."

"Then maybe she'll know where the chief's body is." Despite the calm, rational exterior he held carefully in place, Delroy felt frantic. No one would take Dwight's body. There was no reason. But the body had disappeared and he had no explanation for that. He joined Boone in his search, both of them calling out Jenna's name.

A pile of scrubs lay inside the second room Delroy checked. He froze, not believing what he was seeing. "Cary." His voice was a harsh desert croak that barely freed itself from his lips.

"What?"

"Come look at this. Tell me I'm not going crazy." Slowly, Delroy squatted, hearing his knees pop and crack, because basketball hadn't been the kindest of sports to his body.

Boone joined Delroy in the open hatch. "What?" the navy doctor asked.

Delroy pointed at the blue scrubs lying on the floor inside the supply room. Right on top was a name badge with Jenna Taylor's name and rank on it.

"She left her clothes here?" Boone asked.

"The chief's clothes were still inside the body bag," Delroy said in a low voice.

"That doesn't make any sense."

"No," Delroy admitted. "It doesn't."

Running feet slapped against the steel floor. A young midshipman in scrubs rounded the corner at the end of the hallway. "Dr. Boone," he gasped.

"What is it?" Boone replied.

For an insane moment, Delroy thought the young man was going to say that the chief's body had been found, or that Jenna Taylor—as impossible as it sounded—had been caught streaking through the medical department or had even made it out onto the flight deck. Stress did strange things to people, and the coming hours and probably days of dealing with wounded troops and the battle that raged along the Turkish-Syrian border promised plenty of wear and tear on the nerves.

"They've disappeared, sir," the midshipman said.

"Who?" Boone asked.

The midshipman shook his head. "I don't know exactly, sir. Dozens. I've found piles of clothes throughout the medical department. The missing people are leaving their clothes behind. But nobody's seen them. It's like they disappeared right off the ship!"

❈   ❈   ❈

United States of America
Cheyenne Mountain Operations Center, Colorado Springs
Local Time 2321 Hours

In the last six months of his new posting in the Cheyenne Mountain Operations Center, twenty-eight-year-old U.S. Air Force Technical Sergeant James Franklin Manners had never before seen an attack as large as the one now spinning across the huge wall screen monitors. The feeds came directly from the satellites watching over the action that had broken out along the Turkish-Syrian border. The other men and women around Jim worked diligently at their assigned tasks, collating the real-time information and moving it on to the command post in Turkey.

Buried two thousand feet beneath the mountains that gave the complex its name, Cheyenne Mountain Operations Center remained the backbone of the North American Air Defense Command (NORAD). The United States and Canada had jointly maintained the command post since 1957, with subdivisions responsible for delivering warnings about aerospace dangers, missile attacks launched against North America or the United States, surveillance and protection of U.S. assets in space, and geopolitical events that could threaten the U.S. as well as troops abroad. The command center gathered, assembled, and interpreted data from numerous sources.

Jim tapped commands on his keyboard, bringing up the information from the geosynchronous satellites as well as the low-earth orbit satellites that still maintained a visual window on the aggressive combat theater that had erupted eighty-seven minutes, forty-three seconds ago. He adjusted his headset and listened to the ground communications streaming through the computer links.

"Excaliber, this is Phoenix. Are you prepared to take on wounded?" The transmission was slightly garbled by the cacophony of explosions taking place around the speaker. Despite the dire straits he'd found his group under, First Sergeant Samuel Adams Gander performed his job and reported the events as they occurred.

"Affirmative, Phoenix. Excaliber is ready, willing, and able to transport wounded back to *Wasp*. The cap'n has the ship's hospital standing by if we can't make use of local resources in Sanliurfa."

Jim studied the terrain, spotting the wing units put into the air from USS *Wasp*'s deck out in the Mediterranean. The Marine pilots kept their aircraft flying smoothly, staying close to the hard deck. Tracking the Marine wing had been Jim's primary job, and the task had been relatively simple—until now. Once the Syrian forces were engaged, tracking would become complicated. One of his main priorities was to keep the friendlies separated from the hostiles.

Jim's guts churned as he watched the aircraft moving. He tagged them again with the computer, converting the visual feeds into digital tactical information that showed on the wall screen in front of him. A Syrian MiG popped onscreen as well. Jim noted that he already had a designation for the craft but reaffirmed the tag with frantic trackball movements and a couple keystrokes. He glanced at the computer monitor on his right.

The computer monitor showed the American air forces as blue triangles. The Syrian forces were red. Any unknown aircraft, and thank God there were none of those, would be rendered in green, all of them marked with digital readouts of elevation from the hard deck. The resulting effect would be viewer friendly, like a kid's video game.

Suddenly, many of the blue triangles veered from the LZ the Rangers had set up along the ridgeline behind the border. In a heartbeat, that tightly knit group of helicopters became a tangled confusion.

Glancing back at the satellite visual, Jim watched in disbelief as highly trained Marine pilots somehow managed to crash their aircraft into each other. Only a few escaped the immediate destruction. Even so, others dropped from the sky without ever being touched.

In one split instant, the rescue effort became a catastrophe. What had once been efficient fighting machines suddenly became ripped and twisted debris. As Jim watched in stunned amazement, one of the Cobras blew up when it struck the ground. Somewhere in the areas of his mind that cataloged, identified, and reasoned out such occurrences, Jim knew that the Cobra's ordnance must have blown. Fire wreathed the battered hulk, letting him know there would be few—if any—survivors.

"What just happened?" someone demanded.

"Man, this reminds me of what happened to the Russian air force when they tried to pull off that surprise attack on Israel in January last year."

"Yeah," someone else said nervously. "But that shouldn't happen to us. We're the good guys."

Jim remembered the Russian attack and the way the Soviet aircraft had been swatted from the sky as if by an invisible hand. Footage of the failed attack still rolled on the Learning Channel and on The History Channel when Cold War programs aired.

Spinning in his chair, Jim gazed back at the observation post where the officers stood. Brigadier General Hamilton Farley stood with Canadian Brigadier General Victor Williams. General Farley was commander of the Cheyenne Mountain Command Center and General Williams served as second-in-command. Both men were stern and alert, not showing any signs of having been rousted from bed.

Jim looked for Colonel Morris Turner, the Canadian officer in charge of Charlie Crew, which was currently on duty. Colonel Turner had been standing in his customary position behind Jim, who was the newest member of the team. When he didn't spot the colonel there, Jim glanced around the room. At present time, Charlie Crew consisted of thirty-seven individuals. Even considering that someone might have stepped away from their post, an event that Jim figured was never done during an alert situation because he'd never seen that happen, losing a person in the room was next to impossible.

Then he saw the uniform lying on the floor only a few feet from his chair. Colonel Turner's name badge poked out from one of the buffed shoes.

Despite the training Charlie Crew had undergone, despite the stress that the team had faced on a number of occasions that threatened North American security, the men and women manning their posts came undone. As it turned out, several people were missing.

"It's like they got beamed out of here," Sterling Thompson said. He was a couple years Jim's junior but had such an affinity for all things cybernetic that he had been a natural candidate to post at Cheyenne Mountain. Sterling was also big into science fiction. He pushed his glasses up on his nose and looked at Jim. "There's no other explanation, man. We're two thousand feet down in solid rock, locked up tight behind doors that weigh twenty-five tons each."

"Calm down," Jim advised, pushing himself to his feet. The sat-feeds streaming in from Turkey had faltered as well, but he wasn't sure if the problem lay there or within the Cheyenne Mountain complex. "There's an explanation."

"Yeah," Sterling agreed wholeheartedly. He tapped keys on his keyboard, bringing up a view of space. "And we're going to find it out there. Man, we thought we had problems in Turkey?" He shook his head. "I think we're about to be invaded. These people missing? They're just a sampling for whoever's waiting out there." He pointed at the screen full of stars.

Jim barely handled his own rising panic. He reached down and touched Colonel Turner's uniform, trailing a finger along the edge of the name badge. It felt real, but this couldn't really be happening. He watched as Sterling flipped through the different sectors of space available to them through the satellites they had access to.

General Farley strode from the observation post and stopped near Turner's uniform. "Attention." His voice was crisp and powerful.

The command center crew obeyed immediately. There was nothing like a general's voice to bring an enlisted man up short.

"I've notified security. Whatever this matter is—" Farley glanced down at Turner's abandoned uniform—"it's being looked into by professionals. At this moment, I need all of you to be professional, to be the soldiers you were trained to be in this field, and I need that from you right this instant. Do you understand that?"

"Yes, sir!" The reply boomed from the twenty-three people left in the ranks.

"I need those information lines back up and running," Farley said. "You've got American soldiers and our allies dying over there. If we don't watch over them, give them some kind of heads-up, we're going to lose more of them." He paused. "I'm not going to stand for that on my watch. Is that understood?"

"Yes, sir!"

"Then get back to it. I want everything you can find out, and I want it yesterday."

Jim settled back in at his console. This was why there were generals, he thought. When the world got crazy, an order was still an order. But he remained uncomfortably aware of the vacated uniform lying behind him at the general's feet.

He slipped his headset back on and cued the audible stream.

"Phoenix Leader, this is Alpha Two. We've lost men, Goose." The man's voice cracked with rising hysteria. "They've disappeared! There are empty uniforms everywhere!"

Jim lifted his head and gazed across the empty seat where Donna Kirkland had once sat. She had been warm and friendly and helped him familiarize himself with the demands he faced. Only her uniform remained in the chair now. He locked eyes with Sterling. "You listening to this?"

Sterling nodded. "It's happening everywhere, Jim. It wasn't just us."

For a moment, Jim felt a little relieved that the disappearances weren't held just to the Cheyenne facility. Then, a millisecond later, he realized that the other disappearances indicated that whatever enemy they were up against could strike possibly around the globe—at the very least on the other side of the world—at the same time and with apparent impunity. How were they supposed to deal with something like that?

Even five miles back of the front line and safely entrenched—for the moment, at least—in the abandoned cinder-block building he'd selected as his field command post, Captain Cal Remington could smell the stench of war. Acrid explosive cordite and smoke gnawed at his lungs while dust particles coated the computer screens and irritated the eyes. The wind coming from the south had carried all of those things to them during the last hour and more.

But those things were logged in the back of the Ranger captain's mind. His full attention was divided between the computer monitors and the uniform sitting in the chair where a young corporal had been only moments ago.

The preliminary head count among the intelligence crews showed 20 percent of Remington's on-site teams had disappeared. One moment, those men and women had been at their stations, manning the computers and maintaining the perimeter around the building, and in the next moment they had been gone. All of them had left at once, and none of those who had been left behind had seen anything of the process that had carried those people away. They had left or been taken between heartbeats, as though everyone in the room had blinked at the same time.

Remington chafed over his inability to act on either the missing men or along the front line where his men were. He didn't like taking a hit and not being able to retaliate immediately. But the communications lines had gone down yet again, interrupting the flow of information sent from the Cheyenne Mountain intelligence people as well as the feeds from USS *Wasp*.

The com teams had promised Remington that they would be back on line in a matter of minutes, but the war along the Turkish-Syrian border drew a terrible cost with each second that passed. Men died and military strength withered in seconds. And Remington knew he was losing precious time, resources, and ground that would be hard to do without or nearly impossible to replace.

The monitors relaying the satellite feeds showed grainy pictures of current activity. Bar lines scrolled slowly through the screens, showing the actual repixelization of the digital images passed along.

"Base, this is Cerberus Leader," a voice called over the walkie-talkie headset Remington wore. The field command post's communications still worked up to three klicks away with only slight static.

Five klicks back from the front line, at a time when all the intelligence networks were on the blink, Cerberus was the perimeter security team charged with defending the command post. During the SCUD attack, a few of the missiles had landed nearby, but the cinderblock building had remained standing if somewhat battered.

Until the moment the people went missing from the unit, Remington had felt they were divinely protected, and that was a stretch for him. He believed in God, but he'd never once thought God had any interest in him or knew he'd been born.

"Go, Cerberus," Remington replied.

"You can add three more to that list of MIAs," Lieutenant Don Carmichael told him. "We found the uniforms and gear of one of the outer perimeter guard posts."

"Affirmative, Cerberus Leader," Remington replied. The information continued the trend of confirmed disappearances that had started only minutes ago. Everyone within the three-klick radius who hadn't responded had been verified missing. Remington had ordered the others into search-and-rescue teams to sweep the area and systematically check on units that had gone missing in action. "Secure whatever gear you can salvage and continue your search. Supplies are going to be hard to come by for a time."

"Understood, Base."

The walkie-talkie connection hissed sparks in Remington's ear. He strode again, seeking to neutralize some of the nervous tension that filled him. More than anything, he wanted to hear from Goose. The first sergeant was more than just a friend; Goose was Remington's third hand, the man who could see that things Remington wanted done got done, and that they got done Remington's way.

Remington stepped in behind Private First Class Foster. The private had been on the second team, a step down from the individuals the captain had worked with in the past, but Foster was good with the computer.

"Let's see the archived footage of the helos again," Remington said. "A few seconds before the impact." *We've missed something. We had to.*

"One monitor or both?" Foster asked.

"Both," Remington replied. "Post four quadrants on the screens. All in one-third speed slo-mo."

"Yes, sir." Foster tapped the keyboard. Both monitors ceased struggling with the grainy digital video they were puking over at the moment. The images became crystal clear again, going back to the kind of performance Remington desired and was accustomed to.

The captain stood behind the computer operator and opened his vision. Remington had always been good at tracking more than one thing at a time. That was one of the abilities that had helped him get into OCS and had later helped him make the jump to captain.

The images scrolled again and again, changing by flickers. Besides the ground cams that had been assigned to the Rangers, the U.N. peacekeeping teams, and the Turkish army, several of the arriving helicopters and gunships had been equipped with cams as well. The satellites governed by NORAD's command center had pumped the video and audio transmissions to *Wasp* and to Remington's intelligence teams.

The offered views included ground viewpoint shots as well as shots from inside the helo cockpits.

Remington eyed the screens, blurring his attention and his peripheral vision, not looking at the individual action, but looking through the surface motions for the incongruent actions that didn't fit. Something had gone wrong as the helos had swooped into the LZ, and he was going to see it this time.

The exterior views of the Sea Knight contingent showed the helos descending toward the LZ in perfect formation. The crimson haze from the smoke grenades Goose had used to establish quick visual sighting blossomed against the tops of the smoke clouds from the explosions like blood surfacing from the ocean during a shark attack. In the next instant, some of the helicopters suddenly veered into others.

Two Sea Knights in the lead collided and set off a chain of violence that whipped through the formation. Other helos slammed together in a string of aerial wrecks. Often, the blows were only glancing, or a brief meeting of rotor blades that shattered against each other, not full-blown collisions. Shards of carbonized steel ripped through the helos like fragmentation grenades, slashing through the metal sides and Plexiglas windows like tissue paper. Men died in that moment, and others died immediately afterward as the helicopters broke and went to pieces against the hard earth. Black, oily smoke mixed with flames and obscured the views of most of the few ship-carried cameras that had survived the impacts.

In a brief, frozen split second, the image of Goose on his knees beside a man who had been impaled by a long shard filled one of the helo cams as the Sea Knight heeled over out of control. The image was so stark, so unforgiving, that for a moment Remington was afraid Goose had been killed. He forced himself to remember that he had talked with the first sergeant just after that. When the helicopter made contact with the ground, the camera screen went black.

But Remington had seen something else. The image played at the back of his mind, gnawing like a terrier. He leaned forward. "Stop."

Foster hit the keyboard. All the cycling images left onscreen halted, becoming silent, frozen images of destruction or impending destruction.

"This one." Remington pointed to the lower left quadrant of the left monitor. "Can you identify this helicopter?"

Foster tapped keys and floated a legend into view on the screen. "Yes, sir. That was Lieutenant Briggs's aircraft."

"Can you isolate Lieutenant Briggs's aircraft in that formation?"

"Yes, sir."

"Then show me footage of the approach toward the LZ again and let's see what that helo did."

After a brief intermission for serious keyboarding, Foster put the results up on the right monitor. The helicopters froze onscreen. "This is fifteen seconds before the first crash," Foster said. "And this is Briggs's Sea Knight." The private tapped a few more keystrokes.

A circle, as bright yellow as a tennis ball, surrounded the helicopter.

"Let's go," Remington said, leaning more closely. He watched with interest as Briggs's aircraft suddenly veered out of control and locked rotors with the nearest Sea Knight on the left. Both aircraft fell to the ground like broken birds. "Briggs's craft was one of those that went out of control."

"Yes, sir." Foster nodded. "I've got a list of the others. I can isolate their cameras, too, if you want."

"We'll see. For now, run the footage from the interior camera in Briggs's helo backward. Frame by frame from the impact. You can cross-reference the time-date stamp on the videos, can't you?"

"Yes, sir. That won't be a problem. All the cameras and transmission equipment were calibrated for exact timing." Foster shifted nervously.

"What is it?" Remington asked.

"It's these cameras, sir. The ones used in the helos and by the ground teams? They shoot four thousand frames a minute. Even if you go back thirty seconds, that's two thousand pictures to look at. Frame by frame is going to take some time." Foster sounded apologetic. "Didn't mean to interrupt, sir. Just thought you should know."

Remington nodded. "I needed to know, Private. Can you sort the frames?"

"Sure."

"Let me see every hundredth frame."

Bending to the keyboard, Foster entered the parameters of the search. A new window opened on the monitor, filling with the frozen image of the interior of the Sea Knight's cockpit.

The camera had been mounted inside the helicopter's cockpit roof and peered over the pilot and copilot's shoulders, cutting them out of the picture and not giving a clear indication of what had happened that had made the helo break formation. On normal operations, the Sea Knight carried a crew chief and a mechanic in addition to the pilot and copilot. During hot drops that entailed possible engagements with hostile ground forces, the mechanic was replaced with two door gunners.

Remington guided Foster by voice, flipping to every hundredth frame. Onscreen, the view changed dramatically as the Sea Knight had pitched and yawed in the air. One of the nearby helicopters hung in mid-destruction, the flames and debris hurtling from the craft as steel bent and ripped loose. A hundred frames back, the helo was struck by another helicopter. The copilot's face in the other aircraft was frozen in surprise, one hand pushed to the glass as if to ward off the other helo.

Four pictures—four hundred frames—back, the captain figured out what he was looking for. "Stop here." Remington gazed at the screen, then tapped it. "Can you reimage this? Zoom in and blow it up?"

"Sure." In seconds, the picture grew larger and larger at Remington's direction.

"Do you see it?" Remington stared at the image and felt a cold gust of wind across the back of his neck. He knew that feeling was only his imagination, though. There wasn't a cold wind anywhere in their vicinity.

Foster studied the picture and shook his head. "I see the helicopter that Briggs's aircraft ran into."

"Here." Remington ran his finger over a section of the screen. "Look here and you can see a reflection of the copilot in the Plexiglas." The image looked like a grayed-out photograph against the Plexiglas. "What do you see in the seat next to him?"

"The seat is empty," Foster said in a hollow voice.

"Yes," Remington said.

Foster worked the keyboard, pulling up and scanning *Wasp*'s crew lists on the left monitor. "No, sir," the private said. "That seat wasn't empty. At least, it wasn't supposed to be empty. Lieutenant Briggs was definitely aboard that aircraft. The copilot was Sergeant Julian Mahoney."

Keen-edged interest sharpened Remington's focus. "Go back a hundred frames."

Foster did. The seat remained empty.

Three hundred frames back, passed in increments of one hundred, the view inside the cockpit changed, and the reflection of the interior wasn't displayed against the Plexiglas. Four hundred frames back, the seat was still empty when the reflection formed against the Plexiglas again. A hundred frames back from that point, Lieutenant Briggs, looking dangerously cool despite the immediate pressure he had flown into, sat in the seat with his hand on the control yoke.

"There he is," Foster said.

"Yes," Remington agreed. "Now we roll forward, Private. By tens."

Thirty frames later, Briggs's seat was empty. After a frame-by-frame search, Foster located the two frames in sequence that showed the Marine helo pilot had been in his seat, then gone. Except for the pile made by a uniform, headgear, and boots. The helicopter had gone out of control from that moment and swiftly collided with the nearby helicopter to start off the string of destruction that had rained from the sky.

"Put up both frames," Remington said in a calm, controlled voice. "Side by side. I want to look at them."

Foster tapped keys. The two frames popped into view.

Remington studied the two digital images. Except for the fact that Lieutenant Briggs was missing and his uniform was on the seat, the scenes didn't look different in any way.

Somewhere between the two images, Lieutenant Briggs had managed to strip off his clothing and gear and leave a helicopter 338 feet above an LZ in hostile territory. Remington thought about that, wondering if the lieutenant's body would turn up on the battleground. He glanced at the corporal's clothing in the nearby chair and felt certain there would be no body.

❖   ❖   ❖

When Dockery's hand relaxed in his, Goose felt certain the man had died. However, when he checked the corporal's pulse, he found a flicker of life. The anesthetic had flooded his nervous system and left him limp on the shard of metal that had ripped through his body and now supported him. Dockery's eyes remained open, but Goose doubted the man saw anything.

Goose released Dockery's hand. *God, look over him. Keep him safe till I can get help here, or take him home with You if that's what You feel is best.* Whatever was done needed to be done quickly.

Pushing himself to his feet, Goose looked at Bill's empty uniform. Goose's mind reeled as he tried to accept the evidence lying on the ground.

Bill is gone.

That was the bottom line. No matter how Bill had been taken or killed—*God, please let Bill be alive*—he was gone, and he wasn't there to help Goose now as he had for so many years as a friend and a fellow soldier. The flutter of the wet, dust-encrusted kerchief Goose had tied around his lower face pulled in tight against his lips as he took a deep breath. In that breath, he centered himself, putting on the mental armor of the professional soldier. He spoke calmly into the headset microphone.

"Base, this is Phoenix Leader."

There was no reply.

With effort, Goose turned toward the LZ, where the stricken Marine wing lay shattered. Flames leapt up from the broken helicopters, and the heat created pockets of shifting mirage effects in the air, swirling through the heavy black smoke. A few men stumbled and staggered from the wreckage.

There are survivors. The realization electrified Goose. The fatigue and pain sloughed away from him as the need to act gave him a second wind. He pushed himself into a jog and gazed back along the border.

Two Harriers and one Whiskey Cobra roved through the air, cutting through the ocean of haze that cycled through the air. Roiling waves of fire still scoured the no-man's-land that had been forcibly declared on the Syrian side of the border.

Goose switched his headset over to the general frequency in use by the Rangers. "Phoenix Team, this is Phoenix Leader. Count off."

In quick succession, the team counted off, letting him know that five of the Rangers were still at hand. Dockery and Evaristo were too wounded to help with a rescue effort. Bill Townsend and Neal Clark were missing.

Goose ordered the men to help with the rescue operations among the downed aircraft, then turned his attention to the front line. The Turkish military were still in position there, but he knew he'd feel more comfortable with his teams in place. And he knew that Cal Remington would demand that. "Echo Two. Bravo One."

"Echo Two here, Phoenix Leader," Bernhardt replied.

"Bravo One reads you, Phoenix Leader," York said.

"Hold your positions," Goose ordered. "We've lost com with Base. For the moment, we hold what we have."

Both rifle company leaders agreed.

"Echo Two, is Six still intact and with your unit?" Echo Six was Rick Means, one of the best point men Goose had ever seen.

"Affirmative, Leader."

"Get Six and two men forward," Goose said. "His choice. I need spotters in place. With the com out, we don't have eyes that can see through that haze. I want as much intel incoming as we can get."

"Affirmative, Leader."

"Phoenix Leader, this is Alpha Two. We've lost men, Goose." Sergeant Gunther Slade, the number two in Alpha Rifle Company, sounded hysterical. A ragged breath rattled over the com. "They've disappeared! There are empty uniforms everywhere!"

"Understood, Alpha Two," Goose stated calmly. "Treat them as MIAs for now. Get me a list of missing personnel. Secure any loose weapons and gear. We don't know how soon it will be before we can restock. Charlie Leader, do you copy this com?"

"Affirmative, Phoenix," Lieutenant Harold Wake's deep voice replied. Harry had six years in the Rangers. He was still young in some ways, a graduate of OCS after getting a doctorate in marine biology in

Seattle. He'd attended school with the intention of putting in his time in the military to pay off his college tuition, then get back to the work in the oceans that he loved. Instead, he'd gotten hooked on the Ranger life, drawn to the adrenaline and sense of family that was missing after being raised in state institutions.

"Charlie One," Goose said, "I need you to fall back with your people to aid in the search and rescue among the Marine wing. Grab all the medkits you can get your hands on and head this way."

"Roger, Phoenix," Harry replied.

Goose reached the first Sea Knight. Black spots danced in his vision from the lack of air.

The helicopter sat on the rough land canted over on its right side. A rotor blade had chopped into the hard earth, looking for a moment like it had buried itself several feet with the impact. Then Goose noted the broken stubs of the other rotors and knew that the rotor blade the craft rested on had shattered, too.

Smoke coiled like fat, restless snakes from the helicopter's interior. The Sea Knights carried ordnance, but most of that was secured with the Marines. The downed Whiskey Cobras would be more dangerous.

Dead men lay strewn before the Sea Knight. He forced himself not to dwell on the fact that until minutes ago these men had been alive. Despite the amount of death he had seen in the past two hours, he couldn't distance himself from the horror of it.

And God help me if I ever do, Goose prayed.

After ascertaining that none of the men lying outside the helicopter were alive, Goose ducked down and prepared to enter the open side cargo door. A flash of movement caught his eye, and he was in motion before he recognized the Beretta M9/Model 92F that came up in the hand of the dazed Marine on the other side of the cargo area.

The gunshot filled the tight space inside the cargo helicopter but hardly made a dent in the cacophony of noise that rolled over the battlefield. The bullet slapped into the ground just outside the cargo area.

Goose spun and went to the ground, keeping his assault rifle in his right hand while his left clapped instinctively to his helmet. "Stand down, Marine," he ordered in the voice of authority he'd cultivated while stepping up through the ranks. "I'm Sergeant Gander. With the 75th Rangers."

A choked sob came from inside the helicopter. "Sorry, Sergeant. I'm sorry. I'm hit. I'm hurt bad."

Goose pushed himself up and put his back to the helicopter's body. He kept the M-4A1 canted up. "What's your name, Marine?"

"Lance Corporal Kenny Pierce, Sergeant."

Goose pushed out his breath and stared down at the arm that stuck out from under the helicopter's body. The limb was the left arm. A gold band glinted around the ring finger. *Married.* The realization slammed home to Goose like a hammer falling. Thoughts flickered through his mind, images of Megan, Joey, and Chris. He walled them away with effort. He was a soldier on the battlefield. He would always be a soldier on the battlefield.

"Lance Corporal Pierce," Goose said, "I want you to put your side-arm down."

"Done, Sergeant."

With a quick prayer, Goose heaved off the side of the helicopter, stepped around the dead man's arm, and hunkered down in the cargo door. His eyes took a moment to adjust to the dark interior.

The Marine corporal was young with a kid's features that time in the service hadn't yet erased. Dark brows hung over pain- and fear-filled eyes set in dark hollows. He sat with his back against the opposite side of the helicopter. Blood stained his BDUs. Dead men lay around him. Fuel stink filled the air and let Goose know they were potentially sitting on top of a bomb.

"They're dead, Sergeant," Kenny croaked.

Goose shouldered his rifle and crept forward. The helicopter creaked as the weight shifted but didn't move more than a couple inches. "I know. I lost a buddy of mine."

"I lost my whole squad, Sergeant." The young corporal's face crumpled. He squeezed his eyes shut. Tears tracked down his bloody cheeks.

The young man was lucky to be alive, but Goose didn't mention that. He squatted down near the corporal, aware of the corpses of Marines that pressed in against him.

"Where are you hit?" Goose asked. *Concentrate on the things that you can do. Not what you've lost. That's what Bill always said. Says! That's what Bill always says. You're not going to give up on him, Goose.*

"My legs. I can't move them."

As gently as he could, Goose rolled the corpses from the young corporal, but he was grimly aware that he was still shifting dead weight. Blood was everywhere. He knew he should have at least put on the rubber gloves from the medkit to protect himself, but to be completely protected he'd have had to have a bodysuit. He concentrated on the task at hand, knowing he had to hold himself together for the young corporal.

"What happened to the helo?" Goose took his mini-Maglite from his combat harness.

"Don't know." The corporal yelled in pain when Goose uncovered one of his legs to reveal shrapnel wounds that had to have come from the shattered rotors. All of the men in front of Kenny Pierce were riddled with the jagged shards. More metal stuck out from the helo's interior. "Somebody said the pilot disappeared."

"Disappeared?" Goose opened his medkit and took out gauze and tape, added wraparound compresses, and a pair of scissors. He started cutting the man's pant legs to reveal the wounds. If the metal hadn't ripped through an artery and caused the young Marine to bleed out before now, he didn't want to inadvertently cause that.

"That's what they said."

Goose started wrapping gauze over the compress he'd wrapped around Pierce's lower leg. Letting his hands work through the familiar process, he glanced forward.

The cockpit was visible through the gaping hole left where the bulkhead separating the cargo area had been. The pilot's seat was empty. The copilot lay dead in the other seat with a length of jagged metal thrusting out from under the chin of his flight helmet.

"Did you see it?" Goose asked.

Pierce winced as the bandages were applied. "No."

"If you need something for the pain," Goose offered, "let me know." Shock was sometimes the best pain relief and one of the body's natural defenses. The cuts on the young Marine's legs were bad, but his legs were intact. Without a ready transport to ferry in more medical supplies, they had to conserve what they had on hand.

The Marine nodded. "I can deal."

Goose repacked the medkit. "I've got to get you out of here. Can you walk?"

Pierce tried to shove himself to his feet but couldn't gain enough traction on the tilted, blood-slick metal flooring in his weakened condition. "I can't. I'm sorry."

"Ease up, Marine. We'll all do what we can to see this through. You've done your part." Steeling himself, ignoring the wolf's jaws that wrenched at his bruised knee, Goose gathered the young man up in his arms and ducked down to step out of the helicopter onto the barren earth. The hot wind slapped him, draining his strength. His injured knee nearly buckled under him, but he made himself stand tall.

You survived for a reason, Goose. You survived for a reason and you're going to walk and you're going to do your job. God's hand is in this. Despite everything you see around you, God's hand is in this. Now you be the soldier you signed on to be.

Goose knew the words were Bill's. They must have been from some other time, some other battle when things had looked dark. Goose couldn't remember when that time was. Bill had always said that human beings were venal and unwilling to reach for anything outside themselves. God was there, but most men wanted to understand the nature of God, to know more things than they were ever meant to believe.

"Life comes down to two choices, Goose," Bill had always—has always—said. "You believe or you don't believe. God will test you because He loves you. He will take away everything you think you can know or trust until He reveals that belief to you. One way or another, every one of His children that resist Him is humbled and made to believe again. Look at David. God loved David fiercely, and no matter how many times David turned away from Him, God found a way to turn David back. You can't learn to believe, Goose. You just do. It's the most natural thing in the world if you let it happen."

For a moment, raw pain and fear and doubt crushed Goose as he surveyed the wrecked aircraft and the border such a short distance away where one of the fiercest enemies he'd ever faced waited to kill him and his men.

Holding the young Marine corporal to him, Goose was reminded how Chris had been laid in his arms just after his son had been born. The moment had been overwhelming. Even knowing Megan was pregnant, even feeling the baby kick, it somehow hadn't seemed real.

Then Chris had been there, lying in his arms, so small, so helpless. And Goose swore then that he had felt the hand of God upon him, felt the blessings of God upon him as well as the burden of responsibility. After years in the military, Goose knew he would never be able to keep Chris safe from everything. Goose knew he would never be strong enough or big enough to completely protect his son.

Only God could do that. And in that moment of feeling that God was with him, he knew a covenant had been made between God and him, that they would do everything possible to save Chris in the imperfect world into which he'd been born.

In that moment of grace while holding his son for the first time, Goose had known the truest peace ever in his life. *God, how could I have forgotten that?*

Then Goose realized that he couldn't have forgotten it. God had reminded him of that moment just now, at a time when that memory of faith had been most needed. *God is there. God does see this.*

The fear quieted. *Be still, and know that I am God; I will be exalted among the nations, I will be exalted in the earth.* The passage came from Psalm 46:10. The verse had also been one of those that Bill had always held close to him.

Goose took a deep breath and *believed*, not because he had no choice, but because believing was the *only* choice a man with even a glimmer of faith could do. The pain and fatigue remained with him, but those things seemed more distant. He walked forward, and his injured knee remained strong beneath him. For the moment, that was all he needed.

"Joey!"

Pain filled Joey's head. The throb exploded along his jaw and made his teeth ache. Deafness filled his left ear. Even though his lids were closed, bright light stabbed through his eyes and deep into his brain.

"Joey! Are you all right?"

Someone grabbed Joey's arm and shook him. *Oh, yeah. That helps so much. Thank you.* Fresh agony erupted inside his skull. He groaned and the grip on his arm went away.

"Wake up. We were in a wreck."

Dim images flickered through Joey's mind. Then he remembered the camo-colored Suburban that had been on a collision course with his mom's car. The memory of the crunch and scream of battered and torn metal haunted him. *Man, you are never gonna get out of the house again in this lifetime.*

Then he remembered that Jenny had been in the car with him. He snapped his eyes open, and the blare of car horns closed in on him. The din sounded like he'd set off a shop full of car alarms or stepped into a Klingon trap in a *Star Trek* episode.

Jenny sat in the passenger seat. An ashen pallor colored her face and blood leaked from the left corner of her mouth.

"You okay?" Joey asked.

She nodded. "I think so." She glanced at him. "I was just worried about you. You wouldn't wake up. Are you sure you're okay?"

No, Joey thought, *I'm* definitely *not okay. This is my mom's car, and with my luck tonight, it's probably totaled.* But he said, "Yeah. I'm okay." He turned his head and gazed into the bright headlights of the Suburban shoved against the side of the car. "This wasn't my fault. This guy came outta nowhere."

Checking the right front side of the car, he saw that the impact from the bigger vehicle had shoved his mom's car over into the stop sign. He hadn't even gone forward when his foot had slipped off the brake. The front windshield revealed a road map of cracks and fractures.

Anger swept through Joey. Tonight had been a total bust. Lying about his age and going to the club had been his fault. Not being home at curfew had been his fault. But this.man, this was *so* not his fault. He had just been sitting at the stop sign when this guy had plowed into him. Now he was going to be even later picking up Chris.

Joey unbuckled his seat belt. He felt the bruising across his chest and hip and knew that they had been hit with considerable force.

"What are you doing?" Jenny asked.

"Getting out."

"We should wait."

"For what?"

"The police."

Joey squirmed over the seat. "That jerk hasn't even gotten out of the truck to come check on us. He's probably sitting in there wasted or stoned out of his mind. I don't want him hiding evidence before the police get here."

"It wasn't just him, Joey." Jenny pointed through the cracked windshield.

In the backseat now, Joey paused and looked. Several wrecks sat in the middle of the street. Cars had gone onto the median. Traffic was usually heavy, even at this time of night. Some of his anger melted away as the weirdness of the situation filtered through.

"A whole lot of people wrecked at the same time," Jenny said. "I saw them. It was like those cars just went out of control. Like the drivers just turned loose of the steering wheel."

Fear seeped in through the cracks of Joey's anger, breaking the hot emotion down and filling him with fear. *Something's wrong.* He tried to open the right rear door and found it was jammed. Rocking back, he threw his shoulder against the door. A screech filled the car's interior but the door opened.

Joey stepped out on shaking legs. Out on the street, other drivers and passengers were getting out of their cars. They yelled at each other, cursing, accusing, and sometimes asking if everyone was okay.

Jenny got out but stood behind the safety of the door.

"There's a flashlight in the glove compartment," Joey said. "Would you get it?" Goose had always been a stickler for being prepared. The glove compartment also contained emergency highway flares, and there was a large medical kit in the trunk.

Joey took the flashlight and switched it on. The beam cut through the night that had closed in around them. The Suburban's beams slashed across the top of his mom's car. Joey walked back and peered at the Suburban's cab.

Nothing moved behind the glass. The greenish glow of the dashboard lights outlined the seats and filled the cab. If anyone was inside, he or she had to be lying down.

Joey directed the flashlight's beam into the Suburban. As brave as he'd acted in the car, the last thing he wanted to face was a drunken military guy who wanted to blame him for the wreck. He'd seen young Rangers who'd had too much to drink get into fights, and even somewhat inebriated, those men remained dangerous.

"Maybe the driver is hurt." Jenny came over to Joey and took his arm in her hands. She looked worried. "We need to check on him."

Having the young woman that close, smelling her perfume, Joey felt ten feet tall. He was definitely the guy, and the logical choice to step into the potential danger. "I'll check on him."

"I'm coming with you."

"It might not be safe." Joey hoped that it was, but he wanted her to realize that he might be taking his life in his hands. Well, maybe not his life, but he could get socked. Of course, if he got socked and then was able to restrain the guy the way Goose and Bill had, he'd be a hero, right? Maybe it wouldn't matter so much that he was only seventeen.

"Why wouldn't it be safe?" she asked.

"He could be drunk."

A frown of distaste turned Jenny's lips down. She'd obviously wiped her face because blood smeared her chin. "I've been around drunks before. Trust me, if he's drunk I won't feel like we owe him anything."

Joey started preparing his next argument and Jenny left him standing there. He jogged to catch up. Man, he couldn't figure her out. She'd gone nuts on him in the car, and now she was willing to walk into a situation like this.

On the passenger side of the Suburban, Joey stepped in front of Jenny. She didn't protest. Trying not to shake, Joey directed the flashlight's beam into the big SUV.

No one was inside.

Joey continued examining the Suburban's interior, looking for a bottle or beer cans. Surely there was something that would help his case with his mom when he tried to explain what had happened to her car.

"Did he get out?" Joey asked.

"Who?"

"The driver."

"Did you see the driver get out?" Jenny's tone turned unexpectedly sarcastic.

"I think that was during the time I was kinda knocked unconscious," Joey replied.

"If I'd seen someone get out of this car, I'd have told you." She stepped back from him and crossed her arms.

Joey sighed. Man, there was nothing he could say that didn't lead to a potential argument. "I didn't say that you wouldn't."

"Then what were you saying?"

He turned to her. "Look, Jenny, I'm sorry. I didn't mean for it to come across like that. But there's no way whoever was driving this SUV just disappeared."

She narrowed her eyes angrily. "Then you're saying this car just rolled down the road till it hit us?"

Joey looked back down the street. There were no parking places, no stops along the way where a driver might have left an idling vehicle.

"Something else happened," Jenny said, looking back out at the traffic. "We weren't the only ones it happened to."

Turning his attention back to the Suburban, Joey tried the passenger door. The door opened easily. The SUV had obviously sustained less damage than his mom's car.

"What are you doing?" Jenny demanded.

Joey popped the glove compartment open. "Trying to find out who owns this SUV. A lot of people carry their insurance papers in the glove compartment." He rifled through the contents and found a small expandable file that contained the insurance verification form.

Anthony Macintyre was a sergeant who lived at Fort Benning.

"Hey," Jenny said. "Look in the driver's seat."

Instinctively, Joey started to withdraw, thinking there was something dangerous there. He swung the flashlight beam over the uniform lying on the seat as though the clothes had been driving the car. Before he could move, Jenny shoved in beside him and reached across the passenger bucket seat and plucked the uniform from the driver's seat.

As Joey watched in disbelief, Jenny went through the clothing. She opened the leather wallet. "Sergeant Macintyre, Anthony. That what you found?"

"Yeah. You really shouldn't—"

"Joey, something really weird is going on here. We need to know everything we can." Jenny picked up the guy's cell phone and punched buttons. "The last call he got was from Fort Benning." She showed Joey the glowing screen.

Joey recognized the exchange as one that belonged to the military base even though he didn't recognize the number.

Jenny punched another button and held the phone to her ear.

"What are you doing?" Joey asked.

"Returning the call," Jenny said. "Maybe we can find out who called Sergeant Macintyre, Anthony."

"*What?*" Joey absolutely could not believe it. "Do you know how much trouble we'll be in?"

"Joey, look around. A lot of people are already in trouble. Do you think this many people just happened to wreck all at the same time?"

Disorientation rocketed through Joey as he surveyed the wrecked cars and the milling people. *This can't be real. It can't.*

"No answer," Jenny said. "Just a recording that all circuits are busy."

Joey fished his own cell phone from his jacket pocket. "Maybe it's just that phone. Let me see the number." When Jenny showed him the screen, he entered the number and pressed *Send.*

An automated message came on. "All circuits are busy. Your call cannot be completed. Please try again."

Panic rose in Joey. He dialed his mom's cell phone number.

"All circuits are busy. Your call cannot be completed. Please try—"

He broke the connection and tried again. The same message came on. Working quickly, he flipped through his speed-dial numbers, calling his friends.

"All circuits are busy. Your call cannot be—"

It was a nightmare.

When Joey looked up, Jenny was walking around the back of the Suburban. He caught up with her. "Where are you going?"

"To see if those people need help."

"I've got to go, Jenny. Chris is still waiting—"

An anguished cry interrupted Joey. Startled, he looked over at the woman standing beside a minivan one lane over in the street about thirty feet away. A tow truck had collided with the van's rear, collapsing the van inward and spinning it halfway around. The van's front tires rested on the median and the nose was burrowed into a tree.

"My baby!" she shrilled. "Has anyone seen my baby? Help me!"

Jenny broke into a run. Joey was a half step behind her.

"Can we help?" Jenny asked the woman.

The woman looked like she was in her late twenties and was dressed in a fast-food restaurant's uniform. Her hands shook.

"It's my baby!" the woman cried. "I had the late shift tonight. I belted her in the backseat! I always belt her in the backseat! It's the safest place for an infant!"

Jenny took the woman by the shoulders. "It's going to be okay. We'll find your baby." She looked over her shoulder at Joey. "Find the baby."

Joey hadn't even noticed he'd frozen. He hadn't been around that many adults who were losing it. Seeing such raw emotion from the woman was overwhelming. Anger was one thing. Most people had no problem expressing anger, but fear—

"Joey, find the baby."

"Sure." Joey stepped into the minivan, banging his head against the roof and starting a new crescendo of pain. He played the flashlight over the child safety seat belted into the middle of the van's bench.

No kid.

Then Joey realized that during the impact the child might have gotten knocked out of the seat. That wasn't supposed to happen, but the child wasn't in the seat now. And how would a kid look after she'd been bounced around the interior of a van? The thought hit Joey with staggering ferocity. For a moment he was sure he was going to throw up.

"Joey."

He wanted to snap at Jenny, but he couldn't. He didn't trust his voice.

"Please find her," the woman pleaded.

Reluctantly, desperately wanting to find the baby okay or not find her at all, Joey turned his attention back to the van. He shined the light under all the seats, checked the front to make sure she hadn't been thrown in that direction, then climbed over the backseat to the rear compartment. He found baskets of laundry, a blanket, and a pair of collapsible lawn chairs. But no baby.

"She's not here." Joey turned around and stepped on a small baby rattle, crushing the toy underfoot. "I'm sorry. I didn't see that." The apology, coming at a time when a baby was missing, sounded inane but it was out of his mouth before he could stop himself.

"My baby!" the woman wailed.

The pain and panic in the woman's voice almost broke Joey's heart. He'd never heard his mom sound like that, and he was sure he never wanted to.

"Joey." Jenny's voice was choked and quiet but Joey somehow heard her even over the continuing blare of car horns and car alarms. "Look in the child seat again."

Goose bumps suddenly erupted across the back of Joey's neck, and it felt like an ice-cold fist closed around his heart. His breath locked in his lungs. He didn't know what he was going to find in the child seat, but he was convinced that he didn't want to find it. He suddenly realized the minivan's front windshield was broken out.

Had the baby flown out the window? Was some body part still hanging in the seat? Which body part did he most *not* want it to be? *God, not that! I would have seen that already, wouldn't I? Babies are made of so many different parts.* He knew because he had worked with Chris when Chris was learning to talk, touching toes and fingers and eyes and ears, teaching Chris the names of those parts.

The flashlight beam illuminated the safety seat.

There was no baby there, no baby parts.

Thank You, God. Joey felt tears burn the backs of his eyes.

Then he spotted the pink Winnie-the-Pooh jumper lying on the safety seat. It was strewn across the little chair, just as Sergeant Macintyre's uniform had been in the Suburban. On the front of the little jumper, Pooh sat digging a paw into a honey pot as Eeyore, Piglet, Tigger, and Rabbit looked on. A disposable diaper, folded and creased as though it had just come from a package—a condition Joey remembered rarely seeing them in—lay inside the jumper. A pair of tiny socks spilled out of a pair of *Blue's Clues* shoes.

"She's gone," Joey croaked. "She couldn't have taken those clothes off."

"No!" the woman screamed. She pushed free of Jenny and pulled Joey from the minivan. "My baby can't be gone! She can't be!"

Dazed, Joey stepped back from the van beside Jenny. She took his hand in hers, holding tight. As they stood there, other conversations drifted over them. More people were missing. More piles of clothes had been left behind.

Adults everywhere were losing it. Other people screamed for help, saying they couldn't find their kids.

"What's going on?" Jenny asked.

"I don't know," Joey said. "But I've got to get back to the base. I've got to find my mom and Chris."

"How are you going to get there?"

"The car." Joey looked at his mom's car. The car was smashed, but nothing was leaking underneath. Maybe it was only body damage. He caught himself then, knowing that life had gotten strange, because he would never have thought that his mom's car just having body damage was a thing to be hoped for. "Maybe I can get it free." He looked at Jenny. "You going or staying?"

"I'm going. You don't need to be alone."

Joey led the way back to the car, running fast enough now that Jenny had to struggle to keep pace with him. He opened the passenger door and crawled inside, sliding across the seat to the driver's side. He turned the key, punched the gas, and prayed to God that the engine would catch. Struggling, the engine turned over and started with a shudder just as Jenny pulled the door closed.

"Hang on," Joey said. He put the car in reverse and pushed the accelerator. The front wheels spun, then caught, but the car couldn't break free of the Suburban.

"Cut the wheels toward the SUV," Jenny said, bracing herself. "Floor it."

Joey turned the wheels toward the Suburban then mashed the accelerator to the floor. The engine screamed, sputtered, and then launched into a full-throated roar.

Metal ripped in banshee wails as the car surged again and again. Just as Joey was about to give up, the front left fender tore free and clattered to the ground as the car sped backward. He slammed the brakes on, dropped the transmission into drive, and whipped out around the Suburban. He ignored the stop sign. Everyone out on the street was stopped. New arrivals were getting out of their cars to see what the problem was.

Breathing rapidly, fighting hard not to lose it and start crying like a wimp even though he was more scared now than he could ever remember being in his whole life, Joey sped toward Fort Benning. He glanced at Jenny and saw that she was sitting with her arms folded and tears running down her face.

"Jenny," Joey croaked.

She turned to him, losing part of the tough façade she'd had all evening. "Something's wrong, Joey." She covered her mouth with a hand as she sobbed and her voice cracked. "Something's so wrong. Look at all those cars. Look at all those people."

Glancing at the businesses and houses that lined the street, Joey knew what she said was true. Something *was* wrong. Big-time wrong.

He reached for her hand, folded it into his. "It's going to be okay," he told her. And he felt stupid for saying it because he knew things weren't going to be okay. But he said it because he was a guy and that was something that guys were supposed to say at times like this.

She pulled her hand away. "You don't know that."

"No," Joey admitted, "I don't. I'm just scared and I want everything to be okay."

She hesitated, then put her hand back in his, squeezing tightly. "Me, too."

❋   ❋   ❋

United States 75th Rangers 3rd Battalion
Field Command Post
35 Klicks South of Sanliurfa, Turkey
Local Time 0831 Hours

"How much time elapsed between the two frames?" Remington asked. In the command field post, he concentrated on the pictures the computer tech had isolated of the helicopter pilot seat with and without Lieutenant Briggs of the Marine wing from USS *Wasp*. The legend at the bottom of each picture marked the local time as 08:21:13. The *event*—the Ranger captain didn't know what else to call it—had occurred ten minutes ago and they were only now finding out about the disappearance.

"At this speed," Foster said, "you're getting a frame about every four-tenths of a second."

"Four-tenths of a second." Remington repeated the information in an effort to make it more concrete.

"Yes, sir."

Remington tried to wrap his brain around the idea of the impossible act balanced against the impossible time frame. "So every second there are two frames."

"Maybe three," Foster replied. "Depends on how the time broke down. You could get a frame one or two seconds into the cycle, that still leaves you enough time for two more frames."

"Go through the footage from all the digital cameras we were able to access at this time." Remington tapped the screen showing the two pictures, one with Lieutenant Briggs and the other without. "I want every frame you can pull from every camera."

"Just the helicopters?"

"No. I want the frames from the wing provided by *Wasp* and I want the frames from our men on the ground that are equipped with digital cameras. Get that to me ASAP."

"Yes, sir." Foster bent to the task.

Remington stood and started pacing again, surveying the tech crew around him. None of them seemed to have had much luck with resecuring the computer feeds. He cursed, struggling to hold on to the calm exterior he wore. Everyone remained aware of the piles of clothing that remained of the people they had lost, and the captain knew the questions uppermost in their minds: Is it going to happen again? Will it take the rest of us?

"Captain Remington."

Wheeling about-face, Remington looked at the sergeant he'd assigned to cover the cinder-block building's entrance.

Sergeant Tolliver entered the building in full battle dress, including his helmet and LCE. Sweat beaded his face, attracting a layer of dust. He was a lifer, just as Goose was. But where Goose had the leader's capacity for free thinking and quick decision-making, Tolliver was a plodder. He could be counted on to do things by the book, within reason, and finish an assignment. But Tolliver seldom went beyond the book.

"What is it, Sergeant?" Remington asked. He ignored the fact that all the heads swiveled toward him from the monitors. Everyone in the command post was spooked.

"CIA Section Chief Cody would like a word with you." Tolliver hooked a thumb over his shoulder. "I've got him detained outside."

"I thought Cody had gone."

Tolliver nodded. "He had. He's back."

"When?"

Tolliver shrugged. "Just drove up. We halted him, IDed him, and walked him in from the perimeter."

"Who is with him?" Remington's mind wound around the news, kicking the fact over and looking at all the angles. He had ordered the CIA man out of the command post as soon as the SCUDs had been launched. Cody had wasted no time getting out of the area and heading north to Sanliurfa.

Now the man was back. *Why?*

"He's alone, Captain." Tolliver shifted his assault rifle in his arms.

"But he wasn't earlier."

"No, sir. Verified that through the perimeter guard's notes. That's how I checked his ID."

"What does he want to talk to me about?"

Tolliver shook his head. "He wouldn't say, sir."

Curiosity filled Remington. He knew the agency was a big factor in securing the humint—human intelligence—so necessary in waging the ground war against the Taliban in Afghanistan. During the Vietnam War, the CIA hadn't enjoyed a good reputation, but as far as the Fitzhugh administration was concerned, the agency seemed unable to do any wrong. Remington knew the truth didn't match up with the public image. The undercover agent Goose and his team had extricated only that morning proved that.

"Bring the man in, Sergeant," Remington ordered. "I want him unarmed and under heavy guard. Treat him like a potential hostile."

"Yes, sir." Tolliver saluted, turned a sharp about-face, and left the room.

Remington spun and faced the tech team again, catching several of them just turning away. In the space of a drawn breath, he was staring at the backs of their heads again as they strove fruitlessly to reconnect the lines of communication.

The captain kept his attention forward when the sergeant returned with the CIA section chief moments later. He pushed his breath out slowly and chased his anger and frustration into a corner of his mind. Those emotions had their place, but now he needed the calm cool he was noted for.

"Captain Remington," Tolliver said. "Agent Cody is here."

"What can I do for you, Agent Cody?" Remington posed the question without turning to face the man.

"You can't do anything for me, Captain," Cody stated in his unctuous voice.

Remington spun on the man with the compact ferocity of a hunting cougar. "Then you're wasting my time, mister."

Section Chief Cody flinched and took a half step back before he caught himself. He looked rumpled and definitely the worse for wear. His coat had been taken from him, leaving him in a sweat-stained white shirt and suit pants. His empty shoulder holster hung under his left arm.

"Captain," Cody said, "I assure you that—"

Remington raised his voice, blowing Cody's words away. "I sent my men to recover one of your lost agents just over two hours ago. The hostile who escaped sent a signal that triggered the Syrian attack against Turkey—"

"You don't know that," Cody argued.

Remington cursed, beating the CIA agent down verbally till he closed his mouth in surrender. Embarrassment pinked Cody's ears and cheeks, and he blinked rapidly as he struggled to hold the Ranger captain's fierce gaze.

"I'm thinking seriously of having you placed under arrest and thrown into the brig until we can sort out the disappearances of my people," Remington said.

"What disappearances?" Cody asked.

Remington studied the man. If the CIA agent was feigning surprise, he was doing a credible job. Remington pointed at the stacks of uniforms. Unwilling to release the exact number of losses within his group, he said, "I've had people disappear while they were sitting in front of me. I never saw a thing."

Cody was in motion at once. He walked toward the nearest uniform. "Then it's started."

Remington was so surprised at the man's movement that he was slow to react. Tolliver stepped forward immediately, reversing his weapon and slamming the butt into Cody's head. The CIA section chief dropped. Before he could try to get up, the sergeant placed a foot on the back of his neck, pinning Cody facedown against the floor. Tolliver planted the muzzle of his M-4A1 in the man's left ear.

"What are you doing?" Cody demanded. His voice came out raw and rasping. Panic widened his eyes. His hands flailed.

"Don't move," Tolliver snapped.

Cody froze.

Remington eyed the man with renewed interest. "What's started?"

Tentatively, Cody rolled his head over so he could peer up. "I came here in good faith."

"This time?" Remington showed him a thin smile.

"Both times," Cody insisted. "I was under orders, Captain. Surely you can appreciate that. I was told to keep your knowledge of Icarus's mission to a minimum."

"So you chose not to tell me that the people holding your under-cover guy could trigger the attack?"

"We didn't know that." Blood showed on Cody's cheek where Tolliver shoved the rifle muzzle.

"But you suspected it."

"We didn't know what Icarus had."

"And now you do?"

"No."

"Why?"

"Because we don't know where he is."

Remington digested the news. The communications had been off too long after the initial attack for Remington to tell Goose not to re-lease the wounded agent from his sight. During the confusion of rescu-ing the survivors of the attack on Glitter City, Icarus had disappeared either on his own, with help, or had been abducted by a team Cody had planted with the media people.

"Did you have a rendezvous point set up?" Remington asked.

"Of course we did."

"Then why didn't Icarus make it?"

Cody hesitated till Tolliver prodded him with the rifle barrel. "I don't know."

"What are you doing here?"

"I came back here to offer help," Cody said.

"What kind of help?"

"Your computers have been infected with a virus. Not just the ones here, but all those along the line. Probably all the computers involved in this operation."

"That's not possible. There are security measures, firewalls, all along the way."

"This morning," Cody pointed out, "you would have said that the Syrian attack was not possible."

Remington said nothing.

"The Syrians have been planning this attack for over a year," Cody said. "They penetrated the mil-net at least a few weeks ago."

"With Icarus's help," Remington said, remembering the informa-tion he'd gotten from the man while he'd been in Goose's custody.

"We think they were in before that. The CIA is not totally culpable in this."

"Telling me we've been hit with a virus—even if it's true, which I doubt—isn't help."

"I know." Cody acted patient, like a parent talking to an unruly child, and Remington totally disliked the behavior. "I can give you access to another satellite system."

Remington curbed his frustration with the situation. "What satellites?"

"Satellites leased by the Romanian government," Cody said. "Other satellites that Nicolae Carpathia owns and has offered for your use."

Remington knew the name. Carpathia was an international figure, and part of the reason the U.N. peacekeeping forces and the United States Army Rangers were presently in-country. Carpathia had taken his own country by storm, becoming the darling of the population over the last few years after getting off to a less-than-sterling beginning. Yesterday, the president of Romania had stepped down and suggested that the legislature appoint Carpathia as their new president. In a surprising turn of events, both houses had unanimously done just that.

Before becoming a member of the House of Deputies in Romania, Carpathia had been a shrewd businessman who had his fingers in many international business ventures. He'd gotten rich. Remington wasn't surprised to learn that Carpathia had invested heavily in communications, and satellites would have been one of the most natural investments.

"Why would Carpathia offer satellites he controls?"

"Because he believes in the stand the United Nations and the United States are making here," Cody said.

"Why doesn't he make the offer to the Department of Defense or President Fitzhugh?"

"How long do you think it would take them to make a decision regarding using Carpathia's satellites?"

Remington took in a breath. The truth was, he knew it would take the president, both houses of Congress, and the Pentagon much longer than it would take him to make such a decision.

"You can make this happen?" Remington asked.

"I've got a satellite phone out in my Jeep," Cody said. "Nicolae is waiting for your answer."

Blind and deaf as he was in the current operation, Remington knew he was a sitting duck waiting to be picked off by Syrian troops who would no doubt storm across the border within hours—maybe even minutes. To keep that from happening, the Ranger captain knew he would make a deal with the devil himself if he had to.

"All right," Remington agreed. "Let's see what Carpathia has to offer."

Turkey
37 Klicks South of Sanliurfa
Local Time 0842 Hours

"Is anyone still inside?" Goose jogged toward one of the helicopters that had landed more or less intact. The rescue operation of the stricken Marines arriving from USS *Wasp* was only minutes old. Flames still claimed several of the Sea Knights, and Marine aircraft lay in thousands of pieces. This helicopter's rotors had been broken and the aircraft canted over to the left. Someone had opened the tail cargo hatch, allowing easier egress from the CH-46E.

A Marine staggered out of the tail section while partially support-ing a fellow soldier. Blood tracked the faces of both men. "I don't think so, Sarge. Me an' Kelly, I think we're the only ones that came down in the Bullfrog that made it alive." He glanced at his compan-ion. "An' Kelly, he ain't doing too good."

Goose pointed out the tents that were going up on the northern side of the ridge. "There's a triage station up on that hill, Marine. I've got some of the medics from my unit up there that will take care of you till we get transport units set up to medevac you back to *Wasp*." At least, that was the plan. Goose still had no idea if he could make it happen. Communications with the Ranger command post hadn't happened yet.

The Marine nodded.

"Do you need help?" Goose offered.

"No thanks, Sarge." The Marine shifted his buddy's weight against him, offering more support. "Me an' Kelly walked into this op on our own two feet, an' I reckon we'll finish up our bit of it the same way."

"Fair enough." Goose turned from the two Marines and stepped into the Sea Knight. There were plenty of soldiers who needed help and immediate rescue. And there was a lot of information that needed to be assembled. His boots rang hollowly against the helicopter's metal deck.

Five corpses lay stretched out inside the helicopter. All of them were young Marines. Normally, the sight would have staggered Goose. But now, after seeing the immense landscape of death and carnage laid around him, he was too deadened inside to react. He prayed for them, for God to take their souls into his loving embrace, more out of habit than conviction.

Two uniforms and piles of gear sat near the corpses. They were stark reminders that Goose still didn't know what had happened to Bill.

Goose took the small notebook and pen he'd been using from his combat harness. Working quickly, he jotted down the presence of weapons, ammo, and medical supplies that the Sea Knight carried and noted the two FAVs that occupied much of the cargo space. The Marine fast attack vehicles, built like dune buggies with wide tires and stripped bodies, were armed to the teeth. Both vehicles inside the helo looked salvageable and were still locked into the tie-downs securing them to the deck. Tanaka and Dewey were already coordinating salvage operations from the helos that could be entered and were using every available man who could be spared from the rescue efforts to assemble weapons and supplies. The FAVs would be additional transport as well as prizes in their own right.

Only one of the RSOVs the Phoenix squad had taken for their mission had survived the unexpected aircraft fallout. The other had been buried under tons of flaming helicopter. The surviving vehicle was presently being used to ferry the more gravely injured from the arriving Marines. Other RSOVs were on their way from the front line, but they were bringing wounded from the front lines. Goose had already assigned some of them to help with moving the Marine survivors to the triage and others to help salvage the weapons, ammo, and gear the helos had carried.

Goose also jotted down the names of the dead men, and the names of the two missing men, copying the information on their dog tags. Lieutenant Colonel Troy Folsom had been the commanding officer of the battalion landing team designated BLT 2/6. Three rifle companies—Echo, Fox, and Golf—comprised the backbone of the unit. The heavy weapons company and the light armored reconnais-

sance platoon currently assigned to USS *Wasp* backed the rifle companies. The lieutenant colonel was currently listed among the missing.
His staff sergeant, Delbert Murchison, was severely wounded and lying unconscious in the triage center.

If possible, Goose was going to let the Marines care for their own
dead and select an officer able to collect the dog tags. But if that
wasn't possible and the Turkish, U.N. peacekeeping, and American
forces were routed from the border, Goose wanted an accurate record
of those lost and missing. He'd ordered his men to record the information as well, and the men working the triage were taking down
names of the missing from the injured who were able to give them.

Given the number of empty uniforms being reported, Goose
didn't expect to find them all. The number of missing was staggering.
Nearly one man in three was gone, leaving only his uniform and gear
behind.

Goose worked his way forward to the cockpit. When he looked inside, he saw that both pilots were dead, victims of the shrapnel that
had broken through the Plexiglas. Judging from the deep slashes in
the cockpit, two or more rotor blades from another helicopter had cut
into the area.

Turning from the dead men, Goose headed for the side cargo
door. The headset was filled with constant chatter, squads talking
over each other, somehow managing to pause and listen and swap
the information each needed to get through. Through the myriad
voices, some of which he recognized as men from his own companies, Goose missed Bill Townsend's voice with agonizing awareness.

Before he stepped outside the helo, Goose spotted Dean Hardin
twenty feet away. Hardin was crouched over the broken body of a Marine who had evidently tumbled from one of the helos during a midair collision. At first, Goose thought the corporal was only making
certain the man was beyond help.

Hardin squatted with his assault rifle across his thighs. His head
moved like the heads of squirrels back in Waycross did when they
sensed a predator was in the area. That instinctive wariness on
Hardin's part froze Goose in place, triggering the hunter's skills his father had drilled into him from the time he was eight.

Working quickly, Hardin went through the dead man's pockets.
The corporal scattered personal items from the Marine's belongings
like chaff. Money quickly found its way into a cloth bag tied around
Hardin's neck and tucked into his shirt. Other things quickly followed as Hardin went through familiar motions.

A murderous, cold rage filled Goose. The emotion was an alien thing, something he had never felt before, even in the middle of a firefight. Before he knew it, he was out the cargo door and striding across the missile-blasted ground. His boots scattered aircraft pieces. He didn't know what he was going to say to the Ranger corporal, but by the time he realized that, it was too late.

Hardin heard Goose's approach. He pushed himself up, unsheathing a knife from his boot in a liquid flash of metal.

Goose didn't believe the corporal knew whom he was turning to face, only that someone had seen him stealing from the dead. Getting caught while robbing a fellow soldier, especially a dead one who had given his life for his country and his fellow soldiers, could put a man behind bars in Leavenworth for the rest of his life.

Hardin turned with the knife in his fist and every intention of fighting for his life.

Only Goose's reflexes, honed from years of battles and training, saved his life. He lifted the M-4A1 to block the knife, heard the heavy blade slam into the underside of the rifle's barrel, and felt the vibration of the blow jar along his arms. If he hadn't blocked the wicked knife slash, he felt certain that Hardin would have cut his throat.

Hardin spun away, flipping the knife expertly to his left hand in a motion so quick that most people wouldn't have noticed. His eyes blazed with wolfish intensity and hunger. Then he feinted with his right hand and swept the blade toward Goose in an effort to disembowel him. No remorse showed on the corporal's hard face. Fear tightened his sweat-slick features.

Moving quickly, Goose evaded the knife blow but felt the keen edge sheer through his uniform blouse below the combat vest. The cruel kiss of the knife blade licked fire across his belly but didn't let him know how badly he'd been injured. He stepped back, creating space, remembering even as Hardin launched a boot at his face that the man was also skilled in martial arts.

Hardin's boot caught Goose along his jaw with explosive force that snapped his head around, filled his mouth with blood, and dropped him to his knees dazed. He lost the assault rifle and didn't have time to look for the weapon before Hardin slashed at him again.

Goose fell back out of the way, only inches from death, and swung his right leg around to kick Hardin's feet from under him. The corporal landed face-first on the ground, growled foul curses, and tried to push himself up.

Forcing himself to move, Goose caught Hardin's right wrist in his own right hand, then grabbed a fistful of the corporal's hair in his left. He threw his weight on top of Hardin's head, banging the man's face into the ground. The knife came loose and Goose knocked the blade way, watching it skitter under the helicopter he'd stepped from. Goose wasn't formally trained in martial arts as Hardin was, but he was no stranger to physical confrontations. Back in Waycross, he'd been an all-star wrestler in high school. Once a fight progressed to the ground, as most did, he was in his element. He started running his opponent's body, looking for a hold that would allow him to incapacitate the man.

Hardin's left elbow came back unexpectedly and caught Goose in the face. More blood gushed from his nose, and his eyes filled with tears. Before Goose could recover, Hardin squirmed out from under him and sprang for his assault rifle.

Pushing himself up, Goose reached forward and caught Hardin's foot, tripping the man and sending him sprawling again. Hardin still managed to grab his M-4A1 and roll over onto his back, trying desperately to pull the barrel in line.

Already moving forward, knowing his life was measured in a fraction of the scant time between frantic heartbeats, Goose grabbed the assault rifle's barrel in his right hand and deflected the sudden stream of 5.56mm rounds that spewed forth. The string of reports echoed over the landscape and voices barked out, demanding to know what was going on.

Still holding the heated barrel, knowing the metal could sear his flesh if he held on too long, Goose fell on top of Hardin and hammered at the man with his left hand. He punched the corporal in the face three times, feeling the solid impacts of flesh against flesh. Hardin yowled in pain, then released the assault rifle so he could better block Goose's brutal attack.

Part of Goose knew that he was out of control. A sergeant wasn't supposed to fight with a man of lesser rank, was never supposed to lay hands on a man of lesser rank in anger. He should have pointed his weapon at Hardin and ordered the man to put his own weapons down, then placed Hardin under arrest.

But catching Hardin looting the dead had been too much. Those Marines had given their lives in an effort to come to the 75th Regiment's aid. Watching Hardin steal from them, stripping away the Rangers' dignity, had pushed Goose over the line between civilian and savage that existed within every battle-seasoned soldier.

Goose's breath drew harsh and ragged, burning and drying the

back of his throat. Despite his punishing assault, Hardin got his
hands up to block, then fired the Y between his left thumb and fore-
finger into Goose's throat. For a moment, Goose thought Hardin had
shattered his larynx. He choked, couldn't get his breath, and sagged
back. Hardin lifted a foot and kicked him in the face.

Overpowered by the kick, Goose rolled backwards, managing to
turn the effort into an ugly shoulder roll that was still good enough to
bring him to his feet. Hardin was on his feet as well, already in
midkick. Goose kept his hands in close, feeling his opponent rain
blow after blow into him. His arms kept the punches and kicks from
his face, and the Kevlar vest prevented most of the damage to his
midsection.

Without warning, Hardin turned, evidently giving up on the idea
of chopping Goose down. When the corporal shifted, Goose snaked
his left hand out, caught the man by the right shoulder, and spun him
around. He stepped forward and drove his right fist in a short, tight
arc, twisting his hips to get all his weight behind the blow.

The punch caught Hardin in the middle of his face and lifted him
off his feet. Before the corporal could steady himself, Goose raked the
M9/Model 92F pistol from his hip holster, cupped his left hand under
his right in a modified Weaver stance, and aimed at Hardin's head.

"Don't," Goose said in a cold voice. He somehow managed to
keep himself from shaking with anger or from exhaustion. He was in
no-man's-land as far as the mission went, somewhere deep in the Twi-
light Zone because of the way Bill and all the other missing soldiers
had disappeared, and in uncharted territory in dealing with his command. Never before had he ever drawn a weapon on a teammate with
the full intention of killing the man if he didn't listen.

Hardin's eyes blinked and Goose could see the calculations flicker-
ing in the man's mind.

"You're a dead man if you do," Goose promised. "I swear to God,
Hardin, I'll put a round through your head and drop you like a rock."

Cursing, Hardin lay back on the ground and kept his arms outstretched.

Two Rangers from Lieutenant Wake's Charlie Company rounded
the downed CH-46E. Both men had their assault rifles tucked muzzle
down toward the ground and butt plates resting against the upper
right shoulders, ready to open fire and ride the recoil up any target that
presented itself.

Goose stood with effort. Blood coated his mouth, and he spat a
blob of it onto the dry land.

"Sarge?" Private First Class Darrell Walker stared at Goose. He was twenty years old and new to the Rangers. He'd been recruited only a few weeks out of regular army boot camp for his computer skills.

"Arrest this man, Private," Goose commanded. "I want him held under separate guard back at the triage."

Walker hesitated, as did the other Ranger.

Goose put steel in his voice. "That was an order, Private." Command came when there wasn't time or resources for explanations, and Goose didn't want to talk about the situation till after he'd conferred with Cal Remington.

"All right, Sarge." Walker crossed to Hardin and offered to help the man to his feet.

Hardin shook the offer off and stood with overstated ease. "I don't know why you attacked me, Sergeant Gander," he stated.

Goose looked at him. "Yeah, you do."

"Whatever you think you saw," Hardin said, "that wasn't what was going on."

"Private Walker," Goose said.

"Sarge?" Walker bound Hardin's hands behind him with a pair of disposable cuffs. Ranger scout teams carried them in case they had to take prisoners while working point.

"Corporal Hardin has a pouch around his neck. I want it."

Hardin struggled, but the effort was only token resistance. Goose kept his pistol trained on the man while Walker cut the pouch free, then tossed over the bag.

Goose caught the pouch, leathered his sidearm, and examined the contents. A sheaf of money nearly two inches thick sat inside. There were also rings and bracelets and watches. Dizziness from his injuries, the heat, and everything he'd been through for the past two hours swept over him like a tidal wave.

"I saw what I saw," Goose said.

Hardin wiped his chin on his shoulder. "You're making a big mistake." Naked menace anchored the corporal's words.

"Private Walker."

"Yes, First Sergeant," Walker replied immediately, reacting to the tone in Goose's voice.

"Get that man out of my sight," Goose ordered.

"Yes, First Sergeant." Walker got on one side of Hardin, and the other Ranger mirrored him. Together, the two privates marched Hardin away.

Goose took another look at the contents of the pouch. He didn't understand how Bill Townsend could be gone, other men could be dead, and someone like Corporal Dean Hardin could be up walking around. The fact didn't make sense. He knew he'd never get the image of Hardin hanging over the dead Marine, picking his pockets clean like a carrion eater working the bones of roadkill. Before he knew the nausea was going to hit, Goose was doubled over and throwing up.

After the gut-wrenching attack passed, Goose didn't know if the reaction was triggered by the inhalation of smoke, the stink of the blood and dead bodies, or the fact that he had pulled a weapon on a fellow Ranger. *And been prepared to use it.* The thought remained as sharp and as bitter as the sour taste in his mouth.

He stared up at the blue sky in an effort to center himself. Black smoke stained the clouds and made the air taste thick and acrid. The world had changed, and he somehow knew that things could never go back to the way they had been.

He said a quick prayer, not knowing what to ask for other than his family's safety and the safety of the soldiers who faced death along the Turkish-Syrian border. He found his helmet on the ground, pulled it on his head, and got back to the job he knew and had devoted so much of his life to. Men were left to be saved, supplies salvaged, and plans laid.

And they still had no idea what shape the Syrians were in or if the mysterious vanishings had taken their toll among that army as well. For all they knew, without the satellite communications, the Syrian army was at full strength or had even been the cause of the disappearances.

❀   ❀   ❀

United States 75th Rangers 3rd Battalion
Field Command Post
35 Klicks South of Sanliurfa, Turkey
Local Time 0844 Hours

Staring at the mild-mannered, blond young man on the notebook computer's LCD screen, Cal Remington was surprised to see that Nicolae Carpathia, president of Romania as of yesterday, looked very ordinary. Carpathia was thirty-three years old, broadchested and photogenic in a pleasant sort of way rather than having movie-star good looks. He moved with compact, athletic grace but acted reserved and interested. While CIA Section Chief Alexander Cody had been arrang-

ing the sat-phone/video cam conference call, Remington had gone
through intel files that were locked into his personal computer.

Carpathia's name had been in the news a lot lately, especially as a
diplomat promoting the increase of U.N. peacekeeping efforts, but
Remington had never thought that Carpathia would be on a first-
name basis with a CIA section chief.

The Romanian president stood behind his desk, in full view of the
small video cam connected to the desktop computer monitor. The
connection was good; pixelization only occasionally blurred the re-
ception. Remington's belief that Carpathia could deliver the necessary satellite communications grew by leaps and bounds.

"Good morning, Captain Remington," Carpathia said in a
smooth baritone.

"Mr. President," Remington replied, touching his hand to his hat
brim in a quick salute. He had intended to offer that courtesy from
the start but was amazed at how easily the response came.

The field command post was a beehive of activity. The techs
changed out hard drives of the Crays, using the backup parts that
weren't infected with the virus. Several of them kept an eye on
Remington, still not quite sure of what was going on.

"Your people have quite a difficult road ahead of them,"
Carpathia said. "Of course, whatever help I may be able to offer will
be offered only too gladly."

"Thank you for that, sir. I'm encouraged by your ability to com-
municate with me now."

A slight smile tweaked the corners of Carpathia's mouth, making
him look even younger and very innocent. "Actually, I have a news
team in place near your army, Captain Remington. This communication is relatively simple."

"A news team?" Remington knew some of the media reporters
who had been behind the front lines had gathered around the area
where the Marine wing had gone down in flames.

"Yes. Would you like to see?"

"I'd like that very much."

Carpathia walked to the computer and tapped the keyboard. "I
am conversant with the computer, Captain Remington, but I struggle
with the applications to a degree. Please bear with me."

"Of course, sir." Despite the near-panicked need within him to
have access to the satellite reconnaissance Cody had promised,
Remington felt a little relaxed. Carpathia's obvious command of the
situation was reassuring.

"Ah," the Romanian president said, "here it is." He tapped a key.

The image on the notebook computer shrank to a two-inch by three-inch rectangle on the upper left corner of the screen. The rest of the monitor filled with video footage that had definitely been filmed at the crash site the LZ had turned into. Wounded Marines staggered from the vehicles. Later explosions knocked some of them from their feet. A fuel fire eruption from one of the helos' tanks engulfed two Marines who carried a third man between them. All three soldiers blazed like scarecrows that had caught fire. They ran, but they didn't get far, dropping into writhing pyres that were finally still.

"This is one of the stories that the news team is broadcasting," Carpathia said.

"Is CNN getting this?" Remington asked.

"Yes. FOX News is getting the footage as well. Would you like to see the presentation on either of those channels?"

Either of those channels. Remington heard the offer and couldn't believe it but somehow knew that Carpathia had managed to feed the news stations despite all the chaos that had ran rampant through American and British sources. "No. That will be fine."

"Would you like to hear the audio portion of this footage?"

"No," Remington answered.

"The footage that has been captured is quite dramatic," Carpathia said. "When I saw it, I was moved to contact Mr. Cody and offer the services of my country and myself."

"He hasn't mentioned how he got to know you," Remington said.

"We're the CIA," Cody said with a trace of pride in his voice. "We do business around the world."

"Romania is in a unique position, Captain Remington," Carpathia said. "We are one of the nations that form the bridge between the West and the East. After the Russian attack on Israel fourteen months ago, I happened to be in the unique position to offer Mr. Cody and his associates some assistance regarding intelligence work in the matter."

"How?"

"I own companies that regularly do business with the Russian government. The decision to attack Israel might have been a popular one, but it was not one that met with approval from every politician in the Russian parliament. Mr. Cody and his group felt that knowing who those people were might be fortuitous in the future. I provided that information."

"A favor for a favor?" Wariness vibrated through Remington. Nobody gave anything away for free, just as he was certain the satellite help wouldn't come without some price.

"Nothing so crass, Captain Remington." If Carpathia took any offense at the suggestion, he didn't show it. "I believed Mr. Cody when he presented his case."

"And you believe in the American presence here in this conflict?"

Carpathia nodded. "I do, but I also have friends within the ranks of the U.N. peacekeeping team there. If I help keep you and your people safe, then I will be saving them as well."

"Yes," Remington said. "You will. I can guarantee that, Mr. President."

One of the techs came forward, standing out of sight of the video cam built into Cody's notebook computer. He gave Remington a thumbs-up. Looking past the man, the Ranger captain saw that the Crays were up and running again, but the monitors were all on standby. He nodded at the man.

On the monitor, Carpathia remained in the small rectangle. The bigger picture showed a lone Ranger staggering out of a CH-46E with a wounded Marine in his arms. The shot froze, then closed up on the two men with the twisted wreckage of the helicopter in the background.

Goose! Remington recognized his first sergeant at a glance. Goose was still alive. He breathed a sigh of relief, then checked himself because the time in the lower right corner of the screen showed that the time the footage had been taken had been eleven minutes ago. Eleven minutes was a lifetime on a hot battlezone.

"First Sergeant Samuel Adams Gander," Carpathia said. "I believe he is called Goose."

Remington was astounded by the Romanian president's uncanny knowledge.

Carpathia spread his hand. "Do not be shocked, Captain Remington. The news service has broadcast the sergeant's name. Mr. Cody told me of your friendship with Sergeant Gander, inferred from his observation of you two on a mission this morning."

Okay, Remington thought, *Carpathia pays attention. I like a man who pays attention. He doesn't get surprised much.*

The footage rolled on again, then abruptly ended, leaving Remington ignorant of Goose's fate during the intervening eleven minutes. *Twelve minutes*, the Ranger captain corrected himself. Anything could have happened.

Carpathia leaned forward and tapped a key again. The small rectangle filled the screen again. He stared out at Remington.

The Ranger captain felt the man's eyes boring into his. He could trust Carpathia; he knew he could.

"Are you ready to accept my gift, Captain Remington?" the Romanian president asked.

"I don't have permission from the Pentagon," Remington answered.

"I had thought to contact them," Carpathia said, "but I know how slowly things can happen within the American government. I knew you were in the field and that you could use the information my satellites can bring you."

"Yes," Remington said. And he knew how long it would take for the powers that be to agree to avail themselves of Carpathia's satellites. Men would die during that time, and Remington still felt certain he could drag a victory from the jaws of defeat.

"Captain?" Carpathia said. "I await only your team hooking into the satellite truck I have outside your building."

The truck had arrived only minutes ago. Thick black cables had been run from the Crays to the vehicle, then tied in to the satellite system.

"If you move quickly enough," Carpathia said, "you may still turn this situation around."

"I could," Remington said before he realized he was going to speak. "If that area wasn't lost in darkness to us."

"Do not put up with the darkness," Carpathia encouraged. "You can put an end to it. All you have to do is give the command."

"Bring the satellites on line," Remington said.

The techs worked at their stations. One after another, the monitor screens came on, filling the darkened command post with bright illumination.

"Let there be light," Carpathia said, chuckling a little.

And there was.

United States of America
Fort Benning, Georgia
Local Time 1:46 A.M.

The world had gone crazy.

The radio, back on after sixteen minutes of dead silence that Joey felt certain indicated that the device was damaged by the wreck that had taken out the left side of his mom's car, bore frantic witness to the state of the city.

"—can't call the police," the DJ said. Howler Murphy, the midnight-to-four madman who spun censored rap records and told off-color and suggestive jokes and had earned the ire of most parents of teens around the city, had dropped his radio personality and become a clearinghouse for news. "Most of the phone lines in the city continue to be off-line. If any emergency personnel working to get those lines back up and working would care to drop by the station and let us know what is going on, I'll be happy to give you some mike time."

Driving through the military base, Joey saw dozens of people—maybe hundreds, God, it seemed like hundreds—crossing the streets with flashlights and worried expressions. MPs were out in force, bolstered by additional troops drawn from the personnel who lived on base. Other soldiers living off base came to Fort Benning to find out what was going on or had been called in to help maintain base security. All of them, Joey would bet, had similar stories of disappearances, public utility failures, and mass confusion to relate.

"I have dozens of folks stopping by the station asking to get messages to loved ones who were caught out in traffic," Howler said in an anxious and worried voice. "People, as much as I would like to help, I can't. What I would like to suggest is that those of you who are lost and scared out there stay home."

An MP with an assault rifle slung over his shoulder waved Joey off to one side of the street with a flashlight wrapped in a red plastic cone. Joey pulled the car over to a stop. When he'd tried to roll the window down at the checkpoint gate, the glass fragmented, falling out in chunks the way it was designed to do. The event, something that would have threatened to change his whole life just a few hours ago, had been anticlimactic.

"Can I see some ID, sir?" the soldier asked.

Joey still felt odd at being addressed as sir, but it made him feel kind of grown up while Jenny sat in the passenger seat. He pulled his papers from the dash. The sergeant manning the security gate had told him they would probably be needed as he progressed through the base.

The Ranger corporal glanced at the papers, then compared the driver's license and military ID to Joey. "Are you Goose's kid?"

Joey rankled a little at the "kid" tag. *From sir to kid in nothing flat.* "Yeah." He didn't want to get into the whole stepson issue, and he resented the fact that the corporal might have been only eight or ten years older than him.

"Are you okay?"

Before he could stop himself, Joey touched the swelling at the side of his face. Crusted blood clung to his skin, and his head was still pounding. "I got sideswiped while sitting at a stop sign when all of this started."

"You look like you could use a doctor."

"I'm still standing." That was one of the things Goose said.

The corporal handed the papers back. "Your father's a good man. His unit is having a hard go of it over there in Turkey."

"Have you heard how things are going there?" Joey asked. His interest in Goose's welfare outweighed any slight he might have suffered.

The corporal shook his head. "No. I'm sorry. I'm pulling for him. A lot of us are."

"Thank you."

"Where are you headed, Joey?"

"The special services building. My little brother Chris is there. My mom got called in and had to leave him there." He didn't add that his mom had dropped Chris off hours ago because he just didn't need that kind of guilt.

"Do you know how to get there?"

"Yeah. Take the next right, up three blocks, and the building sits on the left."

"Correct. We're asking that all civilian personnel go to their homes until we get the base back up and running properly. I'll radio up the line, let the guys who are working that area know what you're doing there, but you're only going to get a small reprieve. After that, they'll make you get home."

A rebellious anger ignited in Joey. The world was going crazy, Goose was over in Turkey fighting for his life, and he was being told—in effect—to go to his room. He wasn't a kid; he needed someone to recognize that. Still, he held the anger under control, but only just.

"Don't take the situation personally," the corporal advised, obviously reading Joey's expression. "Anyone who isn't in uniform is being told the same thing. A lot of strange stuff has happened." He sighed and shook his head. "We got people out here claiming aliens have invaded the planet, or that terrorists have set off some kind of electromagnetic pulse bomb that's been coded to DNA sequencings. Base security has got to come first."

Joey let go of as much of the anger as he could. He blew out his breath. "It's cool," he said. "I understand." But he didn't. Nothing made sense. Offered the choice of an alien invasion or terrorists with an EMP bomb coded for DNA sequencing, he didn't want to choose either. There had to be another answer.

The corporal stepped back and waved Joey on.

Slipping the car's transmission back into drive, Joey rolled forward. He couldn't help looking around. Only a little farther on, MPs obviously had harsh words with two men in civilian clothing. The men had no clue about how to act with a sergeant giving orders. Some of the men who lived on base were husbands of military women. Having trouble with male spouses in a military family wasn't new.

Around the corner, Joey spotted a woman almost freaking out as she talked to a two-man team of MPs. She gestured wildly and thrust a baby jumper out at the two soldiers.

"My baby!" the woman wailed through the open window of the car. "Please help me find my baby!"

Before he knew it, Joey's foot pressed a little harder on the accelerator. His mom's car clattered over the speed bumps. He made the next turn and pulled into the emergency services center.

Nearly twenty people stood outside the building, clustered around two Jeeps full of MPs.

Renewed anxiety screamed to life inside Joey, breaking loose like a flood shredding a dam. He turned to Jenny. "Out. Hurry. I've got to find Chris." There was no way Chris could be sleeping through everything that was going on.

A siren screamed only a few blocks over, followed immediately by a voice thundering over a PA system.

If he's not asleep, I can calm him down, Joey told himself. *He'll only have been worried for a few minutes. As late as I am, he's probably already with Mom. She wouldn't leave him here in the middle of this.*

Unless something had happened to his mom. Joey's belly flip-flopped like a bag full of snakes. He started shaking as he jogged toward the building's entrance. Bile bit at the back of his throat with sour venom.

A soldier in uniform stood near the entrance. Tears showed on his cheeks despite the night's shadows. "My son is missing. I left him here. I brought him here myself not two hours ago after I was called in. These people can't just tell me he's disappeared. That every child in this place has just disappeared. They can't make me believe—"

No! Panic burst inside Joey. He stepped up his jog to an all-out run, catching Jenny off guard and powering by her.

"Hey!" A soldier at the entrance grabbed for him.

Joey ducked, going under the soldier's arm and skidding feet-first in a baseball slide. He rose in a bounce automatically when his feet touched the wall at the first hallway. He slapped the wall with his hands, powering himself forward again as the soldier came after him. Another MP reached for Jenny, but she evaded the guy's grasp with athletic ease and raced after Joey and the first MP.

Only a couple turns later, knowing the location of the nursery from past acquaintance with the building, Joey saw four women dressed in scrubs standing out in the hallway. The MP pounded after him, not gaining ground because Joey was so quick.

Holding up his ID to the women as they started to draw back, out of breath, Joey said, "I'm here for my brother. Chris Gander. My mother, Megan Gander, brought him here."

The women stared at Joey, then looked at each other. They all looked shell-shocked.

One of the women, a matronly type with gray hair and bifocals, looked at Joey. "The children aren't here, son."

"Fine," Joey said, breathing rapidly. "I figured my mom would come get him before I could get here." *See? Everything's fine. Chris is fine. Mom is fine.*

But the woman's look told Joey everything wasn't fine. "What's wrong?"

"Your mom didn't come get your brother," the woman said.

"What do you mean?"

"The children that were left here . . . they aren't here anymore."

Panic slammed into Joey. "Then where are they?"

Before the woman could answer, the MP dropped a hand on Joey's shoulder and spun him into the nearest wall. Joey ducked his head back in time to keep his face from smacking the cinder block. The impact knocked some of the breath from his lungs. In the next instant, the MP had levered Joey's right arm so far up between his shoulder blades that Joey felt certain his arm was going to pop out of its socket.

"I've got ID," Joey said, his voice rising to a high pitch because of the excruciating pain. "It's in my shirt pocket. I'm military. I've got a right to be here. I'm here to pick up my little brother."

The MP leaned into Joey from behind, pinning him up against the wall. "We're not letting people into the building. We've got this area sealed up."

"Why?" Joey demanded.

Jenny came running up, only a couple strides in front of the MP chasing her.

"Orders," the soldier snapped. "Ma'am, you stay right there, and I mean *now*."

Looking confused and ticked off, Jenny froze. The other MP arrived and ordered her to turn and face the wall, then put a hand against her back to hold her in place.

"What's going on?" Joey demanded. "You've got no right to do this."

"I've got every right," the MP retorted. "This base has been put on emergency alert. General's orders."

"I just came here to get my brother," Joey said. "I want to *see* my brother."

"What's your brother's name?" the matronly woman asked.

"Gander," Joey replied. "Chris Gander. I'm his older brother, Joey. My mom had to have told you people I would be here after him."

"She did. Corporal, could I see his ID?"

"Yes, ma'am," the corporal said. He took Joey's ID from his shirt pocket and passed it over.

The woman examined the documents. "Corporal, I'd appreciate it if you'd let this young man go."

"Ma'am, this kid just broke through our cordon and I can't just—"

"This kid," the woman said in a stern voice, "*is* a kid. Maybe you need to keep that in mind. He's already gotten through your cordon. I suggest that taking him into custody now isn't going to remove the fact that the cordon was broken, or square things with your sergeant. Now is it?"

The MP was slow in answering. "No, ma'am."

"And his father is First Sergeant Goose Gander," the woman said. "Maybe you haven't heard of Goose, but I can guarantee that he won't enjoy hearing that his son was manhandled by one of his fellow Rangers while he was off in Turkey fighting for his life."

The MP's reply was grudging. "Probably not, ma'am."

"Then let him go. I'll vouch for him."

"Yes, ma'am." The reluctance in the corporal's voice was evident, but he stepped back from Joey and released him.

"When I get through talking to him," the woman said, "I'll send him back out to you."

"Yes, ma'am."

Joey moved back from the wall.

"Is this young lady with you?" the woman asked.

"Yes," Joey answered.

"Is she part of the family?"

Under other circumstances, the question would have embarrassed Joey. All he could think about was Chris. *Missing.* The word hung in his screaming mind like a malignant growth.

"No," Joey answered. "Not family."

"I'm a friend of Joey's," Jenny answered.

The woman looked at the two MPs. "Then I'll need her to stay here as well."

The two MPs touched their hat brims and left. Joey figured they would give him some flack for making their jobs hard, but they didn't. They almost looked sorry for him.

Joey turned to the woman. "Where is my brother? Where is Chris?"

The woman reached out and took his hands. "He's gone, Joey. I'm so sorry to have to tell you this, but he's gone." Fresh tears spilled down her face. Her voice turned into a forced whisper as she continued speaking. "They're—they're *all* gone."

Joey shook his head desperately. "You're not making any sense. My mother called me. She said she left Chris here. With you people. Did she come get him?"

"No." The woman's voice was hoarse. "I pray to God that she had. That all the parents had. But they didn't."

"Then where is my brother?" Joey was almost yelling. Jenny put a hand on his arm and stood close at his side. Joey made himself calm down; he wasn't calm, but he wasn't yelling, even though he wanted to.

The woman's voice wouldn't come. Finally, she took Joey by the hand and led him into a nearby room. The room was filled with beds. A box of preschool toys sat against one wall.

As he entered the room, Joey noticed the empty children's clothing that had been left in each bed. He remembered the woman in the minivan who had lost her daughter. A rush of pain and confusion spilled over inside him, rising with horrifying certainty . The most horrible sight Joey had ever seen waited in the bed the woman guided him to.

There, in the middle of the bedding, Chris's favorite PJs were spread out. The little jammies looked exactly like the other stacks of clothing on the beds and in the cribs. Six or seven grief-stricken parents and family members stood inside the room.

"No!" The cry tore loose from Joey's throat. Before he knew it, his legs went out from under him and he dropped to his knees. *"No!"*

❈   ❈   ❈

The Mediterranean Sea
USS *Wasp*
Local Time 0851 Hours

So many people missing.

The reality of the situation thundered through Delroy Harte's mind as he entered names on the report he was preparing for Captain Mark Falkirk. He entered name after name, finding time and again a familiar name. And the letter remained to be written for Chief Mellencamp. The knowledge lay like an iron anvil in his thoughts.

USS *Wasp* was, in effect, a ghost ship. Nearly a third of her crew had inexplicably vanished. Only empty uniforms and personal items were left behind by the people who had been on board a half an hour ago. With the absence of the Marine wing and groundpounders, *Wasp* seemed to echo hollowly, as if her heart and guts had been ripped from her. The reports from the other ships came through in much the same vein.

CNN and FOX News carried video footage and commentary from a small group of Romanian reporters that had been behind the lines at the Turkish-Syrian border. However, the wisps of information and glimpses of what that area had become were maddening. Not enough information was being received to know what was truly going on over there, and more than enough was being seen to let every crewperson aboard *Wasp* know that the relief effort had failed, becoming a disaster that further weakened the positions of the Rangers, the U.N. peacekeeping teams, and the Turkish army.

"Chaplain Harte."

Surprised, Delroy glanced up and found a young ensign standing in the doorway to his office. The Navy chaplain recognized the young man but hadn't had many dealings with him. Most of the usual staff assigned to him had turned up among the missing. Given what he was beginning to suspect, he found that oddly reassuring and traumatic at the same time. The men who had served with him had been true believers in God, and their faith had been strong.

Stronger than mine, Delroy thought. And for the first time in a long time, he wished that Glenda were there with him. His wife always seemed to be the rock in their relationship. When he fought with his doubts and his fears, when he questioned his own faith in God— *when the time came to bury Terry*—she had stood resolute at his side and seen that things were taken care of.

Her ability to deal with everything through God's grace or her own patience had finally made him see what a drain he was on her. When his pain over his son's death wouldn't go away, when he saw how his own inability to deal with the grief resonated within his wife, he had left Charlotte. He had used her like a crutch, demanding that she make sense of something that made no sense at all. He hadn't been able to deal with his own weakness and his guilt over it.

"Yes, Ensign," Delroy said.

The ensign held up a box. "This was left down in the medical department."

Delroy looked at the box without comprehension.

"Chief Mellencamp's personal property. Dr. Thomas asked me to bring this box to you."

Delroy stood and took the box. During the confusion of the disappearances, he had forgotten about the chief's personal effects. He had intended them to be shipped back with the letter he had yet to write.

"Thank you, Ensign." Delroy hefted the box, surprised to find that so little remained of a man. But Terrence's personal possessions, shipped back after his death, had been few as well. And after Josiah Harte's death, not counting the house and the car and bank accounts and life insurance, not much had remained of his father either.

Just the memories, Delroy told himself. He only had to close his eyes to see his father pounding the pulpit in front of the congregation, or to take Terrence's hand when he'd taught his son fishing. *Just close your eyes and they're right there. But when you open them. God, when you open them.*

"Is there anything else I can do, Chaplain Harte?" the ensign asked. "Coffee, maybe? You look like you could use it."

Delroy placed the box on the corner of his desk. Chief Mellencamp's Bible lay on top of the small pile of family pictures, jewelry, and knickknacks the chief had picked up around the world that Delroy had felt his family would want.

"Coffee would be most welcome," Delroy answered.

"I'll get you some."

Taking the Bible from the box, Delroy studied the simulated leather and gilt lettering. "A moment before you go, Ensign."

"All right."

The weight of the Bible rested comfortably in Delroy's big hands. How long had it been since he had held a copy of God's Word and felt the familiar mixture of euphoria and fear? Delroy still had his father's Bible and the Bible he had given Terrence the day he had taken his oath and become a soldier. Over the years, the Navy chaplain had read from them both, seeking solace and remembrance and understanding of all the terrible things that had happened.

Turning, Delroy faced the young ensign. "How strong is your faith, son?"

"My faith?" The ensign appeared uncomfortable. "In the captain? I have to admit, I've never seen anything—"

"In God," Delroy interrupted. "How strong is your faith in God, Ensign?"

"It's good." The ensign glanced longingly at the door over his shoulder.

"Does the question make you uncomfortable?"

The ensign nodded. "Yes, sir."

"Why is that?"

"I don't like talking about stuff like that, Chaplain."

"But you took an oath, Ensign," Delroy said. "'I do solemnly swear that I will support and defend the Constitution of the United

States against all enemies, foreign and domestic; that I will bear true faith and allegiance to the same; and that I will obey the orders of the President of the United States and the orders of the officers appointed over me, according to regulations and the Uniform Code of Military Justice. So help me God.' U.S. Code, Section 502." He breathed in, remembering his own swearing-in ceremony, remembering Terry's. "Why do you think the phrase, 'So help me God,' is in there?"

"I wouldn't know, sir. I guess it always has been."

Delroy nodded to himself. "You can go, ensign." He glanced down at Chief Mellencamp's Bible in his two big hands.

"Chaplain Delroy."

"Yes, Ensign."

The man hesitated and looked uncertain. "Did I do something wrong, Chaplain? I didn't mean to offend."

Delroy looked up, feeling bad and embarrassed. With everything else going on, the loss of lives along the Turkish-Syrian border and the unexplained disappearances of so many military personnel, it was incredible to see that a crewman could still be concerned with leaving just the right impression on an officer.

"No, Ensign, you didn't do anything wrong," Delroy replied. "This is just a trying time. I only asked because I struggle with my own faith now and again, and it's good to hear others talk about theirs." He held up Mellencamp's Bible. "That was one of the reasons the chief and I enjoyed each other's company so much."

"Yes, sir."

"Would you check on the other lists?" Sweeper teams still moved within *Wasp*. Most of the missing had already been confirmed, but Captain Falkirk had wanted a thorough ship's search before those names were officially designated MIA.

"Of course, Chaplain." The ensign excused himself and left.

Delroy returned to his chair behind the desk. He sat with Chief Mellencamp's Bible in his lap for a time, thinking back on their friendship and all the confusing questions that raced through his thoughts. Then he noticed the paper sticking out of the Bible.

Opening the book, Delroy found several sheets of legal pad paper folded up in Revelation. The chief's Bible had been well used. Mellencamp's neat, precise handwriting covered the generous margins, and the pages were marked with a rainbow of highlighter colors. The chief had his own code for the information he highlighted, but he used it only for proof of his own steel-trap memory.

As chief petty officer, Mellencamp had carried long lists of men, supplies, and necessary tasks in his head. Delroy had protested, in fun between two good friends, that the chief was extraordinarily equipped and his own arguments should be given the benefit of a handicap. But Mellencamp had loved God's Word—the Old Testament and the New—and could quote passages from several books, as well as psalms.

The fact that the chief had been preparing information based on Revelation was no surprise. Lately, every conversation Delroy had entered into with Mellencamp had turned in that direction. The chief had been convinced that these were the end times, that the Rapture—when God would come and call his church home from the earth—was very near.

Delroy's eyes were drawn to the words his friend had scrawled upon the paper.

> We will be called home to heaven. No warning bell. No chance to say good-byes. One moment in this world, the next, standing in God's perfection.
>   And what of the people left behind?

Hypnotized by the question Mellencamp had written across the page, Delroy followed the chief's thinking and found himself flipping through the pages of Revelation. In minutes, he was digging out books from the neat, compact shelves behind him. Fear and horror and hope all began to dawn in his heart.

The end of the world: It was real and it had come. Navy Chaplain Delroy Harte became more convinced of that with each passing minute, and his thoughts became consumed with the carnage, the lies, and the treachery that were in store for those left behind.

United States 75th Rangers 3rd Battalion
Field Command Post
35 Klicks South of Sanliurfa, Turkey
Local Time 0922 Hours

"How bad is it, Goose?" Captain Cal Remington paced the interior of the command post, scanning the computer monitors that revealed the graveyard of helicopters where the LZ had once been. He spoke over the private frequency chipped into his first sergeant's headset, keeping his voice pitched low enough that no one around him could overhear.

"It's bad, sir," Goose said. "About as bad as it could be." The first sergeant listed the details in a verbal code Remington and he had worked out years ago when Remington had taken command of the company.

Anyone listening would have been lost in the gobbledygook of baseball players, stats, records, and play references. After spending so many years together and being used to each other's ways, the Ranger captain translated the code in his head immediately without writing anything down.

After the mysterious disappearances and the casualties along the border during the first wave of the Syrian attack, the Ranger companies were down to roughly a third of their original strength. The U.N. peace-keeping forces were in similar shape. The Marine wing detached from USS *Wasp* was all but decimated from vanishings and the aerial crashes that had littered the dead across the harsh mountainous ground.

The Syrians, though, remained at almost the same strength they'd had prior to the missile launch. Repeated viewings of the footage

Nicolae Carpathia's satellites had captured revealed only a few vanishings from among their ranks. Still, the events of the day had evidently been enough to check the Syrian advance. Enemy troops—Remington felt he could safely consider the Syrians that—continued to reorganize after the disappearances. It wouldn't be long, the Ranger captain knew, before they discovered the extent of the attrition his troops had suffered. And when they did . . .

"Goose," Remington said, only then realizing that silence had stretched between his first sergeant and himself.

"I'm here, sir." Goose's voice sounded flat.

Remington knew the loss of men was getting to Goose. The first sergeant had never taken the deaths of men under his command well. During battle, during the fine-tuning of a tactical op, Goose never let the regret and self-recriminations touch him, but during the fallow times between, Goose struggled with those losses. Marriage and fatherhood had been good for him, binding the wounds and keeping his heart strong. But at the same time, the family that kept Goose together had also created a new weight for the first sergeant to carry into the field.

"We're not going to be able to hold that position."

"I know that, sir. I apologize, sir."

"Knock off the *sir*, Goose. We've been friends a lot longer than I've had these bars."

Goose hesitated. "That we have," he acknowledged. But Remington could still hear the unstated *sir* in his voice.

"You've got nothing to apologize for," Remington said.

"I could have stopped that transmission," Goose said.

"Negative, soldier." Remington made his voice forceful. He strode with his hands clasped behind his back, taking care to step over the bundles of thick black cables that snaked across the floor to the Crays. "The responsibility of that issue does not reside with you or within your purview." The Ranger captain made his voice crisp and clean, ringing with authority. "If the ball was dropped anywhere, it was on my end. I should have asked our alphabet agency more questions regarding the op before I sent your team in."

"They would have lied to you."

Remington knew Goose was offering him a way out, not wanting the captain to take the blame either. A small smile framed Remington's lips. He *had* made a mistake by taking Section Chief Alexander Cody's story on faith. However, Remington didn't have much respect for the CIA.

"If they lied to me," Remington said, "that again would have made it my fault. As captain, I have to be a human lie detector. That power was invested in me by the Officer Candidate School, by the grace of God, and by the board that charged me with my command. No one can lie to me." The sheer brass of the statement was a joke he shared with Goose, but both of them knew that a commanding officer had to have that kind of view of himself to get the job done. "The agency representative withheld the truth from us, Sergeant, and there's nothing we could have done about that."

"No, sir."

"In addition to that, even if you had stopped that call, you don't know that a backup plan wasn't in place regarding a missed check-in."

"I know."

"Then let's worry about the things you do know and the operations that you have some control over." Remington gazed at the monitors.

The display of the images on the screens still astounded him. Whatever satellites Nicolae Carpathia was using brought in imaging—even voices, when cameras were close enough for the microphone pickups to activate—on par with or better than the mil-spec satellites they'd been using for the border op.

The screens constantly shifted perspectives, from ground cameras carried by reporters working the scene to cameras mounted on soldiers' weapons. Goose had one mounted on his helmet at present, providing Remington with a first-person view of everything the first sergeant saw.

At the moment, Goose walked the perimeter of the border the Rangers had been assigned. The first sergeant carried his M-4A1 at port arms just the way the drill instructors back in boot taught. Overturned and burnt vehicles stood out against the broken and cratered earth turned black from missile blasts and fuel-fed fires that had scoured the ground. Teams of Rangers, Marines, U.N. peacekeeping personnel, and Turkish army regulars moved through the debris searching for any that might still be left alive.

"Since we know we can't hold that position," Remington went on, "we need to evacuate."

"I know." The camera shifted as Goose climbed aboard an overturned truck. The view shifted as the camera adjusted to the shade inside the truck's cargo area. Goose's hands holding the assault rifle disappeared for a moment, then came back with a notepad. He sorted through the cargo spilled across the back of the truck and jotted notes about the contents. Later, he would coordinate the recovery of the materials that he deemed necessary and salvageable. "I'm rationing the fuel that we've been able to scavenge, and I've got Henderson and his motor-pool division working on vehicles that might be able to carry wounded and cargo that can be repaired quickly."

"Sounds like you're ahead of me." Remington moved on, checking the screens.

"No, sir," Goose replied. "We've been through situations like this before. This is SOP on a blown mission according to the parameters you've established."

"Actually, Sergeant," Remington said, "I'd be hard-pressed to remember if I came up with those parameters or you did."

"They work," Goose replied. "If it ain't broke, don't fix it."

"Agreed." An image on the screen caught Remington's eye. The banner at the bottom of the screen read TURKISH-SYRIAN BORDER—RECORDED EARLIER.

The image showed Goose carrying a wounded Marine from the burning helicopter. The first sergeant remained frozen in midstep. Pain and desperate resolve were etched on Goose's face. It was one of those images that would end up splashed on the front pages of newspapers and magazine covers back home, Remington could tell.

For a moment, a hint of jealousy flared through Remington. Even when they'd been soldiering together as sergeants, Goose had always seemed to capture the attention and respect of other soldiers as well as the media. He was photogenic and self-deprecating, every inch a team player who sweated blood for the cause.

But Goose would never be an officer. A few times, when his jealousy had risen too high, Remington had consoled himself with that thought. Goose would never be an officer, never be more than the first sergeant that he was. And when he'd had his fill of battle, as Remington suspected Goose soon would now that he had Megan and Chris waiting at home for him, Goose would quietly lay down his arms and concentrate on being a husband and father.

Remington hadn't wanted to deal with any of those responsibilities that would divide his attention and his personal resources. The screen cut away, showing footage of the caravan of vehicles from Glitter City rumbling along the road to Sanliurfa. The refugees had actually reached the city over an hour ago, and more footage showed the arrival of those vehicles inside the city. Several SCUDs had slammed Sanliurfa during the initial attack. Sections of the city were burning ruins now.

"Since we're agreed on the evacuation," Goose said, "all we need is a time frame."

"Part of that will depend on how soon you can get those men ready to go." Remington returned to the screen that showed Goose's point of view.

"We need transportation."

Remington touched the monitor in front of him, loving the power that knowledge gave him. The touch-screen programming that came with the satellite feeds made shifting between perspectives a breeze. Maybe the generals at the Pentagon would give him a hard time about his decision to take the help Nicolae Carpathia had so freely offered, but Remington felt that, in the end, no blame would be laid at his doorstep. Linking with Carpathia had been the thing to do, for just the reasons the Romanian president had gone into.

The monitor cleared in a heartbeat. A long line of military trucks raced along a winding mountain road. The view from the satellite peered down at the countryside. With the magnification available in Carpathia's satellites, Remington could have isolated each truck and shifted over to infrared to discover how many men rode inside.

"Transportation is on the way, Goose," the Ranger captain said. "You'll have it in about five hours. I've got a convoy of trucks aimed in your direction from Diyarbakir."

The distance from the convoy's origination point outside Diyarbakir and the border was 223 miles of treacherous road. The Marine wing from *Wasp* had traveled a little more than that, but the aircraft had been able to fly in a straight line at an average of 150 miles an hour. The land-based support had to travel through treacherous mountain roads further hampered by occasional damage from SCUDs. The five hours Remington quoted to his first sergeant was only if nothing untoward happened during the jump.

"You're stripping the secondary unit, sir," Goose said.

The secondary unit of Rangers in Diyarbakir had been primarily support and supply staff. But they were a fighting unit with heavy field artillery as well, capable of becoming part of a pincer movement should the need arise.

"Superficially," Remington agreed, "the convoy might look like that, but that unit is primarily designated for emergency relief. There is a lot of cargo space aboard those vehicles to help with your wounded."

"What about our dead?"

Remington cursed in his mind, but not one word escaped his lips.

He knew the evacuation would come down to this. A Ranger was trained never to leave a comrade behind, not even a dead one. And the fallback op from the border was going to require more than that from them.

On the move again, Remington walked back to the computer monitor linked to Goose's helmet cam. "We can't take them, Goose."

"Captain, I didn't lead those men here to leave them—"

"You didn't lead them here to watch them die either, First Sergeant Gander." Remington made his voice hard. "Did you?"

The view from Goose's helmet cam lifted briefly to the sky. Traces of smoke still hung in the air. Remington didn't know what answer Goose hoped to find there. Goose still clung to the idea that some higher power actually watched over the world and made decisions about who lived or died. Remington knew that decision rested solely within the individual. A strong man outlived a weak one. A warrior outlived a pacifist. In Remington's book, life's rules were simple. No higher power influenced his life or his rules.

"No, sir," Goose replied. "I didn't lead them here for that."

"*We* didn't lead them here for that, Goose." Remington made his voice gentle again. The commands came naturally. "We cut our losses. We save who we can. We let the others go." He paused, knowing he had to choose his words carefully. "Those we leave behind, Goose, we remember. If we can, we'll return for them and take them back to their families."

"Yes, sir."

Returning for the dead was one of the last things Remington wanted to do. Images of other ops where men had been lost came sharply to mind. Corpses left too long in the sun bloated, became breeding grounds for flies, and turned horrific. A company that had to retrieve its own dead days after the battle, as would likely be the case in this present engagement, suffered mental and emotional damage from that mission that hampered them on the battlefield. If possible, Remington intended to see that someone else was called in for that duty, but at the moment there weren't any possibilities at hand. The mystery vanishings had left everyone strapped for men.

Except the Syrians.

More news about the worldwide event poured into Remington's sat feeds from around the globe. So far, his impression was that Africa and South America had been hardest hit, with Europe next in line, and the Middle and Far East hardly touched. And Remington knew that the full depth of the losses weren't known yet. In some places in the United States, the equivalent of whole towns had vanished. Preliminary reports indicated that China might have lost ten million, but that was merely a drop in the bucket in the population of that vast country. Russia was also lightly touched, at least comparatively.

But despite their seemingly minimal losses, Russia was mobilizing her armies, air force, and navy. That news had filtered down through the command net. What shape those troop movements would eventually take remained to be seen, but the Pentagon was definitely worried. The United States had never been more vulnerable to an attack.

Remington didn't mention any of that to Goose. At present, the first sergeant believed the vanishings to be localized, either the effect of some weapon of mass destruction that the U.S. military hadn't known about or an unnatural phenomenon. Once the news broke that the vanishings had occurred around the world, the Ranger captain knew the battered remnants of the 75th Rangers would lose some of their belief that they would make it out of their present situation alive.

And belief, Remington knew, was necessary in command. Not the kind of faith Goose sometimes talked about that existed between a man and God, but the faith a soldier had in his own abilities and in the orders of his superior officers.

Without a strong command structure, an army was a riot and uncontrolled chaos waiting to happen.

Goose's view returned to the stricken battlefield. He was in motion again, which Remington knew from experience was good. Goose thought best on his feet when he had an objective to accomplish. And Remington intended to keep his first sergeant busy during the long, hard hours it would take to get the retreat organized.

"At first blush," Remington said, "the arriving convoy is going to look like reinforcements."

"What about Syrian intelligence?" Goose asked.

Remington knew Goose referred to the satellites the Russians had allowed the Syrians to use. Since the devastating losses Russia had suffered fourteen months ago during the unprovoked attack on Israel, Russia had sought to rebuild her strength through allies in the Middle East and the Eastern bloc.

The creation of Israel in 1948 had fed the Cold War between the superpowers that had intensified after the Second World War. With the United States backing Israel, Russia had invested heavily in other Middle Eastern countries to offset the edge that the American military had gained in the area. Since Chaim Rosenzweig's formula had elevated his nation's fortunes, Russia had fed the jealousy of the other Middle Eastern nations, gaining many allies that still smarted over past defeats at the hands of the Israelis.

Realizing the Eastern bloc might also be a source of Russian strength, Remington remembered that Romania was part of that sector. The Kremlin's top people would certainly court new president Nicolae Carpathia.

Maybe he already has been courted. The thought was disconcerting to Remington, but as quickly as it had come, the possibility faded from his mind. Even from only the quick conversation he'd had with Carpathia, the Ranger captain had the distinct impression that the Romanian president was very much his own man and would honor any agreement he gave his word to.

The feeling was unusual for Remington. Generally he distrusted most people and often found himself prepared to believe the worst of them. Carpathia, though, was very different. He'd known that even before the Romanian president had lent him the use of the satellites.

"Syrian intelligence has been severely limited," Remington said, addressing Goose's question. "The NSA arranged for key Russian satellites over the border to experience difficulties within minutes of the attack. Syrian military is as blind and deaf as we were. They have no idea how many losses we've actually incurred."

Unless Carpathia gave them access to satellite feeds, as well as Remington. The thought was natural to Remington given the circumstances, but he quickly dismissed the possibility. Carpathia could find a major ally in the United States, and he would be owed big-time after the assist along the Turkish-Syrian border.

Remington turned his attention once more to his men.

"All we've got to do is keep up a strong front along the border until nightfall roughly eight hours from now," Remington said. "You can do that, Goose."

"Yes, sir."

"Keep patrols moving along the border. If the Syrians want more intel, make them pay for it. They'll have to send in men and machines. When they do, take them out. Hold the center, Goose."

"They'll have another wave of SCUDs ready soon."

"Dig in. Tighter than ticks on a hound. As long as they're throwing SCUDs at your men, they can't put an infantry offensive through there. The Turkish military in Diyarbakir are amped up with a supply of Patriot missiles brought in by the United States military machine.

Most of those SCUDs will never make it across the border. And when those gun crews fire, they're going to be targeted in turn. We've already got several emplacements marked."

"Yes, sir."

Goose's camera view swept the ridgeline behind the border. Remington knew the first sergeant was thinking of the men he would lose when those attacks came.

"For now, Goose," the Ranger captain said, "we hold what we've got. The biggest threat there is the Syrian infantry and cav units. Once they start across the border, we can't hold them back."

"I know, sir."

"After the transport vehicles arrive, station them around as if you're preparing to dig in. Get your wounded and your salvaged materials together. After full dark, start loading them aboard the trucks. I want the evacuation underway by 0200. For the moment, we're going to pull back to Sanliurfa."

"Affirmative," Goose replied. "Can we hold Sanliurfa?"

"We don't know yet. That depends on how much the Syrians are willing to invest in this op."

Goose's helmet cam raked the ravaged battlefield. Rangers stayed busy digging their dead and salvageable supplies from wrecks, craters, and piles of stone that had been heavily fortified staging areas.

"They've already invested heavily," the sergeant said. "I don't think they'll back off now."

"Neither do I." Remington scanned the command post, taking in the monitors. "Captain Mark Falkirk is organizing a bare-bones support team aboard *Wasp*. They're going to evac the wounded from Sanliurfa when the transport reaches the city, and they're going to provide air cav to put down any potential Syrian air force units."

"Tell Captain Falkirk that the 75th appreciates the help," Goose said.

"I already have." Remington could tell that Goose had more on his mind. "What are you thinking?"

Without hesitation, Goose said, "I want to stage the evac in two waves. The wounded and the materials go first. The trucks are slower than the RSOVs and APCs we've got. They can leave at 0200 but we won't leave until 0400. We'll cover their retreat."

"That two-hour gap is dangerous, Sergeant."

"Understood, sir," Goose replied. "But the convoy carrying the wounded could break down. If it does, I don't know that I could get the Ranger rifle companies to abandon those men."

Remington knew that Goose was right. And even if he would be successful in ordering fighting men back to leave wounded comrades in the arms of their enemies, the Ranger captain knew that Goose wouldn't be able to leave. After everything those men had experienced today, leaving men behind wasn't going to fit into their acceptable parameters.

"It's forty klicks to Sanliurfa," Goose went on. "If the convoy makes good time, they can reach the city in an hour. That will give them an hour to load the wounded and get the city defenses reinforced before we leave our posts."

"Done," Remington said. "But with you leaving that late, you're going to be hard-pressed to outrun the dawn. Once the sun is up, the Syrians will be better able to see you."

"I know that, sir," Goose said. "I'll talk to the company commanders, but I'm sure they'll agree that the two-stage wave is more doable for them than a mass retreat."

"Carry on, Goose. Let me know what I can do to help you."

"A prayer, sir," Goose said quietly. "Now and then when you have the time, a prayer."

Remington broke the com connection. He had his own preparations to attend to. The command post personnel, including the satellite crew, would pull back after dark. Carpathia already had another crew waiting in Sanliurfa to keep the communications open so there would be no loss of intel.

"Captain Remington." One of the corporals manning the computer terminals waved for the captain's attention. "I've got an encrypted personal message from the Pentagon here, sir."

Irritated, Remington approached the computer. He took his PDA from his pocket and set it in the dock attached to the PC. The machine flashed for a moment as the message was uploaded.

Remington figured the communiqué would be a slap on the wrist for accepting Carpathia's help. That had to be coming. He queued the PDA and read the message, verifying the pass codes that identified the message as legitimate.

In terse sentences, the Joint Chiefs of Staff at the Pentagon had advised him that the military was currently moving to DEFCON 3, the defensive condition defined as *Increase in force readiness above normal readiness*.

The news let Remington know that the theater of action had grown much larger than Turkey, had now, in fact, stretched across the globe. For the Pentagon to declare DEFCON 3, the United States had to fear attack. The only candidates to garner that kind of attention were China and Russia.

Had either of those countries attacked? Were they, not the Syrians, responsible for the mysterious vanishings?

United States of America
Cheyenne Mountain Operations Center, Colorado Springs
Local Time 2429 Hours

"Is this your first time at DEFCON 3?"

The bizarre question chipped through Jim Manners' focus. The technical sergeant wasn't sure if that was the first time the question had been asked or if it was only the first time he'd heard it. He glanced to his right and found Tamara Coleman seated at the console next to him.

Tamara was part of Delta Crew. Her black skin cooled with the green glow of the monitor broadcasting a night-vision display before her. She was in her late twenties and had made technical sergeant three months before Jim had. When he'd first come to the Cheyenne Mountains Operations Center, she'd trained him at his post.

She was chatty and competent and attractive. During the training period, he'd discovered she tried out for the Olympics in the hundred-meter dash and the mile and had nearly snared a position on the American team a few times. Running was one of her passions, and she made it a point to work out in Colorado's high altitudes, hoping to qualify for the American team during the next competition.

"Yeah," Jim answered. "At least, it's my first DEFCON 3 on shift here." He frowned at the monitors. "It's one thing to know we're at DEFCON 3, but it's another to watch it taking place."

"Just be cool," Tamara advised. Her uniform blouse and pants were neatly pressed, her name badge precisely set, and her hair cropped short and styled. She tailored her own clothes and they showed her skill. Almost offhandedly, she shifted between the spy satellites she had access to, using a combination of trackball and keyboard to log information that would be later reviewed by the analysts who had been brought on to sort and distill the huge amounts of intel they were bringing in.

"I am." Jim turned his attention back to his screens. He monitored the various airfields around the world that he was responsible for. "Did you—did you know any of them?"

"Them?" Tamara glanced at him. "Someone who disappeared, you mean?"

"Yeah." Jim nodded. "That's what I mean."

Tamara was quiet for a moment. "I've lost some friends." Her voice was thick. A shimmer of tears gleamed in her dark eyes. "But that doesn't mean they're gone for good. We could find a way to bring them back."

"Yeah," Jim said. He hoped the doubt he felt didn't come through in his voice.

"I was in the break room when it happened." Tamara tapped the keyboard. Delta Crew had been due to relieve Charlie at midnight because they were the next up in the five-crew rotation. Now, however, both teams were at work because of missing personnel. She shrugged. "I always get here early. Gives me time to catch up on my reading and some quiet time for myself. I don't like to be in my apartment when my roommate gets home at night. Gets way too weird sometimes."

"She had a date?"

Tamara smiled a little. "Definitely. New guy she met at the hospital. Tiffany goes too fast in her relationships, then they blow up—usually because she gets bored—and she wonders what happened."

"I thought you were going to move out."

"I thought about it, but I can't. She's like a little sister. After eight months of living with her, I feel kind of responsible for her."

Jim nodded. While they'd been paired for his training, he'd learned quite a bit about Tamara. She was the oldest of nine children, seven of them girls, and she had definite firstborn characteristics. She still sent money back home to her family to help pay the college tuition of her younger siblings. The Air Force had taken care of Tamara's college in exchange for compensatory time in service. Her generosity with her family members had resulted in her string of strange roommates, and her caregiver nature had kept them around. Tiffany was Tamara's latest "lost cause." Tamara was also a Big Sister, and if anyone in the complex had a benefit or fund-raiser going on, Tamara was known as one of the softest touches on the crews.

"So," Jim said, "do you think it will happen?" He stared at the airfields, watching the thermographic displays that showed the crews readying the B-52H Stratofortresses at the Air Logistics Center at Tinker Air Force Base in Oklahoma. Other bases around the United States were making the same preparations with their fleets.

"What?" Tamara clicked the trackball, capturing more images. "War?"

Jim's mouth dried. He didn't know how they could sit there and discuss the subject as calmly as though they were placing a breakfast order. "Yeah. That."

Tamara hesitated. "I don't know." She glanced at her monitor, turning her head just enough to let Jim know she was checking the reflection of Colonel Dan Hatton, the Delta Crew commander who had stepped in to replace the missing Colonel Morris Turner.

Colonel Hatton, an American, was one of the most senior officers at the complex. He stood quietly, granite-jawed with his hands clasped behind his back. During his time at Cheyenne Mountain, Jim was certain Colonel Hatton had seen plenty of DEFCON 3s come.

And go, Jim told himself quietly. All those other DEFCON 3s had come and gone. Otherwise, a nuclear war would have broken out.

The bases Jim watched were strategic. The B-52s were the world's best long-range heavy bombers. Armed to the teeth, a B-52 carried seventy thousand pounds of mixed ordnance, including bombs, mines, and missiles. Air-launched cruise missiles, Harpoon antiship, and Have Nap missiles were standard fare for the big bombers.

The B-52 bomber originally debuted in 1955 as a primary factor in the Cold War. Armed with nuclear weapons, the planes were tasked to fly into Soviet airspace and take out Moscow and other key Russian cities with nuclear weapons. Back in those days, the nukes had still been referred to as atom bombs. Today that arsenal was referred to as weapons of mass destruction, or WMDs. The targets essentially remained the same: deep within Russia or China.

Two B-52Hs—the current updated model with new avionics, defense systems, data-link communications, and precision-guided weapons capabilities—could patrol 140,000 square miles of ocean surface within two hours. Capable of flying at 50,000 feet and at low levels, the B-52 was a dreadnought of air-strike capability. Without being refueled in the air, a Stratofortress had a range of 8,800 miles.

In actuality, the B-52 never had to leave the sky or a threatening posture because the Stratofortress could be refueled in midair. During the Gulf War, the longest strike mission in the aircraft's history was launched by a group of B-52s that took off from Barksdale Air Force Base in Louisiana, flew to Iraq and took out targets, then returned to the home base thirty-five hours later. Only the ability of the crew to function without succumbing to fatigue limited the B-52's performance.

"The Russians have had some disappearances," Jim said, cycling through his list of targets. "I've seen some of the reports. The CIA is feeding information to us from their agents on the ground there."

"I know. That's why the Russian military is in motion."

"Saber rattling?" *God,* Jim prayed, *just let it be saber rattling.* Never before had he felt so vulnerable. Before he'd gotten the Cheyenne Mountain posting, he'd known when international events had turned tense, but he'd never had as great an access to how things were actually shaping up. As a military man, he'd always known that the world hovered daily on the brink of destruction. But settled in at a console in the Cheyenne Mountain complex, he had the distinct experience of being part of the process.

"I don't think so." Tamara's eyes flicked from one monitor to the other. "The Russians are scared."

"Scared? Of what?"

"You know what happened in Israel in January of last year."

"When the Russian fighters got knocked from the air by that freak meteor storm."

"Meteor storm?" Tamara smiled with polite disdain. "Is that what you think happened?"

"That seems to be the best answer."

"Does it? A freak meteor storm that didn't leave any meteors behind?"

"Most people who don't know better just assumed that the destruction of the Russian jets was because the equipment they used was inferior."

"But you don't think that?"

"No way. If those fighters had been inferior, they wouldn't have made the hop from Russia. And for all of them to decide to self-destruct more or less at the same time?" Jim shook his head. "No way."

"So . . . a meteor storm?"

"Well, if the Israelis had used an electromagnetic pulse bomb, we'd have heard about it. And there would have been a lot of power outages at ground zero. There weren't any reported."

"The Israeli military was caught flat-footed. They're more geared for border disputes than aerial combat with the Russians."

Jim felt defensive. "A freak meteor storm that leaves no traces is easier to believe than aliens from outer space."

Tamara nodded to her right. "Sterling wouldn't agree with you. You've heard his theory, right?"

"I have." Jim knew from personal experience that Sterling would expound on the threat of aliens for hours on end if given the opportunity. Sterling was the chief conspiracy enthusiast on Charlie Crew. "Okay, so if you don't think it was aliens or a freak meteor storm or some tactical weapon the Israelis possess that we don't know about, what do you think it was?"

Silence stretched between them for a moment. During the six months he had known her, Jim had seldom seen Tamara think before making a reply. She always had information quickly at her disposal about any number of topics.

"Do you ever read the Bible?" she asked finally.

Jim felt a little self-conscious. He'd seen the tiny cross that Tamara wore on a delicate necklace around her neck when they'd had dinner, lunch, or breakfast after hours to get better acquainted. He'd gone to church when he was a kid, but he'd gotten away from it and resented anyone who tried to shove religion down his throat.

"Some," he said. "It's been a while."

"Ever study the book of Revelation? Daniel? Ezekiel?"

"No."

"Ezekiel 38," she said. "You should take a look at it."

The conversation felt more and more uncomfortable to Jim. He was beginning to feel sorry he'd asked.

"Ezekiel 38 could be interpreted to describe the Russian attack on Israel," Tamara went on. "A great army is supposed to descend from the north and attempt to destroy Israel and take her riches. For years, Israel has depended on outside financial help."

"There are lots of riches there now."

"Because of Rosenzweig's formula, yes. At any rate, during the northern army's attack, when Israel was helpless, God told Ezekiel that He would protect Israel."

"And you believe that's what happened?"

"Not," Tamara stated quietly, "until today."

"When everyone vanished?"

"Yes."

Jim considered her answer and the possibility he knew she was only hinting at. "So if God's hand was in all of the disappearances, where did those people go?"

Tamara looked at him. "Heaven, Jim. They went to heaven." A mostly beatific expression filled her face, but some uncertainty shone in her dark eyes. There was also more than a little sadness.

Even though he had been expecting her to say exactly that, her words still brought a chill that filled Jim's heart. "Why them?"

"Because they were the ones who were deserving."

"Deserving?"

"They *believed*." Tamara shook her head. "Didn't you know some of those people who disappeared from here?"

"Yeah."

"And what were most of them like?"

"They were good people," Jim answered. That was one of the first things that came to mind. Of course, he hadn't known them all, but he'd known quite a few.

"Exactly."

"But there are other good people who are still here," Jim pointed out. "You were left behind."

"Thank you for that, but my faith isn't as strong as it used to be," Tamara admitted. "Or maybe it was never as strong as I thought it was. I don't know." She sighed. "My mother was recently diagnosed with cancer."

"I'm sorry."

Tamara shook her head. "That's not the point, Jim. The point is how I reacted to that news. I'm guilty of holding God accountable for my mom's cancer. I'm not supposed to do that."

"But a feeling like that is only natural."

"Maybe. Other people might blame the environment. I blamed God." Tamara sighed. "I can be mad at God, but I have to understand that the things that happen are for the best. I'm supposed to *believe* in His love." She pursed her lips. "Just last week, I had a disagreement with the pastor at my church. I finally told him about Mom's cancer. He went through the usual spiel, telling me to trust God, that everything was working out according to His plan. I didn't like what he had to say. It's the first time we've ever had any kind of disagreement."

"I would have felt the same way."

"Maybe." Tamara clicked the trackball again, capturing more information. "But my mom didn't. She just accepted the doctor's diagnosis and said that God would figure out what she was supposed to do."

"You've talked about your mom a lot. She sounds like a terrific woman."

"She is. And she's important to me."

"If there's anything I can do."

Tamara nodded. "I'm not going to worry about it anymore. At least, I'm going to try not to. Whatever happens, I really feel like it's in God's hands." She glanced around the room. "Just like the people who disappeared here. I think they're in God's hands." She wiped her eyes. "And you know what else?"

"What?"

Tamara's voice broke, but she recovered. "I think my mom is in God's hands right now, too."

"What do you mean?"

"If this is the Rapture, if God has come and taken His church, I know my mom was one of those."

Tamara's conviction touched Jim in ways he'd never felt before. For a moment, her emotion embarrassed him. When she discovered that what she suddenly found herself believing wasn't actually the case, she was going to be hurt deeply. But a quiet unease had threaded through his thoughts, never to be denied again. *What if she is right? What if God has come for his people?* The thought was terrifying. He felt a cold breeze across the back of his neck. If it was true, then he had been left behind.

"I tried to call home before we were pulled in to fill the vacant posts in here," Tamara said.

"Was your mom home?" Despite his doubts, Jim found himself drawn to the answer.

"I don't know. The phone lines aren't going through right now."

That stood to reason, Jim mused. If the amount of disappearances they were logging in the different military operations they monitored, as well as the disappearances from their own ranks that had left only piles of clothing and tons of questions and fear behind, were reflected around the United States, then the phone companies and communications corporations had been hard hit as well.

"If this event—" Jim started.

"The Rapture," Tamara said.

He nodded. "If the Rapture has occurred, then what happens to us?"

"To the people left behind?"

"Yeah." Just saying that made Jim's mouth suddenly dry. Nothing he'd ever trained for in his life had prepared him for this. Then he remembered all those Sunday mornings in church that he had resented. The sad fact was that he *could* have been prepared.

"The Tribulation."

Jim turned the word over in his head. He had heard the word several times, but it made no sense now. "What is the Tribulation?"

"After the Rapture, God will leave the world more or less intact. The people who are left behind will then have the choice of believing and giving themselves to him, or they can continue to deny His existence and love. During the seven years of the Tribulation, Christians will become more persecuted by nonbelievers than at any time before."

"I thought the believers would have all been raptured."

"They will have," Tamara said softly. "I believe they have been. But there will be new believers, Jim. Don't you see? You're asking questions now that you would have never asked before."

Jim broke eye contact by reaching for his coffee cup. He was surprised at how much his hand shook as he lifted it. This was too much. It was all coming too fast.

When the Klaxon rang, he spilled a little of the tepid liquid in his lap.

"All right, ladies and gentlemen," Colonel Hatton announced over the PA system. "The Russians have taken to the air. We've just escalated from DEFCON 3 to DEFCON 2."

The colonel's words hammered Jim's mind, shattering his thoughts and crystallizing his fear. DEFCON 2 meant that B-52s, escort fighters, and supply planes would take off and prepare to strike Russian targets. He gazed in wide-eyed disbelief as the Stratofortresses he had onscreen suddenly jerked to life and hurtled down runways.

"Jim," Tamara said.

"Yeah," he replied in a thick voice.

"You okay?"

"We're watching what could be the end of the world. Do you know that?"

"It won't be the end," she stated quietly. "There's a lot that will happen before that happens. Things will get much worse."

"Worse than the end of the world?"

"Yes."

As Jim watched, the B-52s leaped into the air, clawing their way into the night skies like birds of prey. Even peering down on them on the large monitor, the flying dreadnoughts looked sleek and deadly when they should have looked more like a child's toys. "Do you think God planned for DEFCON?"

"Yes."

"What do you think happens to the people who die after the Rapture?"

Tamara quietly thought. "I think it depends on how their relationship with God has changed."

"And if it hasn't changed?"

"I don't think things would go very well for them."

Jim nodded. "If we live through tonight, do you think we could talk more about this?"

Tamara reached over and gave his forearm a reassuring squeeze. "Sure."

DEFCON 2, Chaplain Delroy Harte thought to himself as he jogged aft through *Wasp*'s second level. *God, look over me as I strive to bring Your message to frightened and paranoid ears.*

The chaplain hurried through the large mess hall, past the officer's wardroom that functioned as a restaurant or theater or town hall or conference room depending on the scheduled need, until he reached the command and control centers caged protectively under the ship's island structure for extra defense.

The C&C areas remained dark, but the glow of computer monitors and large display screens warred with the gloomy shadows that filled *Wasp*'s bowels. Men spoke quietly, and their voices punctuated the steady hum of computer mainframes and peripheral devices.

Seven theaters of operation existed within the C&C post. The Tactical Air Control Center monitored the airspace around the Amphibious Readiness Group and assigned the daily flight sheets, matching men and machines as well as zones and time frames. The Tactical Logistics Group managed the onboard supplies, weapons, and vehicles as well as the debarkation of the Marine troops. Information was cleared and stored in the Joint Intelligence Center, and hard-drive space was filled with information concerning the world if *Wasp* was ever cut off from the Pentagon as she had been before Captain Remington had managed the coup with the Romanian communications network. The Ship Signals Exploitation Space was shut off from nearly everyone aboard ship because of the degree of secrecy involved in using enemy signals against those enemies. When involved in heavy operations that could threaten *Wasp*, the ARG commander and staff stayed in the Flag Plot deep within the ship where they could most be protected.

The Landing Force Operations Center was jam-packed with high-tech computer systems that tied the Marine commander of the MEU(SOC) with embarked Marine units while away from the ship. From there, fed with the information from spy-sats and in constant communications with his away teams, Colonel Henry Donaldson, the MEU(SOC)'s commander-in-chief, could direct all action his Marines took.

Two Marines stood guard in front of the door. They held their assault weapons at port arms.

"Chaplain Harte," one of the Marines greeted.

Delroy drew himself up tall and straight. Before leaving his quarters, he'd showered and shaved and put on a fresh uniform. Before telling Colonel Donaldson and Captain Falkirk what he had to tell them, he wanted to look his Navy best. Appearance counted for a lot in the military.

But he also carried his father's old Bible. To Delroy, the creases in the imitation leather cover and the dog-eared pages were hash marks and medals of valor in a service that had gone largely unnoticed outside Josiah Harte's community. Maybe the uniform was his armor, but the Bible was his shield and buckler.

"Sergeant," Delroy replied. "I need to speak with Colonel Donaldson."

The sergeant looked uncomfortable. "I'm sorry, sir. Colonel Donaldson left strict orders that he was not to be disturbed."

"'Not to be disturbed?'" Delroy couldn't believe it. His anger and frustration seeped through his grip before he could restrain them. "We just lost hundreds of Marines along the Turkish border, Sergeant. The United States is at DEFCON 2, preparing to possibly go to war with Russia because that country is certain we're responsible for the disappearances that have taken place there. Can anything be more disturbing?"

The young sergeant blinked in shock and confusion. "Sir, I—"

"Sergeant," Delroy put the crisp clear tone of command in his voice as he stepped forward, "do you see these bars and that star on my shoulder?"

"Yes, sir." The Marine backed down slightly but didn't give up much ground.

"I am a commander in the United States Navy," Delroy said.

"Yes, sir. I know that, sir. But I was given orders by my colonel that—"

"Son," Delroy said in a quietly fierce voice, "either you let the colonel make the decision whether or not to see me, or I'm going to walk right over top of you."

The sergeant braced at that. The private accompanying him took a step away and circled Delroy. The chaplain stood his ground. At six and a half feet tall, driven as he was by the need to tell what he knew to be true, Delroy knew he must have presented a fearsome figure to the men.

The ship's crew still told about times Delroy had waded into fights aboard ship and in taverns off base and broke up fights between military personnel. He'd even broken up a fight involving two Navy SEALs that had earned him a lot of respect among his fellow military men, although the number of the Special Forces men had grown in the telling over the years. *Wasp* took pride in having a two-fisted chaplain.

"Sir—"

"Sergeant!" Delroy's voice came out in a bellow. "I said open that door! And I mean *now*, mister!"

The sergeant stood resolute in front of the door, shifting the rifle to better use the weapon as a club if he had to.

Delroy knew he had the attention of several men around him. He almost felt embarrassed. Then he remembered how Chief Mellencamp's body had disappeared from inside the body bag, and how there had been loose piles of uniforms scattered around *Wasp*. The text from Numbers 32:23 came to his mind: "But if you do not do so, then take note, you have sinned against the Lord; and be sure your sin will find you out." He knew he couldn't back away from the task that had been laid before him. The chief's passing and the responsibility of the letter and the disappearance of the body while he'd been there to bear witness; those events hadn't been by accident.

And what about Terry? Delroy's conviction wavered a little when he thought about his son's passing. He steeled himself. Terry's death couldn't mean nothing. He wouldn't let it. Surely even there he would find God's hand. Surely he could believe in that after everything that had happened today.

The door behind the sergeant yanked open.

"What's going on here, Sergeant?" Colonel Donaldson stood ramrod straight, looking fresh as a daisy despite the fact he'd been up long, hard hours preparing for the Marine wing's insertion into Turkey.

Nineteen years a Marine, Donaldson looked every inch of his calling. He stood a couple inches over six feet with the compact and wiry build of a good second baseman. His sandy colored hair was thinning on top, although that was partially masked by the flattop crew cut, and going gray at the temples. Camo BDUs outlined the hard lines of his body.

"Chaplain Harte," the sergeant said. "He wanted to see you."

Delroy's breath came hard and fast, and he could feel his heart blast-pumping in his chest.

Donaldson eyed the chaplain with challenge and curiosity, though there was more of the former than the latter. "Is that right, Chaplain?"

"Yes, Colonel."

Donaldson's chin rose as he stepped out into the hallway. His big hand wrapped around his jaw, and his stubble crackled. "I don't know what could possibly prompt you to interrupt a planning session I'm having, Commander. Especially after I gave specific orders no one was supposed to get in."

"Sir," Delroy said, straightening. "I apologize for the inconvenience, but rest assured that I wouldn't have interrupted if it wasn't important."

"I'll be the judge of that."

For a fleeting moment, Delroy felt afraid. It was a natural reaction, given the circumstances. He'd hoped to persuade Captain Falkirk and Colonel Donaldson to grant him a few minutes alone to explain his reasoning.

He hadn't expected the audience he had in the men stationed in the C&C centers around them.

"Yes, sir," Delroy said. "I wonder if we might talk in private."

Donaldson folded his arms across his broad chest. "This is fine for me, Chaplain Harte."

Delroy felt the colonel's anger, saw the white-hot emotion edged in the sharp angles of the man's body. Most of that anger, the chaplain reasoned, wasn't directed at him but was just seeking a target the same way water constantly sought the lowest level.

"Yes, sir. I see that, sir." Delroy gripped his father's Bible in both hands. He took strength from the book, and in his mind he heard his father, thundering from the pulpit as he presented God's love and the fiery threat of hell and eternal damnation to his congregation.

Terry's voice was in there, too, words ripped from the morning that Terry had shipped out for the battlefield. Despite his training, despite what faith he'd possessed, Delroy had been frightened, and Terry saw that emotion in him. *"Don't be afraid, Dad. I'm not. You see, I believe in you and I believe in God. Between Him and you, how can anything happen to me?"*

But something had happened, and Terry had never come home again. How could God want something like that to happen to a boy who had hardly gotten to live any of his life?

"Well?" Donaldson prompted impatiently.

The colonel's obvious willingness to make an example out of Delroy almost broke his nerve. But he felt his father's hard-used Bible in his hands. Leviticus 5:1 had been a favorite passage of Josiah Harte's when he was talking to his congregation about the need and duty to bear witness to the works of the Lord. *And if a soul sin, and hear the voice of swearing, and is a witness, whether he hath seen or known of it; if he do not utter it, then he shall bear his iniquity.*

"I know how those people disappeared," Delroy said in a voice that almost broke. He felt ashamed of himself. Here he was, testifying to the works of the Lord God, holding his own father's Bible, and he acted as tremulous as a child.

"I'd like to hear this," Colonel Donaldson said. "Especially since military intelligence doesn't have a clue, even with all the technology they control at their fingertips."

"The disappearance of those men wasn't through technology, Colonel." Delroy struggled, barely keeping his voice under control. "Their removal from this world was divine."

Donaldson cursed. "They weren't removed from this world. They were murdered, and—"

Delroy cut the Marine colonel off. "Not murdered. Sir." He took a breath, barely able to maintain eye contact with the man. "Those people who have gone missing around the world, they were taken from this world by the hand of God."

A rumble of conversation from the men in the C&C units filled the hallway.

"Chaplain!" Donaldson roared. "You'll cease and desist announcements like that this instant!"

Mouth dry, heart beating frantically, Delroy said, "I can't do that, sir. God insists that we bear witness to the miracles that He has wrought in our lives so that we might influence others to look within their own lives for works that He has done. If I don't talk about this, I'll be doing a disservice to God and to the men of this ship. I took an oath to serve the people I was responsible for, and from the looks of this ship and the fact that not everyone here was taken, I still have work to do."

"You're out of your mind," Donaldson said hoarsely.

"No, sir," Delroy disagreed. "I've just stopped hiding from the truth. God has shown me something and I am paying attention."

No one spoke in the hallway. Delroy knew he had the ear of every man in the centers.

"Chaplain, I order you to return to your quarters," Donaldson said. "You will remain under house arrest until such time as I—"

"No, sir," Delroy replied.

Donaldson's eyes nearly bugged out of his head. "Are you refusing the direct order of a superior officer, Chaplain Harte?"

"I have been," Delroy admitted, "until today. But I won't turn away from him anymore. Not when there are so many left behind that can be saved."

"Chaplain—" Donaldson's voice raised in obvious warning.

"The proof is right there in front of you, Colonel. You have but to open your eyes to see." Delroy held his father's Bible up before him. "I can show you chapter and verse where God made a covenant to return for his blessed chosen and reap them from this world."

"Chaplain, I don't know what you think you're trying to prove, but—"

"I'm not trying to prove anything," Delroy said. "I am trying to acknowledge the hand of God Almighty in the course of these events that have changed the face of the world in the last hour and a half."

"Sergeant," Donaldson said.

"Sir."

"Arrest that man."

"Yes, sir." The sergeant started forward.

Delroy slapped the Bible against the young Marine's chest, trapping his assault rifle there. "Don't you dare," the chaplain advised.

The Marine halted.

"God put me here today," Delroy said, staring into the young man's eyes, "to bear witness to what has truly happened because there are none so blind as those who will not see." He looked over the sergeant's shoulder at Donaldson. "I want you to listen to me, Colonel. Things are going to get much worse than you see now. The Antichrist will rise up now that the Rapture has taken place. He will rise up and fill the world with lies and treachery for seven years, and the souls of men will be tried as they have never been tried before."

In an obviously practiced move, Donaldson drew the M9 pistol from the holster at his hip. The safety clicked off as the barrel centered on Delroy's face. "Chaplain," the Marine colonel said in a cold voice, "you'll shut your mouth now or I'll put a bullet through your face."

Delroy stared death squarely in the eye and never blinked. He'd been in contact with it before. Each time he'd felt that always-present fear that he wouldn't come back home alive, that he would be crippled for life. But now, staring down the muzzle of the M9, he felt calm and relaxed.

"Thirty-one percent of our crew is missing," Delroy said. "More of them went missing in Turkey, and the survivors are stranded with the very armies they went in to save. Our world is hovering on the brink of a nuclear war between the United States and Russia. And you threaten to kill me?" The chaplain couldn't help it; he laughed, and the sound rolled through the C&C areas. "Have you ever read Revelation, Colonel? Do you even know what's in store for the world now that this has happened?"

Donaldson held the pistol rock steady.

"Threatening to kill me doesn't scare me," Delroy went on. "I was left behind after the Rapture. The only way to my salvation now is through God's love and mercy. And if I can't have those, dying now will be a lot simpler than struggling to live through the dark days that are coming."

Cursing again, Donaldson shoved the sergeant away with his free hand and stood with the M9 held in a Weaver stance. "Disobeying a direct order from a commanding officer during a time that might be construed as wartime can get you executed on the spot."

Delroy gazed at the man, understanding more about what drove him. "You're afraid."

A nervous tic started in Donaldson's left eye. "Shut up," he snarled.

"You've been through battles and wars." Delroy discovered he couldn't shut up. The truth seemed to course in his veins. "But all of that hasn't prepared you for something like this."

"Shut. Up." A slight tremble shook the M9 in Donaldson's grip.

"You feel it, don't you, Colonel?" Delroy asked. "You know that I'm telling you the truth. You *know*."

Donaldson's hand shook more, and his knuckle whitened over the trigger.

"Colonel Donaldson!" The voice whip-cracked through the C&C.

Without turning, Delroy knew Captain Mark Falkirk had stepped out of the Combat Information Center only a short distance away.

The CIC held all the computers and information systems the ship's captain needed to run operations aboard *Wasp* while she was active on a mission.

"Holster that sidearm, Colonel Donaldson," Falkirk ordered. "Operations aboard my ship are going to go by my orders."

With obvious reluctance, Donaldson holstered his weapon. Beads of perspiration covered his pale face. "This man is spouting nonsense, Captain Falkirk. And he's inciting unrest and demoralizing the crew."

Delroy glanced at Falkirk.

The captain was in his early thirties, one of the youngest men to have been appointed to that rank, and the youngest to command *Wasp*. He had a slender build but carried an air of readiness and moved with the fluid grace of a trained athlete. His eyes and hair were dark, complementing the easygoing nature he maintained unless he was irritated or on task.

"Sergeant," Donaldson went on, "take the chaplain into custody and escort him down to the brig."

"Belay that order," Falkirk commanded before the sergeant could get under way. Four Navy security men filed into the hallway, flanking their commander.

"Captain," Donaldson objected.

"My ship, Colonel," Falkirk replied, "and she'll run the way I have her run." He paused. "Are we clear?"

Donaldson clearly didn't like the idea, but he said, "Yes."

Falkirk's eyes flashed. "My ready room, gentlemen. *Now.*"

❄   ❄   ❄

United States of America
Fort Benning, Georgia
Local Time 2:41 A.M.

"Mrs. Gander?"

Megan lifted her head from her arms, startled to find that she had gone to sleep. She'd been sitting uncomfortably at the small conference table in the interview room at MP headquarters and trying very quietly not to go out of her mind with worry. She automatically checked the time, afraid that she had slept past dawn and that Chris would be waking up in the emergency child-care services. When she saw the time, she relaxed a little and prayed that Joey had picked up Chris and they were both now at home.

The MPs had taken her cell phone from her when they'd taken her into custody. She didn't know if Joey had gotten to his younger brother, and she didn't know if Joey was aware that she'd been taken by the MPs. The MPs hadn't called her forced detention an arrest, only that she had been detained for questioning.

The man who stood on the other side of the table was dressed in a fresh Army uniform and wore a lieutenant's bars. He was blond and pale, much too serious for his age, which Megan didn't put much over his mid-twenties. He carried an imitation leather briefcase.

"I'm Megan Gander," Megan said. "Who are you?"

"Lieutenant Doug Benbow, ma'am." He offered his hand.

Megan took his hand and shook briefly. "Are you an MP, Lieutenant Benbow?"

"No, ma'am. I'm with the military justice system. I've been assigned to be your legal representative."

"My attorney?" Megan struggled against the fatigue that filled her mind. "Why would I need an attorney?"

"We can talk about that." Benbow touched the back of the chair across the table from her. "May I sit?"

"Of course." Megan leaned back in her chair and tried to gather her errant thoughts. She was fatigued. Her thoughts swam like fat koi in a deep pond, not quite reaching the surface.

Benbow sat, placing his briefcase on the table, then flipping it open. He took out a tape recorder. "Would you mind if I record our conversation?"

"Why are you recording our conversation?"

The question caused the young lieutenant to hesitate. "I'll be taking notes, of course, but I much prefer to work from a recording. That way I get every word, and I don't miss the nuances a person may use as he or she explains himself or herself." He took out a lined yellow legal pad.

Fear crept in on Megan and the chill in the room seemed like it deepened by the second. "I don't understand."

Benbow clicked the tape recorder on. "I just need to go over tonight's events, Mrs. Gander."

"I've already told the MPs what happened. This doesn't make any sense."

Reaching into an inside jacket pocket, Benbow took out a mechanical pencil and clicked the plunger to expose the lead. "I need to know about the boy, Mrs. Gander."

"Gerry?"

Benbow flipped through pages of notes. His eyes scanned the material rapidly. "Gerry Fletcher. Yes, that's right, Mrs. Gander. You were his counselor?"

Were? Icy jaws seemed to clamp on to Megan's thoughts. "I am Gerry's counselor." *Those were clothes I saw at the bottom of that building. Empty clothes. Gerry fell, but he didn't hit. Thank You, God, he didn't hit.*

"How long were you—have you been—Gerry Fletcher's counselor?"

"About a year." Megan thought furiously, trying to catch up with whatever the young lieutenant was doing.

"Fourteen months?" Benbow's pencil hung expectantly over a clean sheet in the legal pad.

"I'd have to check my notes if you want a definite answer." Megan didn't know why she couldn't remember.

"I have checked your records regarding Gerry," Benbow said. "You've been seeing him for fourteen months."

"You've seen my records regarding Gerry's case?"

Benbow sat up straighter, if that was possible, and regarded her. "I haven't looked through the boy's file, Mrs. Gander. Only your appointments. I found that you first saw Gerry on December 27 two years ago."

The first meeting had been after Christmas. Megan remembered that clearly now. "That sounds right."

"And Gerry has been in your care since that time?"

"Yes."

Benbow scribbled notes and nodded in satisfaction. "During your visits with Gerry, you also came into contact with Private Boyd Fletcher."

Megan nodded.

"Please respond verbally, Mrs. Gander. I may ask that the tapes be admitted in court as evidence."

"Court?" Megan couldn't believe what the lieutenant was saying. "Who's talking about court?"

"The provost marshal's office," Benbow answered.

"Frank Marion is talking about taking me to court?" Unable to sit any longer, Megan stood. Her chair screeched as it shot back. As soon as she stood, she felt light-headed. The scratches along her arm that Gerry had left during his panic before he had slipped from her hand stung.

"I've not spoken with Provost Marshal Marion yet," Benbow replied. "I hope to speak with him in the morning regarding the other extenuating circumstances that have occurred here on base tonight. I don't know how you can be held accountable for Gerry Fletcher's disappearance."

"I'm not."

Benbow nodded politely. "Yes, ma'am. That's why I'm here: to help prove that you were not responsible for what happened to Gerry Fletcher."

"What has happened to him?"

"We don't know, ma'am. The MPs have scoured that building and they've found no sign of the boy."

"He disappeared." Megan forced the words out. "I had him. Then he fell. He just . . . just never hit the ground."

Benbow pushed out his breath easily. "You're sure you had the boy, Mrs. Gander?"

Megan faced the lieutenant and folded her arms. "Of course I'm sure."

"And he was hanging over the building?"

"Yes."

"It's just that—" Benbow hesitated—"I know that things up on that rooftop had to have been confusing. You got called out of bed in the middle of the night after a hectic day, already worried about one of your children who hadn't yet come home, and learned that your husband is engaged in action along the Turkish border before you got up on that rooftop with Gerry."

"What are you trying to say?" Megan demanded.

"I'm trying to suggest that perhaps you weren't at your best, Mrs. Gander. That's all."

"That maybe I wasn't holding that boy? That I imagined all of that?"

Benbow hesitated, then reluctantly nodded. "Yes, ma'am. Without wanting to be offensive in any way, I guess that's what I'm trying to suggest."

"Lieutenant, this is crazy. A waste of your time and mine. There were at least a dozen people who saw Gerry disappear. The MPs had spotlights on Gerry and me. Haven't you talked to them?"

"As a matter of fact, Mrs. Gander, I have talked to most of them. Every man I've talked to has told me that he wasn't sure if you had the boy or not. No one got a good look."

"That's impossible."

"As I said, Mrs. Gander, I know things had to be happening very fast and were probably intensely confusing up on that rooftop."

Megan forced herself to be calm when all she wanted to do was scream. Everything that had gone on tonight, from Joey not showing up at home, to Goose being involved in unexpected action, to the whole situation with Gerry Fletcher, had been overload on her already strained emotions. "And if I didn't have Gerry, what was I holding? What fell from that building?"

"The boy's clothing." Benbow sat quietly. His pencil sat poised over the legal pad. "I've verified that the clothing found at the base of that residence building was the same clothing the boy wore when he entered the hospital."

"They're saying I dropped Gerry's *clothes* over the side of the building?"

Benbow nodded.

Frustration and fright filled Megan. Before she could stop the emotions, some of them boiled over. "Speak up, Lieutenant. The tape recorder only records verbal responses."

"Yes," Benbow said. His tone was totally neutral and he appeared to take no offense. "That's what they're saying."

"Why would I do that?"

"I don't know."

Tears filled Megan's eyes. "I want out of here. Do you hear me?"

The lieutenant frowned uncomfortably.

"I've been here for nearly an hour," Megan said. "Up until the last fifteen minutes, I've been asked over and over where Gerry Fletcher is. I've been asked straight out, and I've had MPs who thought they were very clever try to get me to admit I know where Gerry is."

"Mrs. Gander—"

Megan hurried on, cutting the lieutenant off. "I want to get my baby out of child care, and I want to go home so I can pray for my husband and those Rangers over there in Turkey. I want to know my oldest son is all right. I am a good mother and I'm a good wife, and that's what I should be doing. And despite whatever stories you've been listening to and however you may feel, I am a good counselor." Her voice was thick with emotion. "I did my best to save Gerry Fletcher's life tonight, and I don't know what happened to him."

Benbow was quiet for a moment. "They're not going to let you leave right now, Mrs. Gander."

"Why?"

"Because the provost marshal's office is considering bringing charges against you."

"For what?" Megan's voice tightened into a hoarse whisper.

"For the kidnapping of Gerry Fletcher."

Turkish-Syrian Border
40 Klicks South of Sanliurfa, Turkey
Local Time 0947 Hours

A flash of movement caught Goose's eye. He drew back down to the shelter of the overturned Syrian T-72 main battle tank that had remained remarkably intact after the fusillade leveled by the arriving Marine Harriers and Apaches. A scattering of vehicles, Syrian corpses, and ashes of tents and other flammable materials littered the ground around them.

"Phoenix Leader confirms a hostile," Goose warned over the headset. He brought the butt of the M-4A1 up over his right shoulder, maintaining a tight profile that would allow him to move quickly and sweep the assault rifle up if he needed to, while at the same time remaining a compact target. He peered around the edge of the tank, feeling the hot metal of the tread pressing against his cheek.

Tense seconds ticked by as quiet reigned along the skirmish line that had taken shape on the border. Off in the distance to the north, Goose could hear only a few scattered truck noises, jet engine roars, and the occasional *whap-whap* of helicopter rotors. More noise came from the south as the tanks, APCs, and Jeeps the Syrian army had held in reserve started jockeying for the inexorable push that would come to invade Turkey proper.

Once the armored cav started rolling northbound, Goose knew the Syrians couldn't be held back. The Turkish army, the U.N. peace-keeping forces, and the Rangers had taken huge casualties and lost irreplaceable materials. The Syrian army had taken some incredible losses as well, but the reserve force they'd had outnumbered anything the Turkish defenders had left to give.

There was no way to know what the Syrian military command had intended to do with the army encamped along the border before launching the SCUDs. Remington had stated, during his last discussion with Goose, that he believed the Syrian army would have been pulled back, making it look like they had backed down from the Turks. Then, while the unsuspecting Turkish army was congratulating itself, the SCUDs would have launched and taken out the first line of defense. The Syrians' cav units would have rolled over whatever remained of the defenders.

Intercepting the CIA spy had changed all of that somehow, and Syria had gambled everything on the power of a sweeping first strike. And maybe they had gambled on the disappearances within the border troops as well. However, Remington had mentioned that the disappearances might not be linked to the fighting in Syria, although he hadn't elaborated on that. With long years of friendship and service between them, Goose knew when not to press an issue with his captain.

Exposed on the east side of the T-72, the sun baked down into Goose, and it felt like the heat was leaching the moisture from his bones. Perspiration soaked his uniform and made the dirt that had stuck to his skin beneath his clothing even more uncomfortable. His eyelids felt like they dragged across his eyes in slow motion as he used his peripheral vision to search for the movement he'd caught from the corner of his eye. The heated air seemed too thin and too raw to breathe.

The overturned and burned-out vehicles along the skirmish line formed a deadly maze for the Rangers Goose had led into action. Soot marked the ground in blast patches and made it look like the earth itself had been bruised. Fire and smoke still clung to some of the vehicles and craters. The crackle of the small flames was the only sound coming from close by him.

Movement caught Goose's eye again, drawing him around.

"Goose!" Cusack yelled in warning. The young Ranger brought his weapon up.

But Goose was already in motion as the Syrian soldier thrust his Chinese-made AK-47 forward. Goose turned toward Cusack, whose concern for Goose had left him exposed, fisted the Ranger's uniform in his hand and dropped a shoulder into Cusack's midsection to get him moving.

Bullets traced a white-hot trail along the tank, spinning wildly from the armor. Gunfire and ricochets ripped through the quiet stillness that had filled the area.

Goose shoved Dewey back nearly twenty feet before the Ranger's feet got caught and he fell backward. By that time they were out of range of the Syrian's rifle. Goose's injured knee felt tight under him but held well enough as he pivoted and sprinted back toward the burned-out hulk of a cargo truck.

"Phoenix Base," Goose called as he moved. "This is Phoenix Leader."

"Go, Phoenix Leader. You have Phoenix Base." Remington had assigned a mission control officer to watch over the Phoenix team by satellite while they were in hostile territory.

"Verify hostiles, Base," Goose said. "I need your eyes."

"Affirmative, Phoenix Leader. Base is taking a look-see." Maintaining close surveillance on the skirmish line was a drain on the satcom systems while they tried to monitor the two countries and search for other Syrian troop movements across the border. Remington was doing double duty all the way around by pumping information out to *Wasp* and to the Pentagon. Phoenix Base had been standing by, ready to go close in.

Putting his back to the cargo truck, Goose listened for the Syrians. When he heard no running feet, he dropped into a crouch and peered under the truck from his position beside the slagged remains of the rear tire.

Two Syrian soldiers were prone beside an eight-wheeled BTR-60 armored personnel carrier. Blistered paint bubbled up all around the APC, and the eight tires were withered pools of burnt rubber. With its boat-shaped hull and sloped sides, the BTR-60 was a good swimmer, though that wouldn't do it much good in the desert around them. The vehicle's standard armament consisted of the coaxial 14.5mm KPV and 7.62mm PKT machine guns on the right side. The BTR-60 was by no means cutting-edge equipment, but it was a workhorse on the battlefield.

Goose fired on the fly, aiming for the closest Syrian soldier. A line of 5.56mm rounds from Goose's weapon chewed through the ground even as Syrian fire knocked hunks of rubber from the tire Goose was hunkered behind. Goose's bullets struck the lead man, who jerked with the impacts then lay still.

The surviving Syrian soldier's bullets cut through the air by Goose's head and kicked dirt up into his face. The clear goggles he wore kept the grit from his eyes. The kerchief he wore to filter the acrid smoke covered the lower half of his face.

"Phoenix Leader, Base confirms two hostiles in your immediate twenty," the mission controller said urgently.

"One is down," Goose said.

"Understood. One hostile down. I'm pinging them now, Leader. Your men have engaged thirty-seven Syrian foot soldiers. I'm also reading vehicles that are in motion to your location. I've got ten—no, Phoenix Leader, make that twelve vehicles. They were playing possum, Leader, or they moved up into position during the time we were without sat-relay. Copy?"

"Phoenix Leader copies, Base." Goose checked up the line, making sure all his squad leaders had received the information. Armored cav loose in the Ranger scout forces would be like loosing a lion in a henhouse.

With the vehicle losses the Turkish, U.N., and Ranger forces had already suffered, Goose hadn't wanted to risk losing any more. Even one of the smaller Jeeps or 4x4 transport vehicles would have been hard-pressed to slip through the carnage along the border. And every vehicle they lost on the scouting mission was one less vehicle to help carry the wounded back to Sanliurfa that night.

Intermittent assault-rifle fire opened up in his area. The other members of Goose's twenty-man team, broken into five groups of four, reported engagements as well.

Cusack sprinted to join Goose, taking up position near the front tire of the cargo truck for the limited protection it offered.

"Phoenix Eight confirms two hostiles down," Tanaka reported in a cool voice. The team sniper had taken up a position a hundred yards back on top of a Bradley M-2 APC that had seen its last day. One of the Marines, a sniper with a Barrett M-82A1A .50-cal sniper rifle instead of the more conventional M-40A1 chambered in 7.62mm rounds, kept Tanaka company. Goose had allowed the addition because the man had come highly recommended.

The unique blast of the .50-cal round tore through the battlefield.

"Confirm three down from Eight's position, Base," the laconic Marine stated.

"I need to know about those vehicles, Base," Goose said.

"You'll have it, Leader."

"Phoenix Leader, this is Stonewall Leader."

"Go, Stonewall," Goose replied. Stonewall Leader was the Marine sergeant in command of the surviving troop contingent from *Wasp*. Signaling Cusack, Carruthers, and Jansen, the three members of his own four-man group, Goose sent them around behind the Syrian soldier's position.

"I realize this is your party, sir," Marine Sergeant Deke Henderson said, "but I'd like permission to try my luck with the arriving armored cav. This Barrett, sir . . . well, if you've never seen one in action, you'd be surprised what it will do. Even those later model T-72s can't handle the .50-cal rounds."

"Affirmative, Stonewall," Goose said. "Do what you can. We need to work for a holding position for a while."

"I'll do you proud, Phoenix Leader," the Marine promised.

Gunfire erupted from the Syrian soldier's position. Whirling into action, Goose sprinted for the end of the cargo truck. When he came out around the end, his back pressed up tight against the soot-stained truck, he listened to the Syrian soldier's assault rifle burn through the rest of his clip.

Turning, Goose dropped the M-4A1 into firing position and looked toward the Syrian BTR-60. The sniper lay in a hollowed-out spot in the earth near the APC. Goose directed a stream of 5.56mm tumblers at the BTR-60's sloped sides, counting on the light bullet and the angle of the APC's sides. The lightweight bullets slammed against the vehicle's steeply inclined wall.

Designed to bounce and ricochet after hitting a target, the 5.56mm rounds deflected down into the Syrian soldier. The man pushed himself to his feet, then dropped back and didn't move again.

Goose blinked perspiration from his eyes and searched for more enemy troops. He heard the clank of heavy rolling stock in the distance and knew that the armored cav Base had talked about was emerging from their chosen hiding areas.

The Rangers couldn't back down. Goose knew that. They had to stop whatever contingent of Syrian forces remained in the area here. The Syrians had radio contact with the rest of their army. Remington's intel teams were still assessing how large that army was. If the Rangers backed down, they might trigger a rout that would bring the rest of the Syrians grinding toward them.

Goose turned and signaled to Cusack, Carruthers, and Jansen. The three experienced Rangers moved at double time to fall into position around Goose. He moved Henderson up to take point.

"Take us to the west, Carruthers," Goose said. "We're going to set up a pincer and see if we can't take out some of the cav."

"You got it, Sarge." Carruthers hailed from Big Fork, Montana. He was stocky and solid, slow to speak but quick to act. He was a minister's son, and one of the men that Bill Townsend had spent a lot of time with. He took off, angling to the right, putting the sun to their backs.

Goose readied his M-203 grenade launcher with an HE round. The high-explosive 40mm grenade packed a solid punch that was devastating to the T-55 Russian-made tanks that made up most of Syria's cav, and the round performed well against even the T-72 monsters.

Cusack packed an M-203 as well and readied his own.

"Phoenix Two," Goose called. "This is Leader."

"Go, Leader. You have Two." Eddie Ybarra was a top-notch sergeant from Arizona with twelve years in.

"Set up to the east of the main blockage," Goose said. "Try to outflank the tanks. Your team has two M-203s. I want to catch the Syrian cav in a cross fire."

"Affirmative, Leader. Two is on the move."

When Carruthers waved in warning and went to the ground next to a rocky outcrop, Goose fell into position against a burned-out troop transport that lay in twisted ruin. "Phoenix Three, Four, and Five."

The leaders radioed back in response.

"Hold the middle," Goose instructed. "Take out the ground forces and cover each other. Fall back if you have to. I want to draw the cav in." As those squad leaders responded, he looked around the troop transport, breathing shallowly at the stink of burned flesh coming from within the vehicle.

A hundred yards away, a line of six T-55 main battle tanks, one T-72 main battle tank, two APCs, and three Jeeps formed a pack of hunting steel jackals. Evidently the SCUDs and the carnage unleashed by the Marine wing had struck them, as evidenced by the blast scarring they wore on their armored hides, but they hadn't been disabled. Three T-55 tanks ran the forward line, crunching over broken vehicles and debris as well as corpses of their own dead.

The sight was a vision out of hell as Goose had imagined it back when one of the hellfire and brimstone evangelists had arrived at Waycross, Georgia, when he was a kid. Some of those men had painted word pictures of Satan's dominion, pictures that had been a lot like what he had seen all morning. It was easy to imagine that the whole world had slipped, without knowing or heeding the signs, into the end times, just as Bill had warned.

Syrian troops flanked the armored cav. Some of the Syrian soldiers jogged behind the slow-moving tanks with one hand on the rear so they could take advantage of the cover provided.

"Phoenix Eight," Goose called.

"Go, Leader," Tanaka answered.

"Stay with Three, Four, and Five. I want you providing cover sniping fire."

"Affirmative, Leader, but you're going to be hanging out there."

The clank of the treads and the hoarse rumble of the tanks' V-12 diesel engines grew steadily louder. The T-72 in the second wave stopped, locked down, then belched fire from the main gun.

The 125mm round screamed through the air and struck deep in the heart of the broken and burned vehicles in the Syrian camp. A Jeep jumped into the air, spinning end over end as parts flew off, then landed with a huge crash that shattered it into pieces.

Goose was surprised to learn that none of his team had been hit.

"Phoenix Leader, this is Blue Falcon Leader." The Marine Harrier captain was Dalton Hammer, a Tennessee native. There hadn't been time for Goose to learn much more than that while preparations had been made to save the Marines from the aerial crash site and pull the front line back into a semblance of order.

Remington had managed the liaisons between the U.N. peacekeeping forces and the Turkish army, but Goose had tried to get to know the new commanders. He hardly knew more than their names so far, but each of them had learned in a heartbeat what Goose had expected of them and what he planned to do with their units.

"I want to offer my assistance, Phoenix Leader," the marine captain said. "You and your men are going to get chewed up by those cav—"

"Negative, Blue Leader." Goose put edged ice into his voice. "You will stand down and clear my com. *Now.*"

There was no response.

Goose knew the Marine captain was only concerned about their welfare, but there was no way Goose was going to allow the few surviving aircraft they had left to them to be risked in this engagement. The CH-46Es were going to be needed for evac for the more critically wounded—*provided they lived that long*—and the Harriers and Apaches were going to be used to cover their final withdrawal from the border. Remington had promised additional aircraft would be forthcoming soon from *Wasp*. Though Goose gathered the guys on *Wasp* were having problems of their own.

Knowing his short dismissal was probably going to earn him a grudge match with Dalton Hammer, Goose hoped he'd be alive to mend fences later. The Marine captain wasn't used to taking a backseat to the action. Goose also knew that Remington would support him on any decision he made on the battlefield.

The line of Syrian cav advanced inexorably. Dust rose from the broken ground behind them. The vehicles avoided blast craters large enough to drop Greyhound buses in.

"Phoenix Two." Goose lifted his M-4A1 and curled his finger over the M-203's trigger. Remaining behind cover of the troop transport, he took aim at the center T-55.

"Go, Leader. You have Two."

"HE rounds, Two. First target is the center tank. After reload, take out the tank closest to you in the lead. With luck, the drivers will panic and turn outside. If we get lucky, we'll break a tread and mire those vehicles down."

"Affirmative, Leader. Target acquisition understood. Awaiting your go."

Goose glanced at Cusack at the other end of the troop transport. The lanky young Ranger stood braced with the M-4A1 to his shoulder.

"Affirmative, Sarge," Cusack said. "Locked on."

The tanks continued forward, closing at low speed, bringing in a tide of dust that settled over the trail of dead Syrian soldiers left behind them.

"Stonewall," Goose called. "This is Phoenix Leader."

"Go, Leader. You have Stonewall."

"That .50-cal you're carrying has armor-piercing capability, right?"

"Bet the farm on it, Phoenix Leader."

"Concentrate your fire on the lead tanks. Let's see if we can't jam them up."

"Awaiting your go, Phoenix Leader."

Goose squinted, squeezing out a bead of sweat that had been obscuring his vision. His body was a mass of aches and bruises. He pushed all those feelings out of his mind and prayed to God that he could stand firm and get done what he needed to do.

"Fire!" Goose ordered. His finger drew up the M-203's trigger slack, and he felt the assault rifle buck with grim authority against his shoulder as the 40mm HE round *whoosh*ed from the grenade launcher's throat.

✳   ✳   ✳

The Mediterranean Sea
USS *Wasp*
Local Time 0953 Hours

"God *raptured* his church," Chaplain Delroy Harte stated with more conviction than he'd ever had at any time in his life. "That's why all those people are missing, Captain. The Lord has reached down into this world and taken those believers who walked with him."

But even as the conviction filled the chaplain, he knew the jury was still out for those who watched him. Despite his best intentions, he didn't know if he was getting through to the two men before him. For a moment, he thought he truly knew what his father had gone through on Sunday mornings. Delroy had never met a man who believed in the Word of God more than his father, but even that solid belief—though it had helped shape what Delroy did and his career choices, in fact, just about everything about his life—hadn't been enough to get Delroy into heaven. How had his father gotten up every Sunday morning, hoping that he had discovered a message, a moment in the Bible, that could turn a flicker of belief into a life-lasting flame in those who listened?

Captain Mark Falkirk sat behind his desk and gave Delroy his full attention.

"Captain, are you going to listen to this—this—this *hogwash?*" Colonel Donaldson exploded. He slapped the desk with both his big hands and stood. "You're a military man, Captain, not some wide-eyed kid looking for the supernatural around every corner. Religious magic or whatever hoopdoodle this Bible pounder is pushing isn't going to solve the problems we've got facing us."

Before he could stop himself, Delroy's voice thundered, "God is *not* a parlor trick, Colonel Donaldson!"

"Are you listening to this, Captain?" Donaldson demanded. He looked at Delroy for just a moment as if to make sure the chaplain was staying in place, then turned back to Falkirk.

"I am listening to this, Colonel," Falkirk said.

"You shouldn't be," Donaldson objected. "Do you know the kind of effect the chaplain's ravings are going to have on the crew once this gets out?"

Falkirk remained unflappable. "It appears to have already gotten out, Colonel. Due to you pressuring Chaplain Delroy to speak his mind in front of the crew instead of having a private meeting with him as he requested."

Donaldson swore. "He shouldn't have interrupted my meeting."

"Your meeting," Falkirk said, "wasn't interrupted until you came to the door and entered into a verbal confrontation with Chaplain Delroy."

"If I hadn't gone to the door, he would have come in after me. He threatened to walk through the sergeant I had posted there."

Falkirk flicked his gaze to Delroy. "Chaplain?"

"Aye, sir," Delroy agreed. "I did that."

"Would you have gone through his sergeant?"

Delroy hesitated only a moment. *Stay with the truth, Son,* Josiah Harte had said so many times while Delroy had been growing up. *Always stay with the truth. You'll be judged in God's eyes anyway, and He will know what was in your heart. Hiding the truth from others serves no purpose and sometimes conflicts the works God is trying to do through you.*

"Aye, sir," Delroy answered. "I would have tried. I don't know if I could have. The sergeant is a big man."

Falkirk nodded. "And he's half your age. I would think you'd know better than that."

"Aye, sir." Delroy took a short breath. "But it was imperative that I speak to you and the colonel, Captain. I know the idea of the Rapture is hard to accept, but it's all in here." He held up his father's Bible.

"Oh, spare me," Donaldson growled. "Captain, we're wasting time here."

"Colonel, is there anything else you can be doing right now?" Falkirk's voice was crisp and clear. "Anything for those men over there along the border, or to get the troops here more ready?"

Donaldson folded his arms over his chest. His fists knotted. "No. You know that, Captain."

"I do know that." Falkirk rested his elbows on the neat desk and pressed his fingertips and palms together.

Like a man praying, Delroy couldn't help but observe. *The signs are always there.* His father had always told him that. *A man who learns to walk with God will always find his course charted for him. He just has to pay attention.* The chaplain was paying attention now.

"In addition to putting together relief and help for those Marines stranded along the Turkish-Syrian border, in addition to arranging for medevac ships to get the more critically wounded here when Captain Remington pulls his troops out of the area, I'm trying very hard to understand what happened to a third of my crew and a corresponding number of your Marines," Falkirk said. "Maybe I'm not an imaginative man. I've exhausted everything I can think of, and I can tell you that the Joint Chiefs of Staff at the Pentagon haven't come up with an answer either."

"We don't need this God poppycock running rampant through our men," Donaldson stressed.

Delroy took a deep breath, about to reply to that, but he maintained his silence when Falkirk waved him off.

"Do you know what will happen to the morale aboard *Wasp* if the crew starts speculating like this?" Donaldson continued.

"The morale of this crew has already been damaged," Falkirk stated. "It was damaged when our birds went down in flames over there, and it was damaged when so many of their shipmates vanished without explanation."

"Then it's our job to take that morale and build it back up," Donaldson said.

Anger flickered though Falkirk's eyes for just an instant, then the emotion was gone. "Do you think that you pulling your sidearm and shoving it into Chaplain Harte's face is going to shore up the morale aboard this vessel, Colonel Donaldson?"

"The man simply wouldn't shut *up*," Donaldson roared.

"And if he had?"

"I wouldn't have drawn my sidearm and threatened him."

"So coming to me and requesting the three of us meet to discuss this would have made you happier?"

Donaldson blinked in confusion.

Delroy was also aware that Falkirk had framed the option as a mild rebuke of his actions—that was typical of the way he handled things. *Point taken, Captain.* He breathed out and made himself calm down.

"Because I would have called that meeting at Chaplain Harte's insistence," Falkirk continued. "Chaplain Harte is one of my most valued and trusted officers. I would afford him the same respect I show you."

"You *can't* believe what the man is saying," Donaldson objected.

"You're right," Falkirk agreed. "If I had been a true believer, I probably wouldn't be sitting here in command of this ship right now. I'd be gone with the others."

Donaldson stepped back as though in disbelief.

For the first time, Delroy noticed the Bible lying on the corner of the captain's desk. The cloth bookmark was near the end of the Bible, probably somewhere in Revelation. *Just look for the signs, Son. God will always put them there to guide you.*

"The chaplain is crazy," Donaldson said. "Even if he's not certifiable, he's not in his right mind. He's been up all night. One of his best friends died in medical last night. Sleep deprivation. Emotional turmoil. All the confusion of what has taken place over in Turkey these past few hours. Those things have obviously taken their toll on him. He's lost it."

"The disappearances haven't just been in Turkey or aboard this ship," Delroy said as patiently as he could. "They've happened around the world."

"So what?" Donaldson challenged.

"Seems hard to believe that a weapon could be unleashed that would strike around the globe all at the same time. We don't have anything like that. I don't believe that any foreign power has such a weapon either."

Donaldson breathed heavily, obviously on the edge of losing control. He turned back to Delroy. "How are you going to prove what you're saying?"

"Prove that this was the Rapture?" Delroy spread his arms. "Look around you. The proof is right here. If you want confirmation, read your Bible. Read 1 Corinthians. God states there that He will come for His church." He flipped open his father's Bible to 1 Corinthians 15:51 and began reading in a clear, strong voice. "'Behold, I tell you a mystery: We shall not all sleep, but we shall all be changed—in a moment, in the twinkling of an eye, at the last trumpet.'" The chaplain looked up from the book. "That's how fast it happens, Colonel. In the twinkling of an eye. Just the way those personnel disappeared from *Wasp.*"

"You're insane," Donaldson said, shaking his head. "That book was written back when high technology was getting your household fire stoked by slave labor. The people who wrote it could never have foreseen what's going on today. Crazy talk. That's what this is. Just crazy talk."

"Did you know that Chief Petty Officer Mellencamp's body disappeared in front of me?" Delroy asked. "I was watching when it happened. Have you heard that? Even the dead believers have left this ship. Do you have a better answer for what happened here? What kind of unknown weapon of mass destruction that we agree we don't know about would cause the disappearance of a dead man from inside a body bag without opening the closures or leaving a mark on that bag or on his clothing?"

Donaldson cursed. "I don't need to hear this."

"You do," Delroy said. "You just won't admit to it yet." He opened the Bible again and began reading once more. "'For the trumpet will sound, and the dead will be raised incorruptible, and we shall be changed. For this corruptible must put on incorruption, and this mortal must put on immortality.'"

"Captain," Donaldson said, "are you listening to this load of bull?"

"I am," Falkirk answered quietly. "To every word."

"Then make him stop."

"It's not the Rapture you need to fear, Colonel," Delroy said, drawing the Marine officer's attention immediately.

"I'm not afraid," Donaldson said.

"You're afraid." Delroy felt the strength of conviction flowing through him. Reading God's words, remembering how his father had pounded the pulpit in his pursuit of the salvation of souls, washed away the fatigue and confusion that had filled his heart and his head for so long. He knew those feelings would attempt to return and that he would have to find the strength to stand against them, but he trusted God that he would find the means to do so.

Without warning, Donaldson launched a strong right fist at Delroy's head.

Quickly, faster than he'd ever been before, faster than he'd thought humanly possible, Delroy reached up with his free hand and caught Donaldson's fist with a loud, meaty smack. The blow halted only inches from the chaplain's cheek.

Donaldson's eyes widened in astonishment.

"You're afraid, Colonel," Delroy said. "But that's all right because your fear may cause you to seek comfort in God. You should be afraid, because your immortal soul is going to be the cost of your disbelief."

Donaldson tried to yank his fist back.

Delroy held on to Donaldson with a fierce strength he'd never known. "After the Rapture, God will leave this earth in place for seven years. That time will be called the Tribulation. All those who have not come to know Jesus Christ as their Savior before the Rapture will be given one last chance to make their peace with him and their acceptance of his dominion over their lives. But those seven years won't be easy. The Antichrist will rise up and weave a tapestry of the sweetest lies a man has ever known, and the world as we know it will be changed in ways we never expected."

Donaldson yanked his fist back, and this time Delroy let it go.

"You can't prove a single thing you're saying," Donaldson said.

"You're right, Colonel," Delroy said. "I can't prove it. I'm not supposed to prove it. God isn't empirical. You can't weigh and measure His works against any kind of criteria human beings have ever evolved." He paused, feeling the swell of emotions breaking within him. "That's why they call it *faith*. God is love and trust and acceptance and belief."

Donaldson stepped back, and for a moment Delroy thought the man might reach for his sidearm again. Evidently Falkirk thought so, too, because the captain stood in a quick, fluid motion.

"You're crazy, preacher. Bedbug nuts, if you ask me," Donaldson said.

"If you want a fight, Colonel, it's coming," Delroy said. His voice deepened, and he knew instinctively that he spoke in the measured cadence of Josiah Harte bringing home a fiery invitation. "These next seven years are going to be fraught with peril and dangers beyond man's wildest imaginings. Brother shall be turned against brother, and father against son. And no person will emerge through the Tribulation untouched." He paused. "You won't have a choice about that fight, but you will have to decide which side you're going to be on."

Donaldson trembled in anger, barely restraining himself. From a safe distance away, he leveled a finger at Delroy. "Captain, with all due respect, I request that you issue orders that that man should not be on this ship at this time."

"You're right," Falkirk said. Then he met Delroy's gaze. "Chaplain Harte, go pack your bags. You're leaving in ten minutes."

"Captain—" Delroy protested. He knew there was so much he could do here now that he knew and understood. And there were so many things that he had to work on, to prepare, to research.

Falkirk cut him off. "That's an order, mister, and you're dismissed."

Stiffly, Delroy saluted. "Aye, Captain." He turned a sharp about-face and left the room. Confusion shook him. *God, I thought I understood You. Why are You allowing this?* He couldn't help feeling that maybe he didn't understand at all.

"Would you say that you've had an adversarial relationship with Private Boyd Fletcher?"

Megan looked in disbelief at the young lieutenant who had been appointed her legal counsel. The silence after his question hung in the stark emptiness of the provost marshal's interview room like an echo of her thoughts. Her mind still hadn't gotten around the fact that the lieutenant believed she was going to be arraigned on charges of kidnapping Gerry Fletcher.

"You've read my files, Lieutenant Benbow," Megan said. "What would you say about my contact with Boyd Fletcher?"

"Actually," the lieutenant said, "I've only looked the files over a little. I didn't want to invade the Fletchers' privacy—or yours—unless it became necessary."

"I see." Megan remained calm with effort. She wanted out of the room and to be back home with Joey and Chris. She wanted to know her boys were all right—all of her boys. She wanted to know that Goose was all right despite everything that was going on in Turkey. *That isn't too much to ask, is it, God? Especially not after the night I've been through.* "Even from a cursory view of those files, I'd think that you'd get a sense that Boyd Fletcher didn't care much for my meddling in his family."

Benbow looked at her, his pen poised over the yellow legal tablet. "Is that how you view what you were doing with the Fletchers? Meddling?"

The frustration inside Megan continued to build. "Lieutenant Benbow, how long have you been assigned to your present AOC?" She used military terminology for the area of concentration, basically a job description, to impress on him that she was familiar with army protocol.

"I finished law school last summer, Mrs. Gander," Benbow said, "but I don't see what that has to do with my question."

"Not with your question," Megan pointed out. "The question is all mine. Maybe you finished law school, Lieutenant, but you appear a little naïve."

Benbow colored bright red on his cheeks and ears. He blinked rapidly.

"Let me sum it up for you," Megan said. "Yes, I had an adversarial relationship with Private Fletcher regarding his abuse of his son."

"*Alleged* abuse," Benbow said.

"You're talking like we're in a court of law," Megan said. "Private Fletcher was abusing his son. I knew it. He knew it. Gerry knew it. Helen Cordell at the base hospital knew it. And Dr. Carson was going to file a report with the provost marshal's office tonight—this morning. It's possible that Dr. Carson already did, given Boyd Fletcher's arrest at the hospital. Maybe you should check with the MPs and get a copy of the report."

Benbow scratched the back of his neck with his pencil. "Ma'am, I'm not the enemy here."

"Then act like you're on my side."

After a brief hesitation, Benbow said, "I think we've gotten off on the wrong foot."

"Yes," Megan said. "In fact, I think there are *two* wrong feet involved here." *And neither one is mine.*

Benbow deliberated a moment, then reached over and switched the tape recorder off. "Let's start over again." He stood and offered his hand. "I'm Lieutenant Doug Benbow, Mrs. Gander."

Too surprised to speak, Megan shook the man's hand again.

Taking his hand back, the young lieutenant said, "There's an awful lot of confusion going on around the base tonight. I'm probably not at my best, and I want to apologize for that. I will get up to speed fairly quickly, but I am new to my AOC and the criminal justice court and to Fort Benning. I hope you don't hold that against me for long and that I prove to be a competent representative for you in this matter."

Megan's head spun. "Lieutenant Benbow."

"Ma'am?"

"Sit down."

Lieutenant Benbow paused for a moment, then sat neatly, his knees together and his hands on either side of the legal pad. Megan began to wonder what the mother of this boy was like.

"You'll have to excuse me, Lieutenant," Megan said, offering no apology. "I'm afraid some of my husband's take-charge tendencies have rubbed off on me." That wasn't quite the truth because she had been self-sufficient as a single mom long before Goose came into her life. "Goose is a first sergeant with C Company."

"Yes, ma'am," Benbow replied. "I knew that. I was also told you were a very competent woman. That's why the allegations about you concerning the kidnapping of the Fletcher boy surprised me. Then again, when I thought about it, I wasn't surprised at all." He caught himself, realizing what he had said, and hurried on. "I mean, I could see how you would want to protect the Fletcher boy because everyone says you're that kind of person. A caretaker. A giver. I suppose if you thought hiding Gerry from his father was the only way you could protect him you would do that."

"Lieutenant," Megan said.

Benbow looked acutely attentive. "Ma'am?"

"I *did not* kidnap Gerry Fletcher."

Benbow turned his palms up. "Then where is Gerry?"

"I don't know."

"He was up there on the building with you?"

"Yes." Megan settled into the familiar question-and-answer mode she had been in for the last hour. "Surely by now you've found witnesses who have corroborated that. There were a dozen or more people there."

"Yes, ma'am, I have. And the provost marshal's office has been very helpful in pointing me to them. I intend to interview them all before this investigation is finished."

"But you haven't found anyone who saw Gerry fall from the building?"

"No, ma'am. I had a few say they weren't certain if the boy fell. In fact, several thought they did see the boy on the rooftop and thought he had fallen."

"But now they say they didn't see Gerry fall?"

Benbow nodded. "That's right, ma'am. They said they knew the boy hadn't fallen or jumped when his clothes hit the ground."

"How do they think the clothes got there?"

Benbow licked his lips. "They think you took them off the boy and threw them over the side of the building."

"They believe I stripped Gerry Fletcher down to his birthday suit and threw his clothes from the building?" Megan felt confused and disoriented. In some ways, the present confusion she was going through was worse than watching Gerry Fletcher slip from her grip. That had ended in seconds, and with—she believed with all her heart—Gerry safe somewhere. The conspiracy to make her a kidnapper seemed like an endless loop of madness—madness that just wouldn't stop. "That doesn't make any sense."

"Most of the people involved think you'd do that to protect the boy. The MPs are on your side. They believe that Private Fletcher would have hurt his son if he'd gotten his hands on him."

"They're not on my side if they think I hid Gerry. How do they think I got him down from that building? And without his clothing?"

"There is some belief that you had an accomplice inside the resident building."

"Do you realize what you're saying?" Megan asked. "You make it sound like I had this whole night planned out."

"There are some who think you've had this planned for some time," Benbow said. "I've been told that you were very frustrated with how things were developing with the Fletcher family. Private Fletcher's wife—"

"Her name is Tonya," Megan said automatically. She felt overwhelmed. How could anyone think that she had planned anything that had happened tonight?

"Tonya," Benbow acknowledged, "told the provost marshal's office that you had been acting possessive of Gerry. She states that she started getting the feeling that you would have taken him away from her if you could have."

"Tonya ignored what was happening to Gerry," Megan said. "She knew her husband was abusing her son, and she chose to ignore that."

"Can you prove that, ma'am?" Benbow looked at Megan hopefully.

"She never acted to help the situation or her son," Megan said. "Check through the files I have on Gerry. You'll find that every referral I received came from the base hospital or a base teacher. Never from Tonya. You should have reports in there from Helen Cordell. Have you talked with Helen?"

Benbow regarded Megan silently for a moment. "You don't know what's taking place on the base, do you?"

Megan made herself breathe out. "Lieutenant, Gerry Fletcher fell from that building over an hour and a half ago. He disappeared before he hit the ground. I don't care how incredible you think that event is, it happened. I saw it. Even if you can't find anyone else who will admit that they did." *Please, God, I did see that, didn't I? I haven't gone crazy! How can I take care of my family if I'm insane?* She barely managed to cap the rising panic that filled her. *God, please help me. I don't know what to believe.*

Benbow waited patiently for her to go on.

"I was taken down from that building and brought here," Megan said in a hoarse voice. "I didn't know I was being taken into custody until I wasn't allowed to leave this room without an escort while I went to the bathroom. I don't know anything at all that's happened outside of this room since I was put in it. Nobody's told me a thing. I've got family out there, and I want to know that they're okay. It's driving me crazy to be held like this."

"Then no one has even talked to you about what has happened on the base?"

"No. And I'm starting to worry about that, too. I've noticed a lot of activity outside whenever the door was open. I thought that maybe the MPs were organizing a widespread search for Gerry, since everyone kept coming to me, wanting to know where he was."

"Mrs. Gander," Benbow said in a deliberate voice, "there have been other disappearances on the base. In Columbus as well. In fact, I've heard news stories that say the disappearances are worldwide."

"What? What disappearances?"

Benbow leaned forward. "Gerry Fletcher wasn't the only person to disappear tonight, Mrs. Gander. At about the same time that you're claiming Gerry disappeared, several personnel and civilians around the base went missing as well."

"Who?"

"Helen Cordell was one of those people." Benbow hesitated. "There were others. All of the children on the base seem to be missing. Not just Gerry."

A cold, hard band of fear encircled Megan's heart. She forced herself to speak. "*All* of the children?"

Benbow nodded, flipping through his notes. "The age range of the missing children appears to be from newborn to the age of twelve. At least, twelve is the oldest reported age I have here on base. Some of the radio and TV networks that are still on air are reporting that about the same age group has gone missing throughout the world."

Chris! Sharp pain lanced through Megan's chest. She felt the heat of her son's face against her palm, felt the feathery softness of his breath against her cheek, felt his arms so tight around her neck as he'd rebelled against being left.

The memory of his voice came to her, so innocent and sweet. *"Now I lay me down to sleep. I pray the Lord my soul to keep. I'm just going to sleep for a little while, Mommy, so you can come and get me soon."*

"Lieutenant Benbow," Megan said, her voice thick with emotion, "I have a son—" She meant to say that she had a son in that age range, but she couldn't get the words out.

"Yes, ma'am. I know." The lieutenant referred to the legal pad. "He's here on base. I've cleared him for visitation."

Thank You, God. Thank You that Joey's home safe. Megan tried to speak, but there wasn't enough air in her lungs. Then her thoughts turned to Chris, and the images of her baby tumbled through her head. So many of them included Goose. He had spent so much time with Chris. Was he among the missing? What would Goose do?

"The reports are going to help us," Benbow said. "With the disappearances of these other children, and no real proof that you had anything to do with Gerry Fletcher's abduction, I don't see how this case can proceed into court. I think all the pending charges of kidnapping will be summarily—"

"Stop!" Megan ordered. Tears burned the backs of her eyes but she refused to let them spill. "I—I have two sons. *Two.* I have a five-year-old, Chris. I—I left him with the emergency child-care services—earlier this morning." She sobbed, then hiccuped because she was trying to retain control of her voice. "Do you—do you know anything—about the children there?"

Benbow blinked, then sat as motionless as glacial ice. Finally he said, "All of the children there are reported missing, Mrs. Gander. I'm sorry."

Unwilling to lose complete control of herself right now, Megan took a deep breath. *Later,* she told herself, *I'll look for Chris later.* First she had to get out of here, and this lawyer was her best shot at a ticket out the door. She took another breath, then realized her mistake when her lungs grew too tight. She exhaled slowly, like they'd taught her to do back in childbirth classes. *Oh, Chris.* She put her face in her hands and tried to think through the morass of fear and panic and guilt that overwhelmed her. *Maybe Chris wasn't still there. Maybe Joey got him and took him home. Chris would be safe at home, wouldn't he? But who would take all the children? How could anyone—*

A knock sounded at the door.

Megan heard Benbow get up and open the door.

"Can I help you?" the lieutenant asked.

"I'm Joey Holder. The MPs said my mom was here."

Desperate, wanting to wake so badly from the nightmare she was in, Megan looked up. She stood on the other side of the table and gazed at her oldest son.

Joey stood in the middle of the door. A young woman Megan had never seen before stood at his side. Both of them looked beaten and disheveled. Blood streaked Joey's face. He held out Chris's overnight bag with a look of pure helplessness.

"Chris was gone, Mom." Joey's face crumpled and he began to cry. "I'm sorry. I should have been there. But I wasn't."

Megan was stunned. Tears slid down her cheeks as she went to her oldest son and held him in her arms.

"Chris was gone when I got there," Joey sobbed in a choked voice. "All of them were gone. I didn't even get to say good-bye. I just left the house tonight, left him playing in his room. And I didn't even say good-bye to him."

Megan held her son and smoothed his hair the way she had when he'd been a child. "It's going to be okay, Joey. It's going to be okay." She didn't know how she found the voice to speak the words, didn't know how she found the strength to hold Joey as he shook and shivered and cried. "Everything's going to be all right," she said. But she didn't believe it.

She remembered how Gerry Fletcher had fallen from the rooftop, how he had tumbled in the air, and how he had disappeared, leaving only his empty clothing to strike the ground.

Megan knew in her heart that they wouldn't find Chris.

❋ ❋ ❋

Turkish-Syrian Border
40 Klicks South of Sanliurfa, Turkey
Local Time 0958 Hours

The 40mm grenade streaked across the battlefield, cutting through the smoke and the dust haze, and slammed into the center vehicle of the advancing three T-55 tanks. Orange flames rose in a whirling boil from the impact, then again as Eddie Ybarra's grenade struck home. Two other grenades, one from Cusack's weapon and one from Rusty

Barnes's weapon in the Phoenix Two squad, struck the tank and tore the turret loose.

Goose broke the M-203 open, ejected the spent casing, then shoved another HE grenade into the launcher and closed the breech. Bringing the M-4A1 to his shoulder again, watching as the tanks on either side of the stricken vehicle split off, Goose sighted down the length of his weapon and elevated the barrel a little.

One of the T-55s in the second wave locked down and swiveled the turret toward the overturned troop transport where Goose was taking cover.

"Second target," Goose instructed. "Fire!" The assault rifle bucked against his shoulder and the *thump* of the grenade firing from the launcher sounded a heartbeat ahead of the round from the T-55's main gun.

"Incoming!" Henderson yelled.

At least, that was what Goose knew the man was going to yell before the detonation of the 105mm round filled his ears with the roar of an explosion only a few feet away. The dead husk of the troop transport took most of the impact. The violent rocking of the vehicle when the impact shivered through it made Goose think at first that the transport was going to fall over on him. He braced up against the vehicle, ready to throw himself clear. His fingers worked automatically, breaking the grenade launcher open and thumbing another HE round into the breech. Then he glanced around the still-quivering vehicle.

The Syrian soldiers who had been following the armored cav broke from their positions and streaked toward the Ranger line. Their AK-47s stuttered bull-roar chatter as they advanced.

As Goose brought the assault rifle to his shoulder again, he saw that the first grenade had sped true. Evidently the grenade had struck the T-55's right tread under the armored skirting and blew the track apart. The long metal clanked against the tank and ripped long tears through the skirting before the driver pulled the cav unit to a halt.

The T-55 Phoenix Two's squad had targeted had also lurched to a stop. One of the riskiest design problems with the Soviet tank was the placement of the hatch on the top rather than the rear or underneath. The Syrian crew tried to scramble free of the death trap the cav unit had become. One man raced for the back of the tank while another crawled through the hatch, leaving the other two crewmen in an undetermined state.

Another HE round exploded against the low-slung cupola. The explosion ripped the Syrian soldiers from the tank, throwing them several yards away.

Goose blinked dusty sweat from his eyes. The grainy burn in his eyes told him he hadn't gotten all of it. He aimed his weapon, peering through the open sights left under the mounted scope. He curled his finger over the trigger and squeezed.

The 40mm grenade hit the tank's cupola and exploded. The T-55 shivered slightly. Then the left tread churned again, and the vehicle sped around in a semicircle before the driver realized he was dead in the water.

Goose watched the Syrian soldiers spreading along the skirmish line the Rangers had posted along the scattered wrecks lining the Syrian side of the border.

"Phoenix Three, Four, and Five," Goose said as he fed the M-203 another HE round. Two grenades remained in the bandolier he carried.

The squads responded, letting him know they'd had no casualties.

The sharp, distinct report of the Barrett .50-cal sniper rifle cut through the noise of the diesel engines and clanking treads. One of the Syrian soldiers dropped where he stood, as if knocked aside by a gigantic fist. Almost immediately, the .50-cal banged again and another man went down.

"Three, Four, and Five," Goose called, "be advised that you have sweepers inside your perimeter. Take them down and hold the center."

"Affirmative, Phoenix Leader."

"Two," Goose went on, "we march to the rear. Cut off any retreat."

"On your go, Leader," Ybarra replied. "We're locked and loaded here."

Goose scanned his squad. Carruthers, Jansen, and Cusack were all standing, though they looked like dust-covered wraiths in their BDUs. The three Rangers all nodded.

"Carruthers," Goose said, "you've got point. Jansen, you're walking slack. We're going to hump back to the rear and take out the T-72. They know we're not going to turn our artillery loose on them with squads in the field here."

"You got it, Sarge." Henderson held his assault rifle at the ready.

Goose opened the channel so all the squads could hear him. "One and Two are going to close the pincer. Three, Four, and Five, stand tall. Let's make a statement here, get back some of what we gave up this morning."

"Hoo-rah, Sarge!" Cusack yelled.

Goose rose to his feet from the crouch he'd taken cover in. "Go," he commanded.

Carruthers loped into the lead.

Goose followed the point man. His boots thudded against the spray of loose dirt spread over the hard-packed earth. The motion jarred him, awakening all the aches and bruises he'd acquired since morning, but he denied the pain's hold on him. He'd trained seventeen years for this moment, and he was exemplary at his craft.

While Carruthers negotiated the small maze of wrecked armored cav units and support vehicles that still held dead men sitting inside, two Syrian soldiers broke cover to the left. They were obviously fleeing the tanks where the Marine sniper was taking advantage of every target of opportunity. The big .50-cal rifle sounded like a basso drum rolling in the background.

"Down!" Carruthers yelled, going to cover.

Goose threw himself down and to the left. He shouldered his weapon by the time he hit the ground on his left side, recovered, and squeezed the M-4A1's trigger in three-round bursts. The hail of 5.56mm bullets caught the Syrian soldiers and drove them backward. Their heavier 7.62mm rounds cut the air over Goose's head.

"Up!" Goose commanded, surging to his feet and favoring his injured knee slightly.

His squad came up in unison. Cusack had a neat crease along his helmet where a round had deflected.

"Bucket saved your head," Jansen said.

"Yeah." Cusack reached up and adjusted his helmet. He looked a little pale.

Even after all the death the young Ranger had seen all morning, Goose knew death still became personal when it barely skated by. "Carruthers," he said. "Let's move."

The Rangers raced to the rear of the fire zone and took up a position behind a collection of boulders. Goose and Cusack held to the center while Jansen and Carruthers flared out on either side and slightly ahead to cover their position.

The T-72 looked like a goliath amidst the other Syrian vehicles. Two of the three Jeeps stayed close to the large MBT. The third lay flipped over, fire only now starting to catch under the engine. One of the Jeep's crew attempted to crawl away from the overturned four-by-four, then dropped abruptly. Goose understood the reason immediately when the .50-cal report rolled over his position.

"Two," Goose called. "Are you in position?"

"We're here, Leader."

Snarling like a great metallic beast, the T-72 fired into the mass of destruction lining the border where the Ranger squads battled the Syrian soldiers. Fully loaded, the Soviet-made tank carried forty-five rounds for its main gun, two more than the T-55s. There were also thousands of rounds for the 7.62 and 12.7mm light machine guns. Up and moving, able to fire while in motion, the T-72 was a juggernaut of destruction.

The Syrian tank crew knew the capabilities of their machine, and they were out to make the most of them. Confident of the thicker, layered armor the T-72 carried instead of the lighter armor the T-55s had, the tank drove straight into the teeth of Phoenix Three, Four, and Five.

"Cusack," Goose called.

"Yeah," the young Ranger replied.

"One round into the T-72," Goose said. "To get its attention."

Cusack held his weapon steady and fired. The 40mm grenade covered the ground in a split second and detonated in a wash of flames and smoke against the left side of the turret. Cusack kicked the spent casing free and thumbed another round in as the tank fired while rolling forward. The 40mm warhead only left a smudge of soot across the back of the tank.

"No penetration," Cusack said.

Less than a hundred feet away, the T-72 rumbled maniacally across the field of dead, collided with one of the disabled tanks left from the Ranger squads' earlier attacks, and knocked the T-55 aside. The tank fired, launching a 125mm round into the front of the derelict vehicles. Two wrecked Jeeps and one cargo van shuddered and slid across the ground, leaving deep gouges in the earth for several feet.

Joel Carver, a private with Phoenix Four, took shrapnel through one shoulder that left him too injured to fight or even get himself clear. Phoenix Four had to pull back to take care of their wounded.

Eddie Ybarra's squad took out another T-55 with two grenades, leaving two plus the T-72. One of the surviving Jeeps wheeled and came toward Goose's position, obviously tracking Cusack's shot.

"Didn't get the tank's attention," Jansen yelled, "but we've got people interested. Several Syrian soldiers turned in their direction as well.

Bullets peppered the rocks Goose and his squad used for cover. He kept his head down but watched as the enemy approached.

The Syrian soldier on the Jeep's rear deck stood and fitted a long tube over his shoulder. Goose recognized the weapon immediately as a Soviet RPG-7, a rocket-propelled grenade launcher specially made for taking out tanks and personnel.

The RPG-7 had come out of World War II as an antitank weapon for the German *Panzerfaust*. The Soviet army had embraced the weapon in 1961 and made it their own, then made tons of factory-assembled copies of the weapon that rendered the rocket launcher relatively inexpensive. The Afghanistan rebels had broken the back of the Communist war machine in the 1980s with the weapon, taking out tanks, APCs, and helicopters with the rocket-propelled rounds.

"I've got the Jeep," Cusack said, leveling the M-4A1.

"Leave the Jeep," Goose said. "I need it intact. Take out the troops. Let them know we bite."

Cusack shifted, then squeezed the trigger. The 40mm grenade landed just in front of the approaching line of men. Corpses left the ground and landed in crumpled, smoldering heaps when the HE round detonated.

Staggered but obviously knowing they were fighting for their lives, the Syrians continued their advance.

Goose leveled his weapon and fired, putting another grenade in their midst and only a few yards in front of the Jeep. A small crater opened up, and the concussion took down more Syrian soldiers.

"Fire at will," Goose said, slipping his finger over the M-4A1's trigger. "Stonewall."

"Go, Phoenix Leader. You have Stonewall." The Marine sniper sounded totally cool, utterly competent.

"Stonewall, do you have our position?" Goose peered around cover, dropped to one knee, and swung the assault rifle around. Two three-round bursts took out a pair of Syrian soldiers.

Another Syrian went to ground and skidded to a stand of rocks just before Goose's next burst hammered the terrain in line with where he had been.

"I've got your position, Phoenix Leader," Stonewall said.

"I've got a target for you." Goose shifted, reading the positions of his team and moving to keep the four in a solid two-by-two block of overlapping fields of fire.

"Name it."

"I need the Jeep intact. Then I need coverage till I get to it. The vehicle has ordnance I need to get the T-72 off your position."

"Will do, Phoenix Leader. Stonewall has the ball."

Goose held his position till the first Syrian soldier rounded the rocks. He fired into the center of the enemy, riding the M-4A1's recoil up naturally.

The Syrian's head snapped back, and he fell into a tangled heap with the man behind him.

"Incoming!" Cusack bellowed.

Goose hunkered down on one knee, reached under his jaw for his chin strap, and pulled his helmet down tight to protect him. An RPG-7 antipersonnel round detonated against the rocks and proved to be more lethal to the Syrian troops than to the four besieged Rangers.

"Move!" Goose ordered as he swapped out magazines. "On me!" He led the three Rangers on a charge, peripherally aware that Jansen had taken at least two rounds through his thighs just above his knees. Blood matted the Ranger's pants legs.

Sitting behind the rocks, they'd been sitting ducks for the same kind of pincer movement he'd used against the Syrian armored cav units. The Ranger squads had gotten spread thin, but there'd been no other way to contain the unexpected action from the surviving soldiers.

A Syrian soldier fired at Goose from behind loose collection of boulders. Beyond the man, the Jeep was still in motion. The soldier on the rear deck had the rocket launcher over his shoulder again. Even as he swung around, he suddenly jerked sideways and fell from the moving vehicle.

Goose swept the assault rifle up and squeezed off two three-round bursts. The bullets missed the soldier but struck the rock beside him, driving stone splinters and steel-jacketed lead splinters into his face. The man fell back, slapping his hands over his bloody features and screaming.

Stretching his stride, knowing his team was following at his heels as they'd been trained to do, Goose raced for the RPG-7 that had fallen to ground. The dead Syrian soldier lay only a few feet away.

The Jeep came around in a tight turn.

As Goose watched the Jeep, watched the crew inside it turning frantically to face the Ranger squad, he saw that Ybarra's team had accounted for the other two T-55s. One of the APCs sat in a smoking ruin along the skirmish line. The lead Jeep of the surviving two suddenly caught a 40mm grenade in the grill and became a flaming pyre that slammed into some of the morning's wreckage. The man who survived the initial attack didn't get ten steps from the vehicle before Ranger rifles cut him down.

Only the T-72 remained.

Goose stopped as the Jeep turned. He lifted his assault rifle and took aim. When he squeezed the trigger, the bullets ripped through the windshield and took out both men in the front seats.

Out of control, with no one manning the accelerator or the clutch, the Jeep jerked forward, sputtered, and died.

Recharging his weapon, Goose ran for the dropped RPG-7 and scooped it from the ground, praying to God that the weapon remained intact. "Good shooting, Stonewall," he said.

"I aim to please, Phoenix Leader. Glad you're happy with it. Eight and I have a small problem."

Goose glanced at the skirmish line and saw the Soviet-made tank smashing through the wreckage left from the morning's attack like it was going through wet tissue. The T-72, clad in reactive armor, was nearly invincible on the battlefield and moved through the terrain with impunity.

"I'm working on that now, Stonewall. Two." Goose slung his assault rifle and hefted the satchel of rocket grenades from the dead Syrian's shoulder, then turned and jogged toward the Jeep. He scanned the three Rangers in his squad.

Jansen had the injuries to his legs and was barely holding his own. Cusack had a scalp wound that leaked blood down into his eyes.

"Carruthers," Goose said. "I need a driver."

"You got it, Sarge."

Together, Goose and Carruthers yanked the dead bodies from the Jeep. Carruthers slid behind the wheel and keyed the ignition. Goose clambered onto the rear deck and prepped the RPG-7. He slapped Carruthers on the back of the helmet to signal him. "Let's go."

Carruthers stepped on the accelerator and let the clutch out. The Jeep's four wheels slid through the loose dirt for a second, then grabbed traction.

"Phoenix Two," Goose called as Carruthers steered for the T-72.

"Go, Leader. Two copies."

"That tank's covered in reactive armor," Goose said, squinting through the dust, feeling the kerchief drying around his lower face. "Hit it with everything you've got left and let's see if I can get a clear shot."

"Done, Leader. Three, Four, and Five, if you're anywhere near that tank, get clear."

"We're already clear, Two. There's no way we can stop that thing."

The crunch and shearing of metal filled the air and hurt Goose's ears as he reached into the satchel and took out a rocket. He attached the rocket to the fore end of the RPG-7 tube.

Reactive armor was a fairly recent addition to tank protection. Every tank was covered with metal plates that protected its vital areas of steering, guns, and ammunition storage. Designed by a German inventor in the 1970s, reactive armor consisted of two sets of plates with an explosive between them. When hit by a shaped charge, the explosive would be set off, blowing the outer layer out from the tank and negating most, if not all, of the damage. The RPG-7 rounds could penetrate the T-72's denser armor, but not the reactive armor, in one shot.

And Goose was very aware that one shot might be all he got.

Forty-millimeter grenades slammed into the T-72, but the flurry was quickly over because the Phoenix squads had only five to seven— Goose had lost count—rounds to spare. The onslaught had also drawn the tank crew's attention to their back trail.

The main gun swiveled around on the turret, then belched flame.

Carruthers took immediate evasive maneuvers. The 125mm shot sailed past the Jeep and slammed into a burnt-out troop transport.

Standing tall, taking aim, trying to account for the bumpy terrain, Goose fired the RPG-7 just as the tank's machine guns opened up. A round caught him in the chest and knocked him down on the rear deck, paralyzing his lungs with pain. Even as he fell, Goose saw that his aim had been true.

The rocket impacted the front of the T-72 squarely, leaving a twisted mass of metal where the 7.62mm and 12.7mm light machine guns had been. With any luck Goose had blocked the driver's vision as well.

Incredibly, though wreathed in fire, the T-72 lumbered forward. Goose watched in disbelief as the tank rolled closer. He marshaled his flagging strength and finally managed to draw a breath of air.

"Carruthers," Goose called.

The man sat in the front seat without moving. The Jeep's engine had died somewhere along the way.

"Carruthers." Goose reached for the RPG-7, thanking God it hadn't fallen over the Jeep's side. He found the satchel and took out a rocket.

"Get clear, Sarge," Tanaka advised. "Carruthers . . . Carruthers isn't with you anymore."

Staying low, hands fumbling as he tried to fit the rocket to the launcher, Goose inched forward and looked at Carruthers. At least one round had drilled through his heart, leaving him slack-jawed in death.

God keep him, Goose prayed.

"Get out of there, Sarge," Ybarra said. "Get out of there now!"

Small-arms fire strafed the T-72 as it roared toward the Jeep.

Goose remained with the Jeep. If he tried to leave the vehicle in his present shape, he knew he wouldn't make ten feet before the tank overtook him and ground him under the massive treads.

The T-72 could fire on the move at speeds up to twenty-five kilometers an hour. At present, the armored cav unit was moving faster than that. Or maybe it only looked that way, and the reason the tank crew wasn't firing was because they hadn't reloaded the tank's magazine.

Standing, seeing that the machine guns had been eradicated, Goose tried once more to fit the rocket to the launcher. Before he could accomplish the task, the tank was on him.

In motion, weighing in at forty-four-and-a-half metric tons, the tank was a considerable weapon in its own right.

Dazed, working on fumes, the horror of the moment intensified by Carruthers's death and the pain and fatigue that filled him, Goose realized he only had one chance before the tank ran him down. He gripped the RPG-7 tightly, stood, and stepped forward, timing his approach with that of the tank.

Just before the treads ground over the front of the Jeep, Goose sprinted forward. He leaped from the Jeep's nose to the tank's front skirting, dodged through the flames, tripped over the wreckage of the machine guns, managed two full steps that nearly got him to the tank's rear skirt despite the sudden lunge of motion and mass beneath him, then fell.

He landed on the ground. The horrendous crunching and crashing of the Jeep filled his ears, and he tried desperately not to think of what was happening to Carruthers's body. The impact knocked the kerchief from his face.

As he forced himself to his feet and tried to fit the rocket to the launcher again, he noticed the auxiliary fuel tanks strapped across the T-72's rear skirt immediately behind the turret. He smiled.

Goose slipped the rocket into place and lifted the RPG-7 to his shoulder. He took aim at the back of the turret through the fuel tanks, curled his finger over the trigger as the turret started to turn, and fired.

The *whoosh* of the rocket ended almost immediately as the warhead slammed through the fuel tanks and into the back of the turret. As the Afghanistan mujahedeen had discovered when fighting the Russians, the most vulnerable part of the T-72 was the back of the turret. And exterior fuel tanks just made it that much more vulnerable.

The explosion, coupled with the added punch of the nearly full fuel tanks, blew the turret from the tank. The resulting heat wave washed back over Goose, and his world dwindled to one flash-fried instant.

Then the tank rolled to a halt and exploded again as the ammo stored aboard went off. A roiling mass of fiery clouds, looking like a pillar of fire, streaked from the tank toward the heavens.

Wearily, not believing that he was still alive but thanking God for His mercy, Goose pushed himself to his feet. He peered around at the battlefield. "Base, this is Phoenix Leader."

"Go, Leader. You have Base."

"Do we own this battlefield, Base?"

Cal Remington's voice came over the headset. "You own the battlefield, Phoenix Leader. Good work down there. Establish your perimeter and set up your salvaging operations."

"Understood, Base. Leader out." Goose surveyed the harsh terrain. All they had to do was put up an appearance, keep the Syrian army buffaloed, and survive long enough to retreat during the night.

But night seemed a lifetime away.

The Mediterranean Sea
USS Wasp
Local Time 1017 Hours

Heat shimmered from *Wasp*'s flight deck as Delroy Harte trudged toward the waiting CH-53E Sea Stallion with travel kit in hand. Frustration and anger nearly shackled his mind, blinding him and making him slow to respond to the greetings of the crewmen that he passed.

Despite the horror that had happened along the Turkish-Syrian border, despite the number of personnel that had gone inexplicably missing from the ship and the entire ARG, the ship's crew still had jobs to do. A second wave of aircraft and Marines—cobbled together from Sigonella Naval Air Station in Sicily and MCB Camp Butler in Okinawa—was due onboard *Wasp* in a matter of hours. The ship had to be made ready to receive the new aircraft and troops that would rally to make the next attempt to reinforce the U.S., U.N., and Turkish troops along the border.

The wind from the waiting helo whipped across Delroy with humid intensity that left him perspiring under his jacket. He knew he should feel uncomfortable, and maybe he did, but at the moment, he didn't care.

He also noticed that several of the Marines stared at him with suspicious curiosity and more than a little hostility. *Well, Colonel Donaldson, you certainly get your word around quick.* He held his head high and tried to appear more certain of himself than he was. *God, why did You lead me this far, make me believe in You, and then let me fail at this? I know that you have raptured the church, taken your faithful with you, and I know you left me behind because I have broken the relationship I have had with You. Is this my punishment then, God, for doubting You?*

The insecure feelings came rolling back in, almost thick enough and heavy enough to smother Delroy. As he walked, he carried his father's Bible in his free hand, and he thought about the way Josiah Harte had pounded the pulpit on Sunday mornings, how his father had journeyed to the homes of the sick, and ministered to them until they got better or—as in some cases—how he had helped them let go of the mortal world and not be afraid.

When Delroy was nine, his grandfather had passed. A more bitter, angry, and harsh man had never walked the earth. Delroy had never seen two men less likely to be father and son, or a man more willing to turn his son aside and treasure other children who had turned out to be as godless and violent as he himself was.

During his childhood, Delroy could count on one hand the number of times he'd seen his grandfather. Every time Josiah had taken his family to visit his parents, Jonah Harte had gone away on fishing trips and drinking binges.

Grandmother Harte had tried to fool her husband sometimes by not telling him when Josiah and his family were coming to visit, but there had always been clues: apple pies, extra cookies for the children. So Jonah would load up his tackle box, throw a six-pack of beer in the passenger seat, and be gone for a few days.

In the end, though, Jonah Harte had succumbed to cancer that had broken even his wild fierceness, had melted the unforgiving coldness from his heart. His other children, three sons and two daughters, had wanted Josiah to stay away, but Josiah hadn't. Despite their curses and anger, Josiah had ministered to his father. He knew those curses were directed at him because he could accept his father's death. And because he could offer his father the certainty that if he accepted Jesus Christ as his Savior, he would go on to a better place.

For nearly two weeks, Josiah had stayed with his father, and Delroy had helped. In the South—at least in those days—people died at home in their own beds surrounded by family, not in hospitals with only strangers in attendance. Jonah Harte had died a shipwreck of a man in twisted, sweat-soaked sheets.

But Josiah had never given up on his father or lost his faith in the Lord. That bedroom in the tiny old house had been filled with gospel, with songs sung a cappella, and Delroy had never heard his father's voice sound stronger or the songs sound sweeter. Josiah had talked of God's love, of His sacrifice of his only son to save this world.

And in the end, Jonah Harte's anger and fear and unkindness had shattered. Two days before his death, Jonah had come to Jesus, and he had died almost peacefully in the arms of a son he had never truly acknowledged in life.

Delroy stared hard at the waiting helicopter. *God, take me. Please take me and use me as You see fit. Don't let me lie fallow while there is so much to be done.* But in the back of his mind, Delroy knew he was still angry over Terry's death. *And help me to get over the loss of my son, God. Help me to understand why You took him so that I may stand tall in Your service.*

He almost felt ashamed at the last. God's plans weren't for men to understand. Only glimpses now and then were given to mere mortals. Josiah had taught Delroy that.

As the rotor wash from the helo grew stronger, Delroy tucked his father's Bible under his arm and put his hand to his hat.

"Chaplain Harte!"

At first Delroy thought he had imagined the call.

"Chaplain Harte!"

Recognizing the captain's voice, Delroy stopped and turned around. The rotor wash broke across his back and whipped his jacket billowing before him.

Captain Falkirk crossed the deck in the long, rolling stride of a longtime Navy man. His dress whites shone in the sun, and he looked dapper and resplendent in the uniform. He had his hat under his arm and a pair of blue-tinted aviator's sunglasses on.

Delroy, his hands full with his Bible and his kit, fumbled with his hat and tried to tuck it under his arm so he could salute.

"At ease, Commander," Falkirk said as he reached him. "This is an informal visit." He smiled a little.

"Aye, sir." Delroy stood in the full heat of the glaring sun. He controlled his anger at the man he'd always thought of as a friend, but he couldn't help feeling betrayed. When he'd reached his quarters, Falkirk had already left a message with a young ensign outside his door with instructions to pack only an overnight bag and report to the flight deck immediately. Delroy assumed that the rest of his personal belongings would be shipped to him later. He still didn't know where the captain was sending him.

"I've just come to see you off, Commander," Falkirk said.

"There was no need for that, sir," Delroy replied.

"Angry, Commander?"

"Frustrated mostly, sir."

"But you're angry, too."

Delroy couldn't fathom the captain's easygoing nature. "I think I'm entitled, sir."

Falkirk nodded, and the sun gleamed from the blue lenses. "I think you are, too. Because if you're right and God *has* raptured his church—"

"Begging the captain's pardon," Delroy interrupted, "I *am* right."

Falkirk's gaze behind the blue-tinted lenses was implacable and accusing. "Yet here you stand, in a world that's been left behind, in a world of non- and near-believers."

The captain's words stung. Delroy pushed his breath out. "Sir, I've got a helicopter waiting for me. The longer it sits on that helipad, the more fuel it burns. I wouldn't dare to presume to tell you your job, but I think I'd be a little more miserly with my resources till I figured out where I stood in this thing."

"So why do you think you were left behind?" Falkirk gazed up at Delroy from behind the sunglasses.

"My beliefs are hardly under your purview, Captain," Delroy stated stiffly.

"Aren't they, Chaplain?" Falkirk's voice took on an edge. "You came into my office and started talking, as Colonel Donaldson called it, *crazy* talk. You advanced your theory—"

"It's not a theory. It's the truth."

Falkirk ignored the interruption. "Your *theory* that the world was raptured, in an attempt to explain the disappearances aboard *Wasp* and among the Marines sent to the border conflict. That advancement of said theory places your contentions under my purview." He paused. "Wouldn't you agree, Commander?"

Muscles knotted along Delroy's jaw. He made himself answer with effort. "Aye, sir."

Falkirk looked away, seemingly staring at the whitecapped waves rolling in toward *Wasp*'s bow. "As captain of this ship, I've got a responsibility to the Navy, to the Marines, and to the men and women I serve with."

Delroy remained silent even though he knew the captain awaited a response from him.

"Your view on the happening aboard this ship incited a colonel in the United States Marine Corps to point a gun at your head and later take a swing at you. A *colonel*. Can you believe that?"

"Sir, in my defense, I did not provoke the colonel."

Falkirk swiveled his head and looked at Delroy. "No, sir, you didn't. Your view did."

Exasperated, Delroy asked, "Captain, do you know *why* Colonel Donaldson reacted the way he did?"

"Of course I do, Commander. Donaldson is afraid that you're right."

Surprise stole Delroy's voice.

"The problem is," Falkirk continued, "I am the captain of this ship. I am supposed to set a standard for this vessel and her crew to adhere to. Yet, here are two of the most respected officers aboard my ship, clearly at odds with each other during the greatest crisis this ship—and very probably, the world—has ever faced." He paused. "So I have to make a choice."

"And you chose Donaldson."

"Chaplain, do you know who the most dangerous person on this planet is?"

A multitude of scenarios involving nuclear weapons and biological agents came to Delroy's mind. *Wasp*'s crew knew all about those from intensified studies and debriefs as a result of the current rise in terrorist activity.

"The most dangerous person on this planet," Falkirk continued before Delroy could answer, "is the person who believes he is a pretty good Christian."

At first, Delroy couldn't believe he'd heard right. He thought perhaps the rotor wash had slurred the captain's words.

"Pretty good Christians," Falkirk repeated, "believe they are doing the right thing, living a good life as God would have them do. But they're actually a shell. They live it right on the outside, keep up the appearance, go to church, talk the right talk, do the right things." He paused. "But they don't *believe*. Not where it matters." He tapped his chest over his heart. "Do you know why I'm still here, Chaplain Delroy?"

"No, sir."

"Because I'm a *pretty good* Christian," Falkirk said. "I didn't believe with the strength and the faith and the conviction I was supposed to. And do you know how big that faith is supposed to be?"

"The size of a mustard seed, Captain. At least, that's what my father told me in his church and in his house."

"When I saw Donaldson go at you," Falkirk said, "when I saw the fear in him and I knew in my heart that you were right, I knew if I wasn't careful I was going to watch this ship's crew tear itself apart. Believers, nonbelievers. Christians, non-Christians. Those who were afraid, and those who were not." He paused. "I couldn't allow that to happen. Not on my watch."

"So you decided to jettison me, sir?" Delroy let some of the out-
rage he felt spill into his voice. "And you stand there telling me you
believe what I'm saying is true?"

"Chaplain, the world is living in fear at this moment. Everything
that has happened on *Wasp* has happened in the rest of the world.
Russia stands poised to attack the United States with its nuclear arsenal and take us straight into Armageddon. I'm not willing to go there.
Not without a fight."

"But, Captain," Delroy protested, "I could do a lot of good aboard
this ship. I could counsel the men. I could—"

"You could," Falkirk interrupted in a calm, firm voice, "do a lot
more toward saving lives by speaking at the Pentagon and convincing
the Joint Chiefs of Staff of your belief." He paused. "Of *our* belief,
Chaplain."

Delroy felt as though he'd been poleaxed. "The Pentagon, sir? The
Joint Chiefs of Staff? *Me*, sir?"

"You'll enjoy the joint chiefs. They'll be a tough crowd, but after
watching you witness to Colonel Donaldson in my office, I know
you're the right man for the job. Your father would be proud of you."

The enormity of the task laid before him hit Delroy like a ton of
bricks. "But, sir, my place is here. With *Wasp*. This crew has never
needed me more. And I have never been more able to serve them."

"Are you scared, Chaplain?"

Delroy took a deep breath. "Aye, sir. More than I can ever remember being."

Falkirk smiled a little. "You can do more in Washington right
now, Chaplain, than you can here. Let's work to save lives first, then
we'll work to save souls." He offered his hand. "I made my decision
down in my office. I'd made it before your confrontation with Colonel Donaldson. I was prepared to try to convince you of the Rapture."

"That's why you had the Bible on your desk?"

"That Bible," Falkirk said, "is always on my desk or near to hand.
When I have to deal with problems with personnel, I reach for that Bible before I reach for the Navy manuals."

"I didn't know that, Captain."

"Just as I didn't know if your convictions had strengthened
enough to handle this situation. I know your son's death troubles
you, and I know you've struggled with your own faith."

Delroy's face felt hot. "I'm shamed to know that you were aware of
that."

"We all struggle with our faith," Falkirk said. "I just didn't know if you'd be ready for the task I was going to ask of you. But when I saw you stand up to Colonel Donaldson, when I saw the belief in your eyes, I knew I didn't have to sell you. Just as I know you won't back down from the joint chiefs."

"No, sir."

"Then shake my hand, Chaplain," Falkirk said, "and climb aboard that helo. You're wasting fuel standing here talking, and I don't know that I have the reserves for it."

"Aye, sir. You're right, sir." Delroy shoved his hat under his arm and took the captain's hand. They shook.

"Godspeed, Chaplain," Falkirk said.

"Thank you, sir." Delroy stepped back, saluted smartly, then performed an about-face and jogged toward the waiting Sea Stallion.

Once Delroy was safely buckled in his seat, the pilot pulled the CH-53E into the air and informed him they would be stopping in Greece to pick up the plane Falkirk had requisitioned for the flight to Washington, D.C. The pilot informed him that the plane trip would take fifteen or sixteen hours.

Delroy gazed down through the window, watching as *Wasp* and the rest of the ARG grew smaller and smaller against the blanket of green sea. Seeing the vessels made him realize how small his world really was while he was living aboard *Wasp*.

And how big the problem facing him really was.

But the stakes, God help me, You know what the stakes are. As he bowed his head and began to pray, Delroy was surprised at how quickly and easily the words came to him, but he took strength in them.

❀   ❀   ❀

Edessa Hotel Sanliurfa
Sanliurfa, Turkey
Local Time 2:13 P.M.

"It's hard sitting around watching the news when you don't get to be part of it, isn't it?" The words carried the plummy accent of the finest British boarding schools.

Seated at a back booth in the Edessa Hotel's restaurant, Danielle Vinchenzo swiveled her gaze from the nearby wall-mounted television and looked at the dark-complexioned woman standing in the aisle near her table.

The woman was striking—though her appearance was a surprise. Instead of the fair Sloan Ranger Danielle expected after hearing that voice, she saw a woman who would stand out in any crowd—and especially in a crowd of British blue bloods. She had café au lait skin that gleamed in the light and a mass of black hair pulled up in a style that made her look both professional and alluring. Her dark brown silk business suit was a handmade Italian original that showed off her slim figure. Her purse complemented the look and the suit well. She could have been a runway model for modern businesswomen's attire. Her age could have been anywhere from mid-twenties to mid-fifties. She obviously took good care of herself.

"Do I know you?" Danielle asked.

"Not yet," the woman replied. "My name is Valerica Hergheligiu."

"I'm Danielle—"

"Vinchenzo," the woman said. She smiled. "I know who you are, Miss Vinchenzo. I've seen your work."

"I'm flattered." Danielle sat up a little straighter. The horrific events at Glitter City had taken place nearly seven hours ago. By rights, she felt she should have been up in her hotel room fast asleep. Or even better, in the thick of things, reporting on them.

Only she couldn't sleep. And she couldn't work. She was stuck out here watching the television, being a spectator to the breaking news instead of part of it. Her boss hadn't returned her calls. And her news crew had refused to even think about going to the border where the action was. They'd been too shaken up, between the bombs and the deaths and the bullets and the people who had disappeared from among them. The crew didn't have satellite access for a broadcast anyway. Their equipment was another casualty of this disastrous day.

So she'd been stuck in her hotel. She'd tried to watch the news from her room, but it hadn't been an option because the violence of the morning had seemed to gather around her and wrap her in a cloud of invisible menace. She'd been too uncomfortable alone in her room to be able to watch the news there. She needed lights, people, noise around her—anything to make the world feel normal again. So here she was in a hotel restaurant, with a television tuned to news for company, and a woman trapping her in the booth, wearing clothes that cost more money than Danielle made in a month.

"You should feel flattered," Valerica said. "I've come a long way to find you."

"You have?" None of this was making sense to Danielle.

"Yes, I have." Valerica glanced at the booth seat on the other side of the table. "May I sit down?"

"Of course. I'm sorry." Danielle waved to the other booth. "Please. Make yourself at home." Though if that suit was any indication, home wouldn't look anything like this hotel's restaurant.

The woman sat, then gestured to a waiter. "Have you eaten?"

"No," Danielle admitted.

"That's Turkish coffee you're drinking?"

Danielle glanced down at her demitasse cup. "Yes. I've developed a weakness for it since I've been here."

"Turkish coffee is the milk of chess players and thinkers," Valerica said.

"That's what I've been told," Danielle agreed.

"On an empty stomach, dear girl, that drink is much too sweet and rich."

Danielle studied the woman. She had always prided herself on reading people, had always been quick to figure out an angle someone was about to play. But she couldn't get a reading from Valerica.

The waiter hovered expectantly.

"The mutton shanks kebab with vegetables is very good here," the woman suggested. "Allow me to order for us both."

"All right." Danielle watched as the woman ordered in fluent Turkish, though she had the impression that language wasn't her native one.

The waiter nodded and went away.

"You'll have to forgive me," Danielle said, "but I'm frazzled and not quite myself. It's been an unbelievable day, and I'm about done for. I'm hardly good company right now. I imagine I'm going to appear rude or abrupt."

"Not at all, dear girl." Valerica gazed at her with complete interest. "I'm sure you have questions about many things. Including who I am. Please feel free to ask them."

"Why are you here?"

"In Turkey?"

"Talking to me."

The woman shrugged and smiled as if at her own humor. "Why, I'm here because I want to make you an offer that you can't refuse."

The bald statement made Danielle uneasy, but she couldn't pinpoint why. Maybe it was the too-casual manner in which the woman had made her announcement. She held her silence and waited to see what else this woman had to say.

"You're a media specialist," Valerica continued. "You interview well. You stay current on your assignments and the rest of the world that you're not covering. You look good on camera."

For a moment, the thought that she should get up from the table and just walk away bumped gently through Danielle's mind, like a butterfly banging against a glass window. But it vanished as her innate curiosity took over. There was a story here. She could feel it. There was always a story when she got that cold itch across the back of her neck.

"So?" Danielle said.

Valerica smiled and reached into her purse. She laid a business card on the tabletop.

Danielle read the card. "OneWorld Communications. I'm impressed."

"Not without just cause, dear girl. OneWorld Communications is quickly becoming a media force to be reckoned with."

"Indeed." Danielle searched her brain for background info. "You're owned by Nicolae Carpathia, the man who was made the new president of Romania as of yesterday."

"The very same." Valerica smiled again. "See? You knew that. In spite of everything you've been covering here in Turkey, you knew that. This is one of the very reasons we want to hire you."

"Hire me?"

"As a reporter, dear girl."

Danielle tried to relax. "I'm under contract with FOX News."

"Not anymore."

Panic filled Danielle. She'd prided herself on the work at FOX, but she'd had her share of personality conflicts with the producer who handled her stories. What had happened to her job? "What are you talking about?"

"OneWorld Communications opened discussions with FOX News nearly a week ago with regard to your contract. We wanted to hire you away from them. Less than an hour ago, we managed to buy you out of that contract."

"Without contacting me?"

"It didn't make sense to talk to you until we'd reached an agreement with FOX."

"What kind of agreement?" Worry bounced inside Danielle's head. She had car payments and apartment payments, along with all the other ordinary financial obligations that had to be met. Payments that she could only make if she had a steady supply of cash coming in—and it looked like her job back at FOX had just vanished in the wind. Apparently today's catastrophes weren't over yet.

"We bought that contract out for a princely sum, which I shall not be gauche enough to discuss with you."

"What if I like my job at FOX? What if I don't want to work with OneWorld?"

Valerica smiled. "How can you not want to work with us? OneWorld is going to be one of the biggest media corporations in, well, the *world*."

"That's your opinion." Danielle tried to quell her rebellion but couldn't. She had never liked being dictated to. It was something that had been a part of her character since she was old enough to talk. It was one of the reasons she'd left home the very day she got out of high school—and that she'd made her own way in the world ever since.

"Dear girl—" Valerica's melodious voice took on a slightly icy tone—"that is not my opinion. That is a fact."

Danielle barely noticed the waiter as he returned with another demitasse cup. Her senses blurred. Maybe the sugared coffee was getting to her.

"You were at Glitter City during the attack this morning," Valerica said.

"Yes. Believe me, I noticed," Danielle said. "But let's talk about something more interesting. What happens if I don't accept your job offer?"

Valerica reached into her purse again and took out an envelope. She slid the envelope across the table. "That is a certified check for two years' pay at your present salary, plus a 10-percent raise for your second year with us. If you don't want to work for us, take the money; FOX takes the money we gave them, and you can go back to work for that network. But there's more where that came from if you'd care to join us. We think you have the talent and the drive to be one of the best reporters in the world. You're career will take off for the stratosphere if you work with us. I assure you, you'll never regret taking this offer."

Danielle opened the envelope, looked at the check, and found the amount was exactly what the woman had promised. It was a nice check, with lots of zeros on the good side of the decimal point. She whistled softly. "I'm a bit surprised by this. It's clear from this check that you've planned this in advance and that you're serious about this offer. But why me? What do you want from me? How can I believe you?"

"You're a reporter," Valerica said. "You shouldn't believe me. You should want to check the facts for yourself." She took a satellite phone from her purse, which Danielle was beginning to believe was filled with magic tricks or a hole to another dimension. "Call your news producer."

Dazed, definitely feeling the sugar high from the Turkish coffee, Danielle reached for the phone. She dialed the number and, surprisingly, got through immediately.

"Hello?"

Even though she recognized the voice, Danielle couldn't help asking, "Aaron Diller?"

"Yes. Danielle? Danielle, is that you? Do you have *any* idea of what time it is over here?"

Glancing at her watch, Danielle said, "It's six-nineteen."

Diller swore. "In the *morning*, Danielle! I just got to sleep."

"You're doing better than I am. I haven't slept at all. I've got no sympathy for you, Aaron. My day got kind of ruined when the SCUDs fell all around me this morning and killed my friends and destroyed a bunch of my equipment. Or maybe it was when I got shot at by the Syrian military. Or maybe it was when people all around me disappeared without an explanation. If you want to compare comfort levels right now, Aaron, I'm gonna have the upper hand. Why haven't you called me? Why haven't you answered when I tried to check in?"

"I've been trying to call you," Diller said. "Every time I dialed your hotel, I got a message that the circuits were busy. How did you get this number? This is my *home* number."

"Last year's Christmas party," Danielle said. "You had one drink too many. Or maybe you had five too many. Anyway, you hit on me. Somewhere between offering me more air time on international news spots, a bigger office, a larger and more forgiving expense account, and the keys to your Lexus, you gave me your home phone number."

"Oh. I don't remember that."

"Somehow, I can't forget it." Danielle looked at the woman on the other side of the table. "I want to talk to you about OneWorld Communications."

Suspicion vibrated in Diller's words. "What about them?"

"I'm sitting with Valerica Hergheligiu from OneWorld Communications," Danielle said. "She's convinced that her corporation has bought out my contract."

"Man," Diller said, "they're already *there*?"

"Is it true?"

"Hey, Danielle," Diller said, "in my own defense, I think you're gonna come out of this thing okay. I negotiated pretty good bonuses for all of us that—"

Danielle cut the man off with a hiss too angry to contain recognizable words, then broke the connection. She looked at Valerica as she struggled to get her temper under control. "It seems I'm technically unemployed at the moment. This comes as a bit of a surprise to me. But, even so, I shouldn't have hung up on him. I hope you'll allow me that brief lapse of professionalism."

Valerica spread her hands. "Of course. It sounds justified. But let's talk about your new career with OneWorld."

"I still haven't agreed to accept your offer."

A bright smile split Valerica's face. "Dear girl, you should at least feign interest until you've had time to cash that check."

Danielle couldn't help grinning. "True."

"We want you to continue covering the Turkish-Syrian problem," Valerica said. "And we believe we've found a focal point for your story." She took a mini-DVD player with a superb color screen from her purse, placed it on the table, and switched it on.

Danielle gazed at the gleaming device. "I love the toys already." She'd always been interested in cutting-edge technology.

"Just the tip of the iceberg, dear girl."

The five-inch screen cleared and showed the kind of footage that had aired almost constantly on all the networks over the last few hours. This particular piece focused on the unexplained mishap that had wrecked almost all of the Marine airships coming to the aid of the border forces she'd interviewed so recently.

The camera shot tightened up on a lone Army Ranger sergeant carrying a wounded Marine from a burning helicopter.

Valerica froze the DVD image. "This man," she said. "We want to find out who he is."

After a closer look at the screen, Danielle looked Valerica in the eye and said, "I know who he is."

"Do you?" Valerica smiled.

"Yes. That's Sergeant Samuel Adams Gander of the 75th Rangers." Danielle could still remember how the man's voice had rung out strong and clear as he'd dealt with the slaughter at Glitter City.

"Dear girl," Valerica enthused, "how simply marvelous." She squeezed Danielle's hand. The woman's flesh felt cold as alabaster. "See? Your employment by OneWorld Communications is a thing that had to come to pass."

Danielle looked from the image to the woman. "But why him?

He's a sergeant. A non-com. Why not an officer? The commanding officer of the man's unit is a captain. I know him, too. Cal Remington."

"You do keep up with things, don't you?" Valerica smiled. "Captain Remington will probably march right to prominence as this story develops, but for now, the powers that be want to focus on Sergeant Gander there. He's in the middle of the action, you know. Lots of drama and danger. Very photogenic—all that flame and fury. We want to know who he is and what his story is."

"He could be dead," Danielle pointed out. "When we pulled out, he was already up to his neck in trouble and heading away to find worse. The Rangers were involved in a mission across the border only a few hours ago."

"Perhaps the war has taken him. But perhaps not. In any event, your first assignment—should you decide to accept our offer of employment—will be to discover the whereabouts of Sergeant Gander. Dead or alive. We'd like to get his story."

"I'll have to go to the front?"

"Do you have any objections?"

"Reservations, yes. Feelings of panic, yes." Danielle took a deep breath, held it, then let it out. "But no objections. That's where the story is."

"Then you'll do it?"

"Do you have a camera team available to send with me? My crew and equipment got trashed."

"The camera team is already in place there," Valerica said. "You'll be joining them as soon as—"

"After lunch?" Danielle asked hopefully. Excitement and trepidation mixed within her. "I can be ready then."

"Of course you can, dear girl. Of course you can." Valerica patted Danielle's hand. The gesture was that of a much older woman, almost Edwardian in fact, but judging by her appearance, Danielle knew the woman couldn't be that old.

The waiter brought the plates of mutton on a bed of spiced rice, and Danielle was surprised to find she had an appetite. She launched herself into the meal with gusto, her mind already whirling with how she wanted to work the stories. She didn't even think about the potential threat to her life. She believed the answer to the mysterious disappearances lay along that besieged and battered border. If the answer was there, she'd find it. The answer had to be there. It was the biggest flash point in the world right now. Nothing else had happened around the globe that might trigger such an event.

At least, nothing else that she was aware of.

Of course, here in Turkey, coverage of the rest of the world's news had been spotty, concerned mostly with the disappearances of so many people and all the confusion that had come about because of those missing persons.

It was a mystery, and Danielle loved nothing better than a good mystery—except a good mystery with great ratings potential. Which this story had.

As she ate, Valerica kept talking up the corporation and the new heights of photojournalism they would ascend to together. Danielle couldn't help noticing that the meat on the woman's kebab was still pink, almost ready to bleed.

"Are you sure that's done?" Danielle asked, pointing to the kebab.

"To perfection, dear girl," the woman assured her. "I don't like meat that's been overcooked. I prefer a cut that is still simmering in its own juices, as fresh as though I had sliced it off the living animal myself."

Turkish-Syrian Border
40 Klicks South of Sanliurfa, Turkey
Local Time 1517 Hours

Three squads of Turkish F-4E fighter-bombers from the air base in Ankara roared through the blue sky in tight groups of seven and flew south into Syria. The *Turk Hava Kuvvetleri*, the Turkish Air Force, carried the familiar bull's-eye of two red rings and one white ring that identified them. The fin flashes bore a white crescent moon with a star at the lower point on a field of bright red.

Goose shaded his eyes with a hand and said a prayer for the pilots.

"Those are brave men, Sergeant," Captain Tariq Mkchian said in a sober voice.

"I know, Captain," Goose replied. "Some of them probably won't be coming back."

"Still," the Turkish captain said, "they fly and they go. Just as you and your men stand and fight this day. None of us, it seems, were cut out to break and run."

"Not until we get set for it," Goose agreed.

Mkchian stared down at the line the U.N. forces, the Turkish army, and the 75th Rangers had created behind the perimeter of bombed and broken Syrian vehicles that had been casualties of the SCUD launches. The Turkish captain was a wiry man who stood about five and a half feet tall. Soaking wet, he might have weighed 140 pounds, but he had the carriage of a lion, the mark of a leader of men. Gray marked his dark hair and neatly trimmed mustache. During the cease-fire that had lasted since the earlier engagement, the captain had put on a freshly pressed uniform. He carried his M-16 in the crook of his left arm like a man who had been born with a weapon in his hands.

Farther down the small promontory, three Turkish soldiers who served as the captain's aides stood awaiting orders. All three of them were incredibly young.

Too young to die, Goose couldn't help thinking. But he knew that fact didn't stop death from happening. A number of young soldiers had died or disappeared today, and more probably would join them before the dawn of the next day. That knowledge left a congealed lump of dread in Goose's stomach, and he could only ask God for the strength to get through it.

The sonic booms of the passing jets faded from Goose's ears. His injured knee had swollen further. Thankfully, the screaming pain had died down to a dulled throb, something he could hold at bay thanks to fatigue and analgesics. His clothing remained soaked and gritty despite the dry heat that baked the broken land around him. At least the smoke and dust haze had mostly cleared out. He could take a deep breath without the kerchief on his face and not launch into a coughing fit.

"Our air force will try to keep flights up at irregular intervals until after sundown," Mkchian said. "But if our losses grow to be too great, they will stop sending those pilots."

Goose nodded. He couldn't blame the Turkish military. The F-4Es were their primary offensive and defensive weapons. Every insertion the Turk Hava Kuvvetleri made into Syria that resulted in a lost unit was going to take the Turkish government months—maybe years—to replace. Both planes and pilots were scarce resources, and finding new ones would be difficult indeed.

Valuable resources were being gambled to try to save the embattled Turkish military as well as the U.N. peacekeeping forces and the Rangers. But the Syrian troops were firmly entrenched in the positions twenty klicks behind the border. They'd had all their luck with the ground war, though. Every time the Syrians had tried to send an aerial attack, the remnants of the Marine wing, the Harriers and the Apache gunships, had shot them down. Since then, though, two more of the Harriers and one of the Apaches had been knocked from the sky. Luckily, only one of the pilots had been killed. A few of the Syrian bombs and one of the falling aircraft had resulted in more casualties among the Turkish and U.N. peacekeeping forces. The Rangers, it seemed at the time, had already paid their blood price for survival.

"We'll make the best of it till that happens, Captain," Goose promised.

"I fear your men are pushing themselves too hard," Mkchian said.

Goose surveyed the activity before them. Rangers still led the way on the salvage operations going on among the wreckage left from the SCUD attacks. His men had been busy, scrounging salvageable weapons, ammunition, and foodstuffs. They'd gathered everything useful, from spare tires that hadn't been damaged or weren't too badly damaged to the fuel in Syrian Jeeps, tanks, APCs, and helicopters that could be pumped from the gas tanks into fifty-five-gallon drums to tents, cots, and other gear.

The plan was to pull back to Sanliurfa, regroup, and watch to see if the Syrian forces kept pushing once they made it across the border. After they reached Sanliurfa, the three armies would further retreat to Diyarbakir to figure out how they were going to hold the Syrians from the rest of the country. The thinking was that if the Turkish army stationed at the border, complemented by the U.N. peacekeeping teams and the 75th Rangers, reached Diyarbakir, they could pose enough of a threat of attacking any army that marched on Ankara that the Syrians might not even make the attempt.

The trick lay in getting from their present predicament to Sanliurfa, and from there to Diyarbakir. It wasn't going to be easy.

"Those men are Rangers," Goose said. "When it comes to pushing, they only know one way to get the job done."

"Still, they are doing so much work, and it will be for naught by this time tomorrow."

"If this little ruse holds till this time tomorrow, Captain," Goose said, "I'll be a happy man." *And we'll all be in Sanliurfa.* Then he thought about Bill Townsend, who had vanished, and the other men who had died and gone missing, and he knew that not all of them would be in Sanliurfa. The Rangers would have to leave their dead as well, and that thought pained him because he knew from past experience that the Syrian troops would savage the bodies and use them as psychological weapons.

Along the southern perimeter of the destruction on the other side of the border, the Ranger squads filled sandbags and dug fighting holes. They used Jeeps and the RSOVs to pull wrecked vehicles closer together to form barriers. Long scars showed in the crater-filled earth where wrecks had already been towed.

The media groups had gathered along the no-man's-land that marked the border. Some of them had returned from Sanliurfa with more crew and more equipment. Goose found it hard to believe that the reporters were brave enough—or foolish enough, as some Rangers had openly stated—to risk their lives just to get a story plenty of other people were already getting.

"I could have my men help you," Mkchian offered.

"I appreciate that, Captain," Goose said, "but those men down there are used to working together. They're up against the clock, and they're having to look over their shoulders during that work. It's working right now. Besides the occasional language barrier issues with working with your guys, too many men trying to do everything is going to get someone hurt. So let's leave it. For the time being."

Mkchian nodded. "That was what your Captain Remington relayed to me."

"Captain Remington is a fine officer," Goose said. "He knows what he's talking about."

"Have you served with him long, Sergeant?"

"Yes, sir."

"And you trust him?"

"With my life, sir," Goose answered without hesitation. "And with the lives of my men. If it ever came down to it, I believe Captain Remington would die for the men of his command."

The Turkish captain eyed Goose in open speculation. "Not many soldiers would say that about their commanding officers."

"No, sir," Goose agreed. "Probably not."

"You are a lucky man." Mkchian offered his hand. "I'll leave you to your work then, Sergeant. Thank you for your time."

"Yes, sir." Goose shook the man's hand, then saluted smartly.

Captain Mkchian walked away, already fielding calls from his troops over his headset.

Goose spent several minutes communicating with the men he had out in the field. So far, everything was progressing smoothly. In addition to creating the impression that the Rangers intended to dig in, the squads were also setting up booby traps within the wrecked vehicles creating the barrier. They'd left some nice surprises, including several remote-controlled munitions that would be set off when the Syrians attempted to breech the border. All of those traps and RC attacks were built around ammo that had been salvaged from the Syrian camp that couldn't be taken with the retreat. Later, after the sun went down, his men would put in even more booby traps on the Turkish side of the border with just enough room for the Syrian military to start feeling safe again after running afoul of the first wave.

All those efforts would buy time, not stop the enemy. *But time's all we need*, Goose told himself.

He stayed on the move, not daring to give in to the temptation to lie down or even sit and rest because he was afraid his injured leg would stiffen up on him. He'd gotten a wraparound brace from the medkits to help hold his knee together, and the additional support did provide some relief.

Plus, as first sergeant of the 75th, Goose knew he had no choice but to behave as though he were superhuman. A leader had to lead if he was going to be followed; he couldn't just command. General George S. Patton had put it best when he'd said, "We herd sheep, we drive cattle, we lead people. Lead me, follow me, or get out of my way." Goose tried to live by those words. If his troops saw him start to fall apart, they might not be able to believe in themselves.

He knew that Bill Townsend would have taken umbrage with him over that last thought. Faith wasn't something based on a person or even an idea. It wasn't something that could be weighed or measured. Setting an example was only coaxing others to trust in someone else, someone they could measure themselves against.

Learning to trust others didn't teach a man to look outside himself for the faith in God he needed. For a moment, Goose felt guilty, like he was letting the memory of his friend down, but at the same time he knew that Bill would have forgiven him. That was what Bill was all about. Faith. And leading people in his own way.

I'll get there, Bill. I promise you. I'll get there.

Goose took off his helmet for a moment, slung his rifle over his shoulder, and ran his hand through his sweat-slick hair. The cooling breeze felt wonderful. He wished he could leave the heavy Kevlar-covered helmet off, but he knew that if he did, his troops would follow suit. Every soldier hated the helmets, but the headgear saved lives, and the soldiers knew that, too.

The cannonade of the bombs unleashed by the F-4E fighter-bombers rolled back over the border. The sound came from twenty klicks farther south, and Goose knew there was a time discrepancy between when the bombs were dropped and when the sound reached him.

"Phoenix Leader, this is Quartermaster." The call came over the headset, mixed in with the constant barrage of communications that flowed from the Ranger squads as they went about their assigned tasks.

"Leader hears you, Quartermaster. Go to Tach Two."

Quartermaster was Julian Rodriguiz, a veteran sergeant with Echo

Company. He'd grown up an air force brat and lived on bases all around the world, but when the time had come for him to choose his own vocation, he'd gone army. Besides being a good soldier, a master tactician with small units, and a good cook able to do miracles with things found in the field, he'd also been gifted with a near-photographic memory. Placing him in charge of the salvage operations supply list had been a no-brainer.

Goose switched the headset over to the secondary channel. "Quartermaster?"

"Here, Leader." Julian hesitated. "We've got a situation."

Goose's mind immediately flew to the possibility of small troop incursions by the Syrians. They'd fought off a few such attempts already, and Goose knew there would be more.

"What's the problem?" Goose asked.

"The water supply." Rodriguiz sounded a little tense and unsure of himself, mannerisms Goose had seldom seen from the man even in the thick of battle.

Water was a main consideration to a soldier in an arid climate like Turkey. The dry heat leached the moisture from a man's body, and dehydration was one of the greatest opponents of a fighting man in the desert.

One of the smaller tributaries to the Tigris River flowed south of here, southeast from Diyarbakir north and east of Sanliurfa. Feeding it was a seasonal stream nearly a klick to the east. During the storm season that bridged Turkey's headlong rush from rainy winter to dry summer, with only a brief gasp sandwiched in between for spring, several small streams were born, then quickly withered away. Water was, had been, and always would be a source of contention between Middle Eastern countries. But right now, it was spring and the stream was still running.

During the initial SCUD launch, most of the Rangers' water supplies, as well as those of the Turkish army and the U.N. peacekeeping forces, had been wiped out. All three commanders had sent teams to the stream to replenish their supplies.

"What's wrong with the water supply?" Goose asked. The Rangers had purification tablets to make certain the water was potable, although at the rate they were being forced to use them they wouldn't last long. But the possibility remained that someone farther upstream could foul the water.

"Not the water supply, Leader," Rodriguiz said. "It's Baker." He paused. "They're telling me he's gone crazy."

❀ ❀ ❀

United States of America
Fort Benning, Georgia
Local Time 7:20 A.M.

In the nightmare, Megan was once more atop the residential building. She felt the hard edges of the rooftop cutting into her chest and stomach. Gerry Fletcher again hung at the end of her arm, and his weight was tearing her shoulder apart while slowly dragging her over the side of the building.

Gerry jerked and fought. He slipped from her grip, no longer held by her fist but only by her fingers now. The blood from the long scratches down her arm flowed across their clasped hands. The skin started to slide, to glide, and she knew she was going to lose him. He screamed at her, pleaded with her to hold on, to not let go, to not let him fall.

Somehow, in the nightmare, Megan found the strength to stop Gerry from sliding. She wouldn't lose him this time. Bracing herself, she stopped the inexorable pull that inched her over the side of the building. Then, incredibly, she started to pull Gerry back up.

Without warning, the boy's body split open, the way it might have had Gerry hit the pavement four stories below, and a great snarling beast covered in scales and fur emerged from the lifeless husk. Its triangular head had a low forehead over slitted cat's eyes above a pointed, edged beak filled with monstrous fangs. The thing was almost as big as she was, a cross between a bobcat, a baboon, and a Gila monster.

The creature snapped at Megan's head.

Startled, Megan released her hold.

No longer suspended above the ground, the impossible nightmare thing fell. As it plummeted, the creature started laughing. In the next instant, the creature became Chris. The wind ruffled his blond curls as he fell and screamed in fear. She saw his face, his mouth and eyes wide with fear, and she knew there was nothing she could do to prevent—

"No!" Megan's own hoarse shout woke her. She sat bolt upright in her bed, swaddled in sheets damp with sweat and wearing clothing from last night because she'd laid down certain sleep would never find her. Her heart trip-hammered inside her chest and created a sharp, painful ache. For a moment, she worried that she might be having a heart attack.

Chris!

Pain and anger filled her, bringing stinging tears to her eyes. Her baby was gone, taken by unknown forces. She traced the fresh scabbing that covered the scratches down her arm. It had happened; it was all true.

Resisting the urge to scream, Megan pulled her knees to her chest and wrapped her arms around her legs. She bowed her head and cried as silently as she could.

After the events of last night, after Lieutenant Benbow had finally gotten her released from the provost marshal's office, she'd returned home. She'd had no place else to go. At least, that was how it had felt last night.

Now the house seemed to echo with her son's absence. The family pictures on the bedroom wall—a patchwork of memories picturing Goose, Joey, and Megan from all periods in their lives—had served as a touchstone the three of them had used as jumping-off places for "I Remember" stories they had taken turns telling Chris.

Of course, being only five years old and living with a five-year-old's egocentric view of the world , Chris hadn't believed any of the stories. Joey's baby pictures and soccer seasons, Goose's high school basketball pictures and boot camp photos, Megan's high school swimming competitions and college graduation—none of those events had really existed for Chris's. But her youngest son had listened raptly to the tales all of them had woven sometimes separately and sometimes together.

And mixed in with all those photos of other lives were pictures of Chris. She'd had his picture taken every year on his birthday. He stood or sat or sprawled beside the numbers one through five, all of them as big as or bigger than he was.

There would be no number six.

Megan cried as silently as she could for long, hard minutes. Finally, she felt drained and empty, physically unable to cry anymore. Later, she knew, she would cry and grieve again.

She made herself get up from the bed. If she succumbed to the warm embrace of the bedding, she knew she would have nightmares again—wild visions running rampant through her head. She thought only briefly about peeling out of last night's clothes and taking a shower, but the idea was repugnant. Taking a shower and dressing for the day seemed almost obscene because that would be too normal. Life wasn't normal. It wouldn't be normal again.

Leaving her bedroom, she made her way to Joey's room and

peered inside. His bed was made and unoccupied. The last she'd remembered, Joey had been sitting up with the young woman he'd brought home and watching the news channels. He had promised to wake her if there was any news of Goose.

Panic, tapped from some unknown and bottomless reservoir inside Megan, surged again. She stepped into the room. "Joey."

"He's not there."

Megan whirled at the sound of the young woman's voice and saw her standing in the hallway leading to the living room.

"He's in Chris's room," the young woman said. "I fell asleep on the couch. I woke up just a little while ago and went looking for him." She hesitated. "I didn't intend to spend the night, Mrs. Gander. Especially not without asking. It just happened. I called for a cab, but none were running. And I couldn't ask Joey to take me home. You fell asleep and things last night were just so—so—"

"I know." The young woman's obvious discomfort resonated within Megan, drawing out the nurturer that always lurked beneath the surface. "It's okay."

Jenny crossed her arms, mirroring Megan's stance.

Knowing that the crossed arms were a natural defensive posture, Megan opened her own arms. "I'm sorry. I've forgotten your name."

"Jenny. Jenny McGrath."

"Well, Jenny McGrath, it's good to meet you." Megan extended her hand.

Jenny took her hand briefly. "I'm sorry about Chris."

"Yes." Megan's voice cracked, and if she hadn't already been devoid of tears she knew she would have broken down and cried. "So am I." She blinked her eyes and felt the rough, grainy drag of the lids. "How do you know Joey?"

"We work together. At the Kettle O' Fish."

"I'm surprised he hasn't mentioned you."

"He didn't mention he was seventeen either. Until last night."

"And you're—?"

"Twenty-three." Jenny hurried on. "We're not dating. We just went out together. Last night. First time."

"Out?"

"To a dance club."

The announcement took Megan by surprise. "Joey isn't old enough to go to a club."

"He had fake ID."

Megan took that in. On any other morning while finding all of this out, she would have planned on grounding Joey within an inch of his life. Maybe even until he moved out of the home. But after last night she was going to content herself with knowing he was all right.

Jenny frowned, obviously not happy. "This isn't coming out very good, is it?"

Megan shook her head. "No. Do you drink coffee?"

"Not really."

"Cocoa?"

"Sure."

"Let me check on Joey and I'll make us some cocoa. We can figure out what we're going to do next."

"All right."

Megan went down the hall and peeked in through the open door. Joey was asleep in Chris's bed. He was holding Chris's favorite stuffed bear. The sight broke Megan's heart all over again.

Oh God, why have You let this happen? Have You forsaken us?

Steeling herself, Megan turned from the door and went into the kitchen.

Small and modest, trimmed in yellow and off-white, the kitchen smelled of spiced apples. Jenny sat at the small round table and looked painfully uncomfortable.

Megan switched on the small TV on the baking rack near the stove, then went to the cupboards and started rummaging through them for baker's chocolate, salt, and sugar. She put a cup of water and two squares of the chocolate into a small pan and started to heat them.

"I hope you don't mind if I watch television while we talk," Megan said.

"No," Jenny replied.

The television cleared and showed FOX News. The footage currently rolling involved the disappearances that had taken place around the world. Megan already knew that the incidents were international in scope. She'd watched the news in her bedroom till she'd mercifully fallen asleep while waiting to wake from the nightmare she felt she surely had to be trapped in.

"Joey said your husband was over in Turkey," Jenny said.

"He is," Megan acknowledged. *"Your husband."* Are those Joey's *words or yours?* She knew Joey felt some alienation from Goose's affection. Some of it was because of Joey's age and Goose's frequent absences, Megan was sure. But sibling rivalry was also a big issue, especially at the age Chris was getting to be. Had been. *There will be no number six.*

"So far, the Syrian army hasn't tried to attack Turkey anymore," Jenny said. "The media is reporting that the Rangers are digging in there. There's some speculation that they might try to hold the border, but the experts FOX and CNN has had on say that can't be done."

"Makes you hope the Syrian military command isn't watching the news."

"I know."

Now that the water and chocolate had melted, Megan added a pinch of salt, three tablespoons of sugar, and three cups of milk. "They haven't—" when her voice tightened, she concentrated on stirring— "haven't released the names of any of the dead, have they?"

"No."

"Well, then we still have hope." But Megan didn't know how she was going to tell Goose that Chris was missing. Or how she was going to deal with anything if Goose was one of the casualties of the war that had broken out in the turbulent Middle East.

"Is there anything I can do to help you?"

Bring back my baby, Megan thought immediately. *Let me know my husband is all right.* She took a deep breath and continued stirring. "Look in the pantry, if you don't mind." She pointed the way. "I think there may be some plain bagels in there we can heat up. Even if you're not hungry, you should eat something."

Jenny got up, crossed to the pantry, and took down the bagels. She joined Megan at the counter. Megan handed the young woman a knife and she began slicing the bagels in half, leaving them open-faced.

"Microwave or toaster?" Jenny asked.

"I like mine from the toaster," Megan answered.

"So do I." Jenny popped the bagels into the oversized toaster. "Do you think we should wake Joey?"

Megan considered the prospect only briefly. "No. Let him sleep." There was no sense in getting him up for the day before he was ready for it. They had too much tragedy to face. And Megan already felt a little uncomfortable with the young woman in the house without adding her son into the mix.

"Just so you know, Mrs. Gander," Jenny said, "I had no intention of dating Joey. Even before I found out he had been lying about his age."

"But you went out with him to this club."

"As friends. But I don't think he knew that."

"Oh."

Jenny looked at her. "He may not like me much after he gets up this morning, but after I found out your husband was over in Turkey and that you had called Joey to come get Chris—" she took a deep breath—"well, I didn't want him to be alone."

"That was very considerate of you."

"Joey's a nice guy."

"I'm glad you think so."

Jenny waved to her attire. "It's not that I don't date nice guys, Mrs. Gander. I just don't date."

For a brief moment, Megan saw pain glint in the young woman's eyes. But the emotion was quickly hidden away, like a person with a long-standing injury would pull away from a casual touch from someone who didn't know better.

"Your car wasn't his fault either," Jenny said. "The driver of the truck that ran into us was one of the people that disappeared last night."

Only then did Megan remember that the car was a disaster. "I'll have to call the insurance company."

"I don't know if you'll be able to get through. There are reports all over that the phone lines are messed up. In a lot of places, lines are down due to wrecks, fires, and other kinds of damage. A lot of phone company employees left work after the disappearances happened. Or they disappeared themselves. Nobody wants to go to work today because everything is just so weird."

"I can understand that." Now that the hot chocolate had reached the proper frothy state, Megan removed the pan from the stove. She took two cups down from the cupboard and poured hot chocolate into both. "Were you able to get in touch with your family?"

"Not yet." The toaster popped the four bagel pieces up, and the smell of fresh bread rolled through the kitchen.

"Don't you need to call?"

Jenny was quiet. "If he wakes up, my dad might be worried."

Megan placed the hot chocolate on the table, then found a serving plate for the bagels. "You live with your parents."

"Just my dad. My mom left a long time ago."

"Oh." Megan felt immediately awkward. She took butter, cream cheese, and strawberry and blueberry preserves from the refrigerator, placing them on the table as well. "Have you tried the phone again?"

"A lot," Jenny said. "It won't be a problem till noon. That's probably when he'll get up." She hesitated. "He's kind of between jobs right now."

"It happens." Megan knew there was more to the story, but she also knew Jenny wasn't going to say any more until she was ready.

"With my dad, it happens a lot." A trace of bitterness scored her words.

Megan left the statement alone, sensing that the territory was better left unexplored unless the young woman wanted to go there.

"Let's eat," Megan suggested. They sat at the table.

For a moment, with the bitterness coiled in her heart, Megan considered not giving thanks for the meal. But she knew that was wrong. She had to believe that God had a hand in all the confusion that was now filling her life, even with Chris's disappearance. If she didn't believe that, there was nothing left for her to believe.

She bowed her head and said a brief prayer. When she reached "Amen," she was a little surprised to find that Jenny echoed her.

Jenny took one of the bagel halves and spread cream cheese over the open face. "What do you think happened to all of them?"

"Who?" Megan picked up one of the bagels, too, enjoying the feel of the warm, soft bread in her hands as well as the aroma. There had always been something innately relaxing about fresh bread.

"All the people that disappeared," Jenny answered.

"I don't know."

Jenny nodded toward the small television set. Closed captions carried the news stories across the bottom of the screen. "Some of the people they have interviewed feel like the disappearances were caused by some secret weapon of mass destruction. Others feel like aliens kidnapped all the people. But what if those weren't the answer?"

"Do you have another answer in mind?" Megan caught herself too late and hoped that Jenny hadn't noticed that she had lapsed into counselor mode.

A troubled frown appeared on Jenny's face. The expression looked disturbingly comfortable there. "There was a book in the living room that I found. Something about the end times. The pre-Rapture days, before God comes and takes all the believers from the world."

Megan remembered that the book was one that Bill Townsend had given her to read before he and Goose had left to go over to Turkey. From what Goose had said during that time, Bill had become convinced more than ever that the world was on the eve of being Raptured.

"You read that book?" Megan asked.

"Some of it," Jenny admitted. "It was interesting and really easy to follow. Have you read it?"

"No," Megan admitted. There had never seemed to be enough time, what with holding the household down with Goose gone and trying to meet all her commitments as a base counselor.

"If you do, I'd like to hear what you have to say about it." Jenny pinched a piece of her bagel off and popped it into her mouth. She chewed mechanically and swallowed. "The book really makes you think."

"About what?" Megan asked.

"About all of this." Jenny pointed to the television, then made a vague circular motion. "About everybody disappearing. About only their clothes being left behind. About all the kids disappearing."

"God didn't have anything to do with this." Despite her best intentions to remain neutral during the conversation, Megan heard the coldness in her voice. "God wouldn't have taken my baby away from me."

"Not even to protect him from the seven years of death and destruction that are going to follow the Rapture?" Jenny asked the question calmly and quietly.

Megan glanced away from the young woman and looked through the kitchen window into the backyard. The sun was bright and cheerful. The sky was blue. Outside, it looked like a normal day. Except it was a day without Chris in it. She thought furiously, trying to make what Jenny was saying make sense.

"Do you believe in God, Mrs. Gander?" Jenny asked.

"I used to think so," Megan answered honestly. "But after I was up on that building with Gerry Fletcher, after I had the chance to save him and couldn't—" She shook her head. "After Chris disappeared, I just don't know what to believe anymore."

"I thought about that, too," Jenny said.

"Did you get any sleep last night?"

"Not much. My head is just too full of stuff right now." Jenny took a deep breath. "Mrs. Gander, I hope you'll forgive me, but I think I'm seeing something here that you're not. Maybe it's that book, or maybe it's just that I haven't gotten much sleep. I think maybe you did save him."

Megan clamped down on the angry response that welled in her throat.

"When you were up on that rooftop with Gerry Fletcher," Jenny said, "you caught him. You stopped him from falling."

"Not for long."

"No," Jenny agreed, "but it was long enough that you held on and kept Gerry from hitting the ground before the Rapture occurred. Gerry was taken *before* he hit the ground."

The young woman's words struck home in Megan's heart with the force of a multiton steel vault slamming shut.

"I've never been much of one for God and churches," Jenny said. "After everything I've seen and been through, I really didn't think He cared much for me." Tears slid down her face and her lip trembled. "But I've seen you and Joey. Both of you are good people. For some reason I was with him last night. If I'd been with someone else, maybe I would have been one of the traffic fatalities that occurred when everyone disappeared. Maybe I would never have read that book. I don't know."

"God does love you, Jenny," Megan said, fresh tears stinging her eyes. "God loves all his children."

"Do you really believe that?" Challenge rang like naked steel in Jenny's voice. "Or are you just saying it?"

"I believe it," Megan said, and she was surprised at the strength of the conviction in her voice.

"Do you realize the difference you made in Gerry's life?" Jenny asked. "You held onto him long enough that he didn't die painfully, long enough that God had time to take him in an eye blink."

In that instant, Megan did see that. Some of the anger she felt at God lessened, and even a small part of the pain that she felt over the loss of Chris eased.

"More than that," Jenny said in a hoarse voice, "you got to *see* Gerry disappear. Do you know how many people are reporting disappearances on the television who *didn't* see their family or friends or anyone else disappear?"

"No." Megan reached across the table, drawn by the young woman's pain, and smoothed her hair from her face. *Twenty-three years old; so alone and so scared. What has happened to you?* "No, I don't."

"Hundreds, Mrs. Gander," Jenny said. "Probably thousands. But you saw the disappearance. There was no alien ray beam. No weapon. Nothing. Gerry just—*left*. You were shown what happened to Chris. If you hadn't been called in last night, if Gerry hadn't ended up on that building and you hadn't gone up after him, you wouldn't have seen anything. You would have woken this morning to find Chris vanished and his crumpled clothes left behind in his bed. You wouldn't have had the answer you have now. Don't you see?"

"I do," Megan said, tasting the salt of her own tears on her lips. "I *do* see. I also see that God put you here with me to help me."

Jenny was silent. More tears ran down her face. "I wish I could believe that, because I am *so* scared right now."

"You can believe it," Megan said. "What other reason could there be for you to go out on a non-date with a teenaged boy and his fake ID last night?"

Jenny shook her head. "I don't know. But God—God has never been part of my life."

Megan smoothed the young woman's hair from her face, unable to stop herself, wanting so badly to take her fears and pain away. "God has always been part of your life, Jenny. Whatever you've been through, God helped you survive it to get to this moment. To be with Joey. To read that book Bill left that I have never seemed to find the time to get to." She took a shuddering breath. "To help me believe. And I will help you to believe. I promise."

Unable to sit in her chair anymore, Megan got up and walked around the table. She put her arms around Jenny and held her tight, then was surprised at how fiercely the young woman held her back.

The doorbell rang.

Breaking the embrace after a final squeeze, Megan walked to the front door. After last night, she wouldn't have been surprised to find a group of MPs or Boyd Fletcher on her front porch.

Instead, Melinda Dawson stood there. Melinda was one of the kids that Megan counseled on a regular basis. Tall and gangly, with punk-cut, brilliant red hair and Goth-style clothing, not quite fitting in with the base kids, Melinda was prone to violent displays that unnerved her mother, a single parent who worked at the base commissary.

"Mrs. Gander," Melinda said hesitantly. Then she burst into tears. "My mom is gone! I found her clothes in her bed! She was gone! Just like all the other missing people!" Her voice shattered and she stepped toward Megan with her arms outstretched. "I don't know what to do! Nobody can help me find her!"

Wrapping her arms around the young girl, Megan held her tightly. "It's okay, Melinda. We'll figure out what to do. I promise. We'll figure out what to do."

"I didn't know where else to go!" Melinda said.

"You came here, Melinda. That was the right thing to do." Glancing up from the girl, Megan looked out into the street in front of her house. She saw other kids then, all of them clients of hers. All of them were coming to her.

If Jenny had not helped her see the truth of what had happened, Megan knew she would have been overwhelmed by the arrival of the kids. Instead, she was ready, and she knew then the task that the Lord had put before her.

29

Turkish-Syrian Border
40 Klicks South of Sanliurfa, Turkey
Local Time 1526 Hours

When he topped the small ridge in the Hummer he'd requisitioned from the motor pool, Goose saw that one of the news teams had beaten him to the site and were even now setting up their satellite relay equipment on the big truck carrying the OneWorld Communications logo.

The dirty-brown stream occupied the ragged center of the small depression. Almost thirty feet across and no more than four feet deep, the slow-moving stream snaked through the depression in gentle undulations between the moderately steep sides. In several places, animal runs and bare areas showing high foot and vehicle traffic had scoured the rough riverbank. A few small trees grew along the banks, stubbornly not giving in to the heat and the sun and the barrenness that plagued the land. Weeds grew in clumps, like knotted scabs from a fungal disease.

Over three hundred people—Rangers, U.N. peacekeeping troops, Turkish army soldiers, and even a few nomadic tribesmen who lived outside the cities—stood along the hills leading to the stream. There were a few vehicles, military Jeeps and trucks, but for the most part it was obvious the spectators had arrived on foot. Under the sparse shade offered by the anemic trees, litters bearing wounded from all three military forces sat with groups waiting to move them forward in the long lines that had formed at the stream's edges and met in the middle where Baker stood baptizing people.

Corporal Tommy Bono sat behind the Hummer's steering wheel. He was young and lean, his angular face a mask of dirt and grease. He'd come from Brooklyn, from a long line of firemen, but he'd wanted to see the world before he settled into the old neighborhood at one of the firehouses. His bloody knuckles showed how hard and fast he had been working in the motor pool to get vehicles ready for the night's evacuation.

"Man, Sarge," Tommy said in a dazed voice. "Have you ever seen the like?"

"No," Goose answered. But he'd heard of events like this one. His father had been baptized in the Satilla River in Waycross, Georgia, when he'd been fifteen years old.

The man who had baptized Wesley Gander had been a traveling revival speaker who had worn a white seersucker suit and played a guitar. The man had favored bluesy gospel, and threw in a few hot licks that had scandalized the mothers in the crowds and won over the hearts of the youngsters. He'd arrived in a battered orange Ford pickup that advertised handyman work and carried the tools of his trade in the back. Before doing the revival, the man had worked around town, mending fences, cleaning out garages, and doing small carpentry jobs in exchange for lodging and meals.

On the final day of the week-long revival, after the man had delivered a standing, shouting oration under the tent that had been borrowed from the farmers' marketplace, interspersed the whole time with music and anecdotes, he had called for those who wanted to know Jesus Christ as his or her personal savior. Wes Gander didn't tell the story much, but when he did, Goose was still able to see the fires of conviction in his father's eyes. The revival had been a come-to-Jesus success that was never again equaled in Waycross, Georgia.

According to the local story, there were so many who came forward that day, and the spirit was so strong among them, that the revivalist had led them on a three-mile walk to the Satilla River. There the baptisms had begun. The man had dunked everyone who came forward, the symbolic resurrection of a person after accepting the Son of God's most precious gift.

"Get us closer," Goose said.

Tommy put the Hummer in gear again and crept toward the stream. "What are you gonna do about this, Sarge?"

Goose surveyed all the people around him. "I don't know."

Corporal Joseph Baker stood waist deep in the stream water. Tall and broad with flat features and a round face, Baker looked like a gentle bear. He stood six feet eight inches tall, the tallest man in the company.

Baker gripped the nose and mouth of the man standing beside him, put a hand under his back as the man folded his arms over his chest, and lowered him into the water. A moment later, he brought the man back up.

The man fiercely hugged Baker, then sloshed through the loose mud of the streambed to where he'd left his gear with a compatriot who was already soaked. The freshly baptized man wore the uniform of a Turkish soldier. The man holding his weapon was a U.N. trooper.

Tommy stopped the Jeep thirty yards from the river. "I can't go any farther, Sarge."

"This is good enough, Tommy." Goose lifted his M-4A1 from the floorboard between his feet and slung the assault rifle over his shoulder. He stepped from the Hummer and felt his injured knee nearly buckle under him as it refused to take his weight, even with the brace. But he took another step and the knee loosened up. The pain was sharp and edged enough to bite ferociously.

When Tommy switched off the Hummer's engine, Goose heard the singing.

> "Just as I am, without one plea,
> But that Thy blood was shed for me,
> And that Thou bidst me come to Thee,
> O Lamb of God, I come, I come."

The music swelled across the stream, filling the depression with hope. As Goose slowed and looked around, the music grew stronger as more people joined in.

> "Just as I am, and waiting not
> To rid my soul of one dark blot,
> To Thee whose blood can cleanse each spot,
> O Lamb of God, I come, I come."

For the first time, Goose noticed that the faces of the soldiers and the people around him were free of worry and fear and tension. They weren't like the faces of the soldiers he had left back along the border.

> "Just as I am, though tossed about
> With many a conflict, many a doubt,
> Fightings and fears within, without,
> O Lamb of God, I come, I come."

Electricity scurried along Goose's neck as he listened to the song. In the stream, Bakern kept baptizing the men who stepped forward. He took the first of a line, then switched to the other line. The effort the man made at lowering all those people into the stream water and pulling them back up again was nothing short of Herculean.

> *"Just as I am, poor, wretched, blind;*
> *Sight, riches, healing of the mind,*
> *Yea, all I need in Thee to find,*
> *O Lamb of God, I come, I come."*

The group of OneWorld reporters made their way down through the people on the stream bank. A woman led the way, and for a moment Goose experienced a flash of recognition, but he lost the woman in the crowd. For a second there, he thought he knew her.

Then he spotted Private Braydon Childers, one of the newest recruits to the 75th. Braydon was tall and fit but wore thick army-issue glasses. Stubble showed along his jaw. His uniform was soaking wet.

Goose moved through the crowd. Rangers that saw him looked guilty and turned away, but Goose also noted that they were men who were on break, relieved of digging fighting holes and setting up booby traps.

The only dereliction of duty going on was Baker's water supply team.

"Private Childers," Goose said.

"Yes, First Sergeant." Childers turned in a smooth quarter turn.

"Why isn't that water supply truck moving?" Goose kept his voice level and conversational.

"We were pumping water from the stream, First Sergeant, just like we were ordered. There were already people here. People from the U.N. task forces and from the Turkish army. A few of the nomads. All of them were doing the same thing, First Sergeant."

"Getting water?"

"Yes."

"But that stopped."

"Yes, sir. One of the men of our water detail was talking about Corporal Dockery."

An image of the impaled Ranger filled Goose's mind. From what he understood, Dockery was still alive, though the medical team working him didn't know what was keeping him alive.

"They say Dockery saw Bill Townsend disappear, First Sergeant,"

Childers went on. He looked at Goose. "I was told you were there. Maybe you saw the angel, too."

The electricity skated across the back of Goose's neck again. "What angel?"

"The angel that came and took Bill Townsend away." Childers blinked behind the thick glasses.

Goose shook his head. "I didn't see an angel, Private."

"I was told Dockery saw one. He said the angel came down and touched Bill Townsend on the shoulder and told him it was time to go." Childers searched Goose's face. "Did you see that, First Sergeant?"

Goose hesitated briefly. "No. No, Private Childers, I didn't see that."

A crestfallen look dawned on Childers's face.

"I didn't see Bill Townsend disappear," Goose said. "I turned from him, then turned right back. He was gone that quick."

Childers smiled. "That's when the angel took him, First Sergeant. That's what Dockery is saying." He looked back at the crowd that had formed down at the stream. "One of the guys talked about that. He said that the angels had come and taken the good men—"

"There are a lot of good men left behind here, Private," Goose pointed out.

"Yes, Sergeant. I know that. But what I mean is that the angels came for the believers. Men like Bill Townsend and Conley Macgregor and Stan Thompson. We got to talking among ourselves, and we all kept coming up with the same kind of men. Those that disappeared, First Sergeant, were all men who were in church every Sunday, men who prayed before meals, men who spent time trying to talk to the rest of us and explain about God. They were men who believed absolutely in the Savior."

> "Just as I am, Thou wilt receive,
> Wilt welcome, pardon, cleanse, relieve;
> Because Thy promise I believe,
> O Lamb of God, I come, I come."

"But we didn't listen, First Sergeant," Childers continued. "We didn't believe enough. Most of us, we're good men, just like you say. But we weren't those guys. John Taylor, he spoke up about then and said he'd never been baptized. That's when Jim Yancy said that Corporal Baker had been an ordained minister back in Ohio."

Goose knew that was the case. Bill Townsend had told him the story of how Baker had been a young minister until his wife had died in childbirth. He had left home after her funeral, worked at odd jobs to support himself before he'd enlisted in the Army at twenty-nine.

"John asked Corporal Baker to baptize him," Childers said. "He said he wanted to be saved in Christ before he ended up dead out here."

Goose looked out at Baker as he dunked yet another man. The corporal seemed tireless, like a man possessed. And maybe, Goose admitted, Baker was. The energy surrounding the stream was a strong current, a powerful force that wouldn't be denied. He could feel it.

"At first," Childers said, "the corporal said he couldn't do it anymore. Said he couldn't believe. John Taylor, he asked how could Baker not believe when Dockery had seen an angel, when so many people had disappeared just like is described in the Bible. Gone in a twinkling, that's what Bill used to witness to me."

> *"Just as I am, Thy love unknown*
> *Hath broken every barrier down;*
> *Now, to be Thine, yea, Thine alone,*
> *O Lamb of God, I come, I come."*

"John Taylor," Childers said, "he started losing it. He was afraid." The private's voice broke. "I guess we all were by that time, though I'm ashamed to admit it."

"Fear's nothing to be ashamed of, private," Goose said. "Every man in this op is afraid. I'm afraid."

Childers blinked at him. "You?"

"Yeah. There's something Patton used to say about fear. He said, 'Courage is fear holding on a minute longer.' That's what we're doing out here. Holding on a minute longer."

"Baker finally gave in, First Sergeant," Childers said. "With John Taylor asking him, with me asking him, and the others that hadn't been baptized, Baker couldn't turn away. So he baptized us. And once he started, once all those other soldiers figured out what was going on, they came forward, too. You can't blame Baker. We got it started and he just hasn't had the heart to turn them away." He paused. "Truth to tell, First Sergeant, I think Corporal Baker has found him something out in those waters that maybe he never really lost."

Baker lowered another man into the water and brought him up. As soon as the man was steady, the corporal reached for another and began speaking.

"I still need that water supply truck running, Private," Goose said. "All your crew has been baptized?"

"Yes, First Sergeant."

"Get them together. You're in charge. Get that truck moving again. I'll tell Corporal Baker he's relieved of the water detail and he can continue here."

"I will, First Sergeant." Childers made his way through the crowd and started calling his squad to him.

Goose walked down the hill and stepped into the stream. The water was warm and moved sluggishly, rising to wrap around his thighs. He crossed to Baker, feeling his boots slip on the mud.

Baker paused in his baptism. Water droplets spotted his flushed face. "First Sergeant," the big man greeted him. He looked nervous, but he also looked like a man who wasn't going to be deterred from his appointed task.

Goose was aware of the stares of the other men around them. Fear hollowed all their eyes.

"Carry on, Corporal. I just wanted you to know that you'd been relieved of the water detail."

"I was going to get back to that as soon as I could," Baker apologized. He turned his face toward the stream banks. "But they just kept coming."

"I can see that. I'm going to see if I can find a chaplain or two who can help you. Big as you are, you're not going to be able to carry this load by yourself."

Baker beamed. "It's not just me, Sergeant. God is here with me. I've felt His touch. I knew I couldn't walk away from this and leave it undone."

"Corporal!" Four men carrying a bloodstained gurney charged through the stream, splashing water in all directions. They were part of the U.N. forces. "We need you now! I don't know if Hakim is gonna make it! He wanted you to baptize him!"

Baker stepped toward the gurney.

The man on the gurney was young. His black skin looked ashen. Perspiration gleamed against his shaved scalp, and his head lolled to one side. Bloody bandages covered his midsection and his thighs. His eyes held a glazed appearance, and Goose didn't think the young soldier was going to make it either.

"Son." Baker put his hand on the young soldier's forehead. "Can you hear me, Son?"

"Yes." The young soldier's voice came out as a hoarse whisper. "I hear." He focused his eyes on Baker. "I want—I want God." His breath rattled in the back of his throat. Tremors shuddered through his body and his eyes rolled up into his head.

Baker pinched the young soldier's nose closed and covered his mouth with a big hand. "I baptize Hakim in the name of the Father, and of the Son, and of the Holy Spirit." He nodded. "Put him into the water."

The men holding the gurney lowered the wounded man into the stream, immersing him entirely. Blood floated up from his wounds and formed clouds in the brown water, clearly seen because of the bright sun.

"Bring him up," Baker said.

The men pulled the young soldier back up. For a moment, Goose thought the man was dead.

Baker took his hand back.

"Thank you," the young soldier said. Then a final long breath released from his lungs and the tremors that had coursed through his body ceased. He relaxed in death.

"He held on," one of the soldiers who had carried the gurney whispered hoarsely. "He knew he was dying, but he hung on till we could get him here. He insisted on coming when he heard what you were doing."

Tenderly, Baker shut the young soldier's eyes. "It's done. He's with God now."

"Thank you, preacher," one of the men bearing the gurney said. Together, the four men turned and trudged away with the body of their dead friend.

Tears glittered as they spilled down Corporal Baker's broad face. He swiveled to look at Goose. "I've got to do this, Sergeant. I didn't mean to desert my post. After all these years, God has put His work back in my life."

"I don't think He ever took it away," Goose said softly. "I think He just made you see again." He nodded toward the waiting lines that met in the heart of the stream. "Get back to work, Corporal. I'll see that you get some relief."

Baker shook his head. "I'll welcome the help, First Sergeant, but I won't leave this post. God is making me strong. I'll endure."

"I think you will," Goose said. "As you were, Corporal."

"God keep you, Sergeant," Baker said. Then he reached for the next man in line.

Goose made his way back to the stream bank. Even as he stepped up onto dry land, the woman reporter thrust a microphone into his face. She was young and beautiful in khakis despite the oppressive heat and the dust that constantly carried through the wind.

"First Sergeant Gander," she said.

Looking at her, Goose recognized her from that morning in Glitter City. It seemed like that had been years ago instead of hours.

"Miss Vinchenzo," Goose greeted, though he never broke stride.

"You remember me?" The fact seemed to surprise her and catch her momentarily off guard.

"Yes, ma'am," Goose answered. "I hope you'll excuse me. I've got a job to do." He kept moving up the hill, feeling the sharp ache in his knee as he ascended the grade.

"I'd like to interview you," she said.

"Yes, ma'am. Just not right now. I'll have to clear it with my captain."

"That would be Cal Remington?" Danielle Vinchenzo matched him stride for stride as he marched uphill.

"Yes, ma'am." Goose kept his answers short and clipped. It was a habit. Talk too much and the media could do almost anything they wanted with what was said. He'd been in front of microphones and cameras a lot. Cal Remington loved media attention, and his men sometimes got caught in the glow of the camera, too.

"Do you have anything to say about what is going on here?" Danielle asked.

"No, ma'am." Goose waved to Tommy Bono, who legged it over to the Hummer and climbed in behind the wheel.

Behind Danielle, a cameraman loped along with a camcorder on his shoulder. The man struggled to keep the camera trained on Goose and the woman.

"Baptism isn't exactly standard operating procedure for the army, is it, Sergeant Gander?" Danielle asked.

"No, ma'am." Goose could see that the young woman was getting frustrated with the interview. He also guessed that the transmission was going out live.

Earlier, Remington had warned that many of the reporters had satellite access again and were broadcasting live interviews with the Turkish army, the U.N. task force, and Rangers. Up till now, Goose had kept himself insulated within the closed perimeter of battlefield ops while the reporters had been kept outside the gates.

"A number of people might see this sudden desire to get baptized as an act of desperation," Danielle said.

Goose turned and stood his ground so suddenly that the young woman had to back away to keep from colliding with him. He kept a neutral expression on his face. "Is that what you think, Miss Vinchenzo?"

She froze, not knowing what to say.

"Because if that's what you think," Goose went on, "if you think that those soldiers out there aren't going to hold the line when the time comes . . . well, ma'am, I sure wouldn't be standing where you're standing when the train comes through."

All around them, the men who had been privy to the conversation suddenly erupted in an explosion of applause and shouts of encouragement.

"Hoo-*rah*!"

"That's telling her, Sarge!"

The cameraman behind the young reporter swung around to capture the reactions.

Instead of being angry as Goose had expected, Danielle nodded and smiled in acknowledgement. She switched the microphone off. "Very good, Sergeant Gander. I'm not giving up on getting your story, though. Another time?"

Goose swung himself aboard the Hummer and made his injured knee as comfortable as he could. "At my invitation, ma'am, it would be my pleasure." He touched his helmet respectfully, then waved Tommy into motion.

As they wheeled around, Goose looked at Baker standing in water up to his waist in the middle of the stream, the two lines of men leading up either hillside. At the moment, Goose wasn't worried about the men or even the Syrians. He had no idea what Cal Remington was going to do when he learned that one of his corporals was baptizing men while being covered by international news networks. Or that his first sergeant, the man who knew what he wanted done, was responsible for leaving the corporal in place.

The strains of the invocation somehow remained clear even over the roar of the Hummer's engine, ringing in Goose's ears.

> "Just as I am, of that free love,
> The breadth, length, depth, and height to prove,
> Here for a season, then above,
> O Lamb of God, I come, I come!"

30

Voices woke Joey. He tried to retreat from them and drop back into slumber, where he didn't have to face all the pain that awaited him, but he didn't have any luck. The voices kept intruding because they were voices he didn't expect in his house.

He pushed himself up into a sitting position in Chris's bed. Even after all these years and the nights he'd spent "camping out" with Chris under a sheet while they fought off bears and pirates, he still forgot about the bunk bed above and slammed his forehead into the stout frame. Yelping in pain, Joey rubbed his forehead and ducked under the overhead bed. In a way, that pain felt good. At least there was an understandable reason for that feeling. The pain he'd felt when he woke up was caused by stuff too weird to ever explain. And he knew that the pain in his head would fade in minutes. He didn't think the other would ever go away.

Despite knowing that he wasn't going to find Chris there, Joey still looked through both beds. His heart felt cold and leaden inside his chest. Before he could stop himself, he was crying. His fists knotted in the sheets and he wanted to rip them from the bed.

But the rage inside him died stillborn because he knew the defiance would do no good. He'd dreamed over and over of getting to the child-care facilities. He'd arrived late every time. When he hadn't dreamed about being late, he'd dreamed about leaving the house last night without saying good-bye to Chris. He'd heard Chris in this room, playing with his action figures, doing the voices for all of them.

Some of those voices had even been different. And Joey had slithered out the door like a spy in a James Bond film.

Joey closed his eyes and wiped his face.

All he'd had to do last night was step into the room for a minute. *"Hey, Squirt. I'm outta here. Catch you later."*

And Chris would have said, *"Okay, Joey. Have fun. After while, alligator."*

Now he never would.

Guilt smothered Joey like one of Grandmother Gander's home-made quilts. He didn't know if getting to say good-bye to Chris would have changed how he felt now, but he couldn't get the thought out of his head that he would never have the chance again. He reached down and picked up Chris's tattered teddy bear, then tucked it tenderly under one of the blankets on a pillow.

The voices continued. He thought he heard someone crying.

Thinking about Jenny and wondering if she was still there, wondering if his mom was going to have anything to say or ask about Jenny and not knowing how he was going to handle that, Joey walked out into the hallway in his socks. Last night his mom hadn't asked too many questions about Jenny. Learning that Chris had disappeared had blown her away. He'd never seen her cry so much.

And he couldn't help feeling so much of that was because of him. If he could have told her he was with Chris when he disappeared, maybe it would have helped.

Or maybe he would have disappeared with Chris. *At least then Chris wouldn't be alone, wherever he is.* Joey still had no definite ideas about where that would be.

The news programs all had people on them speculating about why the disappearances had occurred. The theories ran the gamut from aliens from another world to terrorists to some kind of weird fluctuation in the space-time continuum that had drawn the missing people over into an alternate time stream where they were actually supposed to exist instead of the one they were in.

If the guy giving the presentation about the space-time continuum theory had looked more like Commander Data from *Star Trek: The Next Generation* instead of Yoda, Joey might have bought into that one. But the Yoda clone looked like he was a recovering homeless person.

The voices grew louder.

"What am I supposed to do, Mrs. Gander? I need to find my mom."

Bewildered, Joey stopped and stared into the living room.

At least twenty kids were gathered there, some of them flopped on the couch and the easy chair. More of them sat in the floor. Most of them looked like they'd just gotten up from bed. All of them watched the television news footage about the disappearances and the fighting going on in Turkey and Syria, like the TV might hold the answer to all their unsolved problems.

Joey recognized some of the kids from around the base. He recognized others from the files his mom sometimes carried home from work. Of course, he was never supposed to look at those files, but he had anyway because who could have resisted them just sitting there in her file case. He'd wanted to know how messed up other kids' lives were, to get a better idea of where his own life had gone wrong. He felt guilty about looking at the files now.

All of the kids in the files had been dealing with problems: anger management issues, new stepparents, divorced parents, dead parents, parents who cared too much and parents who cared too little, drug problems and drinking problems, poverty, self-esteem, and learning disorders. Compared to them, he was normal. He just wasn't happy about it and didn't know how to change it. He stared at the kids.

What were they doing in *his* house?

"I'll tell you what we're *not* going to do, Anna," his mom said from the kitchen. "We're not going to panic. We're going to take this one step at a time. As soon as the phones come back on again, we're going to find out where your grandparents are and how they're doing."

"My grandparents?" Anna slapped the kitchen table. "Mrs. Gander, I can't live with my *grandparents!* My mom didn't even want to live with my grandparents!" The young teen's voice was almost a shriek.

"Anna," his mom said patiently, "calm down. We're in the damage control phase. You remember the damage control phase from counseling, right?"

Dazed, Joey walked through the living room to the kitchen, having to step over the bodies that nearly covered the carpet. He detected the aroma of fresh-baked cookies. His stomach rumbled in anticipation.

His mom stood at the stove, using a spatula to remove fresh cookies from the baking sheet. She wore an apron. Baking was something his mom used as an outlet for her stress. Joey could always tell when his mom had a bad day because she would turn the stove on, get the apron out, and pull out her to-be-tried recipes. During days when the weather had been too wet or too cold, she'd also spent time baking with Chris. She'd never done that with Joey.

Jenny stood at the counter with a couple of young teen girls. They poured flour and other ingredients into a large mixing bowl.

Other young teens and some older teens sat around the dining room table or on the floor up against the two back walls out of the way of the baking. A young teen girl with braces smiled shyly at Joey. A boy with a sullen expression said, "Mrs. Gander, Joey's awake."

Joey's immediate impulse was to ask the guy who'd made him watch commander, but he curbed the words. No matter what was going on, he had the definite impression that a smart-alecky remark wasn't going to be a good idea.

His mom turned to face him. Flour marked one of her cheeks and her bangs. "Good morning, Joey."

Joey nodded.

"We have company," his mom said.

"Yeah," he said sourly. "I kind of got that."

His mom hesitated, then looked over at Jenny, who was looking back at her. "Jenny, could you talk to Joey and explain things?"

Jenny smiled. "Sure. You've got another batch of cookie dough ready here."

"Good."

Jenny wiped her hands on a dishtowel. "We'll need some more flour and sugar before we make another batch. We scraped the bottom of the canisters to get this one."

"Okay." His mom nodded, already making decisions the way she did when she got on a mission. At least, that was what Goose called it when his mom got into the get-it-done-yesterday mode. "We'll work on peanut brittle next. I was planning to make some for Easter, so I have the necessary ingredients. Maybe Joey can go to the commissary for flour and sugar later." His mom looked at him. "You wouldn't mind, would you, Joey?"

He didn't answer at first, too stunned to reply. Chris had vanished, Goose was in a border war, and she was baking with juvenile delinquents from all over Fort Benning. "Sure. I don't mind." But he did mind. He just couldn't tell her that.

"Let's go, Joey." Jenny looped her arm through his in a manner that was just too familiar after everything they had been through last night. She pulled him after her toward the utility room off the kitchen.

Joey reluctantly followed her, suddenly resenting the fact that

Jenny was still in his house. At the same time, he knew from the looks on the faces of most of the teenaged boys in the kitchen that he was the envy of them all with Jenny on his arm.

Jenny led him through the small utility room and out the back door. They stood on the covered back porch amid the ceramic pots that would hold plants and flowers a month or two from now.

If things ever get normal again.

The outside temperature was still cold enough that Joey could see his own breath for just an instant before it faded away.

"I know things must be confusing for you right now," Jenny said.

"Hey," Joey said hotly, "contrary to popular opinion, I'm not exactly a little kid." The anger and resentment got away from him before he could contain it. "So you can save the baby talk."

Jenny took a step back and wrapped her arms around herself. "What's wrong with you?"

"Me?" Joey couldn't believe it. "It's not me, Jenny." He waved toward the house. "My house is filled with people I don't even know. I can't even talk to my mom without somebody hearing me."

Jenny's eyes narrowed. "Those are kids that your mom is counseling. All of them are missing their parents, brothers, or sisters. None of them had anywhere to turn."

"So they have to show up at *my* house?"

"That's kind of selfish, don't you think?"

"Selfish?"

"Yeah. I think them showing up here says a lot for the kind of person your mom is."

"They're in *my* house!"

Glancing over her shoulder, Jenny said, "Why don't you try to keep your voice down."

"Because I don't want to," Joey said, exasperated. "This is stupid! My little brother disappeared last night! I thought my mom was going to totally freak out!" He let out a pent-up breath because his lungs were suddenly too full to breathe. "I get up this morning, she's got a houseful of strangers. And she's baking cookies like everything is all right. Everything is *not* all right!"

"Your mom is just trying to help those kids." Jenny eyed him deliberately.

"She's my mom. Not theirs."

"I don't think you realize what has happened here, Joey. These disappearances, they happened all around the world. A lot of people are scared. A lot more than just those kids in your house."

"That's not my problem."

"It's a good thing we're not all as narrow-minded as you are."

"Good for who?"

"Those kids in there need help, Joey."

Unable to stand still any longer, Joey stepped off the porch. He gazed at the flower beds, remembering all the times he'd chased baseballs into them when he and Goose had played catch back there. The tire swing that Chris loved so much still hung from the tree above the covered sandbox he had helped Goose build three summers ago.

This was *his* house. *His* yard. And he had been invaded.

"Russia is threatening war," Jenny said. "They think the United States is somehow responsible for all the disappearances. It's all over the news." She paused. "Are you listening to me?"

Joey wheeled on her from halfway out into the backyard. "What are you still doing here, Jenny?"

"I'm helping your mom."

"Last night you seemed like you were in a hurry to get home."

Jenny's voice turned cold and measured. "Last night," she stated, "I offered to come here and help you because your dad is over in Turkey, probably fighting for his life, and to be with you when you picked up your little brother. The only time I was ever in a hurry to get away from you was when I found out you'd been lying to me."

Tears burned at the backs of Joey's eyes but he refused to shed them. "Why are you here now, Jenny?"

"Because your mom could use some help. Because she asked me if I would help her if I didn't have anything better to do."

"And you don't?"

Jenny was quiet for a moment. Her lower lip quivered for just an instant, then stilled. Her gaze turned cold and distant. "No, Joey, I don't have anything better to do. I live with my dad. He's an alcoholic. My mom couldn't take it anymore, so she ran away. At least, that's the excuse she used for leaving us when I was fifteen. I've put myself through school since then, got my dad up and going so it took him longer to finally get fired from jobs that he stopped showing up late to." She took a breath. "I started to work at McDonald's when I was sixteen because somebody needed to pay the rent in those crummy apartments where we lived. I work at Kettle O' Fish to pay the rent in the crummy apartment where we live now. We've lived in that apartment for over two years. That's the longest I've ever lived in any one place."

Joey stared at her, not knowing what to say.

"I have to hide my money around the house because my dad will spend it on alcohol and beer if he finds it. These days, since I've been able to pay the bills, my dad works less and less. I don't go to college because it would cost too much. I change jobs a lot because sooner or later my dad will find out where I work and come in there drunk and cause a scene."

"Jenny, I—"

"Shut up, Joey!" Her voice was fierce. "I don't want to hear 'I'm sorry.' I get that enough from my dad. 'I'm sorry' doesn't pay the bills or put food on the table or give me back any of my self-respect." She paused.

Joey let the silence stretch between them, not knowing what to say. He got the distinct feeling that whatever he said would only cause her to take his head off.

"Do you want to know why I don't date?" Jenny asked in a strained voice.

Joey didn't answer. Too much was coming at him at one time, and he didn't know how to deal with it.

"Because when I dated in the past," Jenny said, "I heard my dad say things to me I never thought he would say. Awful things, Joey. He accused me of stuff I didn't do. Stuff I don't do. He talks to me the way he used to talk to my mom. Only I'm not her; I can't yell back at him the way she did. And even if I did, things would just be worse. I watched each of them put the other in the emergency room when I was little. More than once."

"I didn't know," Joey whispered.

"Of course you didn't know," Jenny snapped. "I don't let anybody know. I don't want anybody to know. You look at me and all you see is a body. You don't even know me, but all of a sudden you're convinced you really like me, or maybe you're even falling in love with me." She let out a ragged breath. "But you don't know me. You don't even try to get to know me. You just like the way I look."

Embarrassment burned Joey's face.

"Guys come around and hit on me," Jenny said. "They think that I need them. I don't need them. I'm making it on my own. Maybe it's not anybody's dream world, but it's what I've got to live with."

Joey waited for a moment, wanting to make sure she was done. He knew he should just wait her out, wait until she went back into the house. Instead, he asked, "Why don't you leave?"

"Leave my dad?"

"Yeah."

"Because he's my dad," Jenny answered. "And because everyone else has left him. My mom. His parents and brothers and sister. His friends. Oh, he still has drinking buddies, but they only come around when he's got money and he's buying." She paused. "Kind of the same way guys come around me because they like what they see and not because of who I am."

"Nobody should have to live like that." Joey thought he was being supportive, but judging from the look of reproach on Jenny's face, she hadn't taken it that way.

"Grow up, Joey," she said. "It's not a perfect world. Sometimes you just have to take what life hands you. If I left my dad, he would die or end up in jail. I hate living with him, but I don't want that to happen." A single tear tracked down her cheek. "He's my father, Joey, and I'm not going to leave him. He's been left by too many people."

Joey shoved his hands into his pockets. His anger had wilted, but the pain inside him still resonated, stronger now because he could feel the pain inside Jenny.

"And you're not the only one with a fake ID, Joey," she said. "I'm not twenty-three. I'm *nineteen*. So if I can handle this, I know you can." She nodded at the house. "I think your mom is a fantastic lady, but she has her hands full with those kids in there. She could use some help." She looked at him expectantly.

Joey stared back at her. "You lied to me. You told me you were twenty-three."

"Isn't that the pot calling the kettle black?"

"No, it isn't. If you hadn't lied to me, I would have never lied to you. And you don't know everything there is about living here."

"And what don't I know?"

Joey thought about the feelings he'd been having for months, about how Chris had seemed to consume the attentions of his mom and Goose, about how he had been relegated to the role of baby-sitter. The way his mom took in the kids who showed up at his house was a perfect case in point.

And now Jenny was using her own problems to try to make his seem insignificant. That was wrong. He was entitled to his feelings, and there was no denying how things had been around his house. Everybody had an excuse for why things had been that way. But in the end, that's all they were: excuses.

Disgusted, frustrated, and hurting, missing Chris, Joey turned away and threw an open hand back at her. "Forget about it, Jenny. It's not worth talking about." He walked away, heading toward the base, not knowing what he was going to do but knowing he couldn't stay there with all the pain and strangers inside his house.

He felt her eyes on his back for a long time, but when he turned around a couple blocks away, she wasn't there. He kept walking, feeling more lost and alone than he ever had.

31

**United States 75th Rangers 3rd Battalion
Field Command Post
35 Klicks South of Sanliurfa, Turkey
Local Time 1542 Hours**

The world hung suspended from a single strand as thin as a gossamer spider web above the gleaming jaws of death.

Cal Remington sat in his ready room in the command post and reflected on that thought. The prose was too purple to put in a field report, but the summation would stand out in a biography or an episode of The History Channel.

The Ranger captain had no doubt that history was being made and that he would probably figure large in that history. A third of the world's population had disappeared with no apparent catalyst—except for a sudden border skirmish that had flared up in the Middle East. The Middle East had been a hotbed of terrorism and world threat for decades—centuries even. But the fighting had never been anything like this. Some weapon of unimaginable power had been unleashed, and Remington had been at ground zero.

Rosenzweig's formula had changed the balance of power within the Middle East. If there was any finger-pointing later, Rosenzweig would surely bear the brunt of the blame. Perhaps the Israeli scientist had come up with the miracle growth serum, but someone else—surely the Russians or the Chinese—had come up with the weapon that had eradicated all the missing people.

But why give it to the Syrians to use?

That was the question.

Sitting behind the desk, Remington rested his elbows on the chair arms and rested his hands together, fingertip pressed to fingertip. He felt tired. He was coming up on almost forty-eight hours without sleep. But he'd never needed that much sleep, and he'd always been able to get from his body what he demanded of it. He wouldn't accept any less now.

He scanned the notebook computer in front of him. The LCD screen filled the small lightless room with soft blue illumination that grayed out all the color of his BDUs and the blue steel of his Colt .45 lying in the modular holster on the metal desk. An earbud connected him to the computer so that he could listen to the files he wanted to without being overheard.

Now that the Crays were up and running at peak performance, Remington had the files archived off-site where he had access to them for reviewing through the notebook computer. He scanned the FOX and CNN feeds coming through, as well as the OneWorld NewsNet footage.

FOX and CNN covered most of the domestic scene in the United States, including the disaster areas that had been declared in all the major cities. Chicago had been hit hard, and Los Angeles had experienced looting, fires, and riots the likes of which even that city had never seen. D.C., New York, Atlanta all had their own share of troubles. The list went on.

The footage rolled, showing wrecked cars, burning buildings, downed planes shattered across airfields and cities. One catastrophe followed another. Martial law had been declared in several metropolitan areas, but the understaffing of the police, fire, and National Guard units that had experienced even larger percentages of disappearances than the population at large had made it almost impossible to enforce.

A knock sounded at the door.

"Come," Remington said.

"Sir," Corporal Waller, one of the computer techs, said, "there's something on OneWorld NewsNet that you might want to see."

"What is it, Corporal?" Remington let the irritation he felt at being interrupted sound in his voice.

Waller hesitated.

"You're burning daylight, mister," Remington warned.

"Yes, sir. Sorry, sir. It's just kind of hard to explain. The OneWorld reporter, she's with the 75th, Captain."

That wasn't news. The presence of the news teams in the area, with the acknowledgement that they couldn't fault the military in any way, had been one of the concessions Remington had granted to Nicolae Carpathia's liaison. Evidently Carpathia was planning to address the United Nations when he made an upcoming trip to the United States. The new Romanian president wanted to use some of the footage of the military engagement along the Turkish-Syrian border to make whatever case he was going to present.

"I knew those people were in the area," Remington said. "As you might recall, I authorized their presence."

"Yes, sir. I know that, sir. But the story they're covering. That's what I thought you might be interested in."

"What is it?" Remington prepared himself to royally chew out his intelligence teams. If he had to learn of an enemy incursion into the protected territories through a news service, heads were going to roll.

"It's the 75th, sir. They're—" the corporal paused.

"Spit it out, soldier." Uncertainty, one of the feelings that Remington most hated in the world, nibbled at the edges of his confidence. The planned retreat from the border was scheduled on a precarious timetable. He wouldn't allow anything to circumvent that schedule.

"Well, Captain, there's a man baptizing soldiers out there."

At first, Remington was certain he hadn't heard right. He couldn't possibly have heard right. "What man?"

"I don't know, sir. One of ours."

"Dismissed, Corporal."

"Yes, sir." The corporal left with alacrity.

Remington closed the windows and opened a live streaming feed from OneWorld. The screen cleared, showing a beautiful brunette standing in front of a slow-moving stream. He recognized her from earlier transmissions that had basically introduced her to the viewing audience and recapped the situation along the border.

"This is Danielle Vinchenzo of OneWorld NewsNet," the young woman said. "We're only a few miles—or klicks, as the soldiers of the United States Army Rangers would say—from the border separating Turkey from Syria. Nearly nine hours have passed since the devastating launch of the SCUD missiles that piled up casualties here at ground zero along the border and several targets deeper into Turkey. The soldiers here—the Rangers, the United Nations peacekeeping effort, and the Turkish army—know they are in for the battle of their lives."

Glancing past the woman, using the zoom function on the video program, Remington focused on the stream in the background. The cameraman almost had the shot in the frame. He couldn't recognize the man doing the baptisms, but his actions were plain enough. Remington saw one line that was on the east side of the stream, judging by the sun's position, made up of soldiers from all three units stationed along the border, as well as civilians. They stood quietly and patiently, and they appeared to be singing.

"Events have gone rather badly for the 75th Rangers," Danielle said, "as they have for every soldier stationed along the contested border. The death count from this morning's attack is still not finalized. Nor have the lists been compiled of those who have simply vanished as has happened around so much of the planet."

Remington clicked the touch pad, bringing the image back to normal.

"But here in the heart of the darkness between these two ancient enemies," the reporter went on, "a man seems driven to snatch hope from the jaws of despair."

The video suddenly cut away and brought up stock footage. Remington immediately recognized the replay of Goose carrying the wounded Marine from one of the downed Sea Knight helicopters.

"So many of you are familiar with the horrible accident that knocked Marine reinforcements from the air only two hours after the blistering attack launched by the Syrian military. Many of you first came in contact with this man then."

The image zoomed in tight on Goose's face, showing the blood and the sand-encrusted kerchief over his lower face, and the haunted blue eyes. The scar along his right cheekbone stood out bloodred against sunburned flesh.

Remington had seen the footage several times. Goose was clearly being molded into a hero by the media. But not Goose's captain. The OneWorld reporter hadn't sought him out for an interview. The fact chafed him. Goose hated media attention, yet here he was becoming a poster child for the Syrian engagement.

"This is First Sergeant Samuel Adams 'Goose' Gander," Danielle said, "of the United States Army's 75th Rangers. He helped organize the rescue of Glitter City, the television and media center north of the border, after the initial SCUD launch, then arrived back at the border encampment to bring in reinforcements from the 26th Marine Expeditionary Unit from the Amphibious Readiness Group in the Mediterranean sea headed by USS *Wasp*."

The video changed again, showing a quick snippet of *Wasp* cutting across the ocean under a full head of steam with helicopters flaring around her.

"In minutes, Sergeant Gander was forced to go from bringing a reinforcement team into the area to helping his flagging troops recover from the devastating attack to rescuing the survivors."

Video footage rolled, showing Marine helicopters exploding.

Then the image changed and showed Danielle standing on the stream bank again. "With the reinforcements they were promised lying either in the triage area they've put together or as casualties across this battleground, with no hope of other reinforcements for some time to come, and knowing that they've been left in charge of defending this country, most soldiers would be daunted to say the least. Others might even give up."

The camera swung past the reporter and focused on the two lines of men that met in the center of the stream. Several of the soldiers carried some wounded on gurneys.

"But the men of the 75th Rangers are not ordinary men," Danielle said in a voice-over. "They are the best of the best. The cream of the crop. Even now, facing tremendous odds with the Syrian army standing down—at least for the moment—on the other side of the border, these soldiers have found a renewed faith."

The camera focused on the huge man standing in the middle of the stream. Remington didn't know the man—yet. But he would, and there would be an accounting two seconds later. The big man placed his hand over the face of a U.N. soldier, then lowered him into the water and raised him.

"I'm told this man, Corporal Joseph Baker, one of Sergeant Gander's handpicked crew, was an ordained minister who had given up his church after losing his wife and child to tragedy." Danielle's voice quieted. "Some said his faith was broken. But Baker has found that faith again, here on one of the bloodiest battlefields that has happened in recent years."

The footage continued to roll. The mountain of a man dealing with the tide of men coming at him from both sides worked like a machine. He talked briefly to each man in turn, covered the man's face with a big hand, and dunked him.

"Most of the soldiers have to hurry back to their posts," Danielle said. "In the beginning, I'm told Corporal Baker simply came here on a water detail assigned by Sergeant Gander. When one of his crew asked to be baptized, Baker granted that request. Other crews from the U.N. peacekeeping forces and the Turkish army were on hand getting water as well."

The camera view pulled back and shifted to show a broader view of the stream. Hundreds of men lined the hillsides.

Remington swore in disbelief. What had Goose been thinking by leaving Baker in place instead of taking the man into custody?

The camera view tightened on Danielle Vinchenzo again.

"Some of the men consented to talk to us," Danielle said. "Although most preferred their experience here today to be kept private." She turned to look off-camera and gestured to someone.

A soldier wearing the familiar baby blue headgear that identified the United Nations peacekeeping teams stepped on-camera with Danielle. He was big and young and nervous and soaking wet. Deep scratches showed on the left side of his face.

"This is Corporal Flannery O'Doyle of the Irish contingent of the United Nations peacekeepers," Danielle said, turning to the man. "Corporal, I'll only take a few minutes of your time. I know you've got to get back to your unit."

"Yes, miss. Me an' the boyos, we've been powerful busy." O'Doyle looked slightly embarrassed. When he smiled, he showed a gap between his two front teeth.

"This assignment hasn't turned out as you expected."

Sadness touched the young corporal's face. "No, miss. I lost three of me mates this mornin', I did. Good men. All of 'em."

"I'm sorry to hear that, Corporal."

"Yes, miss. Thank you, miss." O'Doyle put his hands behind his back at parade rest.

"What brought you here?"

O'Doyle looked over his shoulder, squinting slightly against the sun to the west. The deep scratches on his face showed more. "I heard about a man baptizin' in the stream, miss. An' I had to come."

"Why?"

The big Irishman shrugged. "I was raised Presbyterian, miss. I already been baptized once. When I was just a wee lad. Me ma, she saw to that. She was a right stubborn old lady when she put her mind to it, she was. An' she puts her mind to it often." He pursed his lips. "But I never saw to gettin' baptized on me own. A decision like that, why it seems like it ought to be left betwixt a man an' his Maker, you know?"

The camera tightened on O'Doyle's face. He stuck his chin out, obviously having trouble speaking.

"This mornin', after that ferocious battle, all them men dyin' an' them bombs droppin' from the air, why it was like—" O'Doyle pursed his lips and sucked in a quick breath. Tears glittered in his green eyes. "I held one of me mates when he died this mornin', miss. That's just somethin' you don't forget. But as I sat there holdin' him, feelin' him goin' away from me, I felt like God hisself put it in me heart to get right with him. To come to him on me own two feet." His voice broke.

"And you heard about Corporal Baker," Danielle prompted gently.

"Yes, miss. I did. An' I asked me sergeant if I couldn't come out here an' get right with the Lord. He sent me on, he did. An' I got here an' Corporal Baker, why he rightly baptized me." O'Doyle looked at Danielle. "I tell you, miss, I haven't felt like this in me whole life. I feel like I done been reborn. I come up outta that water, an' I knew everythin' was gonna be okay."

"You mean with the coming battle?"

O'Doyle shook his head. "No, miss. We got a powerful lot of fightin' ahead of this. Our commandin' officers, they all tell us that. I don't know if I'll make it back home or not, but whatever happens, I know it's gonna be all right." He touched his wet uniform. "I'm not alone anymore, miss." He nodded back out at the stream. "Me an' these men what's here, them what has had God hisself speakin' into our hearts, why we'll never be alone on this battlefield again." He shifted his assault rifle over his shoulder and touched his blue beret. "Now, if you'll excuse me, miss, I gotta get back to me unit."

"Of course, Corporal," Danielle said. "Thank you for sharing that with us."

"Miss," O'Doyle said with deadly earnestness, "if you go through somethin' like that back there, bein' saved in the Lord, I mean, you'll find you just gotta tell somebody. It's too big to just keep all to yourself. I'll pray for you, miss, that God will keep you safe in his sight, an' that you'll make your own peace with him." Without another word, he turned and trotted away.

Danielle Vinchenzo appeared to have been caught off guard. She fumbled the smooth transition back to the camera. "This is Danielle Vinchenzo, on special assignment for OneWorld NewsNet, where a miracle is taking shape on a battlefield."

The news channel switched back to the anchor, and the stories moved on to the disappearances that had taken place around the world.

Remington tapped the touch pad and broke the television feed.

He leaned back in his chair and stripped the earbud from his ear. Anger swirled through him. He swore.

The mission had fallen apart. He'd been used by the CIA and didn't know the full extent of his culpability in precipitating the attack, had been in command of the rescue mission that had ended up scattered across the hardpan. His first sergeant was allowing a crazed corporal to baptize the men of three armies while the event was filmed for an international audience.

Remington didn't want to hear about it when the joint chiefs learned of the baptisms. He rubbed his face. More than anything, he needed a win. And to get that win he knew he needed to start putting his foot down and take command of the unit that Goose had let slip through his fingers.

And Remington was going to start by putting an end to the nonsense taking place in that stream.

❖   ❖   ❖

Turkish-Syrian Border
40 Klicks South of Sanliurfa, Turkey
Local Time 1623 Hours

Goose parked the Hummer along the ridgeline overlooking the stream where the baptisms continued. He'd managed to send three chaplains to aid Corporal Baker, drawing from those who manned the triage center. Instead of allowing himself to be relieved, Baker had continued with his work. Seven other chaplains from the U.N. forces and the Turkish army had joined them.

Singing continued to fill the streambed area.

Thankfully, Goose noted, the woman reporter for OneWorld was absent. With Remington stepping out into the field himself, Goose really didn't want her around to witness what he knew was going to be a confrontation.

Feeling the pain of his knee from the driving, Goose stepped from the Hummer. He leaned against the vehicle and stretched the knee out carefully. He'd had similar injuries in the past and had worked through them. The stretching didn't help. What he needed more than anything was rest, a good meal, and eight hours of sleep. Soldiers won wars on supplies like that.

Instead, Goose reached into the pocket of his BDUs and took out a packet of analgesic tabs. He popped the tabs into his mouth, not happy about having to use them because the aspirin in them also thinned the blood and would make any wounds he received bleed more and be harder to staunch.

But being able to move was top priority. He was infantry, after all, not air force or navy. He fought his battles on his feet and he needed two good legs.

He took the canteen from his hip and drank the tabs down in two long swallows. For a moment, he remembered how he and Chris sometimes filled one of his canteens with Sunny Delight—which Chris always called "power of the sun" because he quoted commercials that caught his eye—and "camped out on safari" in the backyard for an hour or two at a time. Chris's vivid imagination always created ferocious beasts, which they tamed or trapped, or swamps filled with alligators, which they avoided. *After while, alligators!*

Joey never hung out there with them because he didn't want to get caught crawling around on the ground to avoid vultures and dragons, but Bill Townsend had. Bill ended up getting to be Chris's horse or camel or elephant a lot. When Joey had been not quite nine, when Goose had married Megan, the backyard had been Wrigley Field or Dodgers Stadium or Fenway Park or Turner Field. Megan had gotten to be the cheering section and umpire, just as she'd always been the "girl" Chris had insisted they rescue from the beasts in the jungle.

A wave of homesickness passed through Goose. He wanted to be back home with his family, to sit at the kitchen table and watch Chris playing in the backyard, to catch a ball game with Joey and work on whatever was creating a rift between them, to have dinner with Megan.

And Goose wanted Bill back here with him.

He pushed the thoughts away and concentrated on the action taking place in the stream. He made himself drink more water. That was one of the things he was pushing on all his troops. Perspiration was the body's cooling mechanism, and drinking water provided the raw materials to get the job done.

A Jeep pulled away from farther up the stream's edge. As the vehicle drew closer, Goose recognized Captain Tariq Mkchian in the passenger seat.

The Jeep pulled to a stop in front of the Hummer. Goose saluted.

"At ease, Sergeant," Mkchian said as he stepped from the Jeep.

"Yes, sir." Goose replaced his canteen on his hip.

Mkchian took off his sunglasses and wiped them free of dust. He put them back on and looked at the stream. "It's an amazing thing, isn't it?"

"What's that, sir?"

"Belief, Sergeant. Belief."

"Yes, sir."

Mkchian looked at him. "I'm surprised to see you here. I'd heard you were here earlier."

"I was."

"And you're back now." The statement came across as a question.

"Yes, sir." Goose wasn't going to tell the man that Remington had ordered him to be there or that the captain intended to put an end to the baptisms.

"I've also been told Captain Remington is en route," Mkchian said.

Goose said nothing.

"My spies, you see," Mkchian said, "are *everywhere*." He grinned as he said it.

Goose knew that the statement was offered in jest, but he also knew that the Turkish captain would have been a fool not to monitor the activities of the Rangers.

"So I had to ask myself," Mkchian said, "what Captain Remington would be doing out here. He has been very adroit at managing intelligence, supply, reinforcements, and renegotiating satellite reconnaissance even though it involved the introduction of the OneWorld NewsNet people among my men."

Goose shifted uncomfortably on his injured knee. Neither sitting nor standing helped with the pain. Only being in motion to some degree helped alleviate the gnawing sensation and the throbbing.

"The only answer I came up with," Mkchian continued, "was that Captain Remington wasn't happy with the events that are currently taking place here."

Goose didn't comment.

"I, on the other hand," the Turkish captain said, "was raised Christian. That's surprising in a country that is 98 percent Islamic. However, many people don't know that Christianity was the chief religion in this country before Islam came in with the Seljuks when they took Jerusalem in 1071."

"Their taking Jerusalem precipitated the Crusades," Goose said.

Mkchian smiled as if in pleasant surprise. "A student of history, Sergeant?"

"My dad was a Sunday school teacher back home, and after the Korean War, he got his doctorate in history and taught college for a while." The university job didn't keep Wes Gander from being a simple man, though. "My dad showed me how Bible history intersects what they teach in public schools."

Mkchian nodded. "My family—according to my father, who takes great pride in these things—insists that we can trace our Christianity back to the early people who first lived in these lands." He looked toward the stream. "This event is an unexpected thing, Sergeant, but I believe it is a good thing."

"Yes, sir."

"But your captain doesn't think so?"

"You'd have to ask him, sir."

"I'll do that, Sergeant." Mkchian looked at Goose. "In the meantime, I've noticed that your leg is troubling you."

"I'm getting by."

"Nonsense. You're in pain. I noticed that earlier and took the liberty of getting a medical kit. Have you ever had a cortisone shot before?"

"Yes." In the past, he'd needed a few cortisone shots to keep that knee functioning.

"I have cortisone. If you'll allow my aide to treat you. I assure you that he's trained to deliver shots like this." Mkchian smiled. "I took a round through my left shoulder a few years ago. The shoulder had to be reconstructed. It still troubles me from time to time, and I have found cortisone to be a good thing." He gestured to the Jeep driver. "Tonight, when we pull back from this border, I would like knowing that you are as able as you can be. To me, such a course of action makes sense because I will in part be relying on you. What do you think?"

Goose hesitated only a moment. "Yes, sir." He knelt with difficulty and unlaced his boot. He pulled his pant leg up and bared his swollen knee.

Mkchian frowned as Goose hoisted himself up on the Hummer's rear deck so his leg would dangle freely. "That knee is in horrible shape, Sergeant."

"Yes, sir. It's not the first time I've damaged it." Goose breathed out and then took slow breaths, pushing his mind past the pain that felt like a rusty bear trap had seized hold of his knee when the corporal gently worked his leg. He continued breathing through the pain of the shots as the man stabbed the needle deep into his knee.

Thankfully, the cortisone was mixed with a local anesthetic and the pain relief was immediate.

"You realize that the cortisone will take the pain away," Mkchian said, "but does not reduce the damage or the amount of damage you can unknowingly do to it."

Goose lowered his pant leg, tucked it back into his boot, and pulled the laces tight. "I know that from past experience, Captain. Thank you."

"It is my pleasure. When we get to Diyarbakir, you should have that knee looked at."

"I will, sir." Goose stood on the leg and tested it. The knee felt numb, like it was a long way away, but he felt his foot just fine.

An engine sounded over the ridgeline. A handful of seconds later, Cal Remington arrived in an RSOV with a full complement of Rangers.

Goose stood ramrod still and saluted. "Sir," he barked.

Seeing Remington in captain's dress still somehow seemed odd after all these years. Goose could remember when they were both coming up through the ranks, both of them breaking in one second lieutenant after another, only to see them go or transfer. But the recognition of the chain of command was immediate.

"Sergeant," Remington said gruffly and fired off a salute while on the move. He looked over Goose's shoulder, and Goose knew exactly what the captain was looking at. "I didn't know we were hosting a revival."

"No, sir," Goose replied. Ever since Remington had gotten hold of him, told him he was coming out, Goose had known what the captain was going to want to discuss.

"If we're not," Remington snapped, "then tell me why I've got a Ranger corporal and three army chaplains hip deep in water handing out baptisms like there was a fire sale."

"Things got out of control, sir," Goose responded.

"Out of control? Sergeant, when things get out of control, you're the first man I expect to put them back under control."

"Yes, sir."

"That's lip service, mister." Remington stood toe-to-toe with Goose, glaring down at him.

Goose knew anger was the most volatile emotion Remington had. In every other department—love, fear, curiosity—he seemed cool, almost dispassionate. Remington and Bill had never gotten along, and Goose had often had to argue on Bill's behalf to keep him with the 75th.

"Who assigned those chaplains to be there with Baker?" Remington asked.

"I did, sir."

"Why?"

"Because I thought it would speed up the process, sir."

"How about ending the process, Sergeant? Did that cross your mind?"

"Yes, sir, it did. However, that seemed to be an unattainable objective, sir."

"First Sergeant," Remington growled, "that's the last thing I want to hear from the man I put in command of my troops."

"Yes, sir."

Remington glared out at the stream. "Those men are slowing down my operation."

"No, sir," Goose said immediately.

Remington turned on him in an instant, shoving his face within inches of Goose's. *"What?"*

Goose met Remington's gaze full measure. For a moment, just the barest hint of a moment that didn't last long enough to cross the line between non-com and officer, they were just two men again.

"The operation has not been slowed, sir," Goose said. "If the captain will check the ops parameters on the mission he has assigned, he'll find that the 75th—despite the loss of manpower and materials—is forty minutes ahead of schedule. The rifle companies are going to be ready to bed down before sunset, sir, instead of working into the night as we had predicted. We will be able to cover the no-man's-land much more effectively."

Remington cursed and drew back. "Those men need to be removed from that stream, Sergeant."

Before Goose could reply, before he could even figure out what he was going to say, Captain Mkchian spoke up.

"Captain Remington, if I may interject."

"You may not," Remington said, turning on the Turkish captain.

Immediately, the men with Mkchian spread out around their commanding officer. Mkchian appeared to take no offense.

"This is a United States Army matter," Remington snarled.

"And this is Turkish soil," Mkchian stated in a calm, even voice that carried naked steel in each word. "You and your men are here at the invitation of my country, because your president believes he has a vested interest in the outcome of things that happen here. I represent the government that invited you here, and as their representative, I'll suffer no disrespect. Is that clear?"

Remington glared at the man. "What do you want?"

"I want this operation to continue, Captain Remington, until it is done. For as long as it takes. You have not seen the effect this is having on the men. Tonight they are going to have to fight for their lives. I would rather they went into that fight believing they could win, or at the very least, survive."

"Getting dipped in holy water and having the name of God spoken over you isn't going to save your hide," Remington said.

Mkchian smiled coldly. "Perhaps their hides aren't what these men are worried about. These men aren't fools. I have talked with many of them. They believe God has called them to this place and to those men in the water."

"Don't give me the God mumbo jumbo. Maybe dipping Achilles in the River Styx made him invincible, but it's not going to do that for those men."

"I don't think they expect that. But I have noticed that many of the men come away from that stream a little braver, a little more clearheaded."

"It's *water!*" Remington growled.

"It's *belief,*" Mkchian said.

"I'm not going to allow this to happen," Remington said.

"And I'm not going to allow you to stop it." Mkchian held his ground.

Remington turned on the captain. "You can't stop me from taking my men."

The Rangers behind Remington, all of them handpicked and all of them discipline problems for everyone but the Ranger captain, flared out, both hands on their weapons.

Unexpectedly, Mkchian clapped his hands and said, "Bravo. Now wouldn't this be a fine finale to the United States Army Ranger involvement in Turkey? My government reluctantly brings you in, and you end up in a Wild West gunfight with the very army you're supposed to be helping. Out of purely humanitarian reasons, of course, as your President Fitzhugh claims."

"No one stands between my men and me," Remington growled.

"Of course not, Captain." Mkchian waved generously toward the stream. "Take your men. By all means. But are you prepared to arrest all of those men you will incite to riot?"

Goose breathed shallowly, stunned by the events taking shape. He'd never seen Remington more on edge.

"And they will riot, Captain," Mkchian said in a softer voice. "Those men are trapped here, and they need something to believe in. Something more than merely military rank and file. A lot of them are dead, but a lot more of them disappeared today without explanation." The Turkish captain raised an eyebrow. "Unless you're prepared to explain that to them?"

Remington didn't answer.

"I didn't think so." Mkchian looked at Goose. "I came here prepared to stop your sergeant, because I fully expected him to try to put an end to these baptisms. He would have tried, despite what you think. He's a good man. I'm glad I caught you at the same time so I don't have to order you restrained."

"If you had done that—"

"I would have," Mkchian said. "You have my promise on that. These men will have their peace, Captain Remington. It is within my power to give them that, and I will." He paused. "Furthermore, if you decide to follow through on this course of action, I will seek out Danielle Vinchenzo, the OneWorld NewsNet reporter that you have sponsored in this area, and tell her exactly what you have done."

A nerve twitched on Remington's jaw. His eyes looked like cold glass as he gave a small, imperceptible nod. "Fine, Captain Mkchian. We'll let you have your little praise party. But I want it over soon."

"As long as it takes, Captain," Mkchian said. "God works in mysterious ways, his wonders to perform. You have your satellites and we have ours. The Syrians won't come this way without being noticed. We'll have time to get into position." He smiled. "There's something you're forgetting, though."

Remington didn't ask.

"Most of Syria is Muslim. Doubtless, they are watching these proceedings on television. In the Koran, it says that the spirits of soldiers who fall in holy battle will immediately go to heaven and be granted special privileges for their sacrifice." Mkchian looked out on the stream where the baptisms continued. "Those Syrian soldiers will see this, and they will think that these men are preparing to make that same sacrifice." He looked back at Remington. "The Syrian soldiers will fear us more for this. They will be afraid because they will think we will know no fear."

The song coming from the men standing in the lines swelled to fill the tense silence that stretched between the two captains.

Turning away, Remington fixed Goose with his gaze. "This is your fault, Goose. You should never have let this go this far. You stay with these people until this is finished."

"Sir," Goose objected, "I should be back at the base."

Remington cut him off. "You should. When this is finished, if you decide you want to be a Ranger again, you come back then."

Before Goose could even attempt a reply, Remington turned and walked away. He boarded the RSOV and didn't look back as the vehicle headed back toward the Ranger encampment.

Goose felt torn. He couldn't disobey an order, but he didn't feel right. He *needed* to be at the Ranger base to make certain everything was getting done.

"Your captain," Mkchian said, "is making a mistake by punishing you this way."

"I knew he wouldn't want the baptisms going on," Goose replied. "I should have stopped them."

Mkchian gazed at him in open speculation. "Then why didn't you?"

For a moment Goose thought the Turkish captain was faulting him as well. Then he saw that Mkchian's gaze was open and honest, without challenge or accusation.

"I didn't stop it," Goose said, "because it felt right."

Mkchian tapped Goose on the chest. "God has touched your heart, too, First Sergeant Gander. No matter how much pain you have to go through to endure, you will be a better man for it. You cannot avoid His touch."

"I don't know, sir. I could have been mistaken about this whole thing."

Mkchian pointed his chin at the men being baptized. "If you are, there are a lot of men with you." He looked back at Goose. "In the meantime, you should know that you have made a powerful enemy today."

Goose shook his head. "The captain's angry, but he's my friend. Not an enemy."

"Sometimes they are both, Sergeant. Just be careful."

Goose tried to find something to say to defend Remington. They had been friends for years. They would be friends forever. He just didn't know how to explain that to Mkchian.

"In the meantime, though," the Turkish captain said, "know that you have my friendship. For what it's worth." He extended his hand.

"It's worth a lot," Goose said, taking the other man's hand. "I don't take friendships lightly."

"Nor do I. God keep you, First Sergeant Gander, for I fear you and I have only begun to see the horrific things that are in store for us." Mkchian released his hand and walked back to his Jeep.

"God keep you, Captain." Goose stared after the Jeep. Unease stirred through his mind, leavening his thoughts and building with each passing second. He was concerned about his relationship with Remington. The captain had been mad at him before, even back when they had both been sergeants, but they had never been in circumstances like these. He'd never seen Remington take things so personally.

Mkchian's final thoughts were very disturbing as well. The man had sounded sure of himself, like he knew what was coming and it was more than just the hasty withdrawal from the Syrian front. And whatever it was, Goose had the definite feeling that it was much, much worse.

United States of America
Washington Dulles International Airport,
Washington D.C.
Local Time 5:43 P.M.

From the instant Delroy Harte left the helipad aboard USS *Wasp* in the Mediterranean Sea and flown west, time turned backward. In Turkey, the clock had moved forward into tomorrow, and the local time there was 0043. He knew that because as he arrived in the restricted airspace over Washington, he realized he'd forgotten to set his watch to local time.

But in the nation's capital, the time was 5:43 P.M., and harsh afternoon sunlight poured through the jet's windows. He'd flown for over fourteen hours, in the helicopter from *Wasp* to the C-9 Skytrain Captain Falkirk had requisitioned for him at Sigonella Naval Air Station in Sicily, Italy. The navy primarily used the Skytrain for cargo and passenger transportation as well as forward deployment logistic support.

Delroy closed his father's Bible gently, pulling the cloth bookmark into place in the book of Revelation. During the long flight he had slept off and on. He'd eaten, too, but the skeleton crew had left him alone.

Large enough to seat 115 commercial passengers, the C-9 was presently set up with half its space allotted to cargo and the other half to passengers. Delroy was the only passenger. It felt odd to be sitting on an empty plane.

Once, about halfway through the flight, he had awakened to find himself alone. He'd remembered how Chief Mellencamp's body had disappeared with him sitting right beside it and how he and the other crewmen aboard *Wasp* sorted through the piles of clothing left throughout the ship's decks after the disappearances. For a moment, he'd thought everyone had vanished from the Skytrain.

Thankfully, that hadn't been the case.

The pilot's cabin opened and a young lieutenant stepped through. Usually the C-9 carried only two pilots and necessary attendants. Evidently this flight was carrying three pilots; this man wasn't one of the two Delroy had seen since the last leg of the flight had begun.

"Chaplain Harte," the young man said.

"Yes?" Delroy scratched his chin, feeling the stubble that had grown there during the flight.

"We're going to begin our descent in five minutes. You might want to put your seat belt on. They had a lot of damage at Dulles when the, uh, *incident* occurred. They haven't gotten it all cleaned up."

"Will there be any problems?" Delroy preferred the sea, calm and wide open. And as long as a person stayed on top of it, the sea was a fine place to be. Flying, in his view, was a necessary evil.

"None that we can see," the lieutenant assured him.

"Thank you, Lieutenant."

"You're welcome." The lieutenant looked at all the papers and books that Delroy had scattered around. "Will you need help putting things away?"

"No," Delroy answered. "No, I'm fine. You go on and take care of your business, Lieutenant."

The lieutenant nodded and started back to the pilot's cabin.

"Lieutenant," Delroy called.

"Yes, sir."

"There is one thing."

"Yes, sir."

"I've got a meeting with the joint chiefs as soon as I can get there." Delroy touched his face. "After a flight this long, I'm not exactly presentable."

"Captain Falkirk had us set up a liaison for you as soon as you're on the ground, sir. You'll be met at the runway with a fresh uniform and toiletries."

"Thank you, Lieutenant." Delroy turned his attention back to his papers. He should have known: Falkirk was a very able and thorough captain.

The C-9 hit a patch of turbulence. His papers and books scattered everywhere. Delroy pushed himself up from his seat and started gathering them. Before he knew it, the lieutenant was kneeling in front of him, picking up the papers and study guides.

"I can get this," Delroy said hurriedly.

"It's all right. Frank can land the plane by himself if he needs to. This won't take us but just a moment."

Then Delroy realized he was trying to keep all of his research to himself. He felt embarrassed to have God's Word scattered around, out there for everyone to see what he'd been doing. Embarrassed—he couldn't believe it. *How long has it been since I felt like that?*

The young lieutenant flipped through the end-times prophecy book Delroy had been referencing "The end of the world, Chaplain?" the lieutenant asked with a small smile. "Is that what you've been reading about?"

Delroy heard the lieutenant's inflection. Was the man trying to be sarcastic? Anger replaced the embarrassment that Delroy had felt. He knew he was having a hard time of it. He'd had little sleep in the last forty-eight hours, what with Mellencamp's death and the flight in to Washington. Colonel Donaldson's response had weighed heavily in the chaplain's mind as well. There was no guarantee the joint chiefs would listen any more than the Marine colonel had. That thought settled into Delroy's brain with a vengeance.

"Yes," Delroy said, "the end of the world. That's what I'm reading about."

The lieutenant handed the books over. "My grandmother used to try to scare me into being a better kid with that stuff."

"With what?" Delroy stared into the young man's ice-blue eyes.

"The end of the world," the young man said. "The—" he held up his hands and made quotation marks in the air— *"Apocalypse."* He laughed. "Like anybody could really believe in that."

"You don't believe the Apocalypse is going to happen?" Delroy stood.

"I think it's a story," the young lieutenant said.

"A story." Delroy couldn't believe his ears.

"Yeah," the young lieutenant said. "Every culture has a story about what's going to happen when the world ends. If you don't like the Apocalypse, maybe you could tune in to Ragnarok. The Norse invented a mythology for the end of the world, too. And if you don't want to hang your hat on the truly ancient beliefs, you can also go for the scientific end of the world as we know it." He smiled. "Take your pick. The hole in the ozone. The melting polar caps. Getting hit by a meteor. Or even the slow death of the sun eventually burning itself out." He shrugged. "The last one could be dull but festive."

"What's wrong with you?" Delroy drew himself up to his full

height, towering above the other man. "How dare you talk to me like that. I am a superior officer, Lieutenant."

"Are you a superior officer, Chaplain Harte?" the lieutenant mused. "You've been sent on an important mission." He made his voice deep. *"Convince the Joint Chiefs of Staff that God has come and taken his children."* He laughed. "Do you know how pathetic that sounds?"

"I'll have your name, mister," Delroy said gruffly.

"Sure. Read it for yourself."

Delroy looked at the man's name badge but couldn't quite make it out. The letters seemed to be squirming, constantly staying just ahead of his ability to focus.

"You don't believe God exists," the smiling lieutenant said. "You've served aboard *Wasp* for five years, and you haven't believed."

"Shut up!" Delroy roared.

"You haven't believed," the man taunted. "That's why Colonel Donaldson didn't buy into your story."

"Donaldson is afraid," Delroy said in a voice that was only somewhat below a shout. He didn't understand why one of the other pilots didn't come back to find out what was going on. *Unless they are all in on it.* The thought filled him with fear.

The lieutenant grinned. He whispered, "Maybe I killed them all."

"Who are you?" Delroy demanded.

The man shook his head. "The question isn't who am I, it's who do you think you are? How can you be a chaplain if you don't believe?"

Delroy walked to the pilot's cabin door and tried to open it. The handle didn't turn. Knotting a fist, he pounded on the door. "Open this door."

"How can you expect anyone to believe you," the man asked, "when you don't even believe yourself?"

Delroy whirled on the man, barely maintaining the panic that filled him. "I do believe!"

"Why? Because a lot of people turned up missing sixteen-plus hours ago and you don't have an answer? Oh, man, if you can't explain it, if things don't go the way you want them to, it must be God. Are ignorance and fear and a need for some kind of immortality what it takes to make you a believer, Chaplain Harte?"

Guilt washed over Delroy, so grim in its perfection that he felt himself crumbling before it like an earthen dam before the raging torrent of an unexpected flood.

The man shook his head. "I can't believe they sent you. There's no excuse."

Delroy trembled, held powerless by the accusations that poured from the man. Every one of them rang true. He had been guilty of exactly what the man said. He hadn't believed. Not for a long time. And was that what it took to make him believe? The disappearance of millions of people?

It only took the death of one to make you doubt. The realization shook Delroy to his core.

"And what message are you going to take to the joint chiefs, Chaplain Harte?" the man taunted. "Lock up the women and children, the Antichrist is coming." He covered his mouth as if in embarrassment. "Oops, forgot. All out of children, aren't we?" He paused. "Including you, Chaplain Harte? God took poor little Terry in the prime of his life."

Tears filled Delroy's vision, and pain wracked his heart.

"That's how you look at it, isn't it?" the man asked. "That God took your son?" He took a step forward, thrusting his face into Delroy's. "Then why doesn't he give him back? What right did he have to take your son?"

The sorrow broke out of Delroy in long, draining sobs. "I don't know! God help me, I don't know!"

"Well, ," the man said in a relieved voice, "then maybe you should give some thought to why you're here." He reached for Delroy's face.

Before Delroy could block the man's hand, it wrapped around his head, smothering him. He felt powerless in the impossible grip, listening to the evil, confident chuckle that sounded right in his ear.

"Go home, *Chaplain,*" the man said in a bestial snarl. "Go home and live in misery the way you have for the last five years. You'll be more comfortable there."

Shoved backward, off-balance, he fell. His head hit the carpeted floor hard enough to send black comets crashing through his vision.

When Delroy's eyesight cleared, the man was gone. Shaking, nauseous, the chaplain pushed himself to his knees. For a moment he thought he was going to throw up. But he made himself stand and go to the pilot's cabin. When he tried the door this time, the handle turned easily. He followed the door inside the cabin.

The two pilots looked back at him with curiosity. Both of them were men Delroy had seen earlier.

"Where is he?" Delroy demanded in a shaking and hoarse voice.

"Who?" the pilot asked.

"The other man," Delroy said. "The other pilot. The one who came back to tell me about the seat belt."

The pilots swapped looks. "Chaplain," the pilot said in a deliberately calm and nonthreatening voice, "there are just us two. No other
pilots. No one has gone back to notify you yet. We were about to."

"I saw him," Delroy said. He felt the man's hand against his face,
and this time he felt the slither of scales instead of flesh. His voice
choked down. "I saw him."

The copilot got up. "Let me help you back to your seat, Chaplain.
If you ask me, you look about done in. Have you rested during this
flight?"

Delroy looked at the two men. They were telling the truth.

"I haven't rested enough," he said. He looked at the pilot who had
offered to help him to his seat. "I'm fine."

The pilot hesitated. "All right, chaplain. But we're going to be
touching down in ten or fifteen minutes. As soon as the tower gives us
clearance. We need you to get belted in."

"All right." Delroy turned and went, knowing that the two men
would probably report this incident to Falkirk. And what would that
report do to the captain's faith?

Delroy returned to his seat and belted himself in. He stared out
the window, feeling the C-9 sink into its final approach pattern only a
few short minutes later. Smoke still curled from fires in the distance
around the city.

Had he been struggling with his own personal demons, trapped in
some warped nightmare of his own doubts? Or had it been something else? If all the believers had been taken from the world during
the Rapture, did that mean that something else might have slipped
back into the world? Something darker? Something evil? Or had that
evil been here all along and only now was freed to rise up?

Delroy didn't know. What he was certain of, though, was that he
was scheduled to speak to the joint chiefs in the next hour—and he
was in no shape for it.

❈   ❈   ❈

Turkish-Syrian Border
40 Klicks South of Sanliurfa, Turkey
Local Time 0101 Hours

The thrum of the generator only twenty yards away rattled through
Cal Remington's skull. His eyes felt like they were filled with broken
glass as he stared at the notebook computer on the small folding desk

he'd brought into the campsite along the ridge overlooking the border area.

His anger was still stoked from the confrontation with Goose and Captain Mkchian that had taken place hours ago. Goose ticked him off plenty. Over the years that they had been good friends, then gotten to be an effective captain and first sergeant team, he and Goose had experienced plenty of differences of opinion. Usually those differences of opinion had taken place over personnel, never over implementation of details of an operation—never over organization or timing or equipment. They'd always disagreed over people.

And those differences of opinion had *never* been publicly aired in any theater they'd been involved in.

Remington accepted some share of the blame. After all, he'd chosen to dress Goose down in front of the Rangers he'd brought with him. Getting the chance to do it in front of the Turkish captain had been a bonus.

That had backfired, though. Mkchian had taken Goose's side, and that had been totally unexpected. Remington had believed the Turkish captain would be against Christian practices.

Since that mistake, Remington had made it a point to research Captain Tariq Mkchian's file more thoroughly. He'd been surprised to learn that the Turkish captain was a Christian. In a country that was overwhelmingly Muslim, the odds were heavily against such an occurrence.

But that was how things were with Goose. He'd always been lucky, always in the right place at the right time. He'd always gotten to know the right people.

Remington knew for a fact that Goose had been recruited for OCS. Goose had turned it down, and Remington knew why. As an officer, Goose would end up dealing with paper more than he dealt with people.

Remington knew the names of every man in his company, but Goose *knew* each man. The first sergeant knew them through families, kids, sports, training, or church.

Remington had never wanted that kind of familiarity with the people he commanded. Familiarity bred contempt. Familiarity forced an officer to think of the unit he was about to sacrifice as human beings instead of numbers that got crunched in the final equation.

The notebook computer screen blinked for his attention. A pop-up menu floated up and let him know he had an incoming call.

Remington pulled on the headset and tapped the *Open* button. He made sure the button cam attached to the notebook monitor pointed at him. The picture at the other end wouldn't be good because the light level inside the tent was low. The light inside couldn't be seen from the outside at all because of the thick tarp.

When the screen cleared, Remington found he was looking at Captain Mark Falkirk. The connection was provided through a sat-phone managed by the Romanian communications company.

"Captain," Remington greeted.

"I take it you're at the front," Falkirk said.

"Yes."

"Intel has marked movement among the Syrian troops."

The message had come in eighteen minutes ago. Remington wasn't surprised that *Wasp* wasn't quite up to speed in the sit-rep along the border. With her manpower cut drastically, *Wasp* been hard-pressed to get set up for the arrival of the Marine Harriers and Sea Cobra helicopter gunships. There were also more Sea Knights providing transportation for Marine troops into the area.

"We got our care package thirty-two minutes ago," Falkirk said. "We'll be sending it along in twenty minutes."

Remington nodded. If the new Marine Wing departed *Wasp* in twenty minutes, they would arrive at the border at 0330 hours, thirty minutes ahead of the scheduled final retreat from the border.

"That's good to hear," Remington said.

"We've just got to hope that everybody's timetable matches up."

"The Syrians are more than likely just getting set up for the morning," Remington said. "And we may have more to fear from the Russians. We're still at DEFCON 2, and that care package you're sending is big enough to attract attention." *Or to trigger an attack all by itself,* the Ranger captain knew. But they had no choice. Without the reinforcements, they wouldn't stand a chance of holding out against the Syrians when they decided to invade Turkey.

And that invasion was definitely coming. All that remained to be seen was how far into Turkey they came before they were stopped. It was possible that the combined forces of Rangers, Turkish army, and U.N. troops wouldn't be able to hold Sanliurfa. They also wouldn't be able to make Diyarbakir City before being overtaken. A number of the mountain roads were out from the SCUDs that morning.

Yesterday, Remington told himself harshly. *Keep it straight.*

One of the other sat-phones he had beeped for attention.

"I have a call coming in," Remington said.

"I'll hold," Falkirk said. "I want to go over the backup LZs we're building in."

"I'll be right back." Remington tapped the mute function on the computer, then answered the sat-phone.

"Captain?" a man said.

"Go, Spotter," Remington said.

Spotter was Nick Perrin, a young lieutenant skilled in urban undercover ops. Perrin was the kind of guy who could walk into a neighborhood, scope out the streets, and let his commanding officer know where potential targets were without ever being noticed.

When CIA Section Chief Alexander Cody had left the command post three hours ago, Remington already had Perrin and his team of hardcases en route to Sanliurfa. Cody had maintained an interest in the missing undercover CIA agent Goose and his team had rescued from the PKK terrorists yesterday morning before the SCUD attack.

"We found the Soupman easy," Perrin said. *Soupman* was their tag for the CIA chief. "Followed him without him knowing. Just like you wanted, sir. He went to an address, a hotel here in the city, stayed inside for a couple minutes, then left."

"Where is he?"

"We've still got him in sight, sir."

"What about the address?"

"That's where it gets interesting."

"I'm listening," Remington said.

Perrin paused a moment, and Remington knew the man was smoking. That was bad news. Perrin only smoked when he got tense.

"I went into the hotel, sir. Took a look around on the QT. There were two bodies in there."

"Who were they?"

"Don't know. We took digital pictures. Either they weren't carrying any ID, or whoever killed them took it when he or she or they left."

"You don't know anything about that room?"

"I didn't want to press outside our operating parameters on the mission, sir," Perrin said. "Asking questions, drawing attention to ourselves, those were definitely out."

Remington's mind raced. Alexander Cody had come out of nowhere with an agent who may have been responsible for triggering the Syrian attack. The Ranger captain wanted to know more about the man.

"Find out who was in the room, Spotter," Remington ordered.

"Yes, sir. How far do you want me to push it?"

Remington thought about that. Cody had an in with Nicolae Carpathia, who had just recently been elected president of his country, a man who was fabulously wealthy, and who looked to be on the fast track to becoming a player in world politics if his announced upcoming visit to the United Nations was any indication. Cody was also operating a loose leash on the man that could have been responsible for igniting the Syrian-Turkey confrontation.

And that man had chosen deliberately to run and hide during the confusion that had taken place at Glitter City. It remained to be seen if undercover agent Icarus had disappeared when all the other people had vanished.

"Push it all the way, Spotter," Remington said.

Perrin hesitated just a moment. Both of them knew that when Remington set him free, someone might die. There had been deaths in the past, enemies who had posed a potential threat to Rangers or had escaped justice in other conflicts.

"Yes, sir," Perrin said.

"Get back to me as soon as you know something." Curiosity ate at Remington. He treasured secrets. Secrets held power. He couldn't help wondering what Cody was hiding.

"Yes, sir," Perrin responded.

Remington broke the connection and turned his attention back to Falkirk on the computer link.

Wasp's captain was looking away when the video feed came back on. He talked with someone off-screen briefly, then tapped the key to open the audio. "Sorry."

"It's all right," Remington said. "The LZs."

"Right." Falkirk looked distracted.

"Is something wrong?"

"Just got a disturbing communiqué on an away op I've got in play."

Remington's senses sharpened. "How will it affect us?" Anything that was going to cause fallout on his Rangers was within his domain.

"This doesn't affect you," Falkirk said. "I was hoping I'd found a way to roll the DEFCON 2 back."

Remington shook his head. "Something like that, you'd need an act of God."

"I know," Falkirk said. "An act of God is what I thought I had in play."

United States of America
The Pentagon, Washington D.C.
Local Time 6:42 P.M.

Delroy Harte sat outside General David Marsden's office and felt the enormity of the mission he'd agreed to carry out for Captain Falkirk.

The fact that the Pentagon was up and running at nearly seven o'clock in the evening when it normally shut down at three-thirty in the afternoon was a prime indicator of how bad things were in the United States. Luckily, the trip in had prepared him for it. Abandoned and wrecked cars surrounded Dulles International. Bulldozers were still at work scraping smashed planes and jets away to free up more runways as the nation slowly reclaimed the air. This time, though, Delroy was certain people would be even less likely to trust air travel.

At 1:21 A.M., when the disappearances had taken place, there hadn't been many flights in the air above Washington, but a hefty assortment of the ones that had been in a holding pattern above, taking off from, or landing at Dulles had come down spectacularly all around the city. The falling passenger jets at the airport had taken out hangars and other jets being serviced and fueled. According to the local news reports, fires had burned at the airport most of the night because emergency services had been even harder hit by the mysterious personnel depletion than the mean averages in the population as a whole so far indicated.

The Pentagon halls stayed busy, and while he waited, Delroy watched the people hustle through. Many messages were still being carried by hand throughout the building because not all of the phone lines were operational again. According to a pamphlet Delroy had found in the seat he'd been shown to by the young Marine lance corporal who had been assigned to him upon his entrance to the heavily secured building, the Pentagon had over one hundred thousand miles of phone lines. He had no idea how many miles weren't working.

Thinking about phone lines made Delroy think again of calling his wife. Or ex-wife, as the case might be. She would have gotten in touch with him if she were going to end their marriage. Then again, he had stopped returning her calls and letters a long time ago. She didn't owe him much courtesy after everything he hadn't done, everything he hadn't said, everything he hadn't listened to her say.

Delroy held his hat in his hands. He was jet-lagged and worn.

And empty, he thought bitterly. The nightmare—he'd almost convinced himself that was what it had been even though he could still feel the man's scaly hand pressed against his face—had beaten down most of whatever belief he had saved up while aboard *Wasp.* He thought about the way he had faced Donaldson while the Marine colonel had pressed his sidearm into his face. He had been so arrogant, so sure of himself. He didn't feel that way now.

Delroy rubbed at his face. He'd shaved with the toiletries he'd been provided after landing, and he'd put on a fresh uniform that Falkirk had requisitioned. It fit him like it had been made for him. As tall as he was, he'd always had to have his pants altered. While he'd been living at home, his wife had taken care of that. The last few years he'd had the ship launderer take care of it for him.

He glanced up at the two young Marines standing outside General Marsden's door. "I'm going to stretch my legs. I've been on a plane for the last fourteen and a half hours."

"Yes, sir," the lance corporal replied. "Please remain within our sight, Chaplain. If you're found in the building without an escort, you'll be locked down."

Delroy nodded. "I'm not going far. Just to the window there and back." He walked slowly, missing the feel of *Wasp's* deck under his feet. He wished he were there now. Then he felt guilty for that wish because he knew it was only because he wanted to crawl into a hole and lick his wounds.

He stood at the window and looked out. Darkness had fallen over the city. Evening still fell early in March. But the night was held at bay by the lights around the city. Searchlights strobed the sky and the light pollution washed away the stars.

Frantic voices whispered up and down the hallways. The pamphlet also said that the corridors measured seventeen and one-half miles long. Yet the farthest distance between any two places in the five-sided building could be easily walked in seven minutes.

The pamphlet was a font of information.

And what do you know? Delroy examined his reflection in the dark glass of the window. The crisp white uniform stood out sharply in the glass and looked like it held a bluish tint. His face, though, was another matter. How had he gotten so old, so worn and used up? He'd never seen that kind of age in his father's face. He had outlived his father, and he had outlived his son.

But it's not just the age, is it, Delroy? You never saw your father this old, but you also never saw him this false. Or this scared.

Fear ached within him, resonating through all six feet, six inches of his frame. He had never been so afraid. What had that nightmare aboard the Skytrain done? Had the nonexistent lieutenant been a figment of his own doubts, a result of the stress he was under, or a mental disorder that was only now manifesting itself?

Confronting Colonel Donaldson aboard *Wasp* wasn't the act of a sane man. No wonder the Marine colonel had been afraid. He wasn't afraid of God's wrath or the Antichrist; Donaldson had been afraid of a madman.

"Go home, Chaplain." The rough voice echoed in Delroy's head. "Go home and live in misery the way you have for the last five years."

The words beat into Delroy, ringing against the immense emptiness he felt inside himself. He wanted out of there. Truly, he did. Falkirk was wrong: he wasn't the man for the job. He was just a deluded fool searching for some kind of meaning over the death of his son.

"Chaplain Harte."

At first, Delroy thought he was hearing the man's words again. Then he spotted the young Marine's reflection moving toward him in the window. He turned toward the Marine.

"Chaplain Harte," the Marine said. "General Marsden will see you now, sir."

"Thank you, Lance Corporal."

Delroy stepped into the general's spacious office and was escorted back to a conference room in the rear.

General Marsden wasn't the only general in the room. Two other men wore stars on their shoulders. All three of them sat at one end of the long conference table.

Coming to erect attention, Delroy fired off a salute at General Marsden. "General Marsden, sir. Navy Chaplain Delroy Harte of USS *Wasp.*"

Marsden was in his late fifties. He had iron-gray hair and quick gray wolf's eyes. He was tall and solid, a big man with a jaw like a 1950s Buick bumper. He returned the salute. "At ease, Chaplain Harte."

"Thank you, sir." Delroy immediately took his hat off, tucked it under his arm, and spread his feet to assume parade rest.

"I'd like to present Generals Todd Cranston and Hubert Mayweather. They are also members of the joint chiefs."

"A pleasure, sirs," Delroy said.

Todd Cranston looked like he was in his late thirties. Cranston had made a name for himself during the latest rash of Middle Eastern conflicts and had turned out to be a media darling. He was also a war hawk with a particular axe to grind regarding Russia. He was blond and rugged-looking. There was talk of a political career once he decided to step away from the military.

"Chaplain Harte," Cranston said.

Hubert Mayweather was older than Marsden, just starting to go to seed. But he remained attentive and had an undercurrent of menace that clung to him. His hair was light brown but gray at the temples. He nodded.

"General Cranston and General Mayweather will be assisting me with this matter this evening," Marsden said, "lending an ear and advice as I need it."

"Aye, sir," Delroy replied.

"You may sit, Chaplain."

"Thank you, sir." Delroy placed his hat on the table and sat a little uncomfortably at the other end of the conference table. The lines had been drawn on the battlefield. The chairs weren't designed for a man six and a half feet tall. He put his hands on the table, the left folded over the right. He tried not to show the tension he felt.

The two young Marines stood at the wall behind him.

Marsden flicked a glance at the Marines. "You'll excuse the extra manpower in the room, Chaplain. Things are, at best, chaotic at this time."

"I understand, sir."

"Captain Falkirk called in a big favor to get you an audience with me at this time, Chaplain."

"Aye, sir. Captain Falkirk wanted me to extend his appreciation, sir. Thank you for seeing me."

Marsden opened a manila folder in front of him. "This is a document Captain Falkirk e-mailed to me." He flipped through pages. "It's a summation of the events aboard *Wasp* and on the ground near the Turkish-Syrian border. After reading the captain's report, I can see that you would appreciate our situation here."

"Aye, sir."

"You lost men aboard *Wasp*?" Cranston asked.

"Aye, sir. And we lost Marines out in the field near the Turkish-Syrian border, sir."

"Soldiers that just vanished?" Cranston asked.

"Aye, sir. And crewmen."

Cranston pointed at the file Marsden had. "And there's nothing in that file that relates anything you might have seen or heard at the time of the disappearances?"

Delroy had read the file during the flight. It was a straight-ahead no-nonsense account of the crashed aircraft and the crewmen missing aboard *Wasp*. "No, sir."

"But you're here in regards to those unexplained disappearances?"

"That's correct, sir."

Marsden looked at Delroy. "According to what I understood from Captain Falkirk's rather cryptic message, you think you have an explanation for those disappearances."

Delroy hesitated. hadn't Falkirk admitted he had the same theory? Maybe the captain wouldn't have wanted to transmit such a message. *Or maybe he didn't want to stick his neck out.* Guilt rattled through Delroy over that one. Even if Falkirk hadn't mentioned that he believed what Delroy had come to say, the captain had stuck his neck out all the same by making certain his chaplain got there to say it.

"Aye, sir. But it's not just an explanation, sir. I believe I have the answer, sir."

Cranston's eyes narrowed. "Chaplain, I have to admit that I have a hard time believing that you have the answer. We've been talking to NASA scientists, military think tanks, and gentlemen in the National Security Agency about a number of possibilities that could have caused the mass disappearances around the world. If you can come up with an answer they haven't thought of . . . well, sir, then my hat's off to you."

Delroy took a sip of breath, feeling as though the room had suddenly constricted on him. He wanted to believe, truly he did. But the image of Terry's casket, the unconscionable grave at Marbury, Alabama, in the family plot where Josiah Harte rested, ran through his mind. It had been raining the day they had laid his son to rest.

"The people who disappeared," he said in a quiet voice, "were Raptured." He wanted to continue, to pour passion into his words, but he couldn't. His throat seemed to dry up and the words just stopped.

Cranston regarded Delroy with a flat gaze. "Raptured?"

"Aye, sir."

"Do you want to explain that term, Chaplain?"

Delroy started to speak and couldn't get the words out for a moment. He cleared his throat and tried again. "They were taken by God, sir."

"Taken by God." Cranston's disbelief was obvious in the hollow tone of his voice, his words driving home like nails in a coffin. He unsheathed the steel of authority when he spoke again. "Did I hear you right, Chaplain?"

"Aye, sir." Delroy sat quietly, aware of how his heart thudded inside his chest.

Cranston glanced down at the legal pad in front of him. "Chaplain Harte, you flew practically nonstop from the Mediterranean, from a ship that is involved in a major military engagement, to bring us that story?"

Delroy had to force his voice out. "Aye, sir."

"And you told your captain this?"

"I did, sir."

Cranston turned to Marsden. "Do you know Captain Falkirk, David?"

Marsden kept staring at Delroy. "Yes. I do. I consider him a very good and very valuable friend."

Cranston shook his head. "Then I must admit, General, that I am confused. I know you must trust him and his judgment, otherwise you would never have wasted my time by calling me here."

"I do trust his judgment," Marsden said. "Captain Falkirk speaks highly of Chaplain Harte. The chaplain has had a long and distinguished career with the Navy."

The words crashed into Delroy's mind. For the first time he realized his career was at stake today. And he had brought them the story of the Rapture, something that he had no way of proving. Perspiration poured down his face despite the room's cool temperature. Had he ever truly believed that? And why?

The mocking voice from the plane tore into his thoughts and wrecked his concentration. *"Because a lot of people turned up missing sixteen-plus hours ago and you don't have an answer? Oh, man, if you can't explain it, if things don't go the way you want them to, it must be God. Are ignorance and fear and a need for some kind of immortality what it takes to make you a believer, Chaplain Harte?"*

Cranston drew lines on the legal pad. "Not to be disrespectful, General, but maybe this should have been a navy matter."

Marsden spoke in a flat voice but didn't take his eyes from Delroy. "General, as you'll recall, Admiral Royce is among the missing. In this matter, I didn't want a stand-in. I wanted us."

Cranston looked at Marsden, then at Mayweather. "Why us?"

"Because we represent a major bloc within the joint chiefs, General," Mayweather said in his honey-soft voice. "When the three of us speak together on something, people listen."

"We don't agree on a lot of things," Cranston said. "The case in point is the situation we need to take regarding Russia."

"We don't know that Russia is behind the attacks that eliminated so much of our population," Marsden said.

"That's bull," Cranston said. "It can't be anyone else. No one else has the technology."

"You know," Mayweather said in a patient father's voice, "that's what Russia is saying about us. That we must be behind the disappearances."

Cranston waved the subject away. "That's just a smoke screen they're broadcasting to the rest of the world."

"They say that's our tactic," Marsden pointed out. "President Fitzhugh's declaration to the American people this morning that we would find out who attacked the United States so savagely and punish those responsible wasn't even a thinly veiled threat."

"Come on, General," Cranston flared. "After what the Soviets did to the Israelis in that surprise attack fourteen months ago, how can you even doubt that Russia is behind this?"

Marsden glanced at Mayweather, then sipped from a glass of water.

Mayweather leaned back in his chair, obviously taking a very smooth handoff. Delroy doubted Cranston caught the transition. The two older generals reminded Delroy of two older deacons in Josiah Harte's church who outmaneuvered the up-and-coming firebrands by double-teaming them so quietly they were never noticed.

"You know, General Cranston, you're something of an accomplished tactician," Mayweather said.

Delroy knew that was definitely an understatement. Shortly after
the Russian attack on Israel and after Chaim Rosenzweig's introduction of the chemical fertilizer that had revolutionized Israel's place in
the Middle East, Cranston had been the man to go to for the answers
regarding questions about those countries. Cranston had helped negotiate the fragile peace that had existed till the Russian attack, then
had helped put the conflicts back into perspective after that attack to
maintain another brief period of bloodless unrest—until the Syrians
had attacked Turkey.

"The accepted view of the failure of the Russian attack on Israel
was because they used planes that were falling apart," Mayweather
said. "Do you really think they would have launched an attack that
was doomed to fail if they had a weapon waiting in the wings that
could vaporize a third of the world's population?"

Cranston remained quiet.

"The Russian military lost a lot of men and machines in that de-
bacle, Todd," Marsden observed quietly. "Men and machines they
could have used to defend themselves in case the United States or
Great Britain or anyone else decided to retaliate."

"Besides that," Mayweather put in, "if I had a weapon that had
made a third of the world's population disappear in a heartbeat, I
think I'd be threatening to use it again instead of denying I had it.
The Russians showed no mercy in their attempted attack on Israel.
Why would you think they would deny possession of a weapon of
mass destruction that worked on a magnitude this great?"

"And American weapon development has run in tandem to Russian research," Marsden said. "They got ahead of us with Sputnik, but
they paid the price for that because they focused the American nation's need to get into the space race instead of allowing the Russians
to get there first. We've never been behind them since."

"Do you think the Russians could invent something we haven't
already had on the drawing boards?" Mayweather asked.

Delroy appreciated the way the two older generals worked. They
were smooth as hand-varnished wood, and they had put the walls
around the younger general with accomplished ease.

Someone knocked on the door. The lance corporal crossed the
room and opened the door. A quiet, quick conversation ensued.

When the lance corporal stepped back inside the room, a young
Air Force colonel accompanied him. The colonel saluted sharply,
feet tight together like he was on parade.

"Colonel Emerson Carter, General Marsden."

"Colonel." Marsden leaned back in his chair. "Obviously you're here on some matter of concern. Otherwise you would not have interrupted a private meeting."

"No, sir," the colonel said. "General King said I was to get a message to you at once, sir. There's a story breaking on FOX that General Farley thought you might want to see, sir."

Delroy placed the name after a moment. The only General Farley the chaplain knew of was General Hamilton Farley, who was in command of the NORAD base at Cheyenne Mountain. Cold fear stabbed through Delroy's heart.

The world was at DEFCON 2, perched at the edge of now and never. Giant airplanes hung like hunting hawks over cities around the world, their bellies filled with nuclear death. Ohio-class and Typhoon-class submarines glided through the oceans of the world, already in position to attack key sites in Russia, Korea, and China. All of those engines of destruction were cutting-edge, built with first-strike capability and armed with nuclear warheads that were designated city killers and could earn that sobriquet in one searing blast.

Marsden punched a button on a keypad built into the conference table. A cube of television screens lowered from a recessed spot in the ceiling. The screens quickly changed to the FOX station.

"—here just outside of Gdansk, Poland," a young reporter spoke into a microphone. "Nobody knows what brought the plane down in this wheat field outside the small city, but speculation exists that there was an aerial battle between American and Russian fighter jets."

The camera view locked in on the raging fire clinging to the unmistakable skeletal shape of a fighter jet. Several emergency vehicles ringed the area. Uniformed men with flashlights worked to keep the small crowds back.

"Will, do we know whether the aircraft was American or Russian?" someone off-camera asked.

The reporter brought the microphone back up to his face. He wore a coat and went bareheaded. He squinted against the wind. "No, Bert. As yet the local authorities haven't gotten close enough to make any kind of identification. Local residents that I've talked to said that they saw streaks that might have been machine gun fire and—"

"When did this happen?" Marsden asked.

Colonel Carter didn't even check his watch. The time stamp was posted on the television program. "Seven minutes ago, General."

"And whose plane is this?"

"One of ours, sir."

Marsden looked at the television screen. "What happened?"

"That plane was a flanker on Bronze Eagle."

Delroy didn't know what Bronze Eagle was, but since the fighter jet was close to Russia, an educated guess told him that the code name was for one of the B-52s put into the air for first-strike capability against Russia.

"The pilot of that aircraft judged that a Russian MiG got too close. Command agreed. The pilot was under clearance to fire a few warning rounds to turn the MiG away. Instead, our pilot was shot down."

"What happened to our pilot?" Marsden asked.

"Dead on impact, sir. There was no seat ejection."

Another young man lost, Delroy couldn't help thinking. He thought of the black coffin Terry had been buried in, thought of the way his wife had taken the flag folded into a tight triangle.

"Of course," Cranston said, "the Russians will say that we reacted in a hostile manner first." He leaned forward on his elbows, his hands wrapped together. "With the jet in Gdansk, not far from the Russian border, that may sell in the public view."

Marsden turned to the Air Force officer. "Was there anything else, Colonel?"

"No, sir."

"You'll keep me apprised of this development? And any others that may happen?"

"Yes, sir."

"Thank you, Colonel. You're dismissed."

With a final salute, Colonel Carter turned on his heel and marched for the door.

Marsden pressed the keypad again, and the television cube disappeared into the ceiling.

"After this," Cranston mused as he watched the screens recede, "the Russians will be in a perfect position to start putting more pressure behind their demands that we give their people back."

"Give their people back?" Delroy didn't realize he was speaking until the words were already out.

"Yes, Chaplain," Cranston said in a hard voice. "The Russians claim we kidnapped their people."

"What about the rest of the people in the world?" Delroy was flabbergasted.

"They don't care about the people missing from other countries," Cranston said.

"What about the people we're missing?"

"They don't believe what they see on television. They think this is all a production. A Hollywood special-effects presentation."

"That's insane," Delroy said.

"Is it, Chaplain?" Cranston sounded sarcastic. "I wouldn't know. Of course, I might mention that people telling me God Raptured the world and took all the believers to heaven sounds insane as well."

Delroy sank back in his chair.

"Unless you can convince me otherwise, Chaplain?" Cranston said. "Maybe you want to trot out your belief for all of us to see."

Delroy tried to speak but didn't know where to begin. What was wrong with him? Why had he come all this way just to sit here like this?

"A message of faith then, Chaplain?" Cranston said.

Face burning, Delroy remained silent.

"Come now, Chaplain Harte," Cranston said. "Surely after the distance you've come with Captain Falkirk's blessing, you can reveal to us your personal visions or prophecies."

"Todd," Marsden said in mild rebuke.

"This man didn't come here to be ridiculed," Mayweather said.

"No," Cranston agreed in a harsh voice. "I'm sure he didn't. But I will tell you this: if he was in my command, I'd have him up on charges of dereliction of duty."

Heaviness filled Delroy's limbs. He felt like he'd been beaten.

"Nothing to say, Chaplain?" Cranston asked.

"No, sir." The answer was dragged from Delroy only by years of training and discipline.

"Then I suggest we call an end to this," Cranston suggested. "With a downed plane in Poland and the Russians hysterical over it, I think we've got more pressing business to attend to."

"Chaplain?" Marsden looked hopeful.

"Aye, sir?"

"Was there anything else you wanted to say?"

Delroy hesitated. He searched his mind for the fire he'd felt back on the *Wasp*. But he couldn't think of a single thing. "No, sir."

Marsden seemed to sag in his chair. "You're dismissed, Chaplain Harte."

"Thank you, General." Wearily, Delroy stood, put his hat on, saluted, and turned on his heel. He walked toward the door in total, agonizing defeat.

❋   ❋   ❋

Turkish-Syrian Border
40 Klicks South of Sanliurfa, Turkey
Local Time 0153 Hours

Goose stood in the darkness at the front of the Hummer. Clouds and dust obscured the stars, and he gave silent thanks for that. If there were any Syrian scouts around that the Ranger perimeter teams hadn't been able to find, the darkness would help cover the fact that the first wave of the retreat was going to start in minutes. Most of the wounded had been loaded an hour ago.

Below in the stream, the final wave of men was finishing up with the chaplains and Corporal Joseph Baker, who had not once stepped from the stream. The big man had at times taken brief respites from the baptisms, during which he had conferred with people he had pulled from the water.

The men held torches they'd made from materials salvaged from supplies that were going to be left behind. The torches flickered in the slow, soft breeze that had turned cold as soon as the sun had gone down. The land was giving up its heat now, and Goose knew from experience that a chill would fill the harsh terrain before morning.

Goose had set himself up on perimeter watch. Movement on patrol helped him work through the anxiety that crashed through him as he wondered how the night's preparations for the evac were going.

Remington's assigning him to the baptism hadn't interfered with carrying out the retreat. Goose knew the Ranger captain had known that when he'd made the assignation. A good first sergeant made his position redundant because he'd trained the men to know what had to be done already and the captain knew everything had already been considered.

Also, Goose had monitored the activities of the different units and squads he'd set up through the headset. His headset was chipped for all the different frequencies in use. He also knew that Remington deliberately hadn't completely cut him out of the loop.

As he walked, Goose kept his eyes moving like he was on point. In the darkness, his peripheral vision was best. He carried the M-4A1 in both hands. At least the cortisone shot Mkchian had been generous enough to give him had kicked in and calmed the damaged knee. The joint still felt puffy and a little leaden but moved well enough, and he felt only occasional twinges of pain.

Other Rangers stood guard as well. Some of them had gotten baptized. Goose could see that their uniforms were still damp, and the men stood huddled in blankets to block the chill wind. On the eastern ridgeline, Turkish soldiers put into by position by Captain Mkchian stood guard as well.

A hundred yards from the Hummer, Goose spotted the hulk of a RSOV. Remington. He knew Remington wouldn't allow anyone else to take one of the vehicles this close to the retreat window. As he got closer to the RSOV, he saw that Remington had come alone.

"Hello, Goose," Remington said, sitting in the seat with both arms wrapped around the steering wheel. His voice was neutral.

"Captain," Goose replied.

"Is this circus about finished?"

Goose looked over his shoulder. Fewer than a dozen torches still burned where Baker and the chaplains spoke to the latest group of men that had been baptized. Pockets of men strode back up the hillsides. One man threw his torch into the stream. The water extinguished the flames at once.

"Yes, sir," Goose said. "I told them they had to be done by two. They finished up about ten minutes ago. They're clearing out now."

Remington sucked air through his teeth. It was one of the few unconscious mannerisms he had, and this one denoted extreme irritation. "You realize we're living out a Chinese curse."

"Sir?"

"Knock off the 'sir,' Goose," Remington said. "This is just you and me."

Goose stilled the immediate "yes, sir" that almost escaped him. Despite Remington's words, Goose knew they would never share the equality they'd had as enlisted men together. Not unless something changed. Goose knew he wasn't going up to officer, and Remington would never willingly leave.

"A Chinese curse?" Goose prompted.

"To live in interesting times," Remington answered.

Goose nodded.

"Of course, some of the men who have been baptized out here have come back talking about these being the end times," Remington said. "I guess Baker and the chaplains are pumping them up about that."

"I wouldn't know," Goose said.

"You mean you haven't been down for a dip?" Remington seemed surprised.

"No," Goose answered. He'd been baptized when he was thirteen, with Pastor Moody on one side and his dad on the other. He could still remember coming out of the water of the baptismal pool and seeing the tears in his father's eyes. Not usually demonstrative in public, Wes Gander had pulled his son to him tightly and hugged Goose so hard he hadn't been able to breathe.

"I don't like this, Goose."

Goose remained quiet.

"I've seen men get religion on the battlefield before." Remington spat the word as if religion was a disease. "A guy sees his buddy get hit next to him. Sees a mortar dig a crater only a few feet away. Gets left out pinned down on a busted op too long. That will change a man's perspective." He paused. "They say there are no atheists in foxholes."

"I've never seen one," Goose replied.

"A guy who isn't sure God is going to get him out of a jam is a guy who's sure God is ignoring him or punishing him," Remington said. "Then he feels like he's jinxed. The guy who figures God is going to save him forgets about trying to save himself. The guy who figures God is out to get him thinks the next bullet has his name on it." He paused. "Either situation makes for a bad soldier and an even worse Ranger."

"Over a third of this unit disappeared yesterday morning, Captain," Goose said. "Nearly that many more people were killed during the SCUD launch. These men can't undergo something like that and walk away unchanged."

"So they decide to get baptized, give their souls to God."

"*Entrust* their souls to God," Goose corrected.

"Semantics."

No, sir, it's not, Goose thought. But he knew the captain wouldn't understand.

Remington nodded at a group of Rangers passing by them only a few feet away. "Now that they're walking out of here, I've got to wonder if they're thinking they're bulletproof or that they've paid up all their dues for a one-way trip to heaven."

"You'd have to ask them."

"I don't want either of those reactions from them," Remington said. "Give me a man who's afraid of dying and wants to make sure the other guy dies first. That's a good Ranger."

Goose disagreed but didn't say so. A good Ranger was a man who got a dirty and dangerous job done as efficiently as he could to save the lives of loved ones and innocents.

"That's why I freed Dean Hardin," Remington said.

Anger flared through Goose. "Captain, that man is a thief, and he tried to kill me."

Remington shook his head and looked away. "That's not how he tells it, Goose. Hardin says you came up on him from behind and surprised him. He had a knife in his hand and he accidentally nearly gutted you. He says he was keyed up from the helicopters crashing and raining down all around you."

"And you believe him?"

"You can't walk up behind a man on a battlefield without giving him some kind of warning, Goose." Remington looked at him then. Accusation showed in his eyes.

"Hardin was stealing from a dead Marine, Captain," Goose said.

"Hardin says he was salvaging resources."

Goose couldn't believe it. "Money from a dead man?"

"Money is one of the best resources a scavenger can find," Remington said. "It converts to any size and works almost anywhere."

"Sir," Goose protested, "those men were our reinforcements. Most of them were little more than kids."

Remington swore. "Goose, listen to me. I know for a fact that you're an organ donor, right?"

"Yes, sir."

"Well, how do you figure on giving someone a heart or a lung without being dead? A kidney or an eye you can maybe spare because you've got a pair. But let's face it: as a donor you're worth more if you're dead."

Goose didn't say anything because he knew where the captain was headed with his logic.

"Those dead men that Hardin took money from were donors," Remington said.

"Was that how Hardin put it, sir?" Goose asked.

"That's how I'm putting it now, Sergeant," Remington said. "And that's how I'm putting it in my report."

"Yes, sir."

"I wanted you to know why I countermanded your orders to hold Hardin. I also talked him out of pressing charges against you for striking him. He'll be with me during the evac."

"Yes, sir." But Goose knew that wasn't the only reason Remington was telling him about Hardin. Hardin was also a man to hold grudges. There was talk, never proven, of a man Hardin had gotten crossways with and ended up killing. When Goose had turned up the scuttlebutt, he'd gone to Remington. Remington had said that men like Hardin, guys who were natural-born predators and survivors, always gathered stories around them. Some of them, the captain had said, were even started by the predators themselves.

"We'll be in Sanliurfa tomorrow morning," Remington said. "We're going to assess the situation and see if we can hold the city, but that will only be a diversion to allow refortification of Diyarbakir."

Goose had figured that would be the case. With the Rangers at Diyarbakir, they'd be able to attack from behind any invading Syrian troops that got deeply into the country and marched on Ankara. For the time they were there, Sanliurfa would also act as a frontier fort where they could arrange hit-and-get missions to disable Syrian cav and missile units.

"You remember the CIA agent you rescued yesterday morning?" Remington asked.

"Yes. Icarus."

"I've had men in Sanliurfa—"

"Perrin?" Goose knew all about Perrin.

Remington nodded. "—and they haven't found this agent."

"Maybe he was one of the ones who disappeared." Goose had heard about losses in nearby areas as well.

"Possibly," Remington nodded. "In the meantime, I find it interesting that the CIA is in the area looking for a rogue agent at a time when something as unexplained as the disappearances take place."

Goose considered that. He hadn't thought about the CIA being somehow involved with the disappearances.

"When you get to Sanliurfa, take a look around. See if this guy turns up."

"I will, sir."

Remington pulled his shirtsleeve back and checked his watch on the inside of his wrist. "Get back to camp, Sergeant. When this thing goes down, I want you where I can use you most."

"Yes, sir."

"And, Goose." Remington fixed him with a hard, flat stare. "This doesn't happen again. Not between us. Not in my command. *Ever.*"

"Yes, sir," Goose said. And he hoped it wouldn't because Remington was his friend, but also because he knew the captain wouldn't allow him to step across that line of command again without severe penalties.

Remington's head whipped away.

Knowing the captain was listening to his headset, Goose quickly went through the channels, flipping over to the main command channel.

"—confirms SCUD launch," a man's high-strung voice announced. "We are under attack! ETA seventy seconds, Captain!"

Goose switched over to the main com channel the Rangers would be using. All the confusion brought on by Remington's actions disappeared in the space of a single heartbeat.

"This is Phoenix Leader," Goose said as he sprinted for the Hummer. He dropped into the seat behind the steering wheel. "The Syrians have launched SCUDs! Dig in! Dig in!" He keyed the starter button and felt the engine shiver to life.

Remington was already in motion, flooring the RSOV so the tires threw out rooster tails of dirt. He would be in touch with the captains of the U.N. troops and the Turkish army, making certain they all had the same information.

Goose shoved the Hummer's transmission into gear and followed. He checked his watch and found that the first evac carrying the wounded was already a few minutes underway. His heart turned cold as he realized those units would be drastically exposed along the roads.

❋   ❋   ❋

United States of America
The Pentagon, Washington, D.C.
Local Time 7:03 P.M.

Nausea wormed through Delroy's guts as he walked from General Marsden's office. His legs quivered and black spots spun in his vision. Perspiration tracked down his face.

People hurried by him, carrying notes and meals. And probably a lot of bad news that was only going to get worse, if the downed fighter in Poland was any indication.

Loosening his tie, Delroy tried to take a deep breath and couldn't. *God, why did You send me all this way to fail?* He couldn't understand it. *How was I supposed to change General Cranston's mind? You're supposed to touch people's hearts. You're supposed to make them change. Not me. God, help me. I can barely keep my own faith together. You know that. You see me as I really am.*

"Are you okay, Chaplain Harte?"

Delroy glanced over at the lance corporal who had been assigned to walk him out of the building. "I don't know."

"There's a bathroom here, sir." The lance corporal pointed to the side of the hallway. "Would you like to stop?"

Delroy spotted the men's room plaque. When it was first designed after World War II, the Pentagon had been designed with men in mind, not women. As a result, the number of men's rooms still far outnumbered those of women.

"You had a long flight, sir," the lance corporal said, "and I know being in that room facing General Cranston like that wasn't easy."

"The general's a hard man," Delroy said.

"Yes, sir. But he's a driven man. If you can get him on your side, he'll go to the wall with you."

"I didn't quite make that happen, did I?"

"No, sir." The lance corporal hesitated. "But I'll tell you something, Chaplain, I believe you're right. I believe the world *has* been Raptured."

"You do?"

"Yes, sir." The young man looked earnest and grim. "My grandmother raised me, chaplain, and she brought me up in the church. If it hadn't been for the church and Pastor Keith, I'd never have made it out of high school. I never would have become a Marine. God works in everyone's lives. It's just that a lot of people don't acknowledge him. Including me, sometimes. But my doubts vanished when I saw what happened."

"Lance Corporal, I wish you had stars on your shoulders." Delroy tried to make a joke of it, but the Marine's forthrightness about his belief made the pain of his failure hurt even more.

"I wish that General Cranston hadn't been the man you needed to win over, sir."

"Thank you for that. And I think I'll take you up on that kind offer. It's been a long, long day for me."

"Yes, sir. I'll be out here if you need me, sir." The Marine posted up beside the door. "So you can take a few minutes to yourself if you need them, sir."

Delroy clapped the young Marine on the shoulder. A regular officer might not be able to get away with that, but as chaplain he could. Even that small gesture, offered out of fellowship and friendship, reminded him how separated he was from the military, how far he was from Cranston's world.

Inside the men's room, Delroy walked to the nearest sink. The door closed behind him and the outside noises went away. The exhaust fan in the center of the room rattled gently.

The bathroom had a dark tiled floor and white walls. Six beige stalls stood at the far end of the room on the other side of a similar number of urinals. The pine disinfectant smell of the room was so sharp it hurt Delroy's sinuses and burned his eyes.

He stood at the sink and looked at his image. His tie hung at half-mast, and his features appeared ashen. *God, forgive me. I have failed You so badly.*

"And where do you go to when you think you're failing, boy?"

Delroy heard his father's voice, a call from his past. That had been one of the things Josiah Harte had asked his eldest son several times as he'd been growing up. As a young boy, Delroy had been a fighter. Being black in Alabama back in those years hadn't been easy. Schoolyard battles had resulted in more than a few white parents showing up at his father's church.

That was what Josiah Harte had always asked when Delroy had come home battered and beaten or battered and victorious. *Battered* had always figured in there somewhere.

If a man fails, Josiah Harte used to say in his occasional sermons when he touched on the subject, *he has nowhere else in the world he can go but to the Lord God Almighty.* The choir would break out in song, a gospel arrangement of "Where Could I Go?"

Delroy shrugged out of his jacket and looked up at the ceiling—and beyond it. "You gotta help me, Lord, because I know I can't help myself. I've gone the distance You asked me to, but I've come up short here." He hung his jacket on the paper towel holder. "I don't know what else You want me to do. You're gonna have to show me what You want me to do now."

He looked at his face in the mirror, wishing there were more of Josiah Harte's features in his. His father's face had been hard and fierce, the face of an avenging angel, Delroy's mother had always said.

Delroy had the face of a boxer. Scar tissue showed under both eyes under close inspection even after all these years. His father had loved watching him box. He'd stood in the corner and worked as cut-man while Delroy had battled in Golden Gloves boxing matches. He'd come to the gym, worked out on the ropes, the speed bag, and the heavy bag with Delroy.

"You're a good fighter, Delroy," his father had told him occasionally, though only when he'd fought in the ring and not in the schoolyard. *"You got a head for it. Always looking for an opponent, always looking. If you*

*ever get your heart wrapped around the Word of the Lord, why, you're gonna
be a champion, boy. But you got a mighty hard head. Mighty hard. Can I get
an Amen on that?"*

Amen, Delroy thought, and he was surprised to see a smile tug at
his lips.

*"You not done, boy. You not done till I throw in the towel or you can't get
up no more. And I ain't throwin' in no towel."*

Delroy remembered the times his father had told him that, times
that he'd been certain he'd been too broken up, too bloodied and battered to go one more round. He'd always gotten up, gone one more
round and sometimes another as long as his father had kept at him.

"I'm not done," Delroy told his reflection. He turned on the cold
faucet, shoved both hands under the stream, and splashed cold water
into his face. The sensation woke him, alleviating some of the nausea
and fatigue he felt. Between that and the memories of his father, he felt
almost human again.

He raised his head and blinked the water from his eyes.

Then he saw the young blond pilot from the C-9 Skytrain standing
behind him. As his vision cleared, Delroy saw that the man wasn't
quite human. Scales covered his flesh, and his amber eyes were set in
elongated slits that ran up on the sides of his head, giving him a snake-
like appearance. His nose was a brief nub above a mouth that held serrated teeth. A black, forked tongue flicked out when he smiled.

"Oh, yeah," the creature said, "you're done. Just stupid, is all."
With blinding speed, the man-creature grabbed the back of Delroy's
head and smashed him forward into the mirror.

Shards of the mirror tumbled into the sink and broke again.
Dazed, Delroy slumped against the sink.

The creature shoved a hand against Delroy's back and straddled his
hips, leaning into him to keep him pinned against the sink. Its other
hand scrabbled in the sink and grabbed a mirror shard from the rushing water in the basin. Hard black talons gleamed at the ends of the
thing's fingers.

"You came into this men's room," the thing said. "You were de-
spondent. You were right to feel that way. And right to do something
about it. After all, nobody believes in you or your God. Everyone will
understand how you felt compelled to come in here and cut your own
throat."

Delroy stared down at the gleaming shard in the creature's hand.
He stared at the inhuman features reflected in the mirror. The black,
forked tongue danced in unholy anticipation.

"You won't be waking up, Delroy, but I'm your nightmare."

Twisting quickly, Delroy brought his left elbow back into the thing's face. It seemed stunned by the blow but didn't release him. Delroy brought his elbow again, feeling the dense bone of the thing's head.

With an angry squall, the creature fell backward. Delroy pushed himself up to his feet, bringing his fists up in front of him automatically.

"Give up, Chaplain," the thing snarled, raking its empty hand across its features. "Give up and I'll kill you fast."

"No," Delroy replied.

"You want to give up." The thing swiped at him with the mirror shard. Light splintered from the gleaming surface. "It's too hard for you to believe."

"I struggle with my belief," Delroy said. "I strive to be stronger in my belief. It's what every good Christian does."

"Really?" the thing mocked. "I got a news flash for you, ace. All the good Christians have done left the planet. You people that are left here, you're prey." The creature uncoiled, almost like a snake uncoiling in a strike.

Delroy caught the creature's shard-wielding hand by the wrist with his left hand. He jammed his right forearm up under the thing's jaw, catching it so fast that the serrated teeth closed and chopped off part of the black tongue.

The creature head-butted him.

Dazed, Delroy went backward and slammed against the wall. The creature was at his throat immediately. With raw, savage strength, the thing shoved him down to the cold tile floor. Pieces of the broken mirror scraped against the floor and cut into Delroy's back.

The thing straddled Delroy. It grinned. "You're going to die, chaplain. Ersatz faith never protected anybody."

Delroy struggled, but every time he got set and pushed, the creature moved fluidly and countered his strength, keeping him pinned to the floor.

"You're nothing, chaplain." The creature smiled and the slitted eyes gleamed. "Your son was nothing. He's gone and you'll never see him again."

"God took my son," Delroy said.

"Bullets blew your son's heart out, Chaplain. Don't fool yourself."

"I'll see him again," Delroy said. "I'll see Terry again."

"Want to try for tonight?"

Delroy yanked his right hand free and drove a punch into the thing's face, catching it off guard. When the creature shifted, he rolled, getting over on top of it. But the thing slithered away, scrabbling up another mirror shard. Losing was only a matter of time. Dying lay an inch behind that.

"Die tonight, Chaplain, and you get to see your boy earlier, right?"

"I can't," Delroy said. "God has a purpose here for me." He shook his head. "I'm not done yet." And suddenly he believed it. Believed it right down to the core. He found the will to pray, really pray, for help. *God, help me, in Jesus' name.*

And the bathroom door opened. Looking over the thing's shoulder, Delroy saw General Todd Cranston's jaw drop in surprise.

The creature hissed like a scalded cat, curled in on itself, and faded away into the shadows.

Gasping for air, Delroy struggled to his feet. Chest heaving, he stared at Cranston. "You saw that."

"No." Cranston shook his head.

"Then what did you see?"

"You," Cranston said. "I came in. You must have fallen. That's all." The general reached for the door.

"No." Throwing out a big hand, Delroy caught the door and shut it. "You saw it. There are no aliens, General. No mystery weapons that the Russians dreamed up."

"You're crazy."

"Those people that are missing were taken by the Rapture," Delroy went on relentlessly.

"No."

Delroy leaned into the man, invading Cranston's personal space the way he had seen his father do with reluctant parishioners. "Do you know what we're up against, General?"

Pounding sounded on the door. "General. General Cranston. Are you all right, sir?"

Delroy recognized the voice of the young Marine. He ignored the demands. "If you don't recognize what is before you, General, if you don't help curb the DEFCON 2 status we're at, you're going to help the enemy win."

"The enemy?"

"The Antichrist," Delroy said. "He's coming. You just saw one of his minions. Now that the Rapture has occurred, the Antichrist will rise and take everyone and everything he can in the next seven years before the Glorious Appearing of Christ."

More pounding hammered the door. "General!"

"We're soldiers, General," Delroy implored. "We're supposed to be good soldiers. The first line of defense for civilians and those who are too weak or unable to defend themselves."

"General!" The door jumped as someone tried to force his way in.

"You took an oath," Delroy reminded. "You took an oath before God to serve this country. God is part of every military creed and duty we have. You can't turn your back on him, General."

The door flew open as Marines boiled into the room. Delroy didn't know how many of them there were. They hit him and knocked him down, driving him to his knees and pinning his arms behind his back. One of the Marines held a Colt .45 to the side of Delroy's head.

Cranston stared back at him with an unaccustomed pallor.

"God put me here tonight," Delroy said. "I came a long way to be here. And the only reason I'm here is to get you to do something that you can do." He breathed hard, twisted painfully by the Marines. "I heard Him and I believed Him and I came. And He put you through that door at that moment to see what you saw, General. If you don't believe that, then you're lost. And if you're lost, that thing wins."

Cranston shook his head and wiped his mouth.

"What did you see, General?" Delroy asked. "You've got a third of the people missing around the planet. Countries armed with nuclear weapons pointed down each others' throats. Doesn't that sound like Armageddon to you?"

"General," the lance corporal said. "Why don't you get out of here and let us handle this? We've got him."

"No," Cranston said. "Let him up."

"Sir?"

"Get off him, Marine. That's an order."

"Sir, yes, sir."

The Marines released Delroy. Weakly, the chaplain tried to get to his feet.

"Here, Chaplain Harte." Cranston extended his hand. He still looked uncertain.

Delroy took the man's hand and let Cranston help him up.

"I don't know what I saw, Chaplain Harte," Cranston said, "but whatever it was, I'm willing to listen."

"Thank you, sir."

"Grab your coat and hat," Cranston said, "and let's go find out if I'm as influential as you seem to think I am."

"It wasn't me thinking that, sir," Delroy said. "I just carried the message."

Turkish-Syrian Border
40 Klicks South of Sanliurfa, Turkey
Local Time 0217 Hours

Pillars of fire leaped up from the ground in front of the ridge overlooking the Turkish-Syrian border.

Goose drove the Hummer flat out, feeling the vehicle claw over the broken ground, then go airborne a couple times. Less than a hundred yards from the ridge, a SCUD missile slammed into the front of the hill where the Rangers, the U.N. troops, and the Turkish army had pulled back to holding positions. Rock and dirt rained down over Goose, peppering his helmet and his body armor. His face and hands took hits as well, but those were more annoying and scary than damaging.

The battlefield, less than a day old from the previous morning's attack, only hours older than the disappearances that had caused helicopters and planes to rain from the sky, erupted again as the new wave of devastation tore into the area. Smoke and dust occluded the landscape in less than a minute, forming a thick, drifting acrid fog.

Goose flipped through the headset frequencies, tuning in to the com channel set aside for the Marine wing survivors. He jerked the wheel as a large boulder smacked into the ground ahead of him, but he wasn't able to entirely avoid the mass. The right front end of the Hummer kissed the boulder and the headlights on that side shattered. The sudden jarring rocked Goose in his seat, but the belts kept him in place till he regained control over the Hummer.

The Marine Harrier and Sea Cobra gunships leapt up from the LZ that had been made earlier. The pilots' voices sounded anxious as they formed up. One of the helos disintegrated as a SCUD hammered it from the sky. Pieces of the Sea Cobra rained down in flaming shards. Then the Marine wing was engaged, streaking over the border into Syria to hunt the SCUD launchers, targeting them through the satellite reconnaissance being done from the field command post.

Remington drove his RSOV just back of the ridgeline and parked.

A hundred yards away so that both vehicles couldn't be lost in one SCUD blast, Goose parked the Hummer and leaped out. He kept his head down, one hand on his helmet, and ran for the ridge. The Ranger rifle companies lay spread out along the ridgeline, taking what cover they could behind natural fortifications, husks of downed planes and helicopters they'd pulled into position, and behind sandbags they'd spent the afternoon filling.

Goose hugged the ground and prayed for his teammates and the Marine wing that had flown into enemy territory. As infantry, the only chance the Rangers had was to dig in and try to survive. Again and again, the earth shook beneath him. He kept his face buried in his arms, choking on the dirt and the dust that stayed stirred up. He kept praying, hoping to get home to Megan, Joey, and Chris.

In less than a minute, the Marine pilots were confirming successful strikes against identified SCUD launchers. Unfortunately, the pilots in turn were being targeted by ground antiaircraft guns. As Goose listened to the frantic radio chatter, he realized the attrition rate among the Marine wing was fierce.

"Marathon Leader, this is Blue Falcon Leader," the Harrier pilot called.

Marathon Leader was Captain Remington's call sign. The operation had been designated *Marathon* because of the long run the Rangers would have to do to get to Sanliurfa. The Turkish military had moved extra troops into the city to help hold the Syrians back until the next fallback to Diyarbakir could be arranged.

All we've got is forty klicks of bad road, Goose told himself. *We can do forty klicks.*

"Go Blue Leader," Remington replied, "you have Marathon Leader."

"Marathon Leader, be advised that the hostiles' infantry and cav units are in motion."

"Roger that, Blue Leader. Can you confirm twenty from the line?"

"Twenty from the line is ten klicks."

"Roger ten klicks, Blue Leader. Marathon One, did you copy?"

"Affirmative," Goose responded. "Marathon One copies. Roger ten klicks."

If the Syrians were ten klicks out, Goose knew it wouldn't take more than seven to ten minutes to cover the distance. He looked back over his shoulder at the mountain road the fleeing transports carrying the wounded had taken earlier in the day.

Goose couldn't see any of the trucks, Jeeps, and Hummers that carried the wounded, but he knew they didn't have a big enough lead to make an escape. If the drivers didn't maintain a grueling pace, the approaching Syrians would quickly overtake them. And the same grueling pace they had to maintain might kill many of the injured.

At least when the Syrians got close to the border, the SCUD launchers would have to stop firing at them. But the medevac units would remain fair game for the missiles.

Six minutes later, the command post personnel radioed that the Syrian cav should be visible from the Rangers' positions. That was the bad news. The good news was that the SCUD launches were down to practically nil. Between the attacks by the Marine wing and the probability that the Syrians had expended most of their arsenal the previous day, they obviously hadn't had much to give.

Goose crawled to the ridgeline and peered over. Through the smoke and the dust haze, he spotted the front line of the approaching Syrian cavalry. The tanks and APCs looked monstrous in the darkness, briefly lit up as their cannon and machine guns opened fire. Orange gouts of flame rent holes in the darkness.

"Incoming!" someone yelled, and Goose didn't know if someone else had yelled or if he was only hearing his own voice.

In the next instant, the cannon rounds impacted against the ridgeline. A few others exploded farther back behind Goose. A fresh wave of falling dirt and rock rained down over Goose's back.

Then the line of advancing cav broke up as they hit the first of the M-18A1 claymores the Rangers had positioned in the area in front of the burned-out hulks of Syrian vehicles left from the initial attack yesterday. The mines slowed the tanks and APCs for a moment as the drivers feared broken treads or blown tires in the case of some of the APCs.

The Syrians had been expecting the traps there, Goose knew as he took out his night-vision binoculars, but the next layer was down and dirty, stuff that wasn't found in the textbooks.

As the Syrian cav units stood down to send infantry ahead to search out the claymores that could cripple the APCs and tanks, Remington gave the order to begin the second wave of the evacuation.

The U.N. forces departed first, sagging from the middle of the confrontation zone as Remington had worked out. Even with all the casualties they'd had, the Rangers stood the best chance of surviving bringing up the rear. The U.N. forces hadn't been bloodied as frequently or as harshly as the 75th, and the Turkish army was more equipped and trained to attack en masse rather than by small, swiftly moving special forces units.

The U.N. forces sped through the night, getting away smoothly in spite of the blistering attack that had taken place. If the Syrians hadn't moved forward and forced the confrontation, Goose felt certain they could have made the retreat as easily as a practiced circus act.

The vehicles drove without lights because that would have drawn Syrian fire immediately. With the heavy dust and smoke streaming across the battlefield, the vehicle's lights wouldn't penetrate and would only blind the drivers. Small reflectors had been placed along the mountain road for the first five klicks, till the road disappeared up into the mountains high above the border.

The Syrian infantry advanced cautiously against the threat of the claymores. Using rifle-fired grappling hooks, they shot the heavy hooks into the area methodically, crisscrossing the lines and dragging the hooks back through. As they hit claymores, the explosion threw dirt and rock into the air. Occasionally, some of the Syrian soldiers were hit, but not often. Thousands of dollars of munitions were going up with nothing to be gained for it.

Except time, Goose reminded himself. Time was the one priceless commodity a soldier needed. The ability to control time was a dream.

The Syrians continued advancing, firing the grappling hooks, dragging them through the claymores, advancing, reloading, and firing again.

They were, Goose had to admit, remarkably efficient. In a handful of minutes, groups of men had cleared tank-wide paths through the open area to the maze of broken vehicles. The tanks and APCs inched forward, still comfortable out of range of the Rangers' M-203s.

"Snipers," Goose called.

The sniper teams along the ridgeline, composed mostly of Marines who had survived the crash of *Wasp*'s Marine wing responded.

"Targets," Goose commanded. "Fire at will."

Almost immediately, the snipers opened fire. The heavy reports of the 7.62mm rounds from the M-40 sniper rifles and the .50-cal cartridges from the Barrett popping off with measured cadence seemed barely noticeable after the thunder of the exploding SCUDs. The M-

40s were ranged out to a thousand yards. The Marines handling the Barretts claimed hits had been confirmed out to a mile.

Syrian infantrymen dropped in their tracks. In less than a minute, the Syrian tanks locked down and started firing, punching rounds into the ridgeline. The Syrian infantrymen moved quickly through the remaining ground to the abandoned vehicles, thinking they were safe from the sniper fire as they continued searching for a way to the border.

"Marathon Fire Control," Goose called. His voice sounded hollow and far away. Ringing rolled inside his ears from the explosions that had fallen all around him. "This is Marathon One."

"Go, One. You have Fire Control."

"Do you have your target?"

"Roger target, One. Fire Control is up, fully loaded, and hunting bear."

Tension knotted Goose's stomach. He stared down at the broken maze of shattered Syrian vehicles. The Rangers had taken as much fuel as they needed to get their own transport back to Sanliurfa and hadn't tried to carry any extra. If they made Sanliurfa, the objective and the necessity would be to hold the city, not abandon it immediately.

With that operating parameter in mind, the Rangers had devised crude napalm bombs using the leftover fuel from the downed aircraft that hadn't exploded or ruptured their tanks. Aviation gas was the most combustible liquid they had. While they had been filling jerry cans with salvaged gas from the Syrian vehicles, they had also been refilling those gas tanks with a mixture of aviation gas, detergent, and oil from the motor pools of the Rangers, U.N. forces, and Turkish army. Adding remote-control detonators and wiring them to go off in select areas gave them an added arsenal.

With the snipers driven back by the tank support cannonfire, the Syrian infantry moved deeper into the maze of vehicles. None of the soldiers seemed to notice that the vehicles had been positioned to lead to strategic locations.

"Fire Control," Goose said, "light up the primary zones."

"Fire in the hole, One."

Goose dropped the night-vision binoculars so the incendiaries wouldn't cause temporary blindness when magnified through the lenses.

The near-napalm, as the Rangers had termed the explosive mixture, detonated, blasting free of the constraining spaces where it had been held. Huge gouts of flaming liquid spewed through the air, covering several of the Syrian infantry.

Goose's heart almost went out to the men. God help them, it was a horrible way to die. But he turned off his feelings. If the Syrians weren't stopped here, at least for a while, they would roll over the Rangers, the U.N. forces, and the Turkish army. Not even the wounded had a chance of escaping. Goose knew they wouldn't hesitate about killing everyone. After the bloodthirsty attack with the SCUDs yesterday morning, he knew there would be no Geneva Convention rules.

The battle was a basic one. The winners lived and the losers died.

Syrians covered in the sticky flames created by the mixture of fuel, oil, and detergent turned into human torches. Panicked, they ran in all directions. Some of them tripped claymores, proving that the threat still existed within the maze of vehicles.

Still, the Syrians regrouped and came inexorably forward. When the tanks were certain the claymores had been cleared, they rolled ponderously forward.

"Fire Control," Goose called.

"Go, One."

"Zone Two. Now."

With the tanks and APCs in the heart of the maze, the secondary explosives, blocks of C-4, diesel fuel, and fertilizer, detonated from ground emplacements. The rolling cav halted again, but only for a moment. Evidently knowing they had no choice but to push on through, the tank commanders engaged again and rolled forward.

"Blue Falcon Leader," Remington called. "This is Marathon Leader."

"Go, Leader. You have Blue Falcon."

"You're up."

Goose glanced to the east and saw the few Harriers and Sea Cobras sweep in toward the tanks and APCs. The Marine wing had few bombs left after attacking the SCUD launch sites, but they unlimbered everything they had. The effect left several APCs and tanks disabled or heavily damaged.

"Marathon, this is Blue Leader. We're tapped, guys, and running on fumes."

"Get clear, Blue Leader," Remington said. "Thanks for the assist."

"I've heard that Rangers lead the way," the pilot said in a gruff, friendly voice. "Didn't know they stayed to close the door."

"We're a full-service corps," Remington said.

"God keep you, Marathon. We'll be waiting on you in Sanliurfa."

The surviving Harriers and Sea Cobras turned north and disappeared into the black sky.

"One, this is Leader."

"Go, Leader," Goose responded.

"Let's break it off by the numbers."

Calmly, Goose called out the evacuation units, sending the Rangers into full retreat in waves. He was aware of the RSOVs, Hummers, and Jeeps departing in an organized fashion. He stayed with Fire Control.

When the Syrian army hit the abandoned Ranger, Turkish, and U.N. vehicles, they hesitated. There were no claymores in front of the wrecked vehicles, but the near-napalm and C-4 was in place. Thunder and flames shredded the night again. When the tanks tried to rush through, they found claymores staggered and waiting on the other side that blew some of the treads.

"All right, Fire Control," Goose said. "We're done here. Retreat." He turned and stayed low, running across the broken ground.

The twenty Rangers of the fire control unit ran for the waiting vehicles a quarter mile distant as the Syrian cav opened fire again. The tanks and APCs fired blindly, though, lobbing shells into the ridgeline where they believed their tormentors were, and put very few over the top.

We're going to make it, Goose thought. He was covered with grit and perspiration. The pain in his knee was more fierce now, but it held together. His breath burned the back of his throat dry.

Twenty-one men piled into three RSOVs, leaving the other Jeeps and Hummers behind. The fact that those vehicles weren't going anywhere offered mute testimony that several soldiers who had held the line at the ridge weren't going to make it to Sanliurfa.

Private John Brady from backwoods North Carolina took the wheel of the RSOV and aimed them at the reflectors that had been set up to mark the road. He was a seasoned driver, a good wheelman, and claimed to come from a long line of moonshine runners and NASCAR racers. Goose didn't know if the claim was true, but the man knew how to handle a vehicle.

The three RSOVs sped toward the winding mountain road.

Goose sat in the passenger seat and tried to find a comfortable position for his injured knee.

"They're coming, Sarge," Corporal Travis Madden called from the back of the RSOV. He was one of the best electronics-on-the-run guys the Rangers had ever turned out.

Twisting in his seat, Goose peered back at the ridgeline and saw the first of the tanks, APCs, and Jeeps pull into view. There was no hesitation; the Syrians came on at full speed now, a rolling onslaught of armor and firepower.

They're not going to stop, Goose thought. *They are not going to stop.*

In the darkness, with only indirect moonlight and starlight illuminating the night, the Syrian cav took on the appearance of monsters, merciless juggernauts on the trail of weakened prey.

There was no certainty that they would be able to hold Sanliurfa without the reinforcements from *Wasp*.

"Marathon One," Remington called.

"One reads you, Leader."

"Are you underway?"

"Closing ground," Goose assured him. He held his M-4A1 butt to the floor next to his seat and held his shoulder strap with his other hand. The RSOV jumped, jerked, and bounced as it flew across the terrain.

The road turned narrow as the grade inclined, and it twisted like a broken-backed snake. Loose rock made the going more treacherous, and Goose felt even the RSOV's four-wheel-drive struggle to keep traction.

"Sarge!"

Whipping his head around in the seat, Goose looked at Madden.

The corporal was pointing behind them. "We lost Sullivan."

Only a short distance behind them, Goose watched as the rear RSOV tumbled down the steep mountainside. The drop had to have been a hundred feet, with nothing but broken rock at the bottom. The vehicle rolled twice, then came to a stop wedged precariously against a rocky outcrop.

"Stop the vehicle," Goose ordered.

Brady slammed on the brakes.

"Back up," Goose said.

Brady rammed the transmission into reverse and backed down the steep grade. The Syrian cav units could still be seen in the distance, making good time now.

"One, this is Leader."

"Go, Leader," Goose responded. "You have One."

"My intel team tells me you've halted."

"They should have also told you that we lost one of our vehicles over the side."

"Leave it, Goose. You've got no margin there to effect a rescue. Those hostiles are going to be on you in minutes."

Goose peered through the darkness. He fully expected that Remington was right, figuring that the men had been thrown clear of the RSOV. Then he saw one of the men moving, still belted into his seat.

"At least one of them is alive, Leader," Goose said.

"Get clear, Goose."

Brady braked the RSOV adjacent to the vehicle.

"I can't, Leader. I've left enough men behind on this mission. I can't leave any more."

"You're going to die there with them."

Goose didn't reply, giving orders to get the other Rangers moving. They took ropes from the RSOV's equipment compartments and tied onto the rear. Wrapping the rope around his waist, Goose rappelled face-forward the way the Australian special forces did, moving the fifty feet down to the wedged vehicle in three long steps.

He landed on the steep rock face just above the vehicle. Rocks skittered beneath his feet, almost causing him to fall.

"Hold up, Sarge," one of the Rangers said. "Don't touch the RSOV or we'll fall."

Taking out his mini-Maglite, Goose surveyed the vehicle and saw that it actually swayed a few inches on the rocky outcrop. Even more incredible, Corporal Joseph Baker had clambered out and was using his own strength to keep the balance. He was dug into the mountainside like Atlas from Greek mythology, taking enough of the weight of the RSOV to keep it balanced.

From the pain-filled look on the big man's face, Goose knew the balance was a fleeting thing. No one aboard the RSOV dared move.

"I need more rope," Goose called up. He tied himself in place and caught the rope that was thrown down to him. "Secure the other end to the RSOV up there." He stepped to the rear of the RSOV where most of the weight displacement was. "Hold on, Baker."

"I'm holding, Sarge. God's with me. I'm not going to let them fall." The big man's face was a map of agony, but there was a quiet kind of strength there, too. No fear, but a confidence that Goose couldn't believe.

As he worked to tie the other lines to the wedged RSOV, Goose heard the growling thunder of the approaching Syrian cav. In less than a minute, he had the support ropes in place.

"Okay, Baker," Goose said, giving himself more slack as he made his way down to the big man. "Turn loose."

Gingerly, not trusting the ropes, Baker turned loose and nearly fell.

At his side, Goose grabbed the man's combat harness and steadied him. Trusting his own weight to the line around his waist, Goose tied a final line to the corporal's harness. Together, they started climbing up the ropes.

Goose's muscles strained and ached. His knee protested with waves of throbbing pain. *God, help me. Just a little farther. I want to make it back home. I want to see my family again.* His arms and legs trembled from exertion. Darkness clouded his vision.

Just as they were about to reach the top, the wedged RSOV shifted, throwing down wheelbarrows full of rock. Maybe it was the vibration of the tanks rolling across the mountain, or maybe the RSOV it was tied onto had been subtly shifting the whole time. The lines couldn't be cut because the other Rangers were still climbing them.

Deep, cold conviction filled Goose that they weren't going to make it. The RSOV slid a few inches. The closest man was still more than ten feet from the road's edge above. The RSOV slid again, a whole foot this time, coming to within ten feet of the edge. The Rangers up top grabbed the vehicle and tried to brace it, but the effort was no use.

Then headlights flared around the bend in the mountain road. A RSOV sped down the grade. Without hesitation, the driver put his vehicle behind the sliding RSOV.

The two vehicles came together with a grinding crash. Goose skidded three feet down the mountainside. For a moment it looked like the new arrival's attempt to block the sliding RSOV was doomed to failure.

Then, unbelievably, the RSOVs all came to a stop. The late arrival held steady with one front wheel hanging out over open space.

"Climb," a familiar voice ordered. "Climb those ropes, Rangers, because if I have to climb down there and hump you up here myself, you'll be peeling potatoes for a year."

At the top of the climb, Goose looked into Remington's face. He reached up and took his friend's hand, remembering all the times they'd had each other's backs in a dozen different countries on a hundred different missions.

No matter what other mysteries the world offered, no matter what other changes occurred, Goose knew that the friendship between them was enduring. Different than the one he'd had with Bill Townsend, but no less vital.

"Thanks," Goose said, leaning into Remington's strength and letting the man help him up the mountainside as his knee threatened to completely go out from under him.

"I didn't want to finish this one up by myself, Goose. And it would be hard to break in a new first sergeant."

Dean Hardin sat in the passenger seat beside Remington, though. Hardin's face still bore the bruises that Goose had inflicted. The man's presence reminded Goose that even though the friendship was unique, it also came with problems.

"Move, soldier," Remington growled. "You're letting the entire Syrian army catch up to us."

Goose hobbled painfully to his RSOV as Brady and Madden cut the fallen RSOV free. The vehicle tumbled end over end down the mountain and burst into flames.

Remington took the lead, causing Brady to comment in wonderment at the Ranger captain's skill. Both vehicles battled the grade, lunging like quarter horses, then shimmying like cats on a hot roof as they fought for traction on hairpin curves.

Baker sat behind Goose.

"Are you okay?" Goose asked.

"I am." The man smiled. "I'm more okay than I've ever been, Sarge. God is with me. He made sure I was in a position to stop that RSOV's fall, and He gave me the strength to hold it there." He shook his head. "God didn't put us here to fail, Sarge. He has something planned for us."

Goose felt certain the man was delusional, perhaps hurt in ways he didn't know yet. But yet, at the same time, Goose felt an unexplained absence of fear. He glanced back over his shoulder and saw that the tanks and APCs were only a short distance behind. They'd lost a little of the advance they'd gained because the vehicles couldn't negotiate the turns like the RSOVs.

"Marathon One, we're blocked! We're blocked!"

The announcement filled Goose with dread. And in the next moment, the run through the mountains came to a grinding halt.

"What happened?" Remington demanded.

"One of the transport trucks lost an axle. Locked up and flipped. It's crossways in the road."

"Get it out of the way," Remington ordered.

Goose forced himself to stand in the RSOV's seat. Looking ahead, he saw the switchback where the transport truck had overturned.

And the mountain vibrated with the weight of the approaching Syrian armored cav.

"We're trapped," Madden said. "Man, we almost made it." Anger fired the corporal's words.

"No," Baker said. Even in the darkness, black bruises could be seen forming on his neck and face and across his shoulders through the tears in his shirt.

How had he taken that kind of punishment? Even in the face of the approaching maelstrom of Syrian cav, Goose was blown away by the memory of Baker standing under the RSOV, holding the vehicle up to save his friends. Then Goose remembered all the long hours that Baker had stood in the stream doing baptisms.

Baker looked at Goose, his moon face as calm as a child's. "It's God, Sarge. Can't you feel Him around us? We don't have to worry about the Syrians. All we have to do is trust in Him."

The big man pushed himself out of the RSOV, leaving his M-4A1 behind.

In disbelief, Goose watched as Baker walked fifty feet away, then knelt down on the hard rocky road. Baker held his hands out, his palms turned heavenward.

"I'm giving myself to You, Lord," Baker said in a strong, clear voice. "Take me and use me as You will. But I ask You to protect me from my enemies, and to protect the men with me."

Other Rangers went forward, all of them men Baker had baptized in the last two days.

The Syrian armor came on.

A dozen men knelt on the rock with Baker, all of them holding hands, forming a line of human beings across the road. Baker led the men in prayer, his voice strong and resonant. He spoke the verse, and they followed him.

"The Lord is my shepherd," Baker said, "I shall not want."

More men came forward, knelt and took hands. The prayer grew louder.

The vibrations from the Syrian cav units grew stronger.

"He maketh me to lie down in green pastures," Baker went on.

Goose glanced forward and saw that several Rangers were frantically working on the overturned transport truck.

"He leadeth me beside the still waters," Baker said, and the men joined him immediately. More Rangers stepped forward, filling in the human wall that separated them from the advancing Syrian vehicles. "He restoreth my soul."

Some of the pain went away in Goose's knee. A calmness came over him even though he knew the Syrian guns were already sweeping the fragile flesh-and-blood wall.

"He leadeth me in the paths of righteousness for his name's sake."

"Sergeant Gander!" Remington's voice cut through the descending tranquility. "Get those men on their feet!"

Goose couldn't move.

The Syrian tanks spread out along a wide place in the mountain road. The road was wider at this bend, overshadowed by a huge stone ledge. The tanks stood four across, and APCs ranked behind them.

"Yea, though I walk through the valley of the shadow of death, I will fear no evil: for thou art with me."

Drawn by the feeling that touched his heart, Goose went forward. Taking up arms against the tanks wasn't going to stop the heavy rounds that would rip them to shreds. Even bringing the RSOV's TOW missile launchers to bear wouldn't stop the carnage that was about to be unleashed.

Remington swore and came after him. "Sergeant! I gave you an order!"

"Thy rod and thy staff, they comfort me."

And Goose repeated the words with the men. He heard the words of the psalm rising into the night sky. His burden of worries was lifted from him. This was right. He just wished that Remington could see it. Something in the world had changed; it had grown darker and more bright. He missed Bill Townsend, but at the same moment he felt like Bill was with him, kneeling with the dozens of men praying with Corporal Baker.

"Thou preparest a table before me in the presence of mine enemies."

Goose heard Remington ordering the other Rangers into a defensive posture.

"Thou anointest my head with oil. My cup runneth over."

Then a peal of thunder took away all sound.

"Ready!" Remington shouted into the silence that followed.

The gunners adjusted, taking advantage of the higher incline where the Rangers were.

"Aim!" Remington roared.

For a moment Goose felt fear worm into his heart as he considered that he might not ever see Megan, Joey, or Chris again. Before the fear could grow, though he heard a voice, calm and powerful.

"Be still and know that I am God!"

The voice took Goose's breath away. In the next instant, the huge stone ledge jutting out from the mountain tore free and skidded down the mountainside, triggering an avalanche of rock and boulders that gained mass and speed. To Goose, it looked like the whole mountaintop toppled and fell.

And when the mountain fell, it swept the Syrian cav away, rolling tanks and APCs and Jeeps over the edge like they were a child's toys. When the mass of rock stopped moving, a thirty-foot wall of stone and dirt stood where the enemy had been only a moment ago.

For a moment, the silence was almost complete except for the rolling thunder of the echoes of the avalanche passing through the mountains.

Baker began again. "Surely goodness and mercy shall follow me all the days of my life, and I will dwell in the house of the Lord forever."

Drained but uplifted, First Sergeant Samuel Adams "Goose" Gander bowed his head and gave thanks to his Lord.

EPILOGUE

Church was held under a canvas tent near one of the walls of the city.
Benches had been fashioned out of ammo lockers and boards salvaged from the wreckage of buildings that had been hit by SCUDS.

Corporal Joseph Baker, heavily bruised from the action that had
taken place only twelve hours ago, stood at the front of the congregation and talked about the miracle that had leveled a mountain and
turned back the Syrian army.

Several of the men in the group were reinforcements from Ankara
and from *Wasp*. They hadn't seen the mountain leveled, but they had
been drawn to the story.

Goose stood at the back of the group. His injured knee throbbed
maniacally and he kept most of his weight on his good leg. He knew
that if Remington saw him favoring the limb that the Captain would
order him to the temporary hospital area for treatment.

Until his unit was safe, Goose couldn't rest. He stood in the baking heat that hung over the wrecked city and hoped that what he'd
been told about the coolness of the approaching evening was true. So
far the Syrians hadn't tried to invade the country any farther and the
sat-recon systems were all back on-line. With the reinforcements in
place from the United States, the United Nations, and the Turkish
military, Goose was certain the Syrians wouldn't try anything until
they were able to mass an overwhelming attack. At best guess, he and
his men—and the Allied forces as a whole—had a few days of breathing room.

But the attack would come. Goose was certain of that, too.

Baker described the power of the Lord, how He had reached down and saved the 75th Rangers as they'd fought and struggled to escape the Syrian forces. As he talked, media people shot footage of the Rangers.

"Probably just a Syrian missile," one of the reinforcements said ahead of Goose. "You know. Those Syrians probably launched a SCUD up into those mountains, and instead of taking our guys out it started a fissure that caused the whole mountaintop to crumble."

One of the men sitting in front of the new guys turned around and grabbed his arm. "Back off, man," the private snarled. He wore a bandage around his head and had his other arm up in a sling. "You weren't there. I was. I saw Corporal Baker start praying to the Lord. I heard his words as he called out for our salvation. That prayer—Corporal Baker's, and the prayers of every man out there—got answered. God reached down and spared us."

"Let go of me." The reinforcement brushed the other man's hand away. "I don't need to hear any preaching."

"Then what are you doing here?"

As quiet as the conversation was, the confrontation spread quickly. Several of the new men aligned themselves with the reinforcement, and men who had been in the retreat last night stood with the wounded private.

In another minute, Goose realized, the pushing and shoving would start. Military men standing down while in war zones didn't wear well. And there was always resentment between men who had been blooded in a conflict and those who had not. The tension was a product of testosterone and fear, all mixed into a combustible concoction that would spill over onto everyone around them if somebody didn't stop it right now.

Goose stepped forward, trying not to limp. He carried his M-4A1 slung over his right shoulder, barrel pointed up, his pistol holstered on his hip, and had the chinstrap of his helmet looped over his left shoulder.

Even as Goose started to move, epithets and curses erupted between the two groups. Hands curled into fists.

Goose pushed his way in between the men. At first they resisted, but they gave way immediately as soon as the soldiers caught sight of his stripes. He put steel in his voice. "Stand down *now.*"

"Yes, Sarge," the private said.

"Understood, Sergeant," the other man said.

Goose swept the men with a gaze, feeling the eyes of everyone else under the canvas watching him. They were all waiting to see which side he would be on.

"You men are gathered here as brothers," Goose said. "Sworn to fight a common enemy. That enemy lies just outside the gates of this city, and he'll be coming again in just a matter of days."

Sweat beaded the faces of the men watching him.

"I've left dead men scattered from here to the border," Goose went on. "Something I swore as a Ranger that I would never do."

Guilty looks on the faces of some of his men made it clear he wasn't the only Ranger regretting this.

Guilt stung Goose, too, but there was nothing he could do about it. "Those men stood together," he said. "They fought together and they bled together and they died together." He paused. "I'm going to tell you now that you men don't stand a chance if you don't stand together. If you're going to stand together when we're attacked or—God willing—when we take the attack to them, then you'll start standing together now."

Silence filled the canvas canopy.

"Is that understood?" Goose growled.

"Yes, Sergeant," all of the men chorused.

Goose looked back at Joseph Baker. "Sorry to interrupt your service, Corporal. Carry on."

Baker smiled and saluted with his Bible. "Thank you, Sarge."

Turning, feeling pain bite into his knee, Goose walked back toward the rear of the tent.

Captain Remington, resplendent in a fresh uniform, stood there looking at him. Dark aviator sunglasses hid his eyes, but Goose knew from years of friendship that Remington wasn't happy.

"Could I see you a moment, Sergeant?" Remington asked as Goose joined him.

"Yes, sir."

Remington turned a cold, perfectly executed about-face and walked out from under the tent.

Goose followed. As he moved out of the shade, sweltering heat hammered him, boiling up from the parched earth. Micro-mirages danced above broken street sections that thrust up out of the ground like rolling sea caps.

The latest Syrian SCUD attack had been partially directed at Sanliurfa and had leveled much of the city. Many tall buildings lay scattered in ruins. Military and civilian crews worked to clear the blocked streets. Other crews fought to contain and extinguish the fires that still burned among the piles of rubble.

Carrion birds gathered throughout the city, perching on broken buildings and swooping from the sky, looking for the victims of the attacks. A third contingent of workers followed the birds, looking for the dead.

When bodies were found, they were piled into the backs of cargo trucks and driven to mass burial sites. Even though Sanliurfa would not in all probability be held for long, the dead had to be cleared out to prevent the spread of disease, and some attempt had to be made to identify the corpses, though most were burned or crushed too badly for recognition to be easy. Goose moved upwind from a group of those searchers.

Remington stopped by the Hummer he was using as his personal vehicle. Anger showed in the set of his shoulders and the stiffness of his neck. He swung around on Goose and pointed toward the canvas church. He swore. "*That*, Sergeant, is precisely the reason I didn't want this stuff started."

"Yes, sir," Goose responded, staring at the twin reflections of himself on Remington's sunglasses. He didn't try to argue with the captain. Both of them knew the free time the men had was their own. Arguing with Remington wouldn't have gotten anywhere anyway.

"And don't tell me that all this Bible thumping is good for the morale of the men."

"No, sir," Goose said.

"What happened on that mountain last night," Remington said, "was not some kind of mystical event. No Second Coming."

Goose remained silent.

Remington swore again. "Baker is pouring this swill out like slops to hogs in a trough, sergeant. Don't tell me you believe in this nonsense."

Goose measured his words carefully. "That mountain fell, sir. I saw it fall."

"And what made it fall?"

Goose hesitated. "I don't know, sir."

"But you believe God caused it?"

"Yes, sir."

"Then I'm also going to hold God responsible for the deaths of all those Rangers we left behind, Sergeant."

Goose felt an immediate surge of anger. That wasn't what God was about. He'd learned everything he knew about God from his father in Sunday school, and from Bill Townsend during the last few years. God hadn't killed those men they'd been forced to leave behind.

"Sir—"

"Don't you argue with me," Remington interrupted. "Don't you even dare."

"No, sir."

"You can't have it both ways, Sergeant. If God was responsible for our salvation last night, then why didn't He save those men we lost?"

Goose didn't have an answer for that. He felt there was still so much he needed to learn.

Remington shook his head. He cursed and paced for an instant, then swung back on Goose. "This is a bad business, Sergeant. Bad business. Those men in that tent are there because they want to feel special. Like the hand of God Almighty has touched them. Like they're invulnerable or something."

Goose stood his ground. His knee throbbed.

"Is that what you want them thinking, Sergeant?" Remington demanded. "That they're invulnerable?"

"No, sir."

"You're right, 'No, sir.' Because thinking like that will get those men killed."

"Yes, sir."

Remington took in a deep breath, held it for an interminable moment, then released it. His dark lenses turned toward Goose again. "I am their commanding officer, Sergeant. I want them believing in me. Is that clear?"

"Yes, sir."

Remington flicked his gaze back to the tent. "Let Baker talk for now, Sergeant, but I want this shut down. We've got chaplains for this kind of thing. I don't need some holy-roller stepping up from the enlisted to go on a private crusade to save the souls of the men I'm leading into battle."

Personally, Goose disagreed with that. Since they had been in camp in the city, Baker had continued with the baptisms for a while, till no one else had come forward. Then the big man had started witnessing to those who were interested.

"I want Baker's little tent revival closed down," Remington went on.

"Sir, this is Baker's personal time."

Remington wheeled on Goose and thrust his face forward, stopping less than an inch from Goose's face. Goose never moved. He shifted his gaze, staring through the captain's head the way he'd been trained to since Boot Camp.

"That man owes me five hours of sleep, Sergeant," Remington said. "I want them. Starting now."

"Yes, sir."

"Dismissed."

"Sir." Goose saluted sharply. "Yes, sir." He turned an about-face and headed for the tent church. Remington was wrong about his assessment of God's fault in the deaths of the men they'd lost, and Goose knew that. But he also knew he couldn't argue the point.

❈   ❈   ❈

**United States 75ᵗʰ Army Rangers Temporary Post
Sanliurfa, Turkey
Local Time 1612 Hours**

"Sergeant Samuel Gander." The woman in the Red Cross uniform looked around the room that had been set up as a communications center. She was middle-aged, a brunette with twenty extra pounds on her and a calm, confident demeanor. She held a hand over the phone handset she held.

Heart beating frantically, Goose limped forward. "Here." He held up a hand so the woman would see him in the crowd of men that filled the building near to bursting. "I'm Sergeant Gander."

The phone service coming into Turkey was abominably slow. He knew there were problems stateside, too, but he didn't know why. He'd been busy. And news was filtering through the military ranks slower than usual because there was so much weird stuff passing through with it that one knew what to believe.

The phones had been put in immediately upon the arrival of the American military reinforcements. Communications were being routed through one of satellites donated by Nicolae Carpathia until the American satellites were back on-line.

The Red Cross had manned the phones, answering and putting through calls as quickly as they could for servicemen in the immediate area. Goose had established a relief crew that swapped out with men at post so they could take phone calls from home.

The building was an auditorium that had been gutted of furniture to make room for the phone equipment. Soldiers sat on the floor or leaned against the walls while they waited to take calls that had been put on hold.

The woman handed the phone to Goose. She smiled, but she looked tired and worn. Not all news coming from home was good, and not all of it going back was either.

"It's Mrs. Gander, Sergeant," the woman said.

Thank You, God, Goose thought silently as he accepted the phone. He nodded at the woman. "Thank you, ma'am."

The woman hesitated. "Please try to be brief, Sergeant. I know that's asking a lot, given our present circumstances and everything that has been going on. But there are a lot of other men that need to speak to their families as well." The speech was the same one Goose had heard her dole out every time she handed over the phone.

"Yes, ma'am," Goose said. He pulled the handset to his ear and felt trapped by the cord. "Megan?"

"Goose? Goose, is it really you?" Megan's voice cracked and he heard her crying at the other end of the connection.

"It's me, Meg." Goose barely swallowed the lump that was in his throat. His eyes burned and he felt the unshed tears he wouldn't let fall because men were watching him. Everything he had planned to say to her evaporated the instant he heard her voice. But he did know what mattered. "I love you."

She cried for a moment. "I . . . love . . . you, too."

They were silent for a while, and Goose felt terrible that this time looked so wasted. But just hugging the phone like that made him feel like Megan was right there, like he could reach out and touch her or smell her hair.

"How bad is it there, Goose? I've been watching television. That's all anyone has been doing over here. It looks really bad."

"It probably looks better than it is," Goose said.

"But you're all right?"

"Yes." Goose shook his head, feeling the weight of everything that had happened. "I am. But there are a lot of guys over here, Meg, that aren't all right."

"I know. I've been praying for all of you."

Goose took a deep breath, struggling to keep himself centered. "Bill—" His voice broke. "Something happened to Bill."

"Is he hurt?"

Fatigue muddled Goose's thoughts. He didn't know how to explain what had happened. "He's not hurt. At least, I don't think he's hurt. He—he disappeared, Meg. I was right there beside him. He was there, then he wasn't. Nobody here knows what happened."

"I know," Megan said. "It happened over here, too."

Goose tried to focus on what she had just said. "What happened?"

"The disappearances," Megan said. "The news is full of it."

The horror of a worldwide epidemic of disappearances surged through Goose. They still didn't even know who had taken the missing men—or how. He'd heard pieces and fragments of conversations about people missing back in the United States, but he'd been too busy to follow up on the scuttlebutt. He did know that DEFCON-2 had been pushed back due to something that had happened in Washington, D.C., and for that he was grateful.

"We haven't got much access to the news here," Goose said. "The disappearances have happened over there, too?"

"Yes."

Goose thought about his dad and Megan's parents. "Have you heard from your mom and dad?"

"Yes. They're fine. Just scared. The way most of us are. Nobody really understands what has been going on."

"It's okay," Goose said with more confidence than he felt. "We'll find out. The captain tells me the military intelligence teams are working on it. They'll find an answer. Maybe we can get those people back."

"I don't think so, Goose. Really, I don't." Her voice broke again.

"We'll get through it, Meg," Goose said. "I promise."

"We don't have a choice. I know that. I just don't understand why all the children had to be taken." Her breath rattled as she inhaled deeply. "Well, I mean I do understand, but it's just so hard to accept."

"What?" Panic exploded Goose's heart. "What about the children?"

Megan cried for a moment, then got herself together. "The children, Goose. All of the children are gone. Didn't you know?"

"Meg." Goose's voice faltered and he thought for a moment he was going to go insane. None of this made any sense. "Meg, there aren't any children in the 75th." Then he realized that he hadn't seen any children in the city streets either. But that hadn't been too surprising. Parents would keep their kids inside, especially with a foreign army occupying the city. "Where are Joey and Chris? Are they all right?"

She was quiet too long.

"Meg?" Asking again hurt him. Pain welled in his throat. Tears blurred his vision.

"Joey's here," Meg answered. "It's Chris, Goose. Chris is gone. Our baby is *gone!*"

To Goose, it seemed like all the air in the room suddenly went away. Then his injured leg went out from under him. All of his reserves seemed to collapse and dwindle into the cold, hard center of himself that manifested.

"Goose? Goose!"

Hurt took away Goose's voice. And even if he could have spoken, he didn't know what he would have said. All he could think about was Chris, how he might never hold his son or speak to him again. Bill's disappearance had seemed so grim, so final.

And now Chris. *God, what have You done? What have You done?*

❋   ❋   ❋

United States of America
Ft. Benning, Georgia
Local Time 9:46 A.M.

Megan dumped the dirty clothes into the washer, added detergent, then closed the lid and started the cycle. Doing ordinary things—cooking, cleaning, getting kids to bathe—all felt reassuring. While she was doing those things, she could pretend everything was all right in the world, that the stories of the mysterious disappearances and all the tragic deaths that had happened the night before were all fantasies and lies. Propaganda, even.

Except that she knew it wasn't.

Even more upsetting, Joey hadn't come home last night. Megan had no idea where her eldest son was. He'd talked with Jenny—argued actually, Megan knew, because she'd heard them—yesterday morning. He hadn't come back since.

She'd tried to find him. Megan had gone through the list of acquaintances she'd had for Joey. For the most part, she'd discovered that her son no longer hung out with the same kids. And how had she not known that? Guilt washed over her as she listened to the washer's agitator kick to life and start whacking the laundry.

"Megan?"

Hearing Jenny's voice, Megan looked up and saw the young woman standing in the utility room doorway. "Yes."

"Bathroom's free," Jenny said. "Your turn in the shower."

Jenny had stayed last night to help out with the kids that had had nowhere else on base to go. Megan had been in touch with some of the other counselors and the volunteer staff to establish a system to start taking care of all the kids that had been left bereft of parents, either through the disappearances or because their parents were away on military assignments and the guardians they'd had had disappeared. Keeping enough hot water in her household to meet the needs of all the kids she'd taken in was impossible. She'd set the washer for cold.

"A shower, huh? Do we still have hot water?" Megan asked. She wanted a shower more than anything. She'd missed taking one last night with all the extra kids to care for.

"Some," Jenny answered. "If you make it quick, it might last."

Megan sighed and nodded. "I've got Kelly and Regan's things about to come out of the dryer."

"I'll take care of it," Jenny said.

Megan nodded thanks, then headed back through the house. Kids were clustered around the table with Monopoly and Life. Board games helped give the younger teens focus. Others crowded around the television in the living room, watching the news from around the country.

She wanted to pull them back from the television, because she knew the images of downed planes, wrecked cars, burning buildings, and riots in the larger metropolitan areas would live with them forever. But those images would be mixed with footage of the terrorist attack on the World Trade Center, people jumping from the top of the buildings, and the sight of the space shuttle *Columbia* breaking up over Texas. These kids weren't completely unprepared for tragedy.

The world had changed. It had changed during those events, and it had changed yet one more time.

Megan couldn't help wondering how many more changes were coming, but she knew they would be there. How long had it been, she wondered as she crossed the living room and gently removed Tabitha Welch's feet from her couch, since there had been a true innocence in the world?

Tabitha apologized and Megan felt guilty. She told the girl everything was all right. Tabitha hugged the throw pillow she was holding more tightly.

The doorbell rang.

Josh Webb, who had two parents overseas and his grandparents missing, answered the door. He talked for a moment, then looked at Megan. "Mrs. Gander, it's for you."

Two uniformed MPs stood at the door. Both of them looked haggard and worn, much older than they should have.

"Mrs. Gander," one of them said.

"Yes."

"I've got a warrant here, ma'am." He offered her a piece of paper.

"A warrant?" Megan knew what the word meant, but she couldn't make sense of it.

"Yes, ma'am," the MP said. "This was issued by the Provost's office. Gives me the right to search the premises."

"Search for what?"

The MP looked past her at the kids that had gathered behind her. "I'm looking for Gerry Fletcher, ma'am."

This is insane, Megan thought. But she said, "Gerry isn't here. He was one of the kids that disappeared last night." God, how could she say that so off-handedly? Chris was one of those that disappeared. It wasn't natural; she'd never accept it as natural even if, as Jenny suspected, God had had a hand in it.

"Yes, ma'am." The MP nodded. "You're probably right, Mrs. Gander. But I was ordered to search the premises."

"My son." Megan's voice became a hoarse, tight whisper. "My son Chris was one of the children that disappeared." She could still remember the deep sobs that had racked Goose at the other end of the phone connection. How could they be so far apart when there was so much to deal with? They needed each other. She knew that her husband needed her as much as she needed him.

"Yes, ma'am," the MP responded. "I know." He looked upset and uncomfortable. "Mrs. Gander, I still have to look."

Wordlessly, Megan stepped back.

The teenagers stepped back, too.

The MPs filled the room. They looked big and alien and uninvited. The weapons they wore seemed threatening.

"Any of you guys Gerry Fletcher?" the MP asked.

A chorus of "nos" followed the question.

"Well, then," the MP said, "I'll have to look around."

Unable to speak, Megan waved them on into her house. She couldn't believe what was happening. She had tried to rescue Gerry Fletcher the night before last. Now she was being treated like a criminal.

The search, thankfully, was thorough but brief. Jenny treated the men with icy, reproachful stares during the time they spent in the house.

At the door again, the lead MP held out another piece of paper. "I was also ordered to give you this, Mrs. Gander."

Tears leaking down her cheeks, Megan took the paper with a shaking hand. "What is it?"

"It's a summons, ma'am. You're being ordered to appear in the provost's office."

"Why?"

The MP shook his head. "I wouldn't know, ma'am. That's all I was told."

In disbelief, Megan opened the paper. There, in big bold letters, were the words ORDERED TO APPEAR and DERELICTION OF DUTY. She looked up.

"Ma'am," the MP said. He seemed hesitant. "I know your husband. I don't know Goose well, but I know that he is a good man and he's doing his job over there. I don't know if you can get through to him about this, but if you'd like some advice . . ."

"Yes, Corporal," Megan said. "I'd very much like some advice."

"Get a lawyer, ma'am," the MP said. "The military will probably give you one, but I'd hire an outside attorney to help represent you. The provost marshal, I don't know what's got him so hot on this, but from what I saw this morning, he's going to be coming after you. And he's going to try to nail you."

Oh, God, Megan thought, *what else are You going to put my family through?* She made herself nod. She made herself say, "Thank you, Corporal," then she made herself close the door because she didn't know anything else she could do.

"Megan," Jenny called.

Unable to speak, Megan waved the young woman away. Aware of the teenagers staring at her, Megan went to her bedroom. She tried to gather clothes to take with her to the shower, but she couldn't. She saw Chris' pictures hanging on the wall, all the birthday pictures from age one through five, and knew there would be no picture for age six.

Dereliction of duty.

It didn't make any sense. But she knew if she were found guilty she would be locked up. A sentence that could last for years.

Was that what life—what God—had in store for her? Years spent in a military prison without her sons, without her husband?

She knelt beside the bed and tried to pray. But she couldn't. The words wouldn't come and she felt horribly betrayed.

✷   ✷   ✷

United States 75ᵗʰ Army Rangers Temporary Post
Sanliurfa, Turkey
Local Time 1956 Hours

Goose sat at the bar in a tavern that had been resurrected that afternoon. The furniture had been cobbled together from wreckage that had been nearer to ground zero of several SCUD strikes.

Other men sat around him. Some of the men were military, from the US, from the UN, from the Turkish army, but others were citizens, displaced villagers, media personnel, and hucksters trying to make money. No one tried to sit with him. He'd claimed a small table as his own and every man there read the warning signs.

Cigarette smoke hugged the dark ceiling where stains and residue from millions of other cigarettes had left permanent marks. The smell of beer and alcohol pervaded the tavern. The place felt like a thousand other places around the world that Goose had been in before he'd met Bill and Megan. It even reminded him of the beer halls his father had hung out in back in Waycross when Goose was a kid.

Jeeps and Hummers and cargo trucks rolled by outside as the military continued putting down sandbags and shoring up defensive postures in case the Syrian military decided they felt lucky despite the turn of events on the mountain. Those soldiers worked by lanterns and Kleig lights now. The night had fallen nearly an hour ago. Or maybe it only seemed like an hour ago. Goose wasn't sure.

He turned his attention to the beer bottle sitting on the table in front of him. Then he looked at the picture of his family, taken only last summer at a backyard barbecue. Even though he wasn't in the picture, Bill Townsend had been there. Bill had taken the picture.

In the picture, Goose held Chris tightly in his arms. Chris loved being out in the sun, and his hair was bleached so blond it was almost white. Megan stood at Goose's side with Joey next to her.

Gone.

The word hammered into Goose's mind and sent a stake through his heart one more time. How could his son just be gone? How could Bill just be gone?

Footsteps sounded behind Goose and he recognized the measured stride immediately. He would have recognized the stride in a parade march. He sat quietly, waiting.

Remington came around the table.

Reluctantly, Goose came to his feet and saluted, then stood at attention.

"At ease, Sergeant," Remington said. "This is a social call."

"Yes, sir." But Goose knew that Remington had waited until he'd gotten to his feet and saluted before telling him that.

"Sit down," Remington said.

Goose sat.

"Mind if I join you?"

"No, sir."

Remington hooked the chair on the other side of the table and sat. He folded his hands on the tabletop. "I heard about Chris."

"Yes, sir."

"Knock off the 'sir', Goose. This is me and you."

"All right."

Remington took a deep breath, looked away and let it out, then looked back at Goose. "I had to find out about it from someone else. I should have heard about it from you."

"You were busy."

"Not too busy for you, Goose," Remington said. "I'm never too busy for you."

Goose knew that wasn't true. There had been times in the past when he'd had to wait for Remington's attention, sometimes for days.

"How are you holding up?" Remington asked.

"Not good," Goose answered.

"Can you do your job?"

"I don't know."

Remington's voice crackled with authority. "That's not the answer I was hoping for, Sergeant."

"No, sir, it's probably not."

Anger darkened the captain's features. "Don't you sit there and feel sorry for yourself, Goose."

Goose held back an angry response, because Remington was a friend as well as a commanding officer.

"What happened to Chris is a bad thing," Remington said. "But, from what I understand, that happened to every kid out there."

Goose controlled himself with effort. Remington didn't have kids.

"I don't know what you're going through, Goose," Remington said, "but if I could share part of the burden of it, I would."

Shame cracked Goose's anger a little because he believed Remington might have tried. But in the end, all the same, he knew that Remington wouldn't have been capable.

"I don't know what happened to those kids," Remington said. "I don't know what happened to those men everyone reported missing. But there are some things I do know." He ticked points off on his fingers. "There's an army waiting out there thinking they're holding a sword to our bared throats. They're waiting for us to make a mistake. They're waiting to grow brave again. I've got busted rifle companies out there that are undermanned, under-equipped, and some of them scared out of their minds, scratching around in the dirt looking for Jesus to come bail them out." The captain took a ragged breath. "I can't have that, Goose. And you know I can't have that."

"Yes, sir."

Remington looked at him. "I need you, Goose. I need you to be strong."

Goose paused. "I don't know if—"

"Then you figure it out, mister!" Remington's voice grew loud enough to quiet the men around them.

Goose was conscious of the unwanted attention.

"You're a soldier, Goose," Remington stated in a harsh voice. "You're a sergeant. A leader of men. More than that, you're *my* sergeant. You'll get those Rangers up and running, and you'll stand tall when I tell you to."

"Sir, yes, sir." Goose's response was automatic, ingrained by years of military training.

Remington exhaled again and leaned back in his chair. "I shouldn't even be having this talk with you, Goose."

"No, sir."

"You've been hurt before. You've been scared before. When those things happen, there's one thing that you've always been able to hold fast to."

Goose remained silent.

"You're a soldier, Goose. You've always been a soldier. You were a soldier waiting to happen back in Waycross. You're a soldier now. You'll be a soldier the day you die."

"Yes, sir."

Remington's voice softened a little. "And when you die, Goose, you're going to die standing tall, facing whatever enemy you're up against that day, and you're going to die believing that you're doing all you can do." He paused. "That's all a professional soldier can ask for. And before you're anything else, Goose, you're a professional soldier. Probably the most professional soldier I've ever seen."

"Thank you, sir."

Remington pursed his lips. "You've got some downtime coming, sergeant." He glanced at the picture on the table. "Get this straight in your head. Figure out what you can do something about and what you can't. Don't let the world get so big you can't deal with it. One thing at a time. One opponent at a time. One mission at a time. One battle at a time. One war at a time. That's how we've always done it." He paused. "It works. That's how we'll continue to do it."

"Yes, sir."

"We'll get through this, Goose." Remington stood, and Goose stood with him. "We will because we don't have a choice. Get some sleep, then get back out there. We've got to make this city look like we're going to hold it. That way Ankara and Diyarbakir City will have time to get ready to deal with the Syrian invasion when it comes. And it will."

"Yes, sir."

The captain hesitated. "I also want Baker and his snake-oil show shut down."

Goose took a moment to consider, wanting to make sure he had his words right and wasn't too confrontational. "I don't know if I can do that, sir. The men have a right to peaceably assemble on their own time."

"Back home, sure, but this is a war zone, sergeant. They can assemble only when I say so. Remember that."

"I will, sir."

Remington grimaced. "If you can't shut the man down, Sergeant, at least limit him."

"Yes, sir."

"I don't want an army full of zealots," Remington said. "After last night, stories have passed all through this command about how God reached down and saved the 75th."

Goose nodded.

"I've also heard that God took all those missing people."

Goose didn't say anything. Megan had tried to tell him that, too, but she'd sounded more like she was trying to convince herself.

"Including your son," Remington said.

Reaching into himself, Goose made his face stone.

"I don't believe that, Sergeant," Remington said. "I believe if you'll think back, you'll remember that several SCUDS hit that mountain before we got there. SCUDS that didn't make it to their target destinations. I know that's what I saw."

Goose knew that was true. The SCUDS had gone everywhere again for a while. The second attack was what had damaged Sanliurfa so much. But he could also remember the feeling, the euphoria, that had filled him when Joseph Baker had led the Rangers in prayer.

"You have to ask yourself, Sergeant," Remington said, "that if you want to believe that God cares about the 75th so much that He would save us from the Syrians, why would He see fit to take your boy?"

And that, Goose knew, had been exactly the question he had been wrestling with while he'd sat there and contemplated drinking that beer. He faulted himself for being so weak. Yet he forgave himself immediately. The God that he had been brought up to recognize wouldn't have just taken Chris away. Would He?

Would He?

Indecision chafed at Goose's thoughts. Baker seemed certain of what had happened. *But you no longer are, are you?* The saddest part of that was that Goose honestly didn't know. If Chris hadn't been taken—

But he had. Chris was gone. Megan had told him that.

Remington dropped a hand to Goose's shoulder. "And if you need anything, let me know."

"Yes, sir. Thank you, sir." Goose watched Remington go, feeling the distance that now lay between him and his friend.

Outside the door, still in Goose's sight, Remington's Hummer rolled forward. In the glare of the lights against the night, Goose saw Dean Hardin sitting at the steering wheel as Remington climbed aboard the vehicle.

Hardin showed Goose a cold smile and tossed him an insouciant two-fingered salute. In the next instant, the Hummer pulled away.

For a moment, Hardin's presence drew Goose's mind from the despair that filled him. Hardin was a dangerous man, and one that didn't easily forgive grudges. He was the kind of man that would put a knife in another man's back the first time a chance presented itself. During the upcoming battles with Syria, Goose knew there would be plenty of chances for Hardin to find him.

"Some piece of work, your captain there," a quiet voice said.

Goose turned back to the table and found a man sitting in the chair Remington had vacated. Although the hours that stretched between their previous encounter seemed several lifetimes long, Goose recognized the younger man.

"Agent Icarus," Goose said softly.

The young man smiled through a mask of bruises. "Yes." He glanced furtively around the tavern. "I know your captain is looking for me, Sergeant."

Goose nodded. "So is the CIA."

"I expected as much."

Goose started to get up.

"Don't, Sergeant." The young agent placed a hand on the table, safely out of reach of any sudden move Goose might make without getting up from his chair. Inside the hand, an electronic detonator blinked a red warning light.

Goose froze.

"Do you know what this is?" the young agent asked.

"Yes."

"Good. I have the explosive planted in this place. If you move, a lot of people, perhaps even you, are going to die."

"What are you doing here?"

"I came to speak with you."

Goose inhaled and exhaled, taking time to think about that. "Why?"

"Because you impressed me yesterday. I think you're a good man."

Goose shrugged. "You could be wrong."

"I know." The young agent shook his hand holding the remote control detonator. "That's why I came with insurance."

"I'm listening," Goose said. Using his peripheral vision, he glanced around the room, hoping he would spot a member of his unit that he could give hand signals to.

The young man looked worn and much the worse for wear. Goose doubted he'd seen a bed since his squad had rescued the man from the PKK terrorist cell. "Things aren't exactly what you think they are."

"That transmission initiated the attack," Goose said.

The young man nodded. "That was all planned. My capture. You being there to stop the PKK cell. All of it."

Goose listened, thinking the younger man was delusional.

"They're very good at what they're doing," Icarus said. "Of course, they've been waiting for that moment yesterday for decades. They've had time to think and plan and get ready for the final confrontation."

"What confrontation?" Goose asked. "The Syrians?"

Icarus shook his head. "The Syrians are actually only a small part of it, Sergeant. The fate of the world hangs in the balance here." He smiled in self-deprecation. "Or at least the next seven years of it. As well as the souls of all those who have been left behind."

"Who was left behind?" Goose struggled to find the thread of logic in the man's words.

"The non-believers," Icarus said. "And those who only gave belief lip service. And those like yourself who had doubts."

"About what?"

"God."

A cold chill spiked through Goose's belly.

"I heard about what happened out there on that mountain, Sergeant."

"It was just a fluke," Goose said. "The mountain had been shelled. It was ready to fall. When the Syrian heavy cav came through there, the fissures gave way and the mountain fell."

Icarus smiled. "I'd heard it was the hand of God that spared you." He shook his head. "Maybe I heard wrong." He gazed into Goose's eyes. "What do you believe?"

Goose hesitated. "I don't know," he replied.

"If it was just that the mountain that chose that time to fall, or some kind of uninvolved fate that simply occurred at that moment, the timing couldn't have been any better for you and your men."

Goose couldn't argue with that, so he didn't.

Icarus glanced around the room. "I was fooled, Sergeant. I was used."

"You need to talk to the CIA."

"I can't. No one there will believe me. And if Cody finds me, I very much believe he will kill me." Icarus smiled. "I think you and your team were better than he bargained for. I don't think I was supposed to survive the rescue yesterday. But I did. And now he's afraid of me because of what I know." He paused. "Cody had a team waiting for me here. They captured me. I had to kill them to escape. Cody's looking for me. And I know your captain has men out looking as well."

"Why talk to me?" Goose asked.

"Because you seem like a good man," Icarus said. "I've seen few enough of them my life that I've learned to know one when I see one. Your friend, Bill, is a good man, too."

"He disappeared," Goose said.

Icarus nodded. "I can't say that I'm surprised."

"Do you know where he is?"

"Yes."

Blood thundered through Goose's temples. If the man knew where Bill was, then maybe he knew where Chris was. "Where?"

Icarus studied Goose for a moment, then shook his head sadly. "You're not ready." He shifted the detonator in his hand. "I'll tell you this, though. As bad as you think things have been, as bad as you think they're going to get, they're going to be even worse. Worse than you can ever imagine. Seven years of lies and subterfuge and unspeakable horror, Sergeant. Only those who find the truth will be spared. And even after everything that has happened, there are going to be so many that don't believe."

"Don't believe what?"

"That's what I'm talking about, Sergeant. The proof is lying before you, and still you refuse to see. That's what the Antichrist is relying on."

Goose studied the man. "You don't have a bomb."

A smile flitted across his face. "Of course I have a bomb."

Goose shook his head. "You come in here worrying about the souls of people you don't even know, and you claim you're prepared to destroy this place and kill everyone in it? I don't believe you."

"Listen to me." Icarus looked even more nervous, and he was scared now, too. "You've got to listen to me."

"No," Goose said. "No, I don't have to listen to you." He surged up from the table. Then his bad knee locked up in a blaze of pain that took him to the ground. He fought his way through the agony, willing himself to stay conscious.

By the time Goose got to his feet in the crowd of confused and concerned tavern patrons, Icarus was gone. Goose limped through the crowd to the back door to the alley.

Nothing moved in the fetid shadows that filled the narrow alley. Icarus was gone as if he'd never existed, but his words hung in the air.

"As bad as you think things have been, as bad as you think they're going to get, in reality they're going to be even worse. Seven years of lies and subterfuge and unspeakable horror, Sergeant. Only those who find the truth will be spared."

Goose limped out into the alley. Overcome, nearly exhausted, hurting over his losses and more confused and lonely than he'd ever been in his life, he sat in the alley with his back to the wall.

He looked up at the star-filled sky and wished he could believe the way that Bill had, wished that he could hold Chris again, wished that he *knew.*

And only a sheer effort of will and years of training kept him from screaming in frustration. Still, just as Remington had said, he was a professional soldier. No matter what happened, he knew his place in the world.

But sometimes—sometimes when they were hurt and lonely and scared and confused, when there was no fighting to be done, sometimes soldiers cried.

ABRIDGED AUDIO Available on three CDs or two cassettes for each title. (Books 1–9 read by Frank Muller, one of the most talented readers of audio books today.)

AN EXPERIENCE IN SOUND AND DRAMA Dramatic broadcast performances of the best-selling Left Behind series. Twelve half-hour episodes on four CDs or three cassettes for each title.

GRAPHIC NOVELS Created by a leader in the graphic novel market, the series is now available in this exciting new format.

LEFT BEHIND®: THE KIDS Four teens are left behind after the Rapture and band together to fight Satan's forces in this series for ten- to fourteen-year-olds.

LEFT BEHIND® > THE KIDS < LIVE-ACTION AUDIO Feel the reality, listen as the drama unfolds. . . . Twelve action-packed episodes available on four CDs or three cassettes.

CALENDARS, DEVOTIONALS, GIFT BOOKS . . .

FOR THE LATEST INFORMATION ON INDIVIDUAL PRODUCTS, RELEASE DATES, AND FUTURE PROJECTS, VISIT

www.leftbehind.com

Sign up and receive free e-mail updates!